VOLUME
ONE

Sa

IMAGE COMICS, INC.

www.imagecomics.com

ISBN 978-1-60706-601-9

SAGA, VOLUME ONE. Third printing. July 2013. Published by Image Comics, Inc. Office of publication: 2001 Center Street, Sixth Floor, Berkeley, CA 94704.

FOREIGN LICENSING INQUIRIES WRITE TO: foreignlicensing@imagecomics.com

BRIAN K. VAUGHAN
WRITER

FIONA STAPLES
ARTIST

FONOGRAFIKS
LETTERING+DESIGN

ERIC STEPHENSON
COORDINATOR

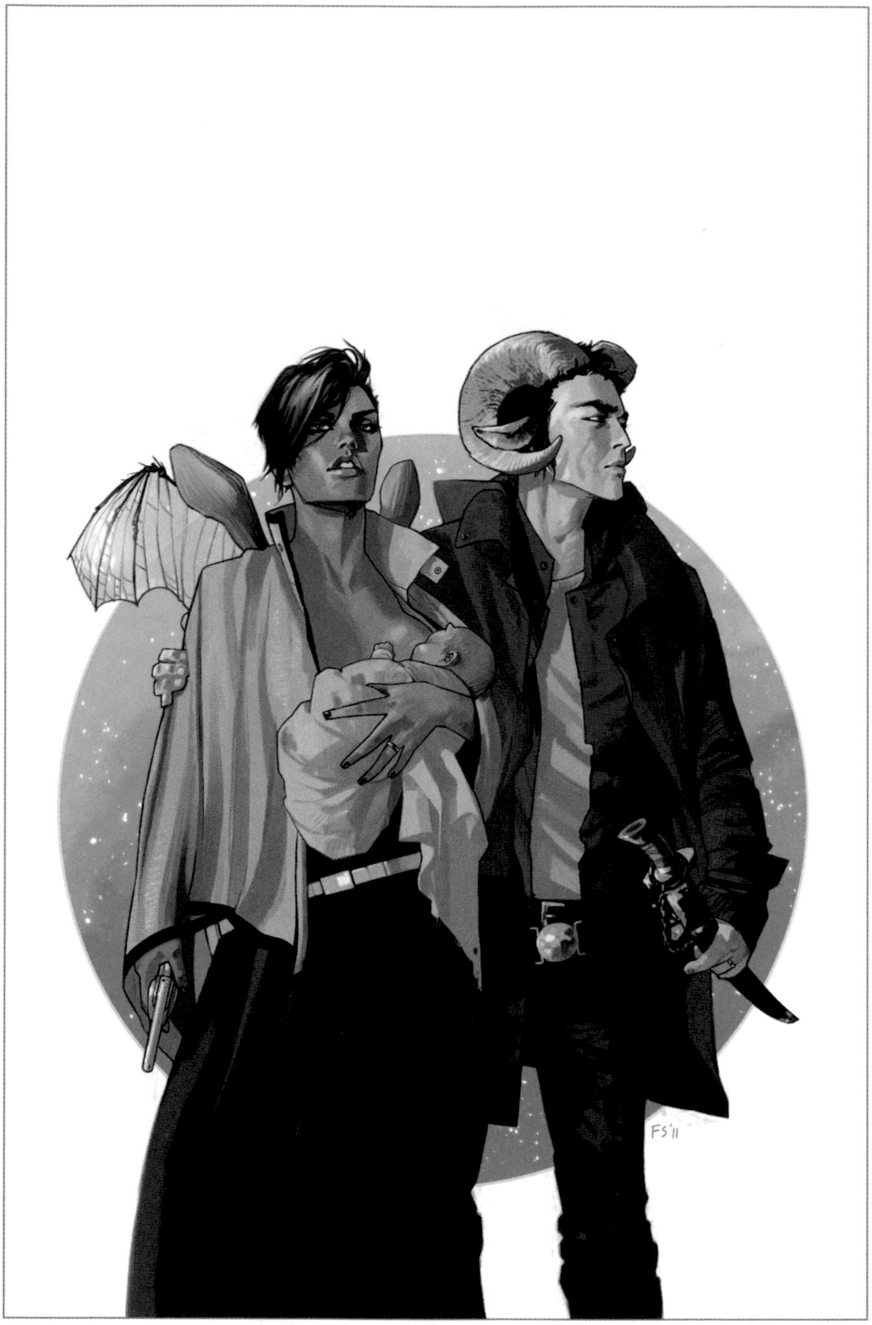
FS'11

CHAPTER ONE

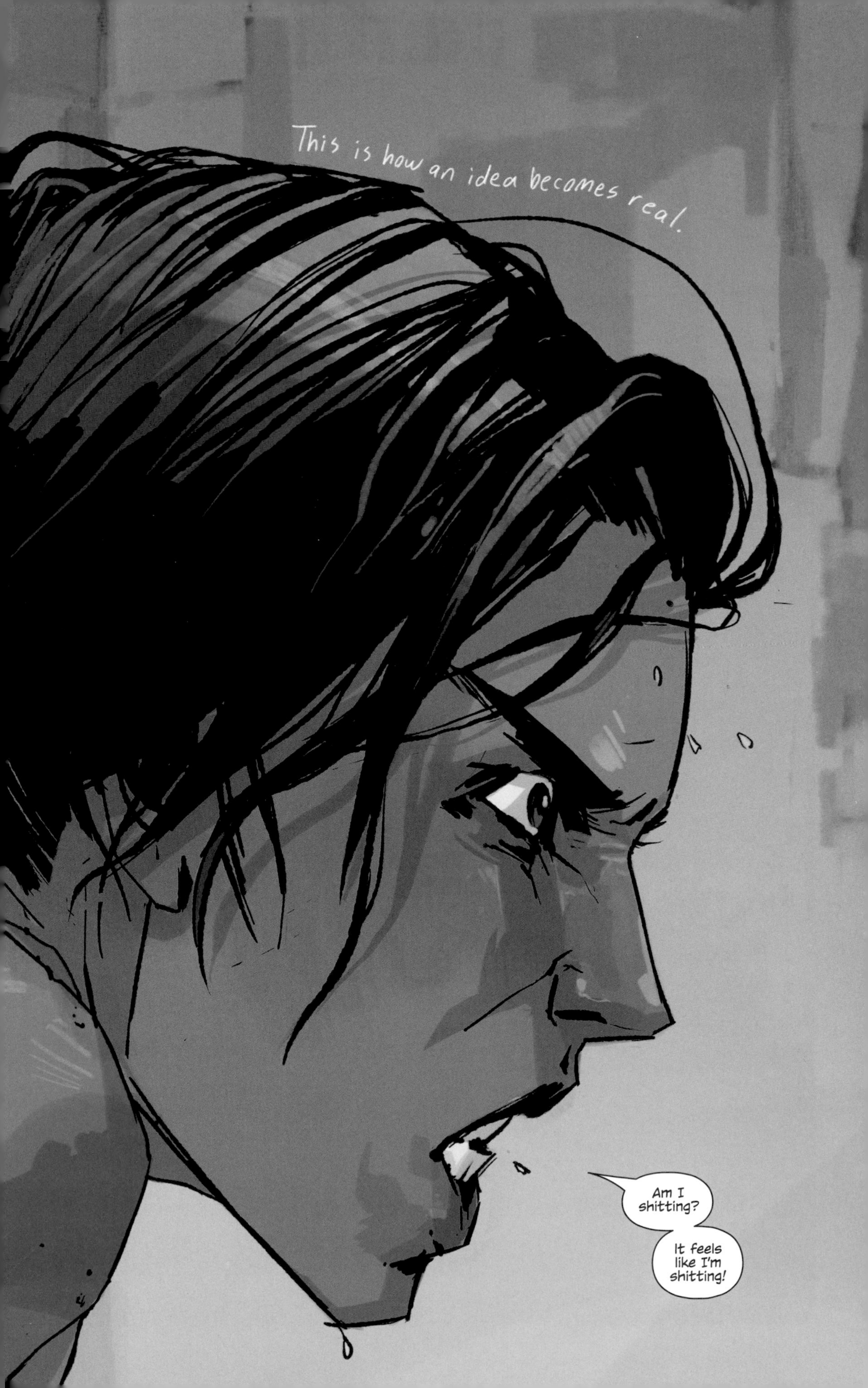
This is how an idea becomes real.
Am I shitting?
It feels like I'm shitting!

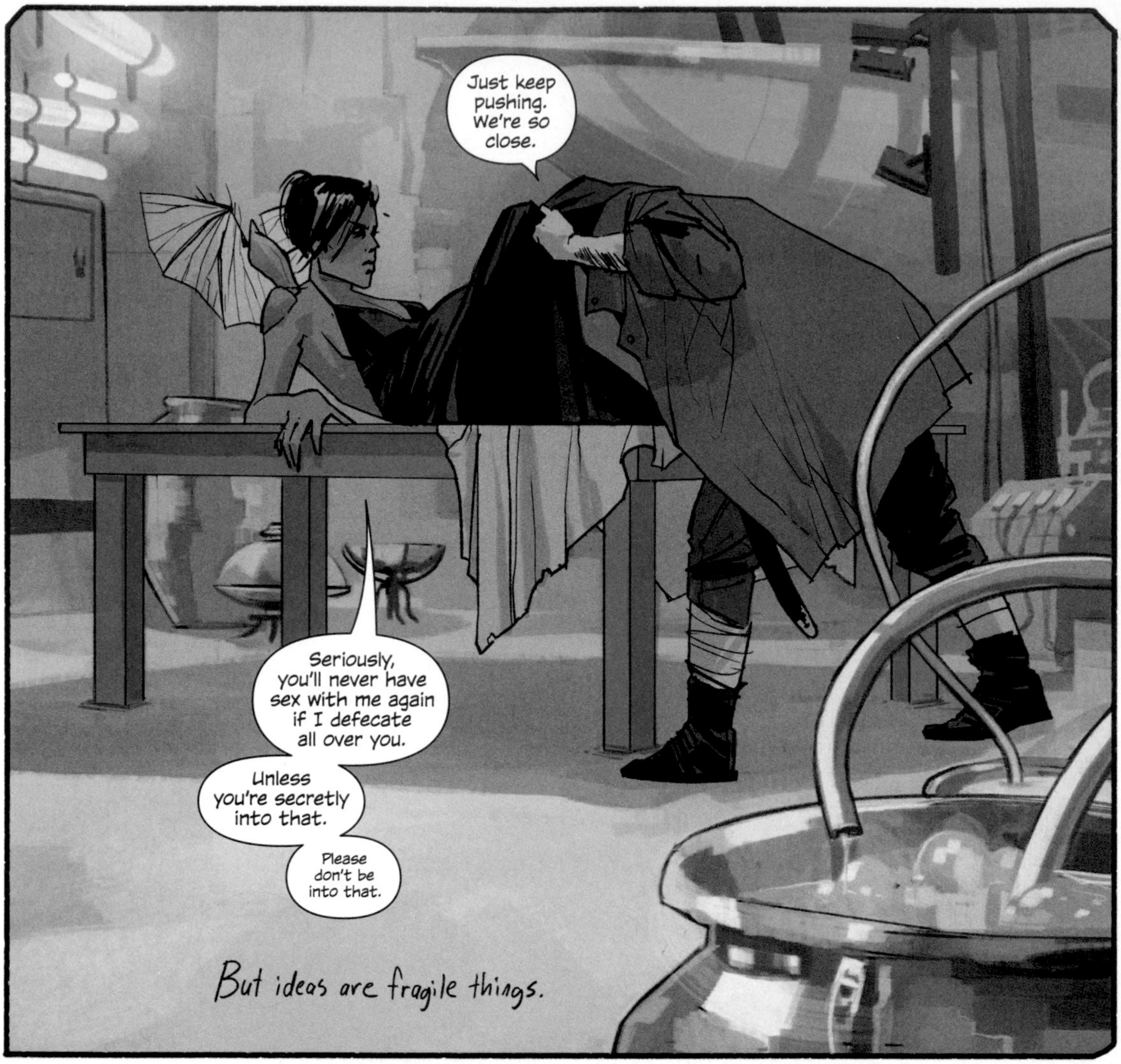
Just keep pushing. We're so close.
Seriously, you'll never have sex with me again if I defecate all over you.
Unless you're secretly into that.
Please don't be into that.
But ideas are fragile things.

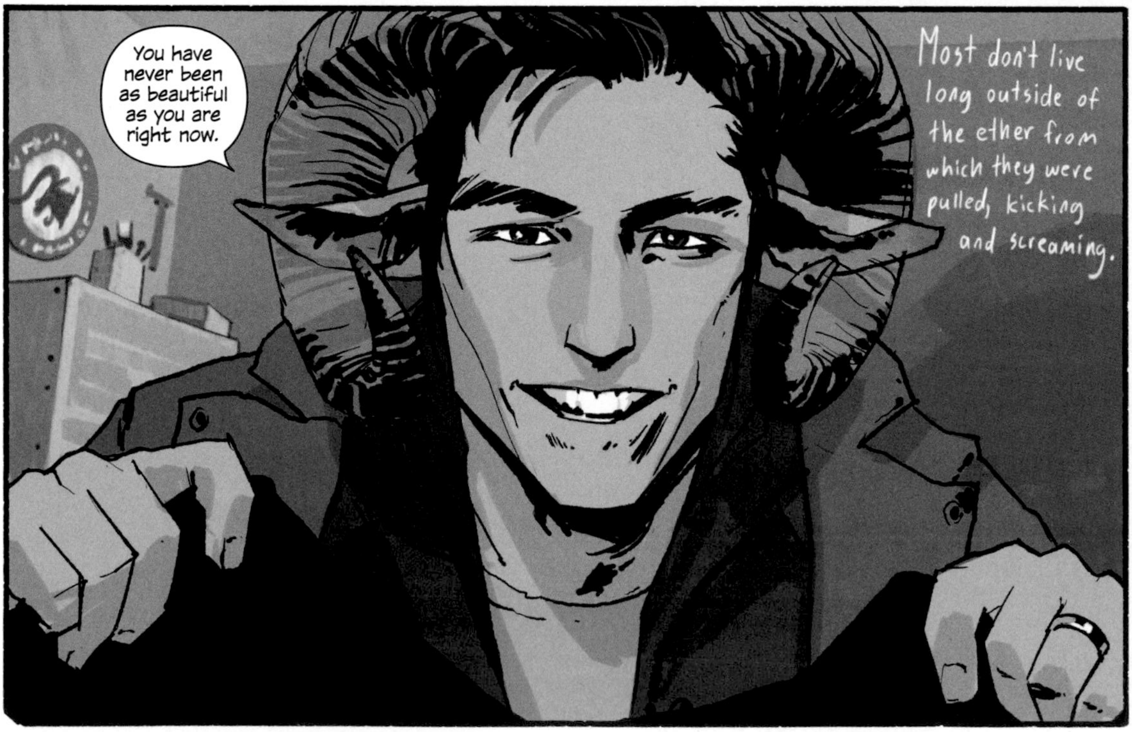
You have never been as beautiful as you are right now.
Most don't live long outside of the ether from which they were pulled, kicking and screaming.

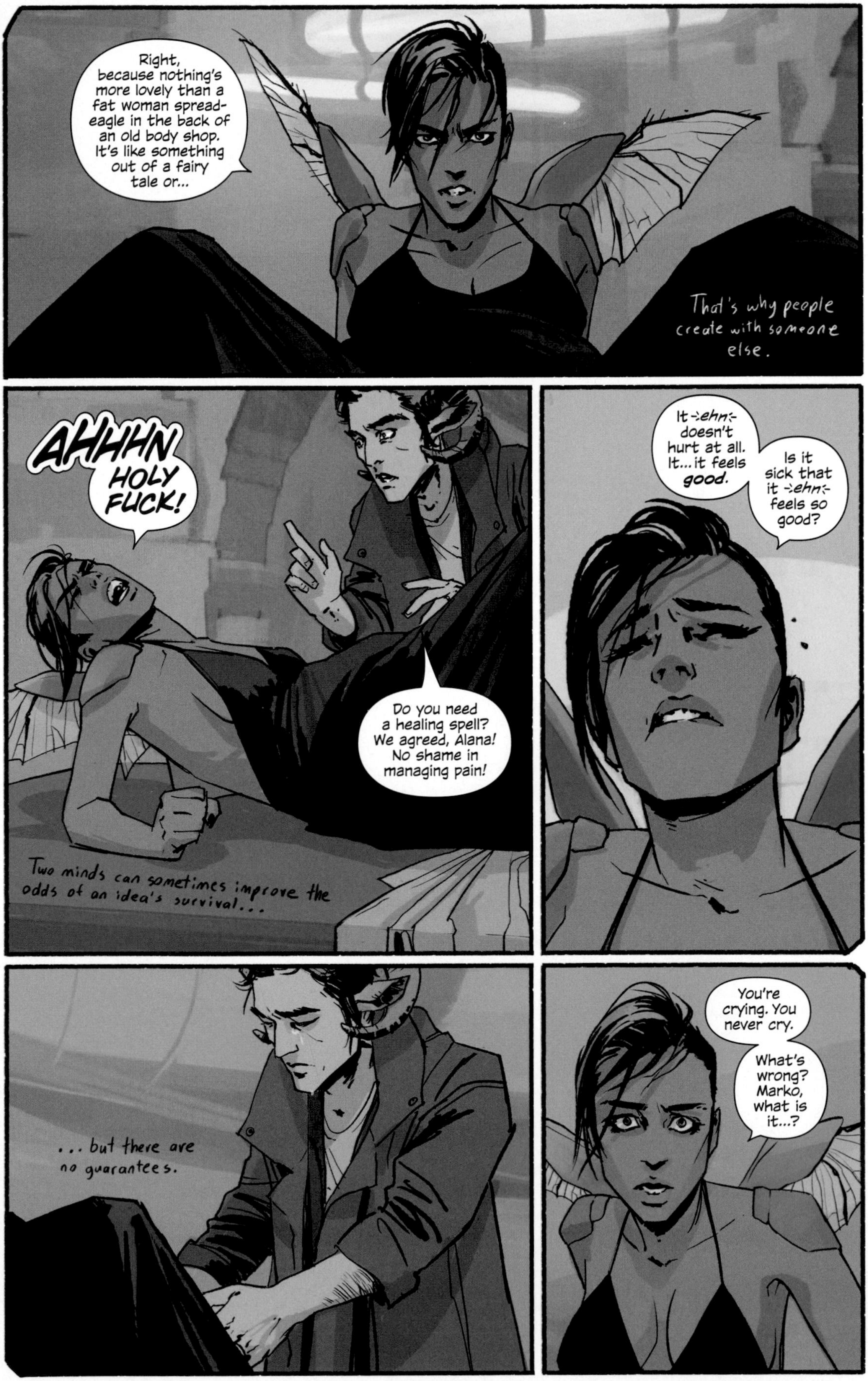

Right, because nothing's more lovely than a fat woman spread-eagle in the back of an old body shop. It's like something out of a fairy tale or...
That's why people create with someone else.
AHHHN HOLY FUCK!
Do you need a healing spell? We agreed, Alana! No shame in managing pain!
Two minds can sometimes improve the odds of an idea's survival...
It -ehn- doesn't hurt at all. It... it feels good.
Is it sick that it -ehn- feels so good?
...but there are no guarantees.
You're crying. You never cry.
What's wrong? Marko, what is it...?

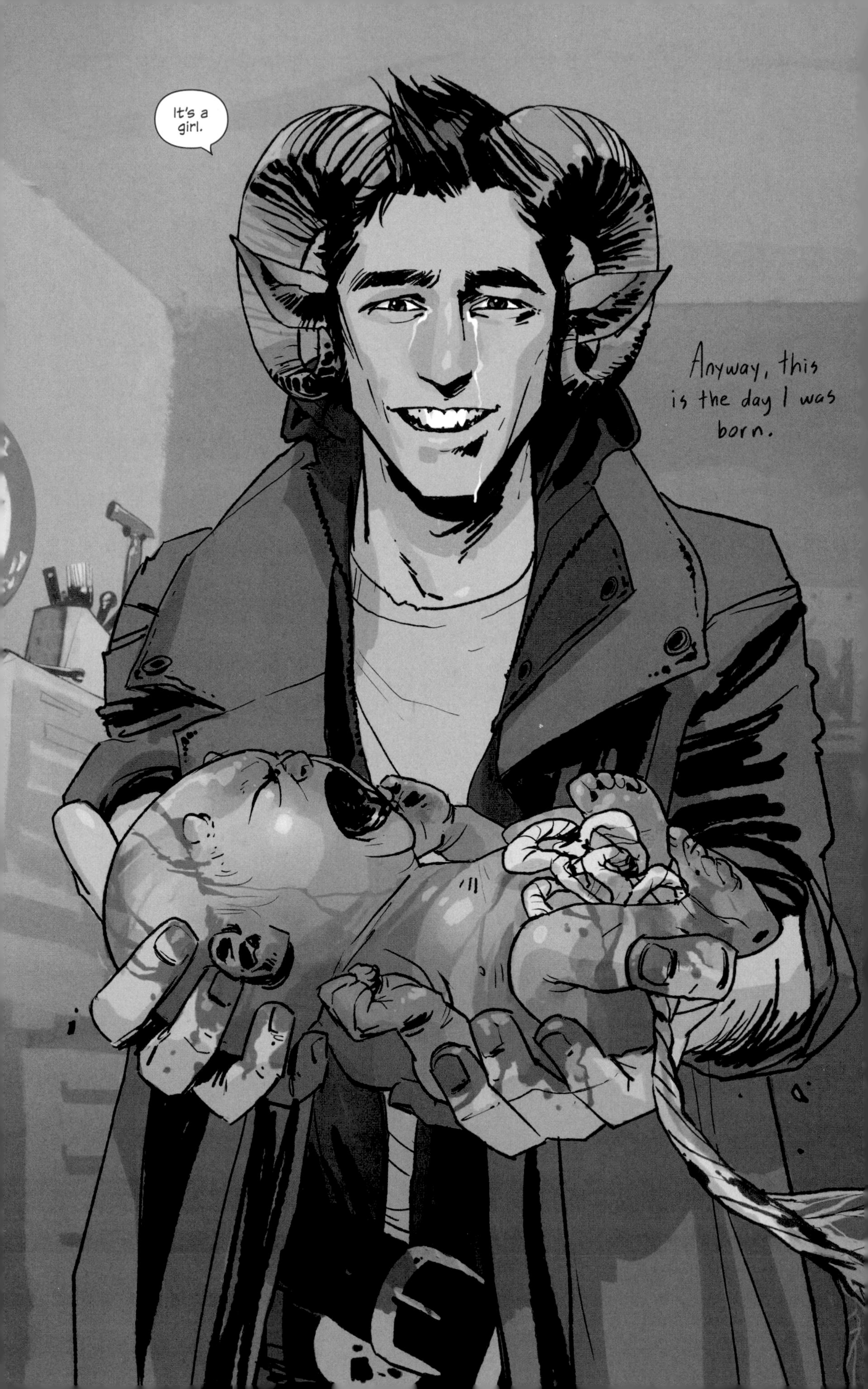
It's a girl.
Anyway, this is the day I was born.

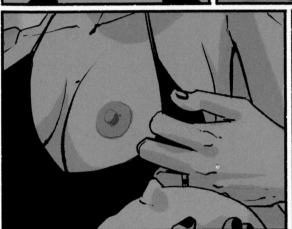
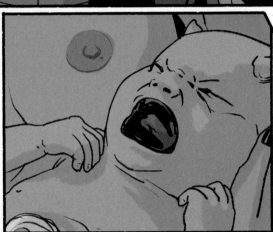

She's perfect.

Look, she's gonna have your horns.

And your wings.

But what's up with those eyes...?

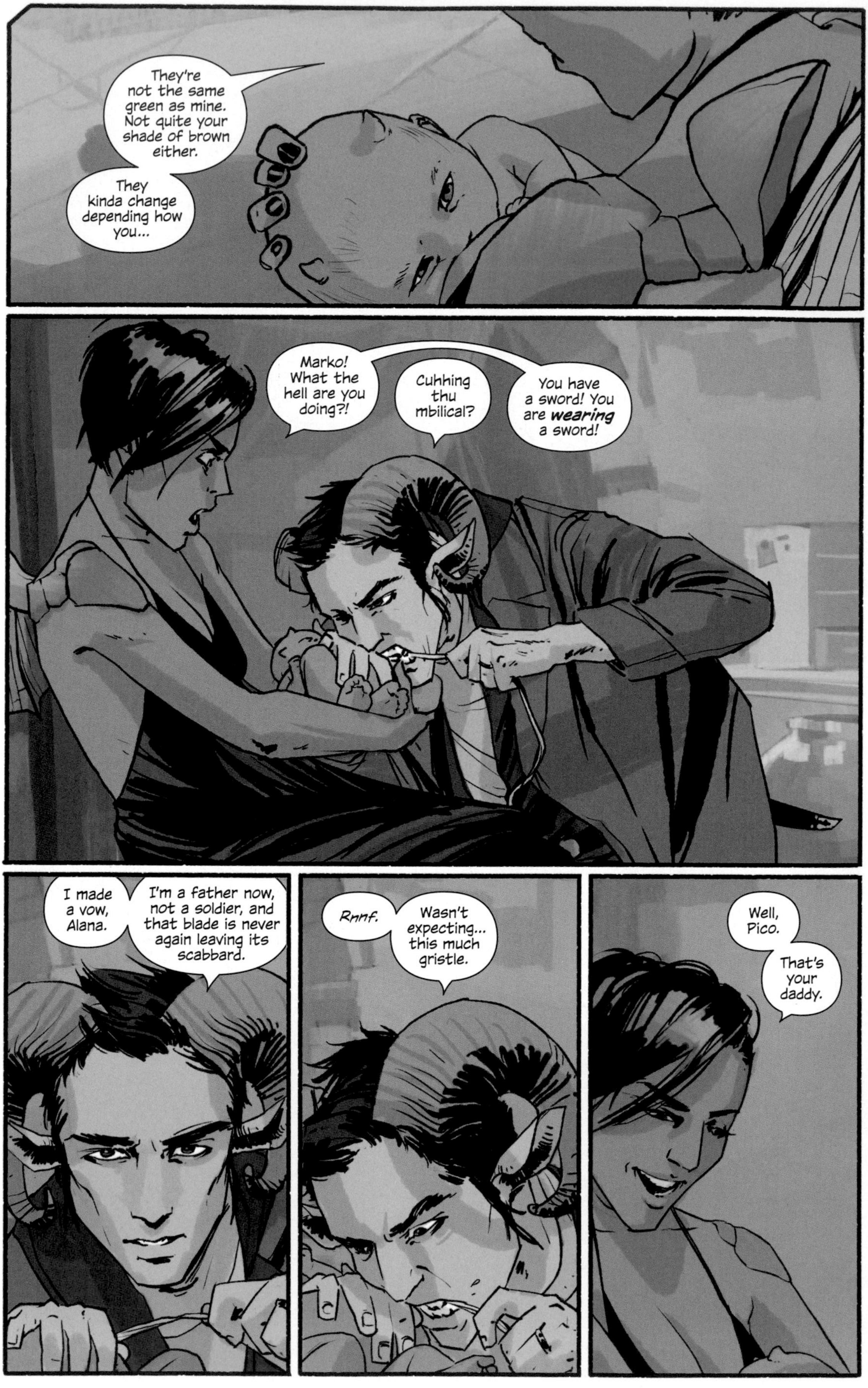
They're not the same green as mine. Not quite your shade of brown either.
They kinda change depending how you...
Marko! What the hell are you doing?!
Cuhhing thu mbilical?
You have a sword! You are *wearing* a sword!
I made a vow, Alana.
I'm a father now, not a soldier, and that blade is never again leaving its scabbard.
Rnnf.
Wasn't expecting... this much gristle.
Well, Pico.
That's your daddy.

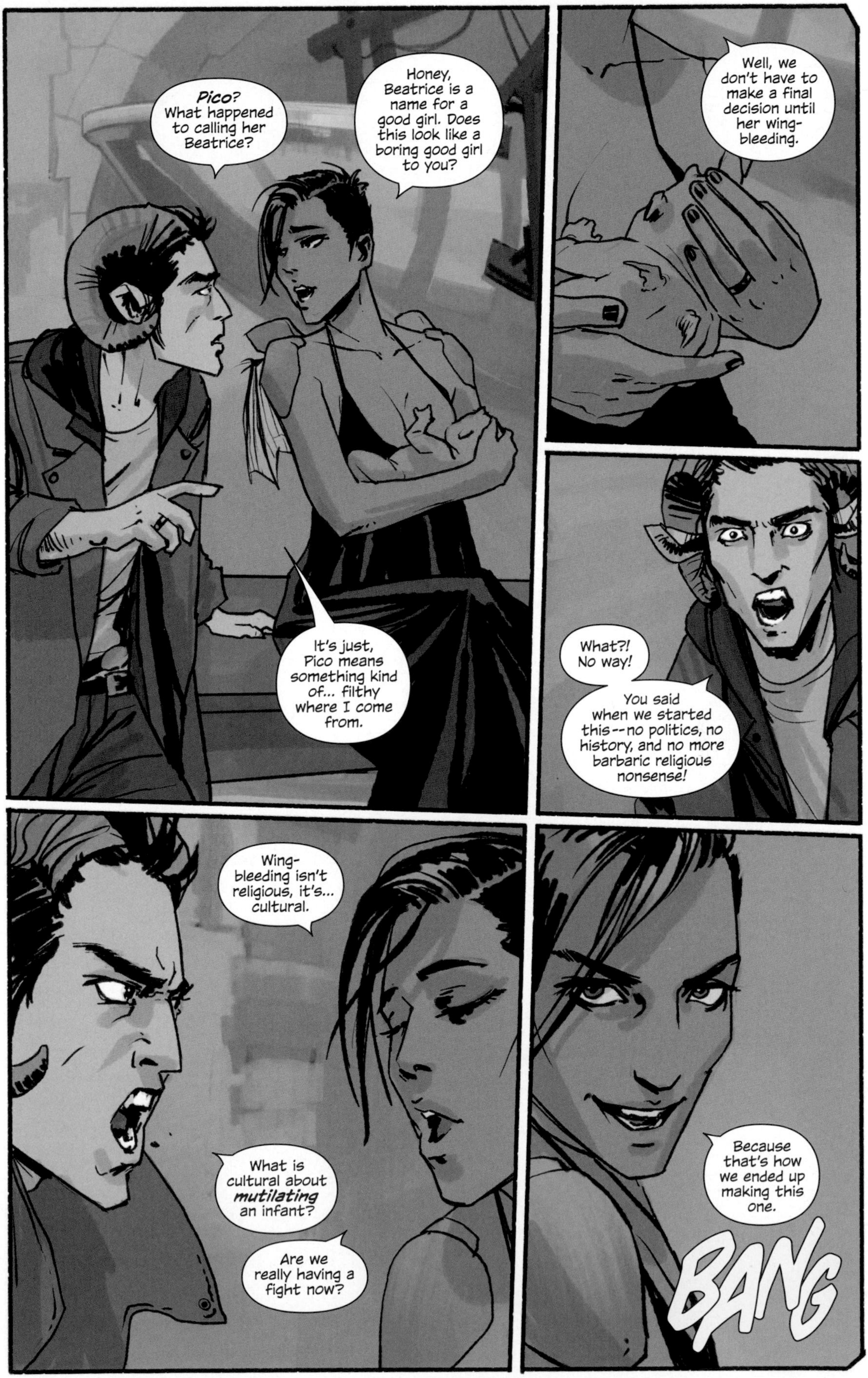
Pico? What happened to calling her Beatrice?
Honey, Beatrice is a name for a good girl. Does this look like a boring good girl to you?
It's just, Pico means something kind of... filthy where I come from.
Well, we don't have to make a final decision until her wing-bleeding.
What?! No way!
You said when we started this--no politics, no history, and no more barbaric religious nonsense!
Wing-bleeding isn't religious, it's... cultural.
What is cultural about *mutilating* an infant?
Are we really having a fight now?
Because that's how we ended up making this one.
BANG

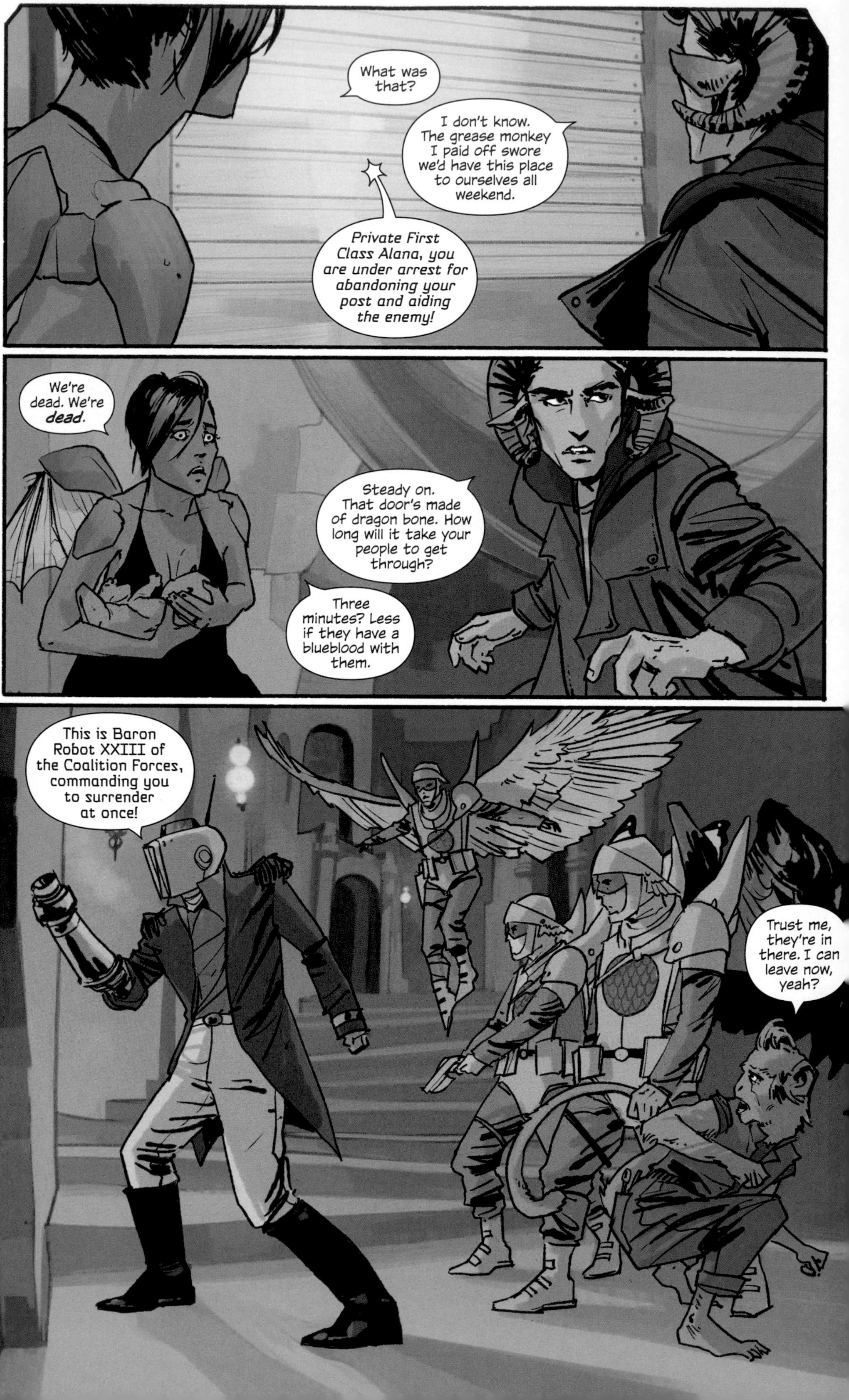
What was that?
I don't know. The grease monkey I paid off swore we'd have this place to ourselves all weekend.
Private First Class Alana, you are under arrest for abandoning your post and aiding the enemy!
We're dead. We're *dead*.
Steady on. That door's made of dragon bone. How long will it take your people to get through?
Three minutes? Less if they have a blueblood with them.
This is Baron Robot XXIII of the Coalition Forces, commanding you to surrender at once!
Trust me, they're in there. I can leave now, yeah?

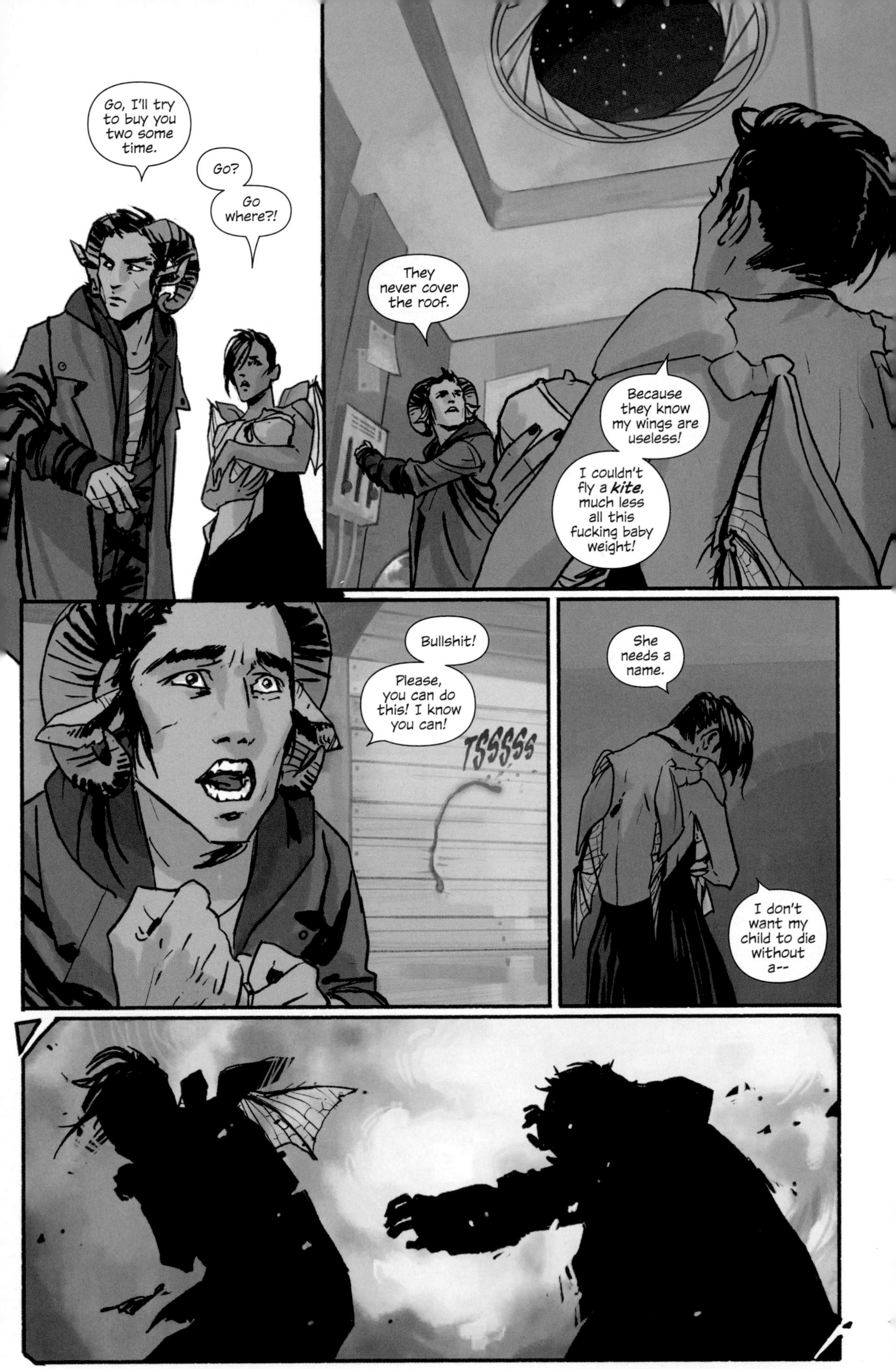
Go, I'll try to buy you two some time.
Go?
Go where?!
They never cover the roof.
Because they know my wings are useless!
I couldn't fly a *kite*, much less all this fucking baby weight!
Bullshit!
Please, you can do this! I know you can!
TSSSSs
She needs a name.
I don't want my child to die without a--

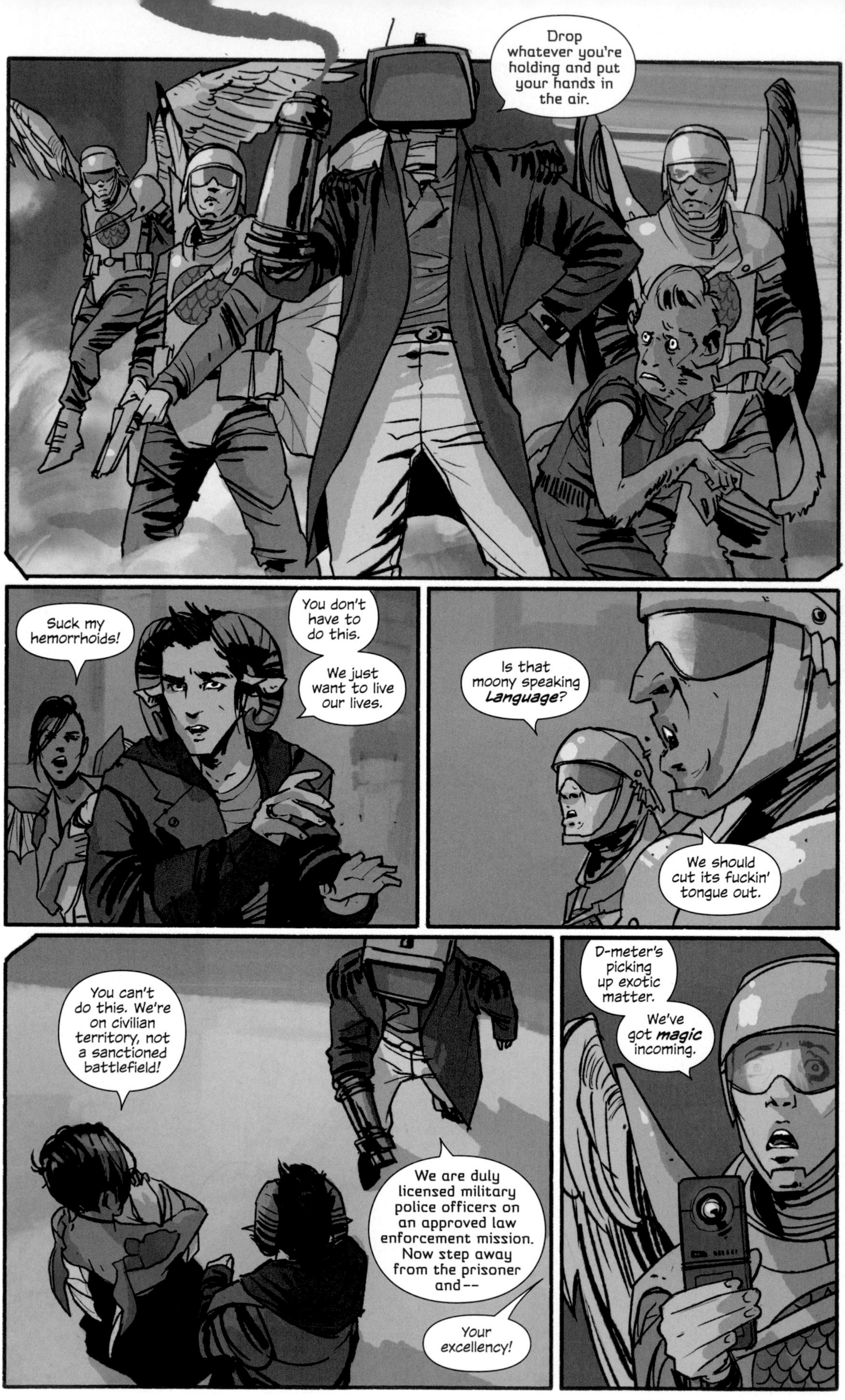
Drop whatever you're holding and put your hands in the air.
Suck my hemorrhoids!
You don't have to do this.
We just want to live our lives.
Is that moony speaking *Language*?
We should cut its fuckin' tongue out.
You can't do this. We're on civilian territory, not a sanctioned battlefield!
We are duly licensed military police officers on an approved law enforcement mission. Now step away from the prisoner and--
Your excellency!
D-meter's picking up exotic matter.
We've got *magic* incoming.

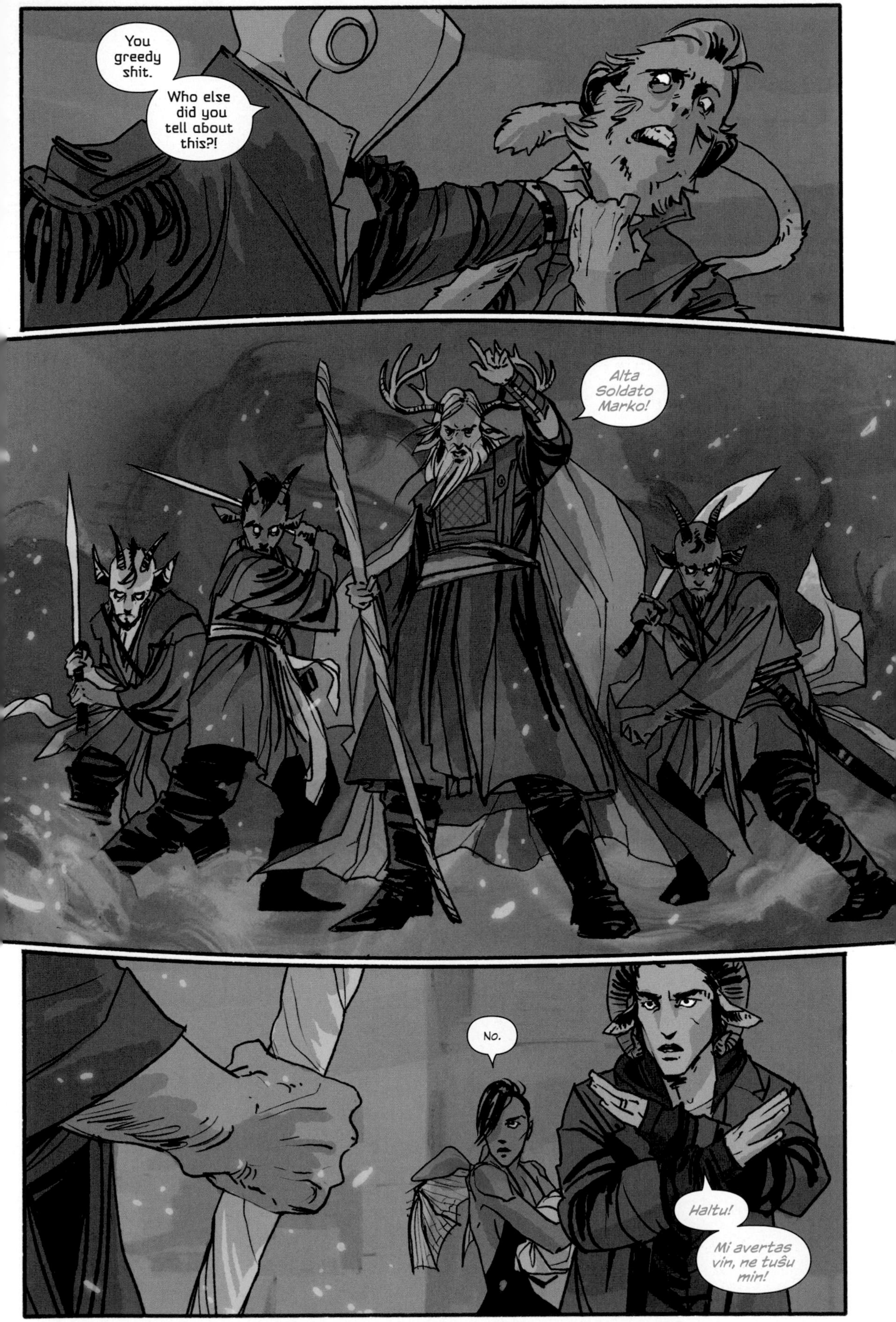
You greedy shit.
Who else did you tell about this?!
Alta Soldato Marko!
No.
Haltu!
Mi avertas vin, ne tuŝu min!

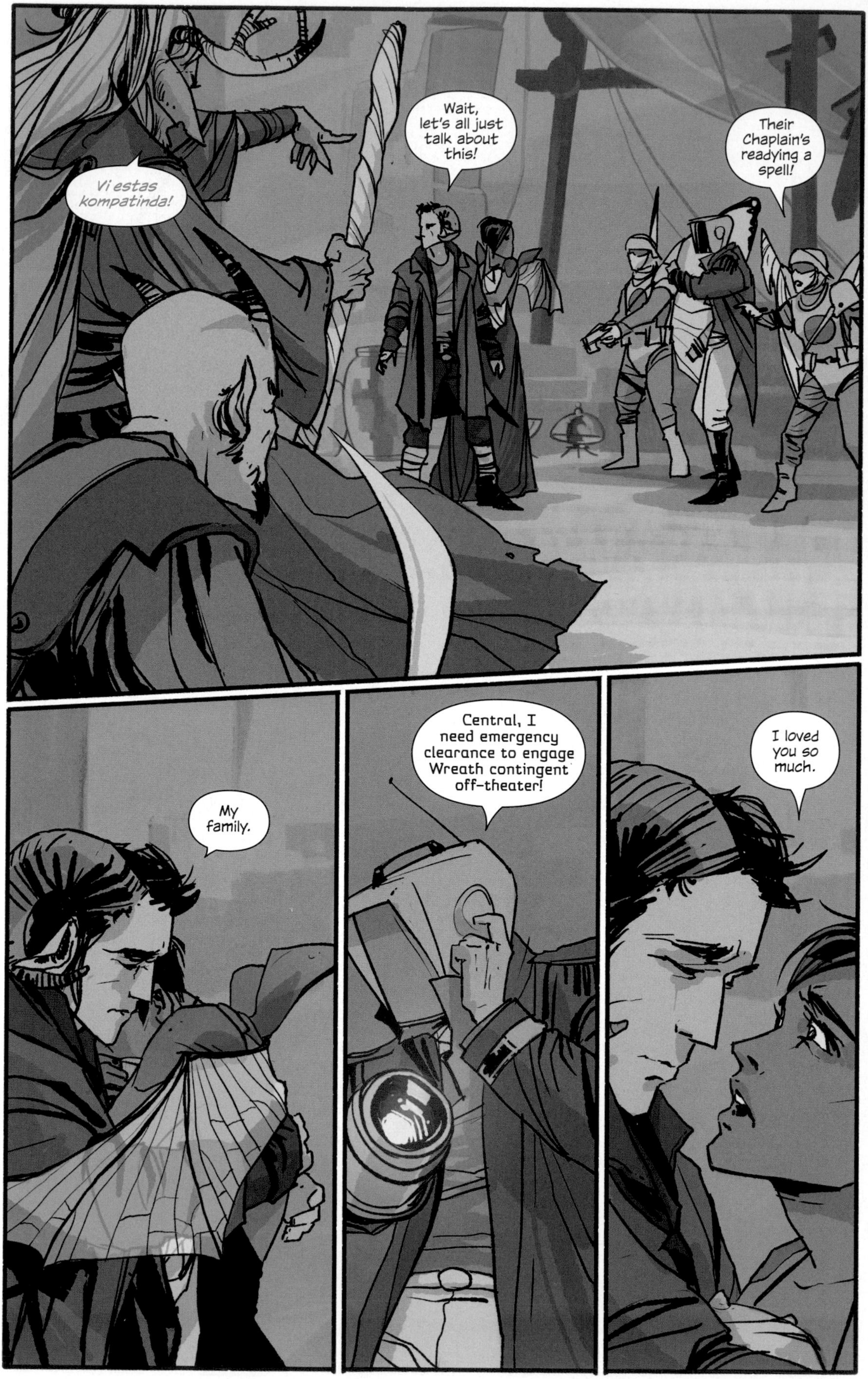
Vi estas kompatinda!
Wait, let's all just talk about this!
Their Chaplain's readying a spell!
My family.
Central, I need emergency clearance to engage Wreath contingent off-theater!
I loved you so much.

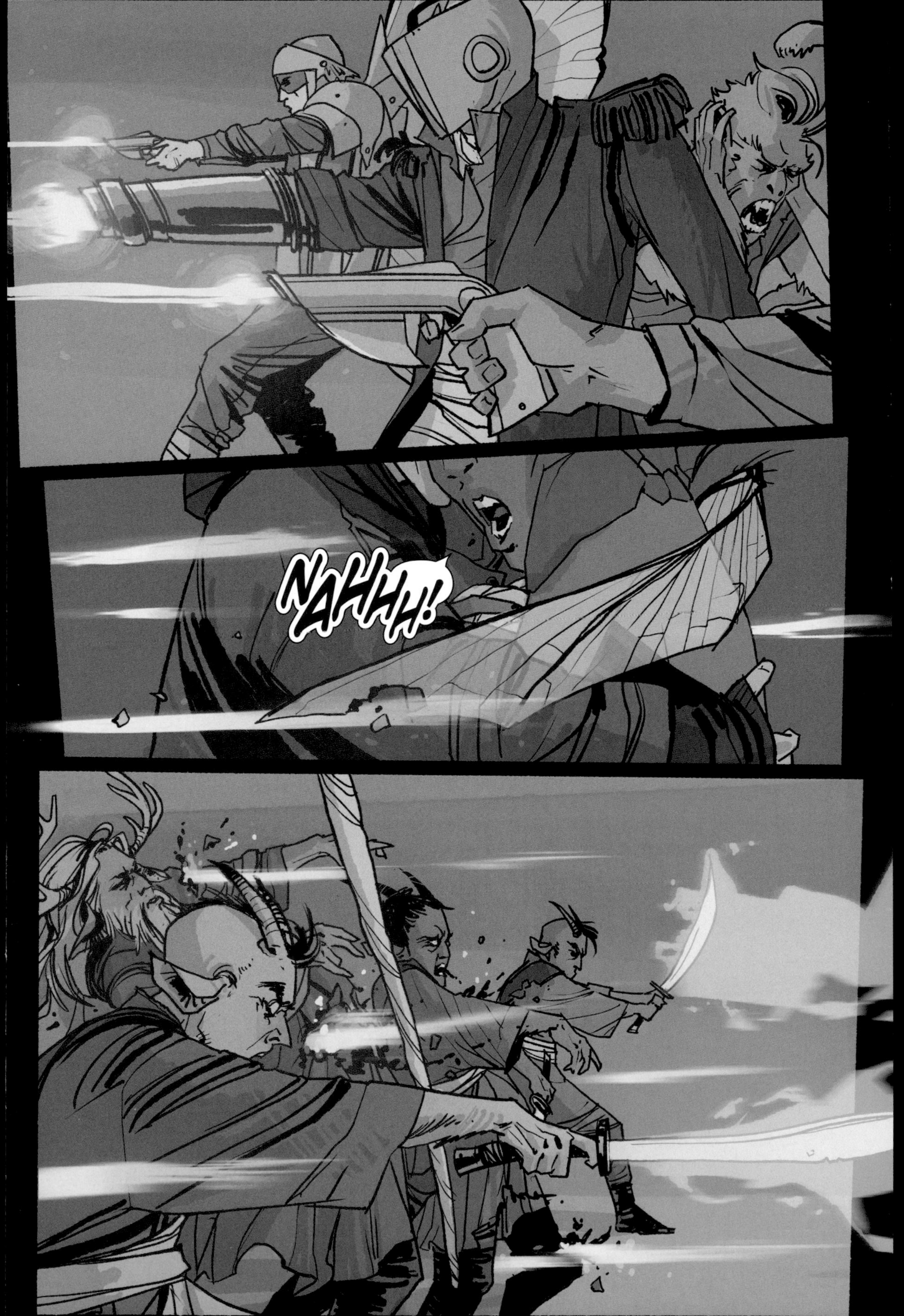
NAHHH!

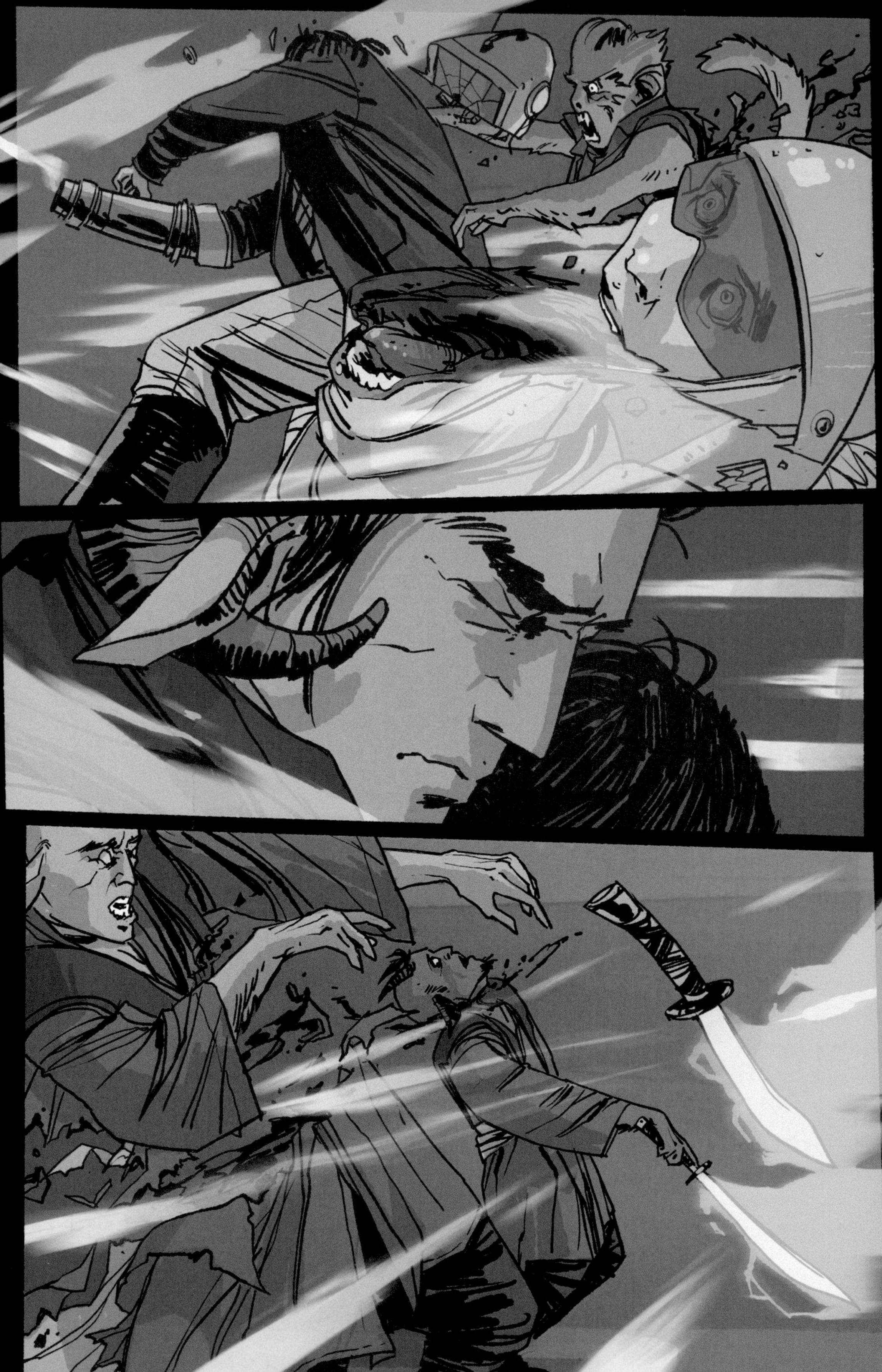

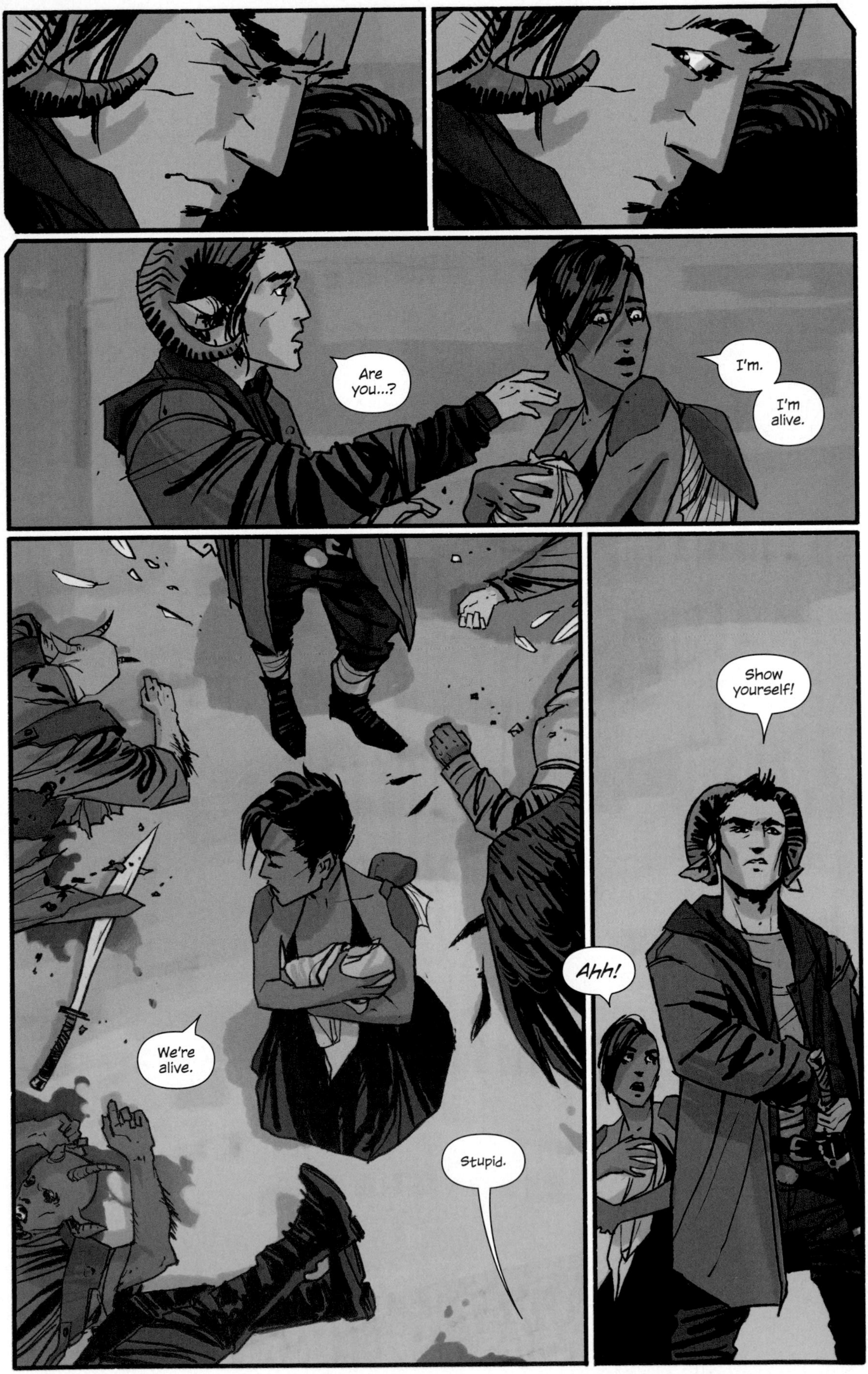

Are you...?
I'm.
I'm alive.
We're alive.
Stupid.
Show yourself!
Ahh!

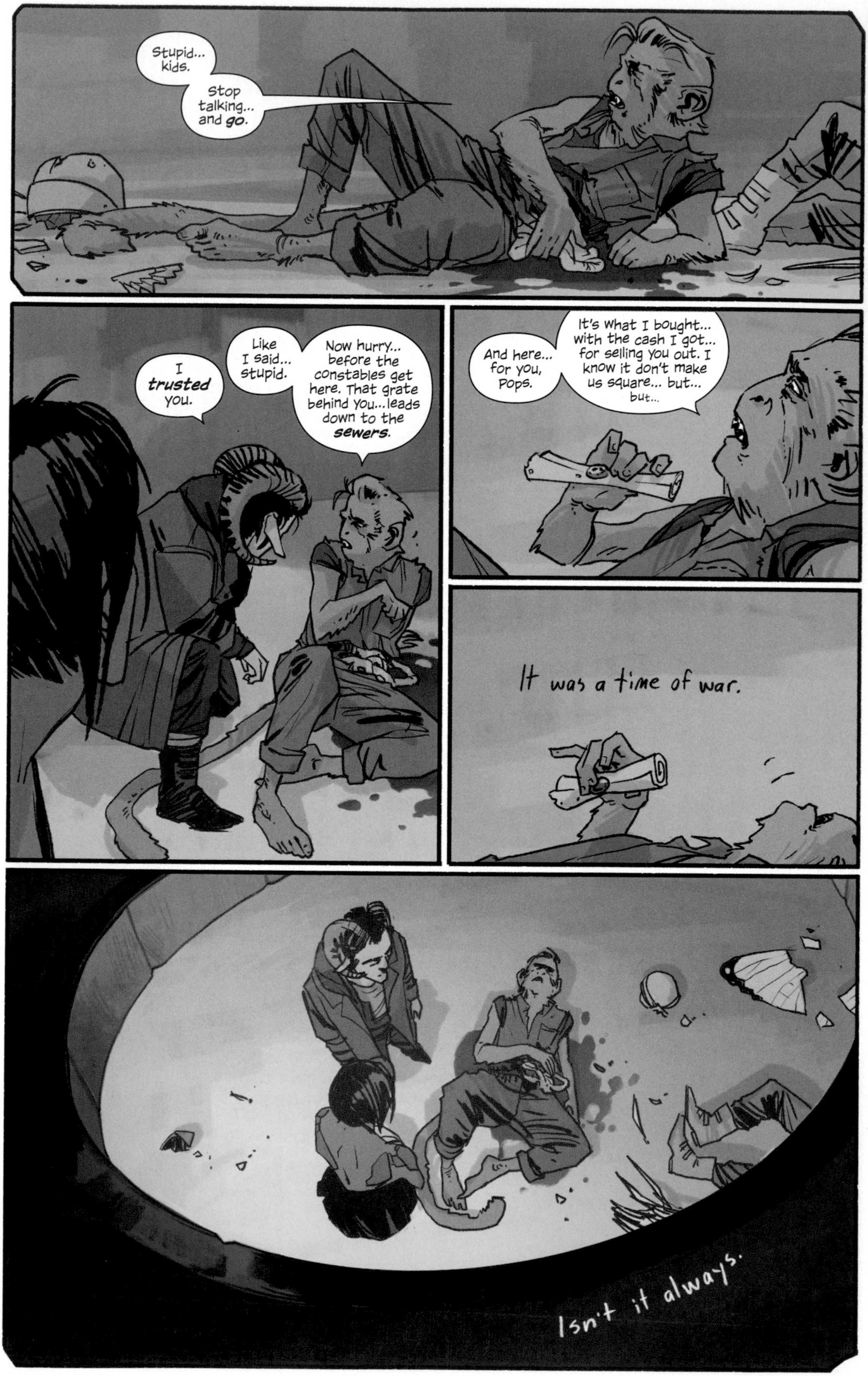

Stupid... kids.
Stop talking... and go.
I trusted you.
Like I said... stupid.
Now hurry... before the constables get here. That grate behind you...leads down to the sewers.
And here... for you, Pops.
It's what I bought... with the cash I got... for selling you out. I know it don't make us square... but... but...
It was a time of war.
Isn't it always.

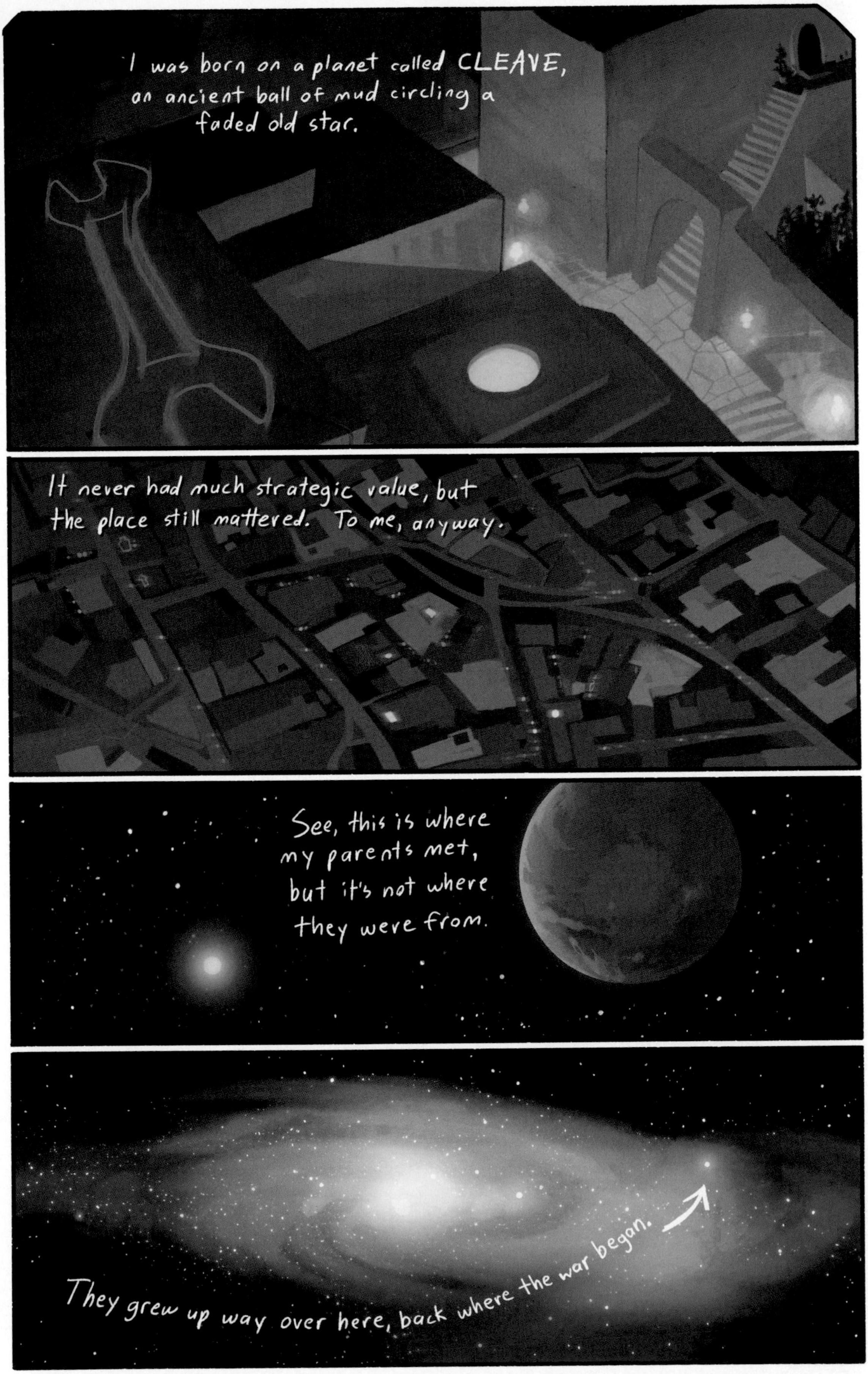
I was born on a planet called CLEAVE, an ancient ball of mud circling a faded old star.
It never had much strategic value, but the place still mattered. To me, anyway.
See, this is where my parents met, but it's not where they were from.
They grew up way over here, back where the war began.

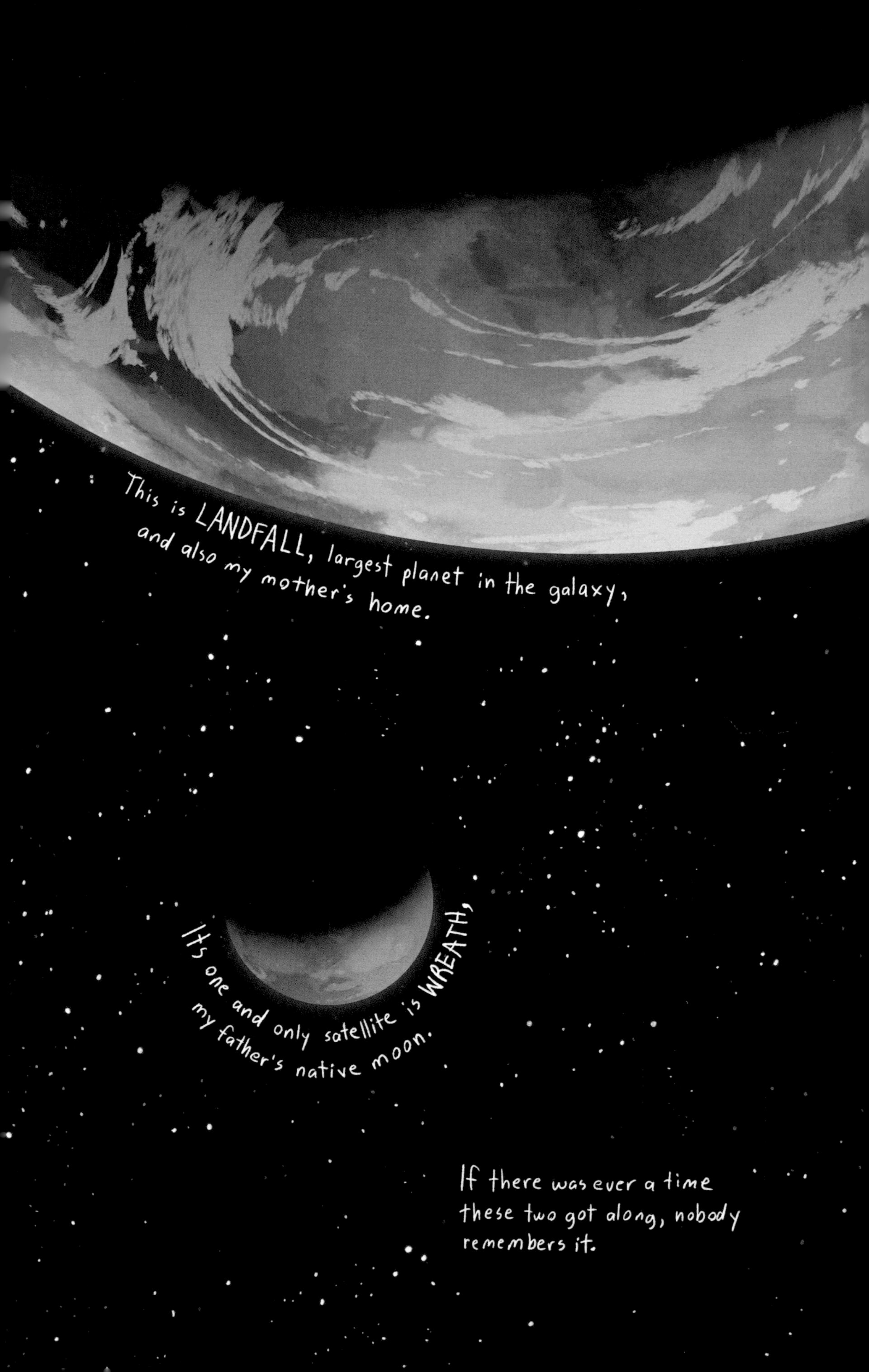
This is LANDFALL, largest planet in the galaxy, and also my mother's home.
It's one and only satellite is WREATH, my father's native moon.
If there was ever a time these two got along, nobody remembers it.

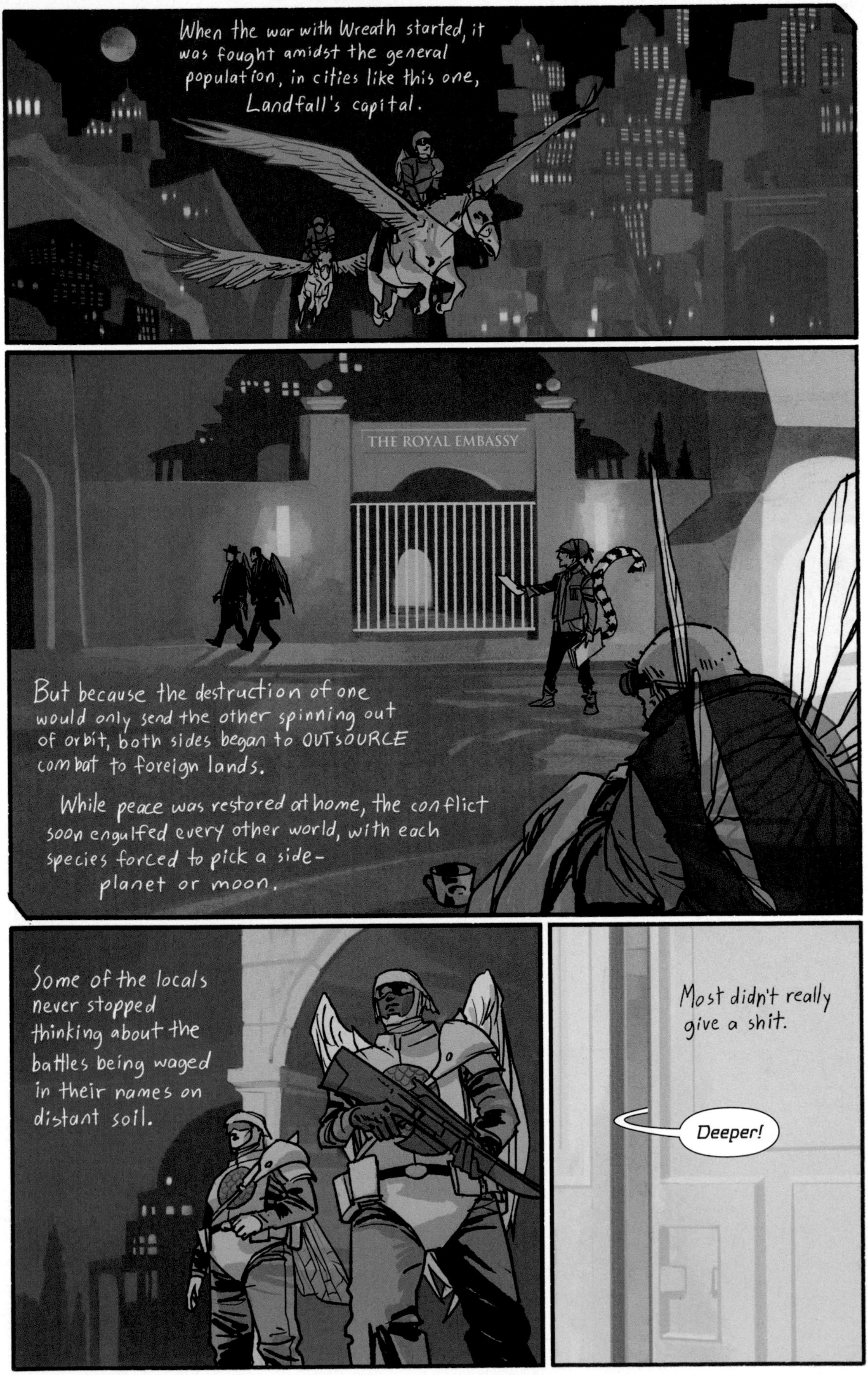
When the war with Wreath started, it was fought amidst the general population, in cities like this one, Landfall's capital.
THE ROYAL EMBASSY
But because the destruction of one would only send the other spinning out of orbit, both sides began to OUTSOURCE combat to foreign lands.
While peace was restored at home, the conflict soon engulfed every other world, with each species forced to pick a side-planet or moon.
Some of the locals never stopped thinking about the battles being waged in their names on distant soil.
Most didn't really give a shit.
Deeper!

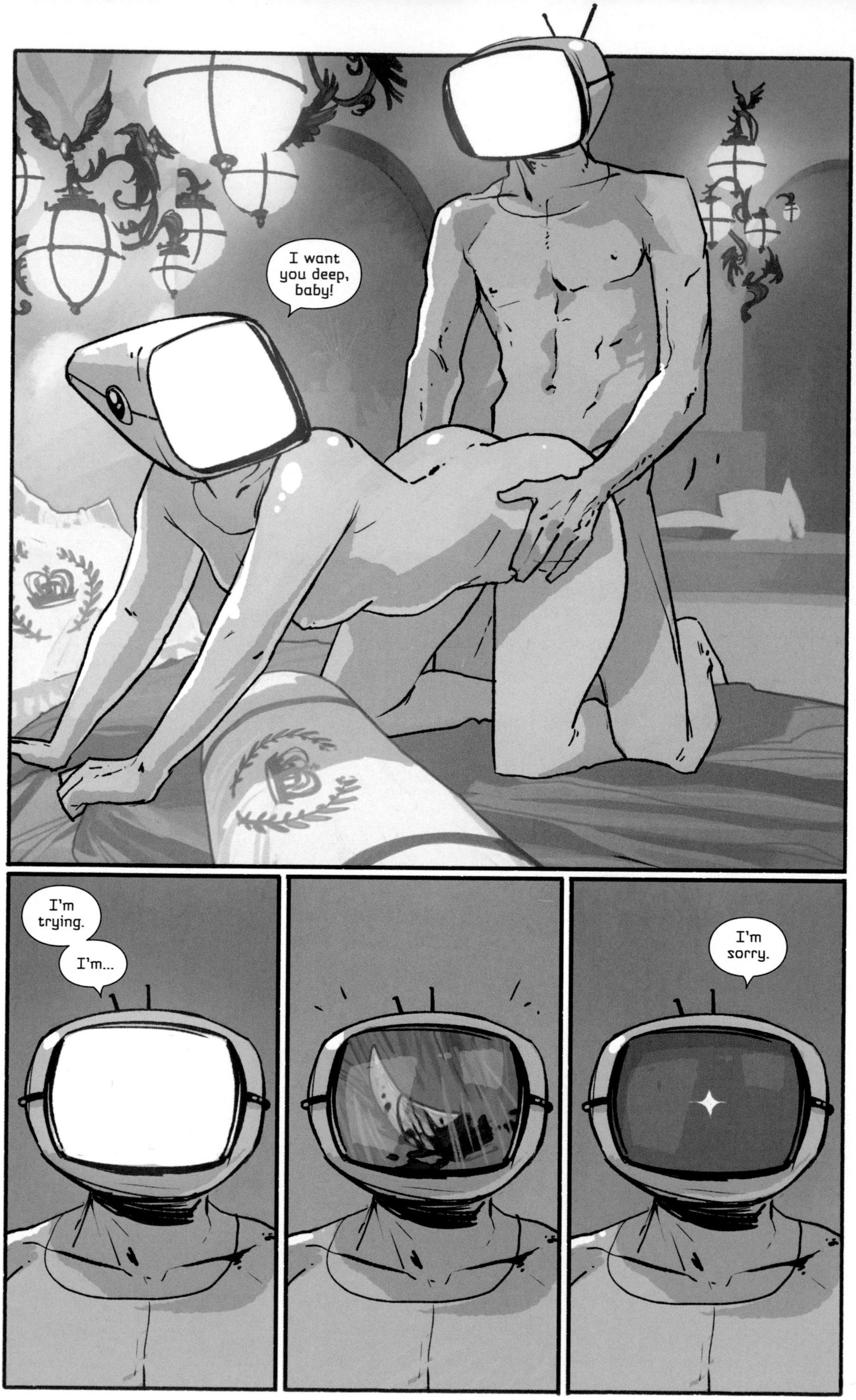
I want you deep, baby!
I'm trying.
I'm...
I'm sorry.

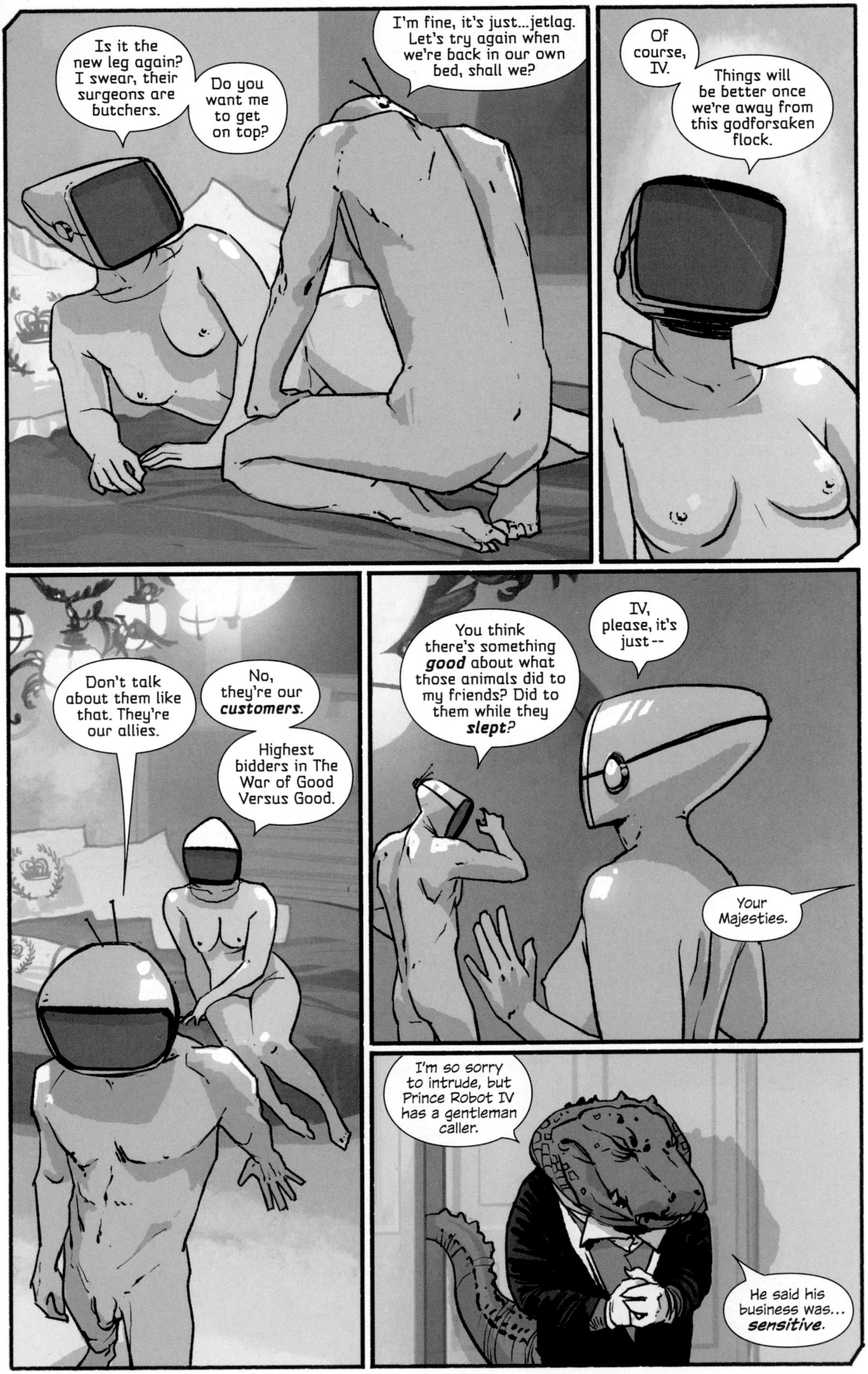
Is it the new leg again? I swear, their surgeons are butchers.
Do you want me to get on top?
I'm fine, it's just...jetlag. Let's try again when we're back in our own bed, shall we?
Of course, IV.
Things will be better once we're away from this godforsaken flock.
Don't talk about them like that. They're our allies.
No, they're our **customers**.
Highest bidders in The War of Good Versus Good.
You think there's something **good** about what those animals did to my friends? Did to them while they **slept**?
IV, please, it's just --
Your Majesties.
I'm so sorry to intrude, but Prince Robot IV has a gentleman caller.
He said his business was... **sensitive**.

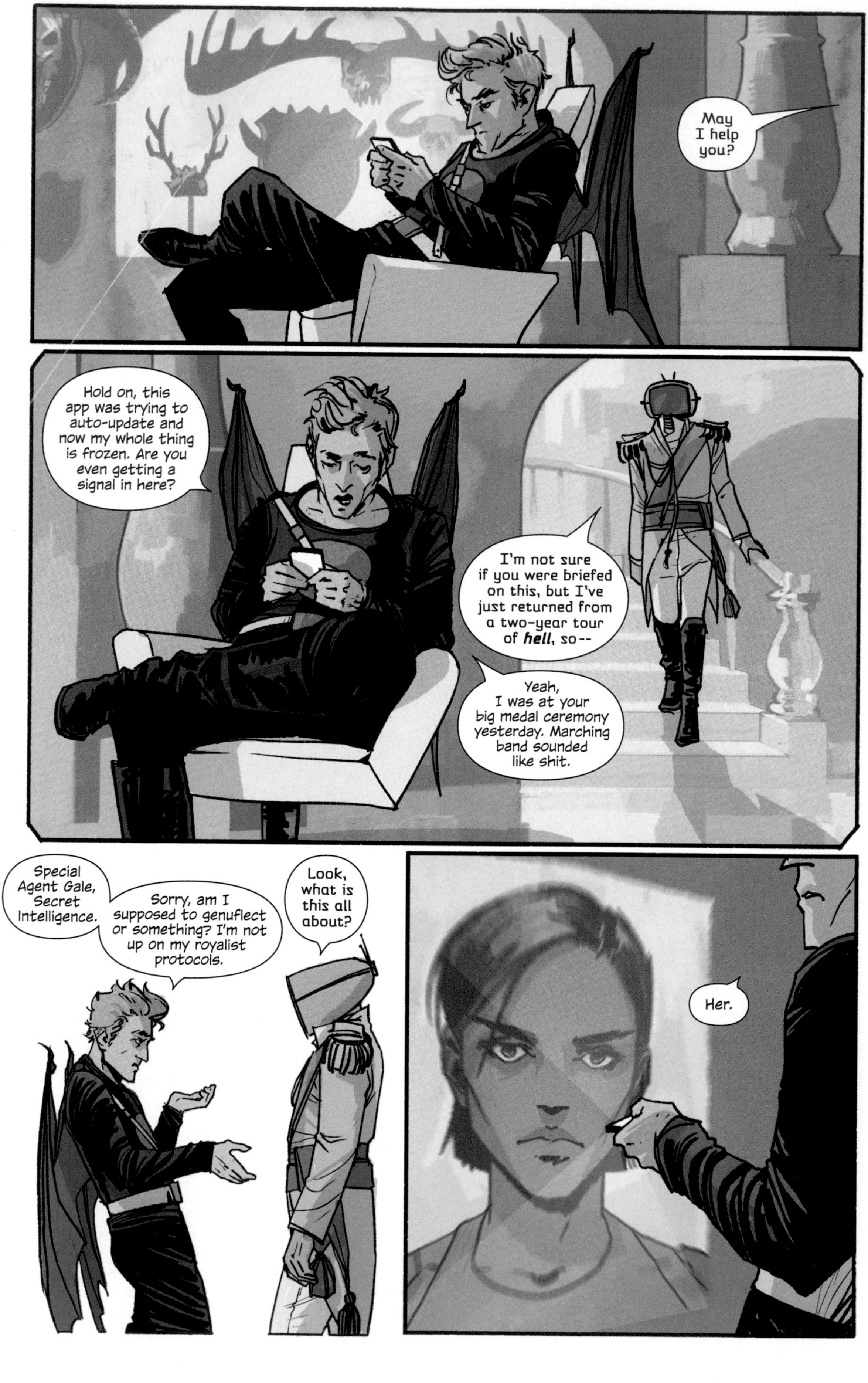
May I help you?
Hold on, this app was trying to auto-update and now my whole thing is frozen. Are you even getting a signal in here?
I'm not sure if you were briefed on this, but I've just returned from a two-year tour of **hell**, so--
Yeah, I was at your big medal ceremony yesterday. Marching band sounded like shit.
Special Agent Gale, Secret Intelligence.
Sorry, am I supposed to genuflect or something? I'm not up on my royalist protocols.
Look, what is this all about?
Her.

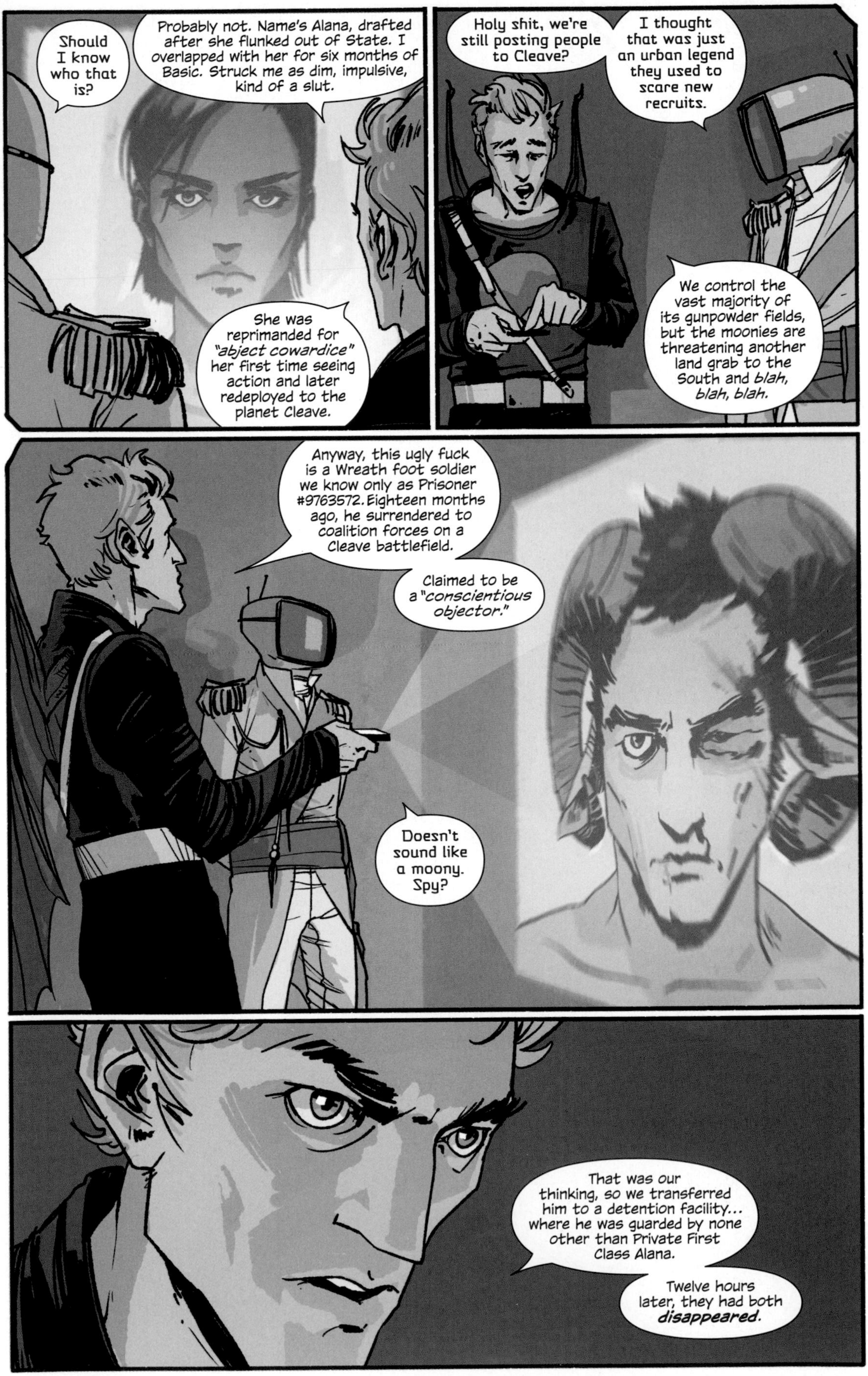
Should I know who that is?
Probably not. Name's Alana, drafted after she flunked out of State. I overlapped with her for six months of Basic. Struck me as dim, impulsive, kind of a slut.
She was reprimanded for *"abject cowardice"* her first time seeing action and later redeployed to the planet Cleave.
Holy shit, we're still posting people to Cleave?
I thought that was just an urban legend they used to scare new recruits.
We control the vast majority of its gunpowder fields, but the moonies are threatening another land grab to the South and *blah, blah, blah.*
Anyway, this ugly fuck is a Wreath foot soldier we know only as Prisoner #9763572. Eighteen months ago, he surrendered to coalition forces on a Cleave battlefield.
Claimed to be a *"conscientious objector."*
Doesn't sound like a moony. Spy?
That was our thinking, so we transferred him to a detention facility... where he was guarded by none other than Private First Class Alana.
Twelve hours later, they had both ***disappeared.***

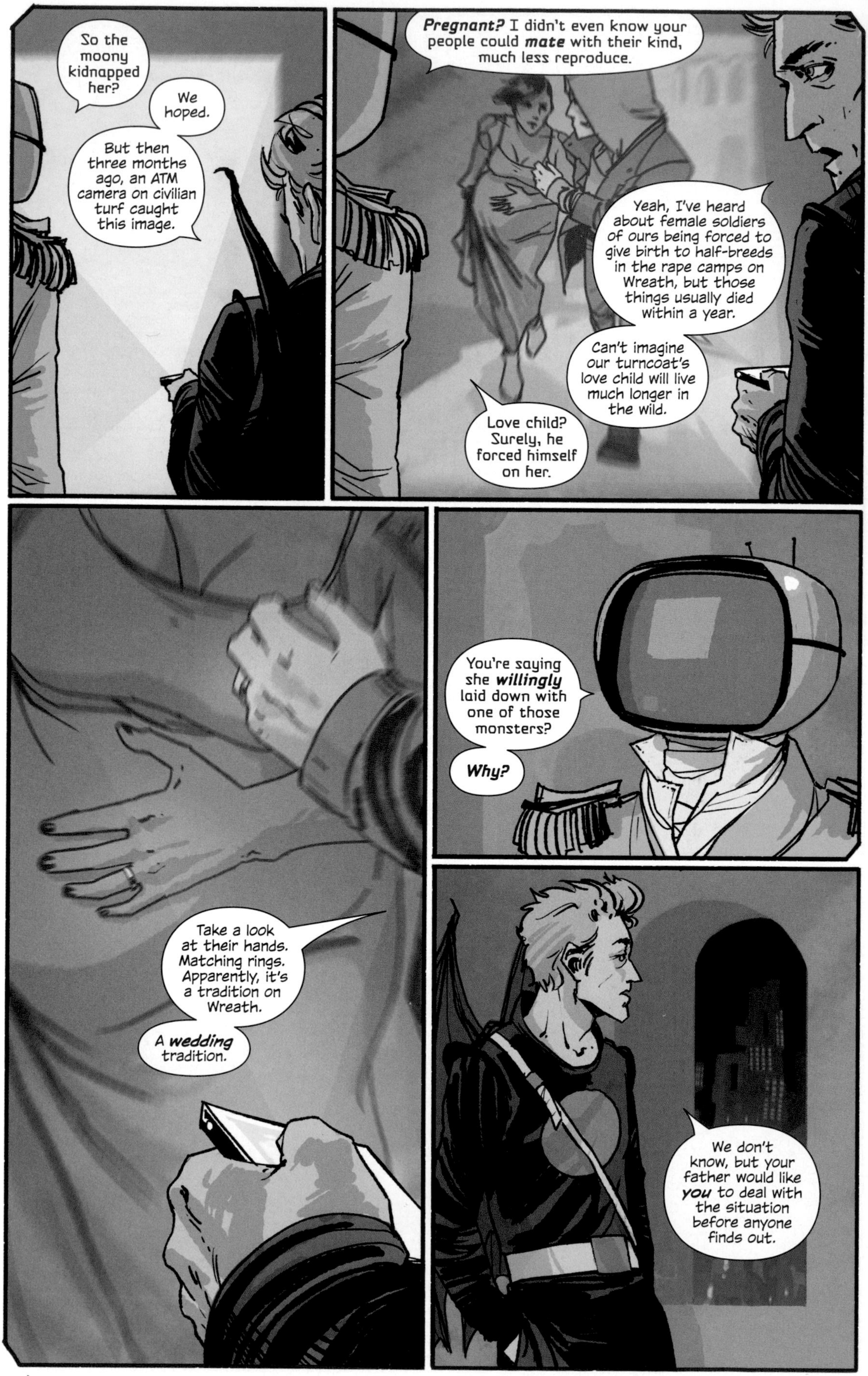

So the moony kidnapped her?
We hoped.
But then three months ago, an ATM camera on civilian turf caught this image.
Pregnant? I didn't even know your people could mate with their kind, much less reproduce.
Yeah, I've heard about female soldiers of ours being forced to give birth to half-breeds in the rape camps on Wreath, but those things usually died within a year.
Can't imagine our turncoat's love child will live much longer in the wild.
Love child? Surely, he forced himself on her.
Take a look at their hands. Matching rings. Apparently, it's a tradition on Wreath.
A wedding tradition.
You're saying she willingly laid down with one of those monsters?
Why?
We don't know, but your father would like you to deal with the situation before anyone finds out.

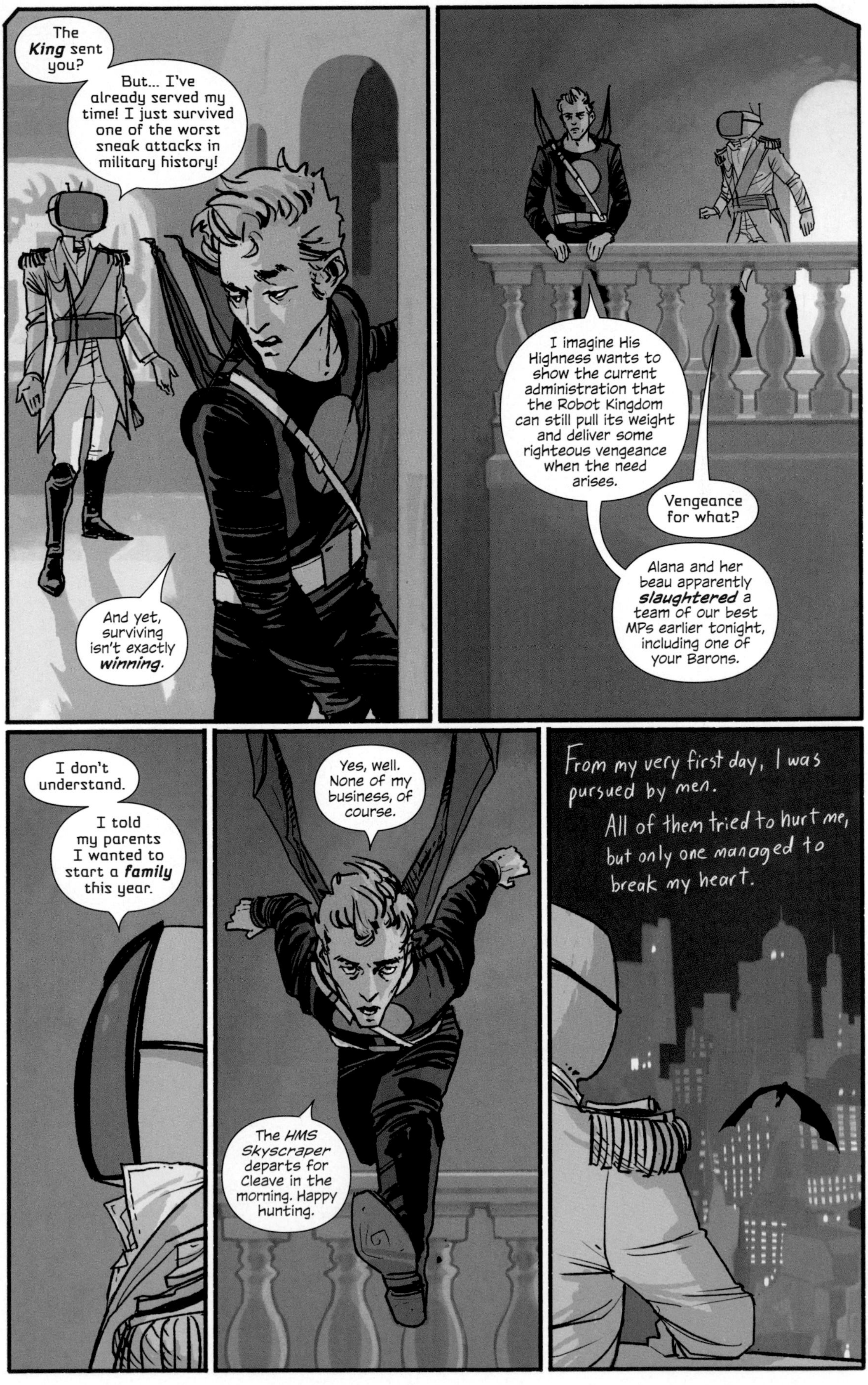
The *King* sent you?
But... I've already served my time! I just survived one of the worst sneak attacks in military history!
And yet, surviving isn't exactly *winning*.
I imagine His Highness wants to show the current administration that the Robot Kingdom can still pull its weight and deliver some righteous vengeance when the need arises.
Vengeance for what?
Alana and her beau apparently *slaughtered* a team of our best MPs earlier tonight, including one of your Barons.
I don't understand.
I told my parents I wanted to start a *family* this year.
Yes, well. None of my business, of course.
The *HMS Skyscraper* departs for Cleave in the morning. Happy hunting.
From my very first day, I was pursued by men.
All of them tried to hurt me, but only one managed to break my heart.

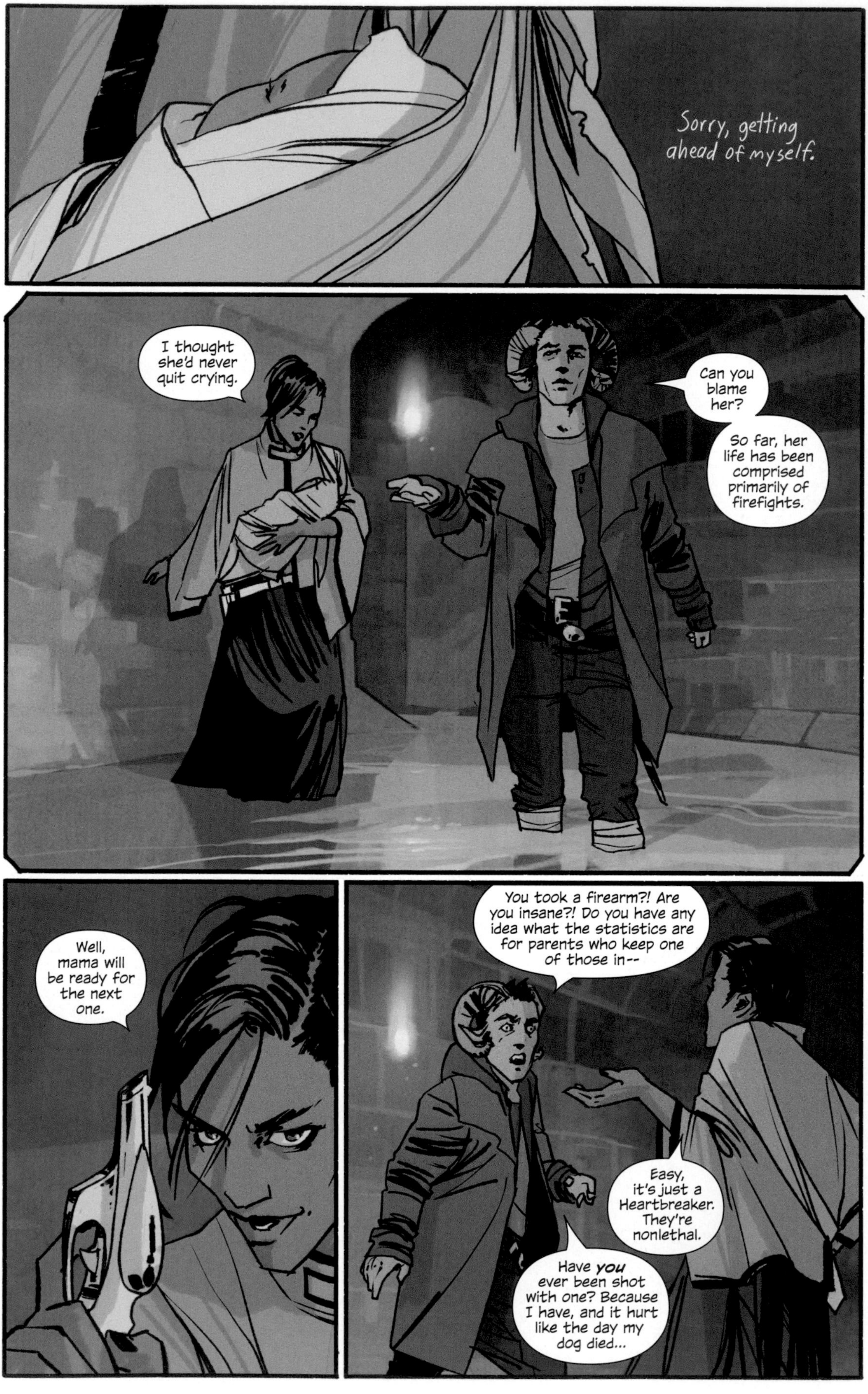
Sorry, getting ahead of myself.
I thought she'd never quit crying.
Can you blame her?
So far, her life has been comprised primarily of firefights.
Well, mama will be ready for the next one.
You took a firearm?! Are you insane?! Do you have any idea what the statistics are for parents who keep one of those in--
Easy, it's just a Heartbreaker. They're nonlethal.
Have *you* ever been shot with one? Because I have, and it hurt like the day my dog died...

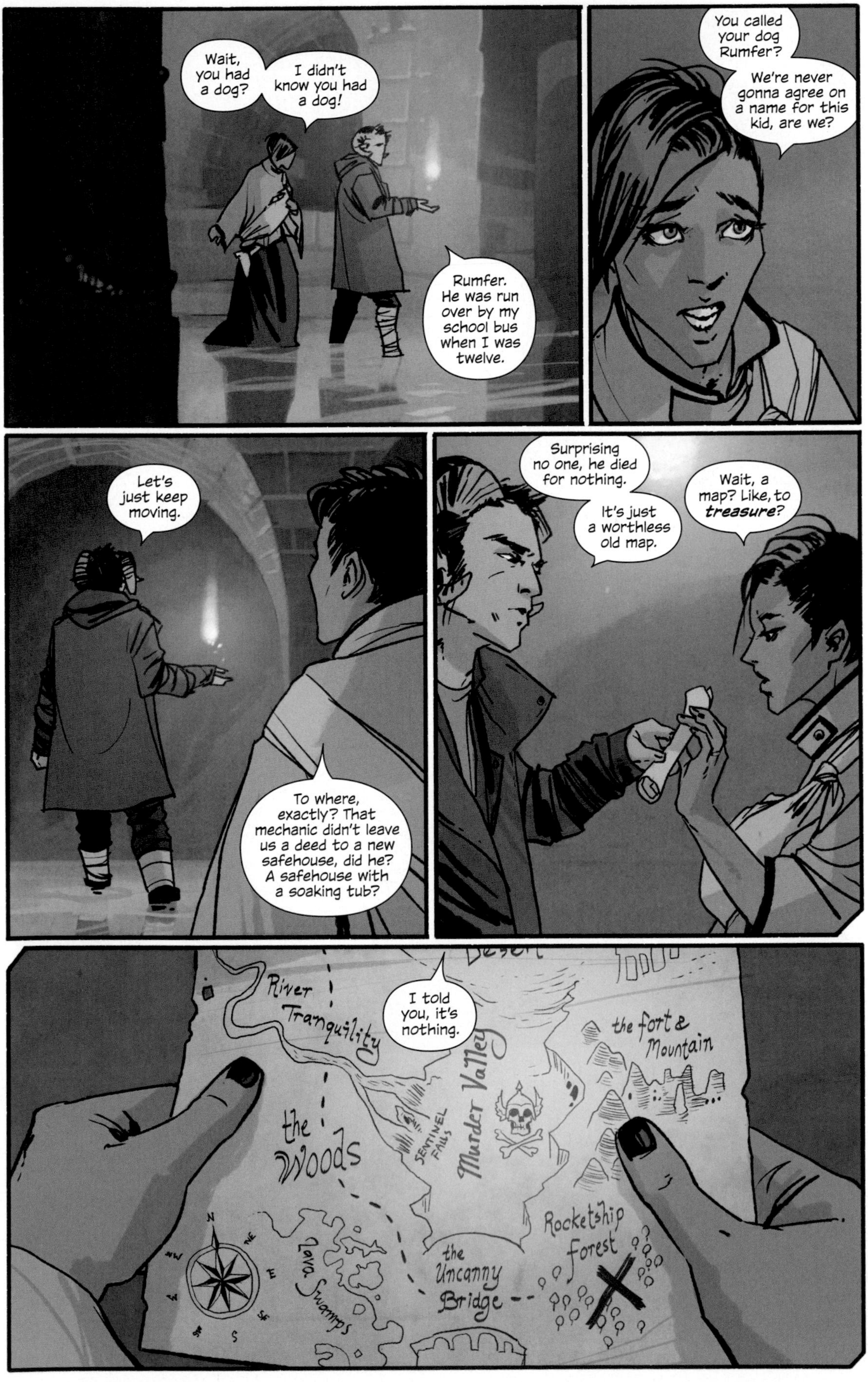
Wait, you had a dog?
I didn't know you had a dog!
Rumfer. He was run over by my school bus when I was twelve.
You called your dog Rumfer?
We're never gonna agree on a name for this kid, are we?
Let's just keep moving.
To where, exactly? That mechanic didn't leave us a deed to a new safehouse, did he? A safehouse with a soaking tub?
Surprising no one, he died for nothing.
It's just a worthless old map.
Wait, a map? Like, to *treasure*?
I told you, it's nothing.
River Tranquility
the fort & Mountain
Murder Valley
Sentinel Falls
the Woods
Rocketship Forest
the Uncanny Bridge
Lava Swamps
N
E
S

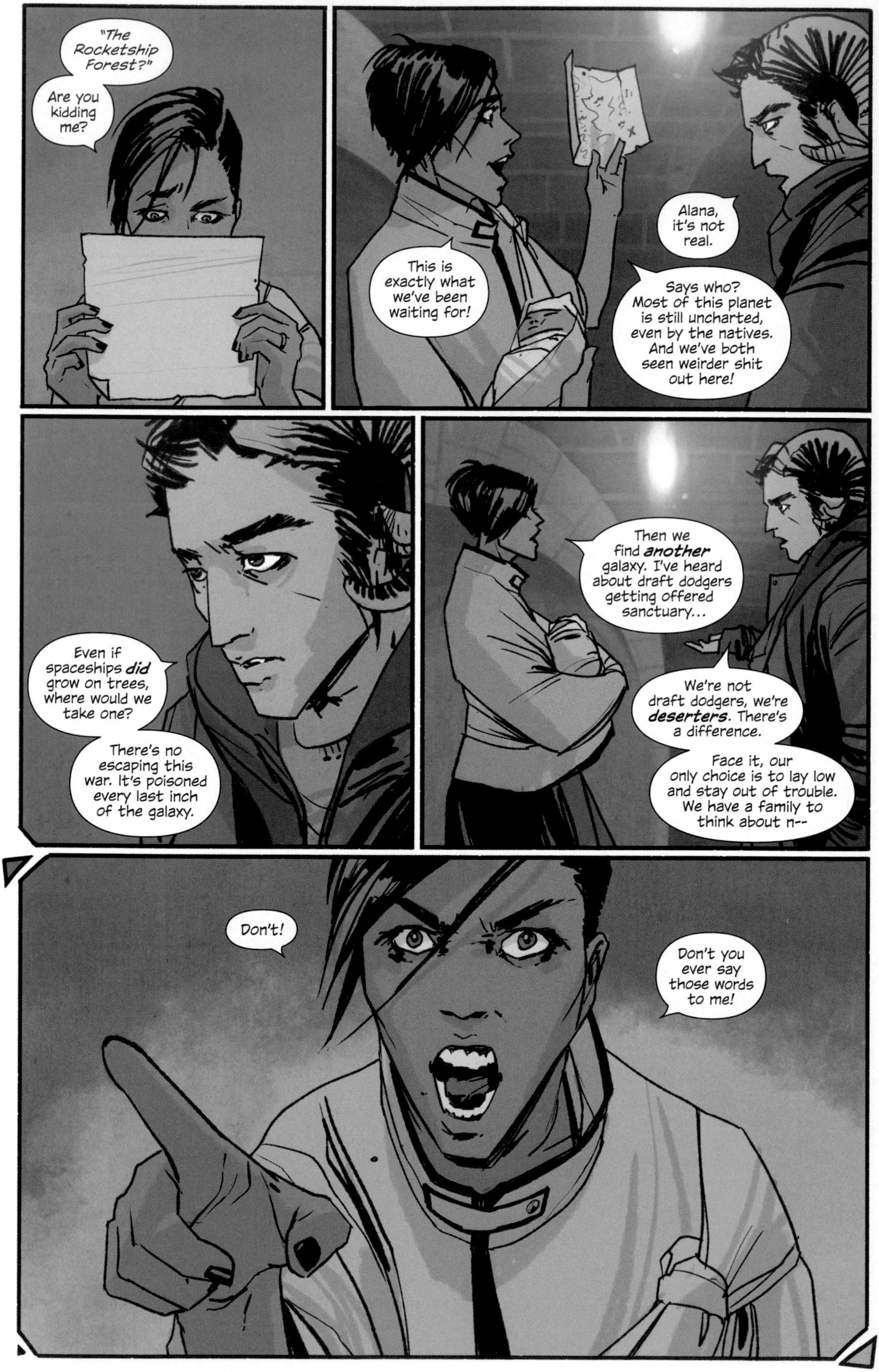

"The Rocketship Forest?"
Are you kidding me?
This is exactly what we've been waiting for!
Alana, it's not real.
Says who? Most of this planet is still uncharted, even by the natives. And we've both seen weirder shit out here!
Even if spaceships *did* grow on trees, where would we take one?
There's no escaping this war. It's poisoned every last inch of the galaxy.
Then we find *another* galaxy. I've heard about draft dodgers getting offered sanctuary...
We're not draft dodgers, we're *deserters*. There's a difference.
Face it, our only choice is to lay low and stay out of trouble. We have a family to think about n--
Don't!
Don't you ever say those words to me!

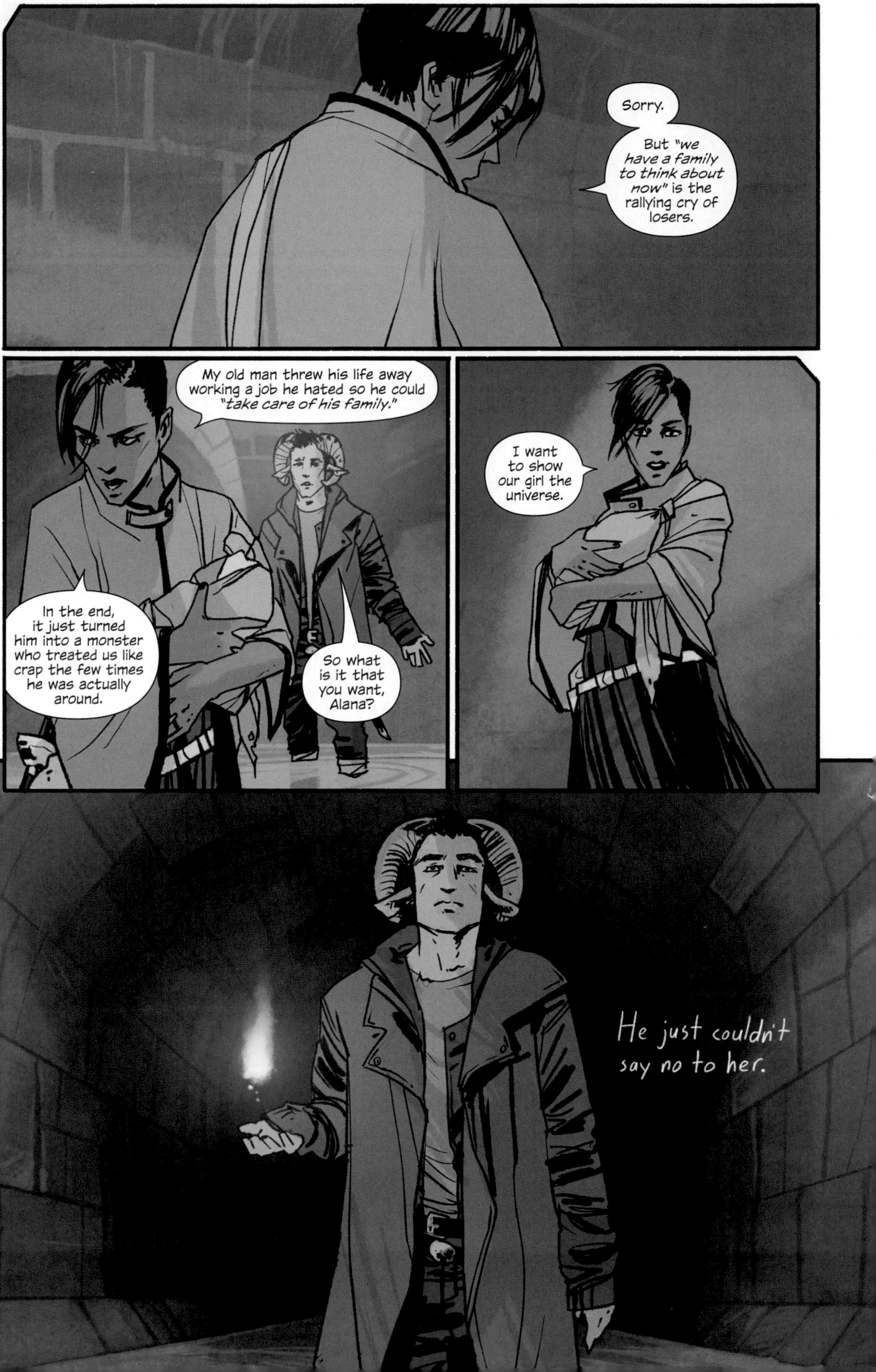
Sorry.
But "we have a family to think about now" is the rallying cry of losers.
My old man threw his life away working a job he hated so he could "take care of his family."
In the end, it just turned him into a monster who treated us like crap the few times he was actually around.
So what is it that you want, Alana?
I want to show our girl the universe.
He just couldn't say no to her.

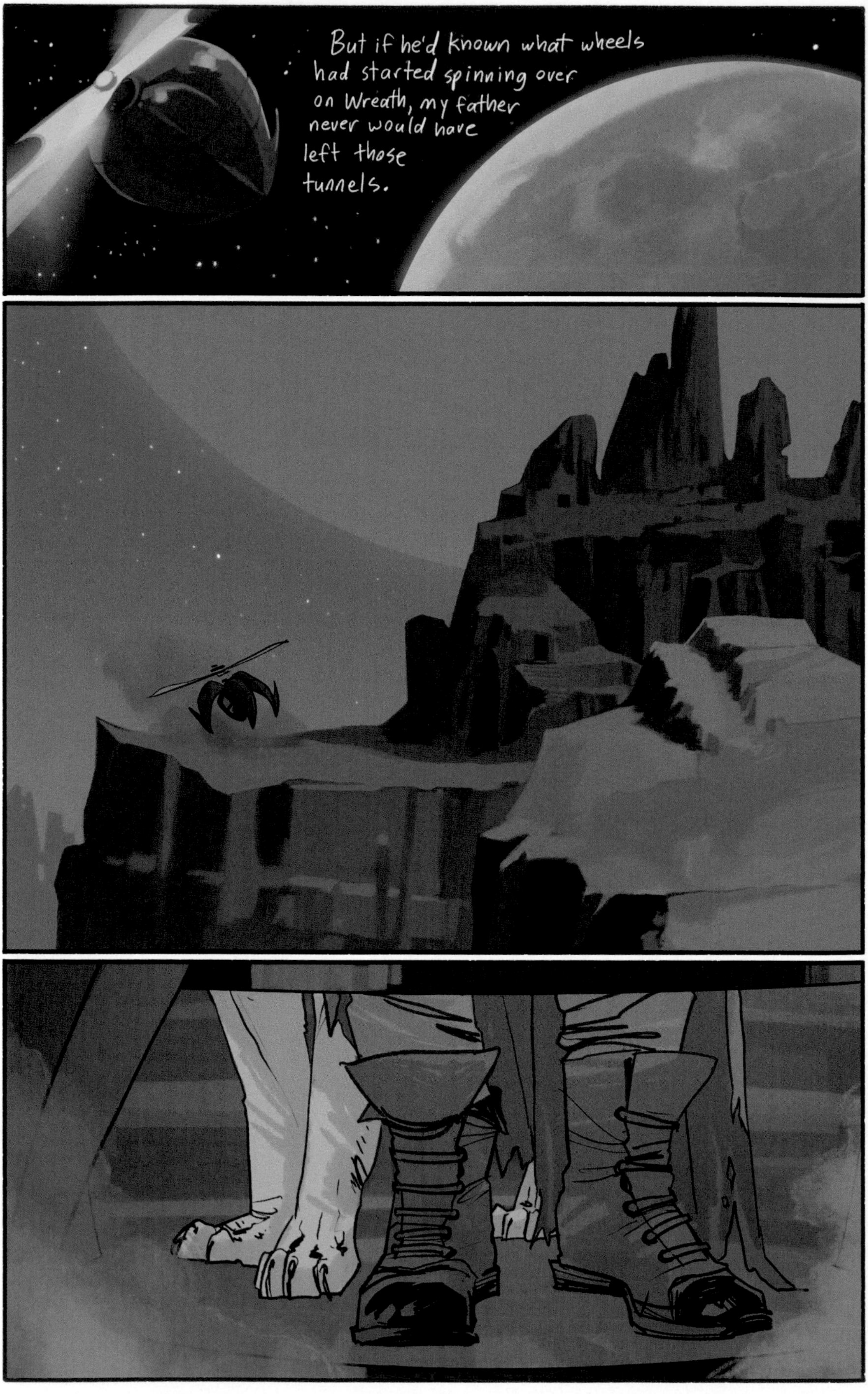
But if he'd known what wheels had started spinning over on Wreath, my father never would have left those tunnels.

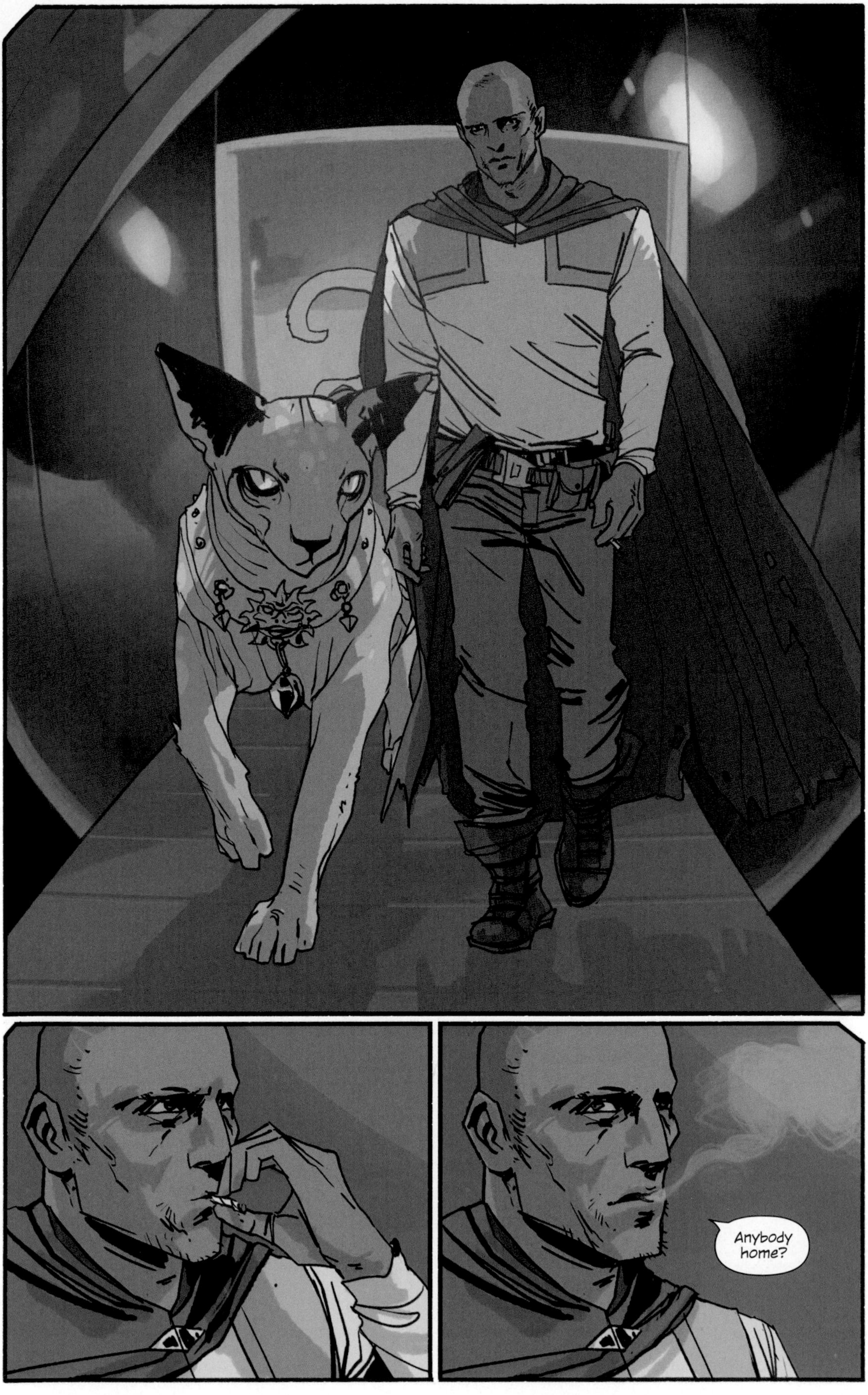
Anybody home?

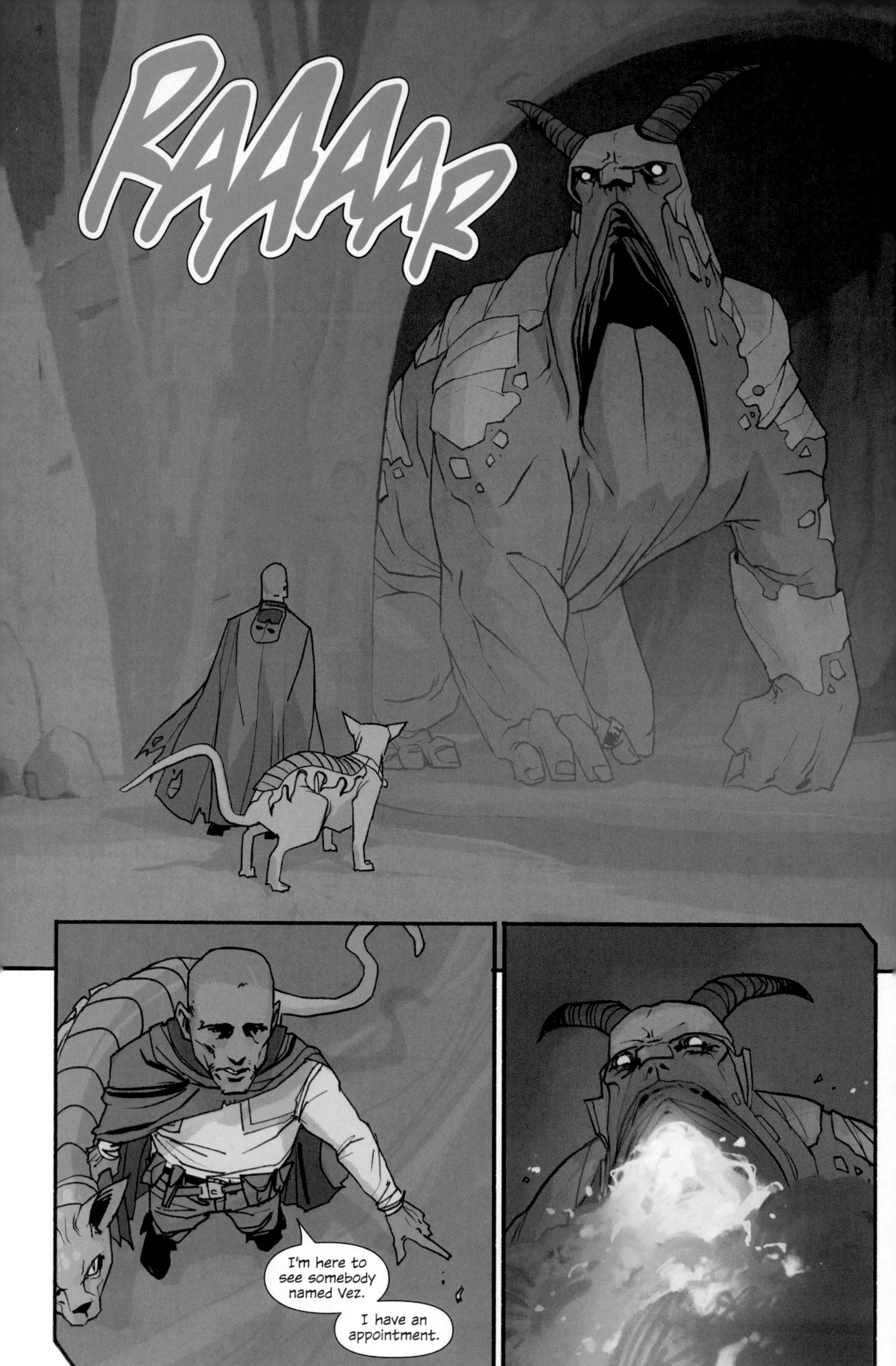
RAAAAR
I'm here to see somebody named Vez.
I have an appointment.

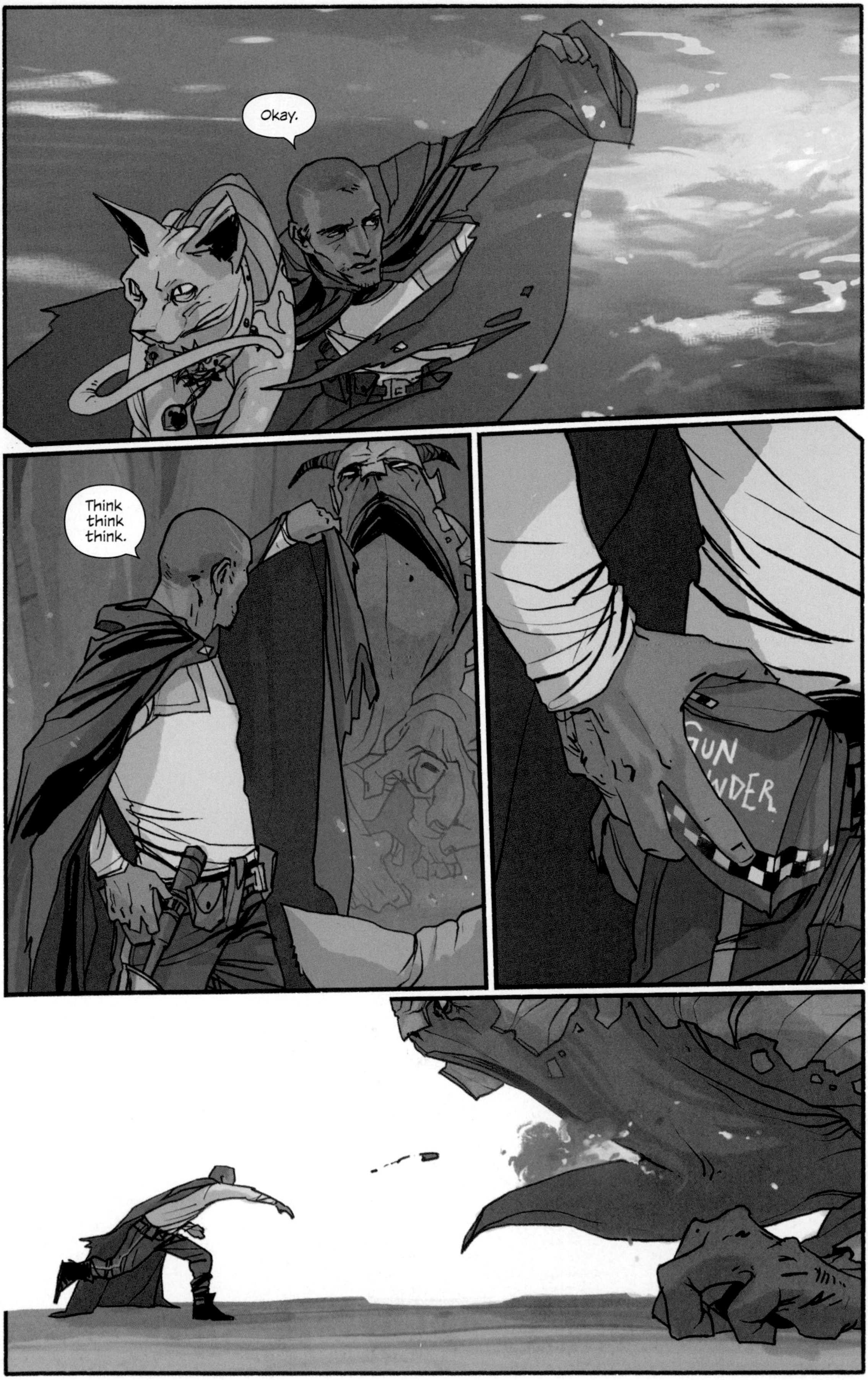
Okay.
Think think think.
GUN

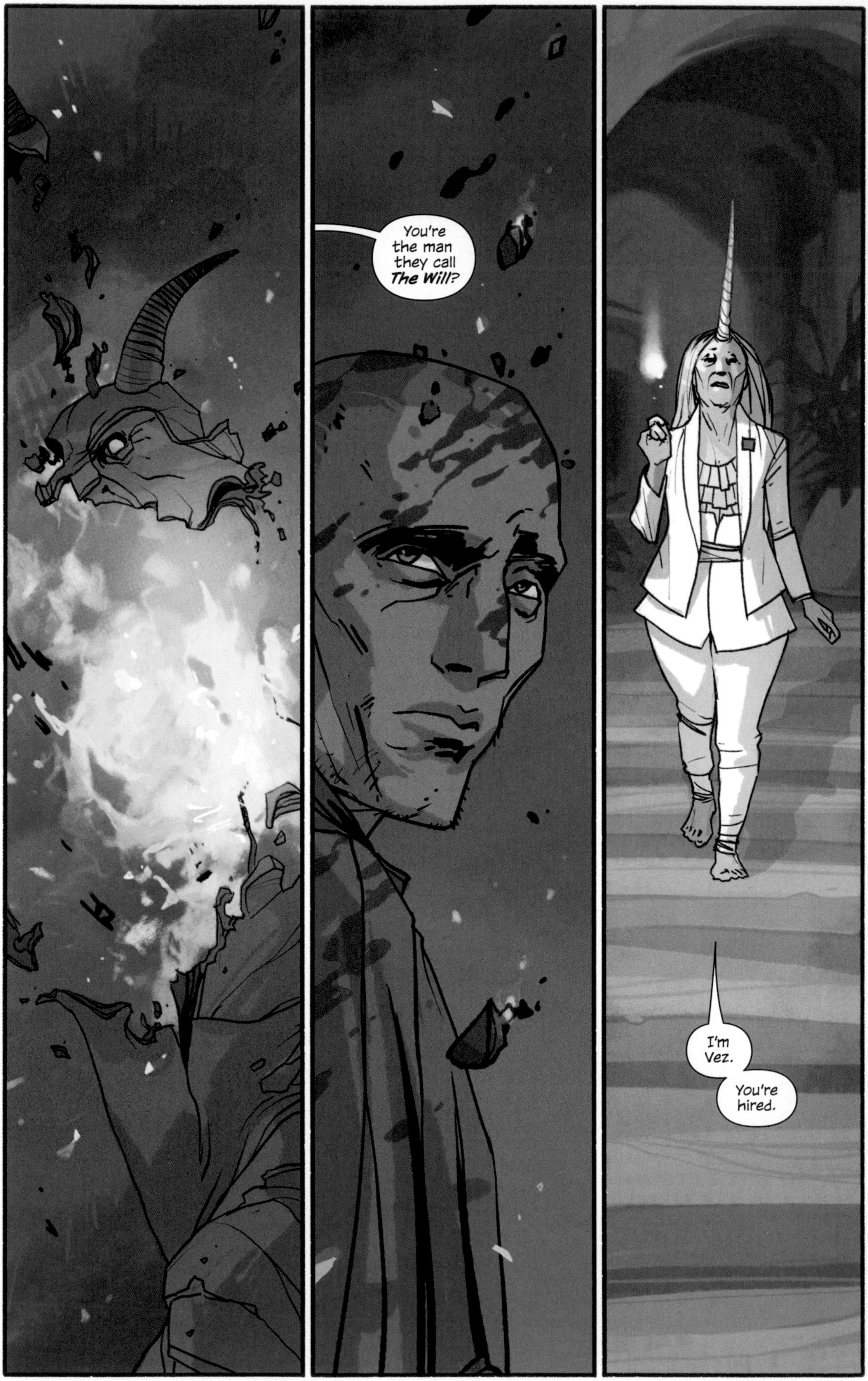
You're the man they call *The Will*?
I'm Vez.
You're hired.

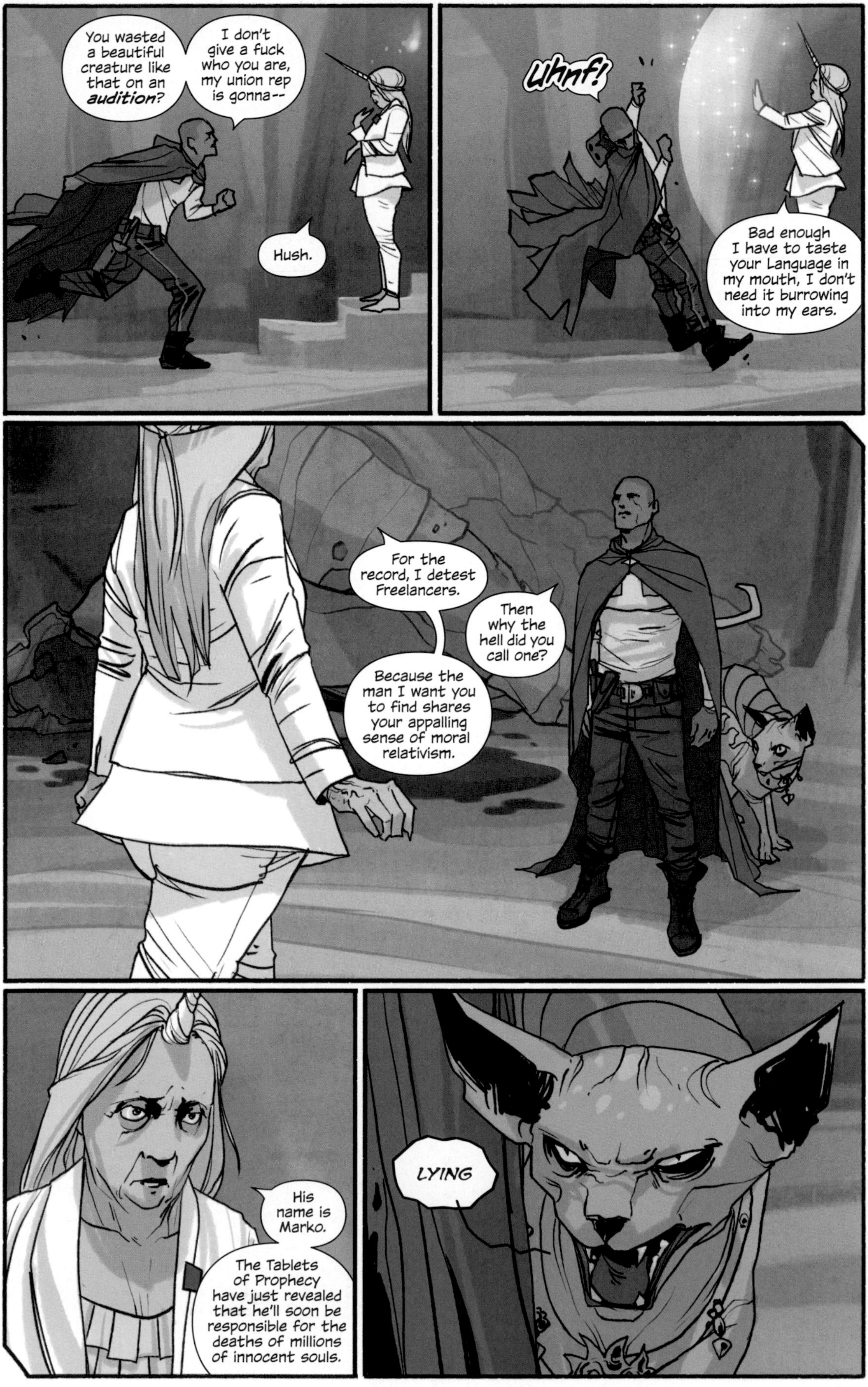
You wasted a beautiful creature like that on an *audition*?
I don't give a fuck who you are, my union rep is gonna--
Hush.
Uhnf!
Bad enough I have to taste your Language in my mouth, I don't need it burrowing into my ears.
For the record, I detest Freelancers.
Then why the hell did you call one?
Because the man I want you to find shares your appalling sense of moral relativism.
His name is Marko.
The Tablets of Prophecy have just revealed that he'll soon be responsible for the deaths of millions of innocent souls.
LYING

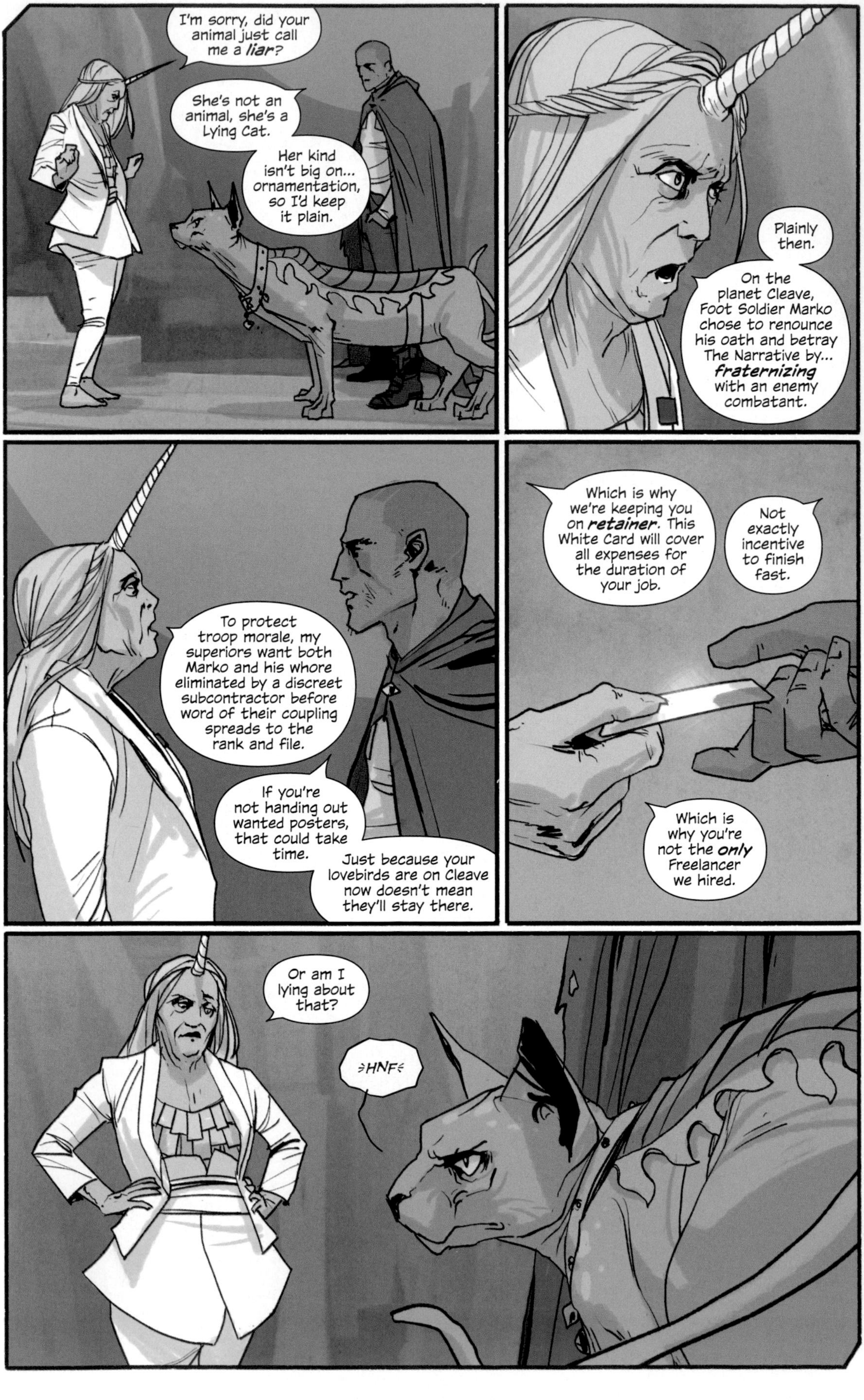
I'm sorry, did your animal just call me a *liar*?
She's not an animal, she's a Lying Cat.
Her kind isn't big on... ornamentation, so I'd keep it plain.
Plainly then.
On the planet Cleave, Foot Soldier Marko chose to renounce his oath and betray The Narrative by... ***fraternizing*** with an enemy combatant.
To protect troop morale, my superiors want both Marko and his whore eliminated by a discreet subcontractor before word of their coupling spreads to the rank and file.
If you're not handing out wanted posters, that could take time.
Just because your lovebirds are on Cleave now doesn't mean they'll stay there.
Which is why we're keeping you on ***retainer***. This White Card will cover all expenses for the duration of your job.
Not exactly incentive to finish fast.
Which is why you're not the ***only*** Freelancer we hired.
Or am I lying about that?
HNF

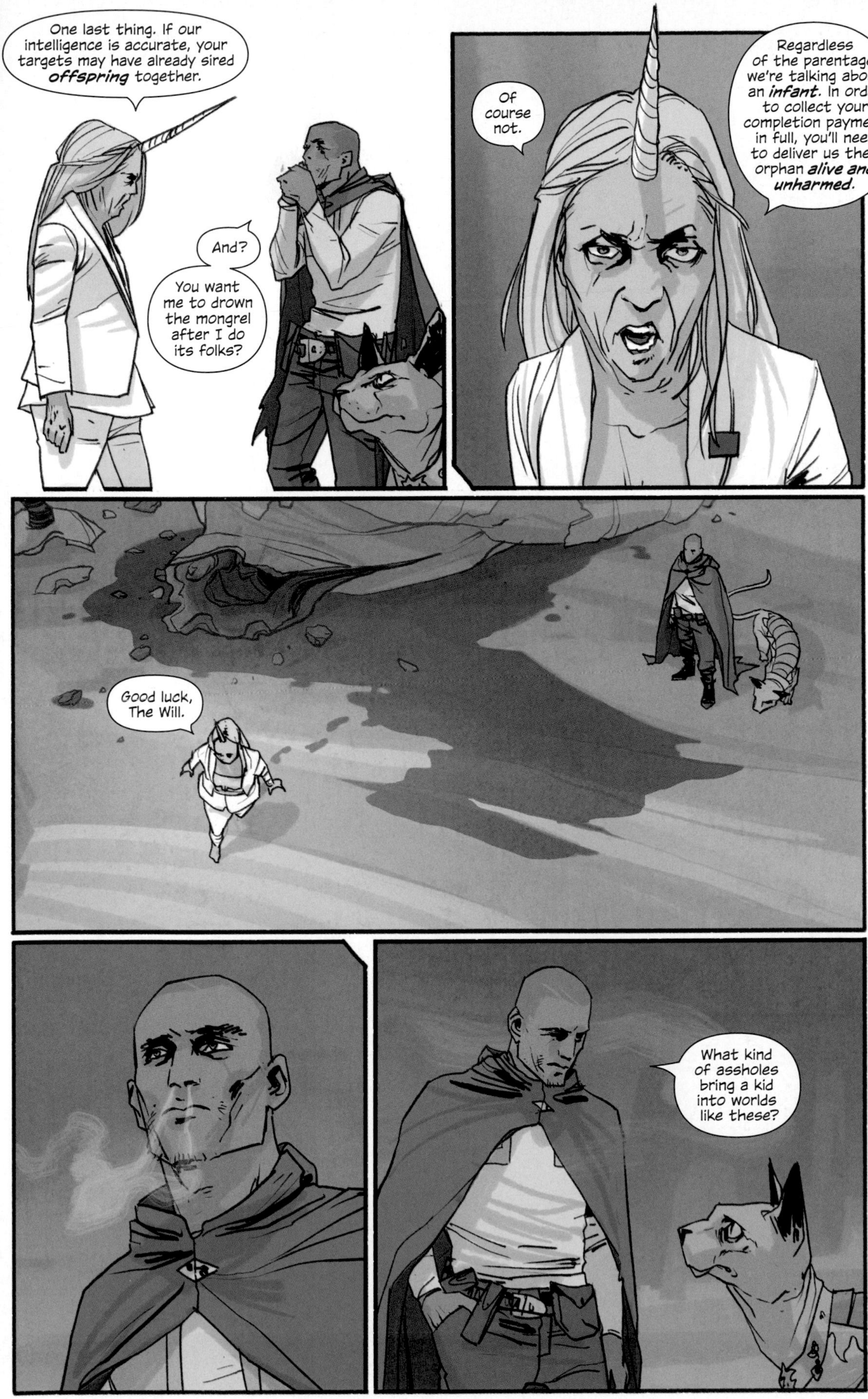
One last thing. If our intelligence is accurate, your targets may have already sired ***offspring*** together.
And?
You want me to drown the mongrel after I do its folks?
Of course not.
Regardless of the parentage, we're talking about an ***infant***. In order to collect your completion payment in full, you'll need to deliver us their orphan ***alive and unharmed***.
Good luck, The Will.
What kind of assholes bring a kid into worlds like these?

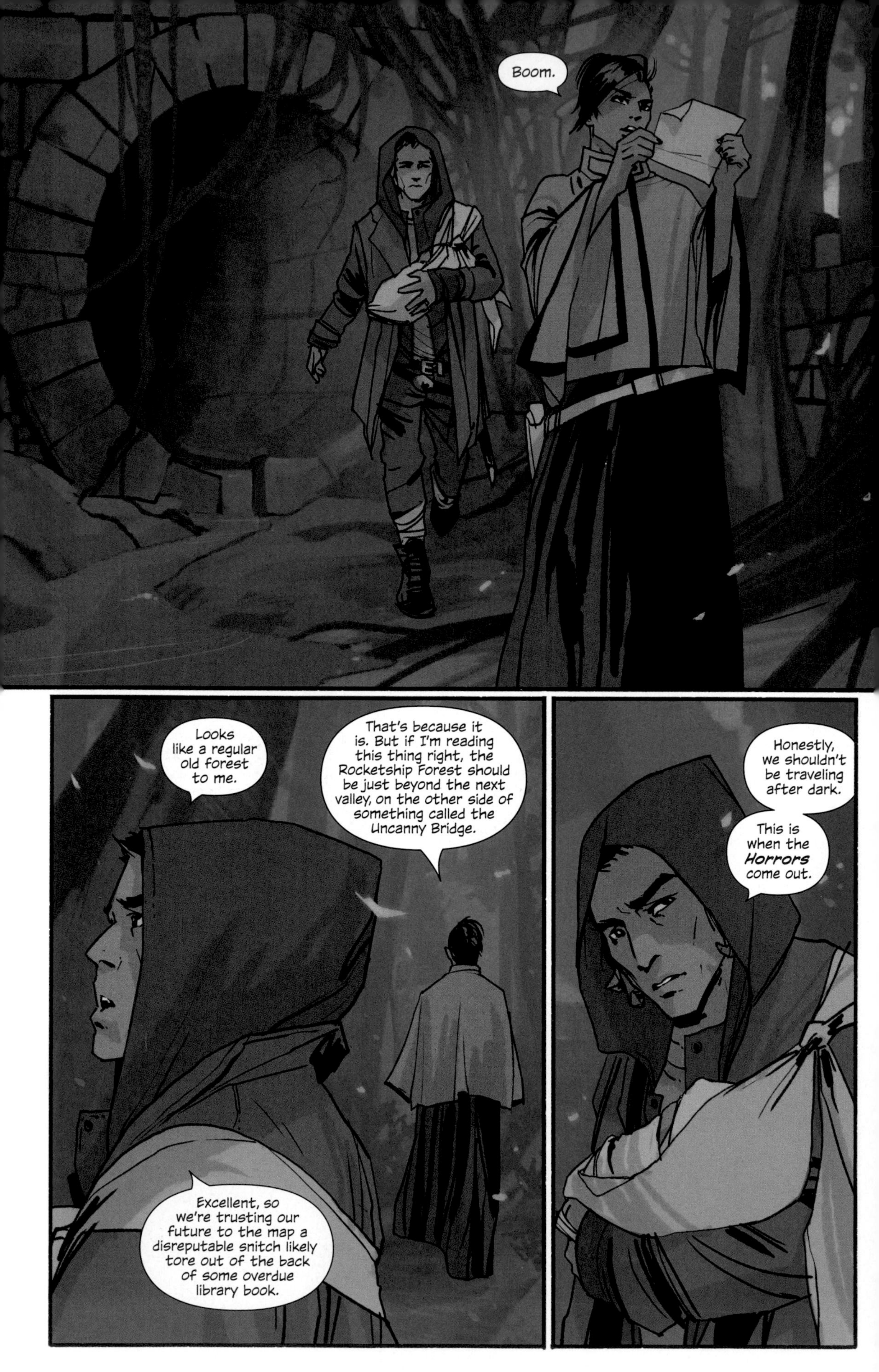
Boom.
Looks like a regular old forest to me.
That's because it is. But if I'm reading this thing right, the Rocketship Forest should be just beyond the next valley, on the other side of something called the Uncanny Bridge.
Excellent, so we're trusting our future to the map a disreputable snitch likely tore out of the back of some overdue library book.
Honestly, we shouldn't be traveling after dark.
This is when the ***Horrors*** come out.

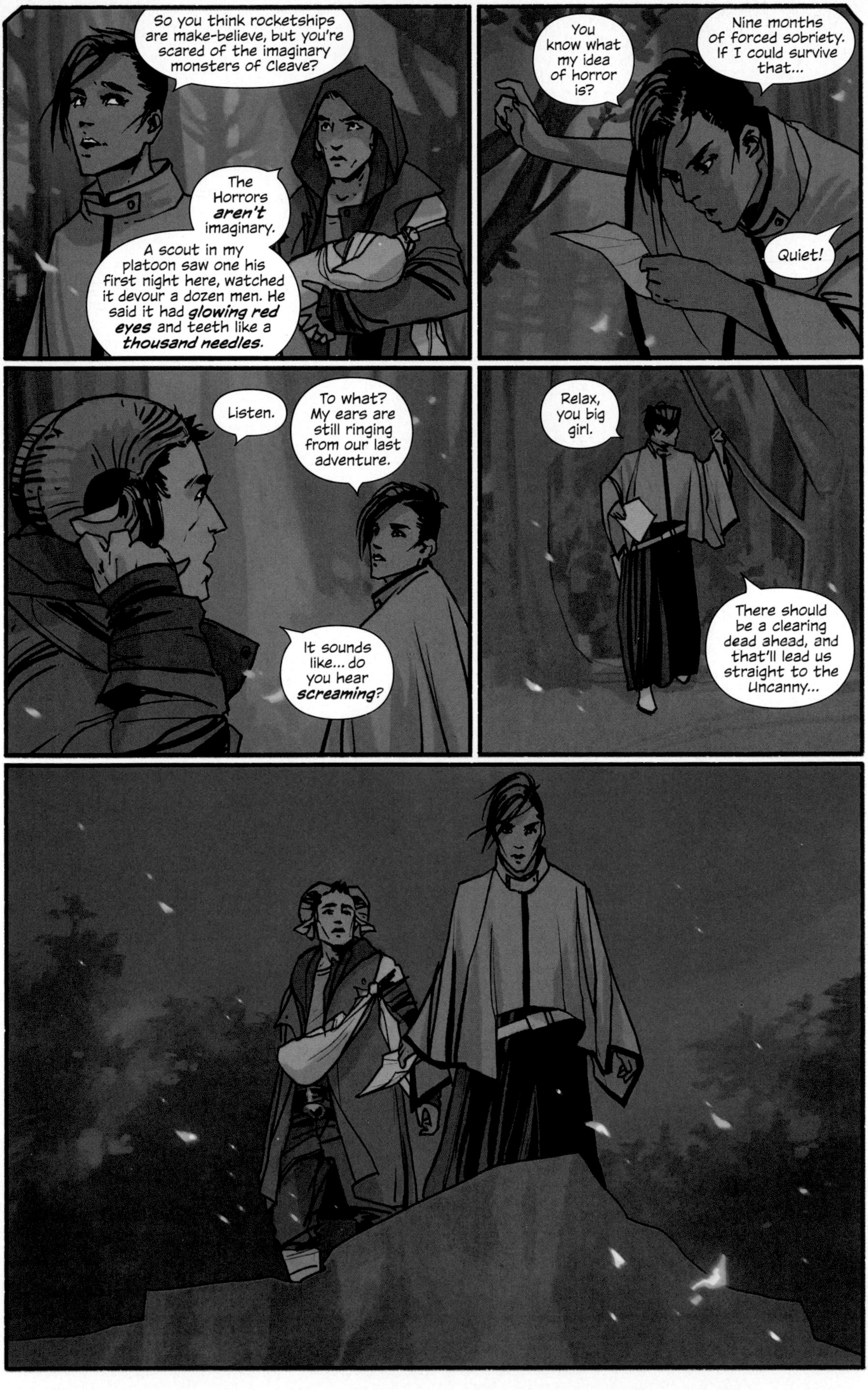
So you think rocketships are make-believe, but you're scared of the imaginary monsters of Cleave?
The Horrors **aren't** imaginary.
A scout in my platoon saw one his first night here, watched it devour a dozen men. He said it had **glowing red eyes** and teeth like a **thousand needles**.
You know what my idea of horror is?
Nine months of forced sobriety. If I could survive that...
Quiet!
Listen.
To what? My ears are still ringing from our last adventure.
It sounds like... do you hear **screaming**?
Relax, you big girl.
There should be a clearing dead ahead, and that'll lead us straight to the Uncanny...

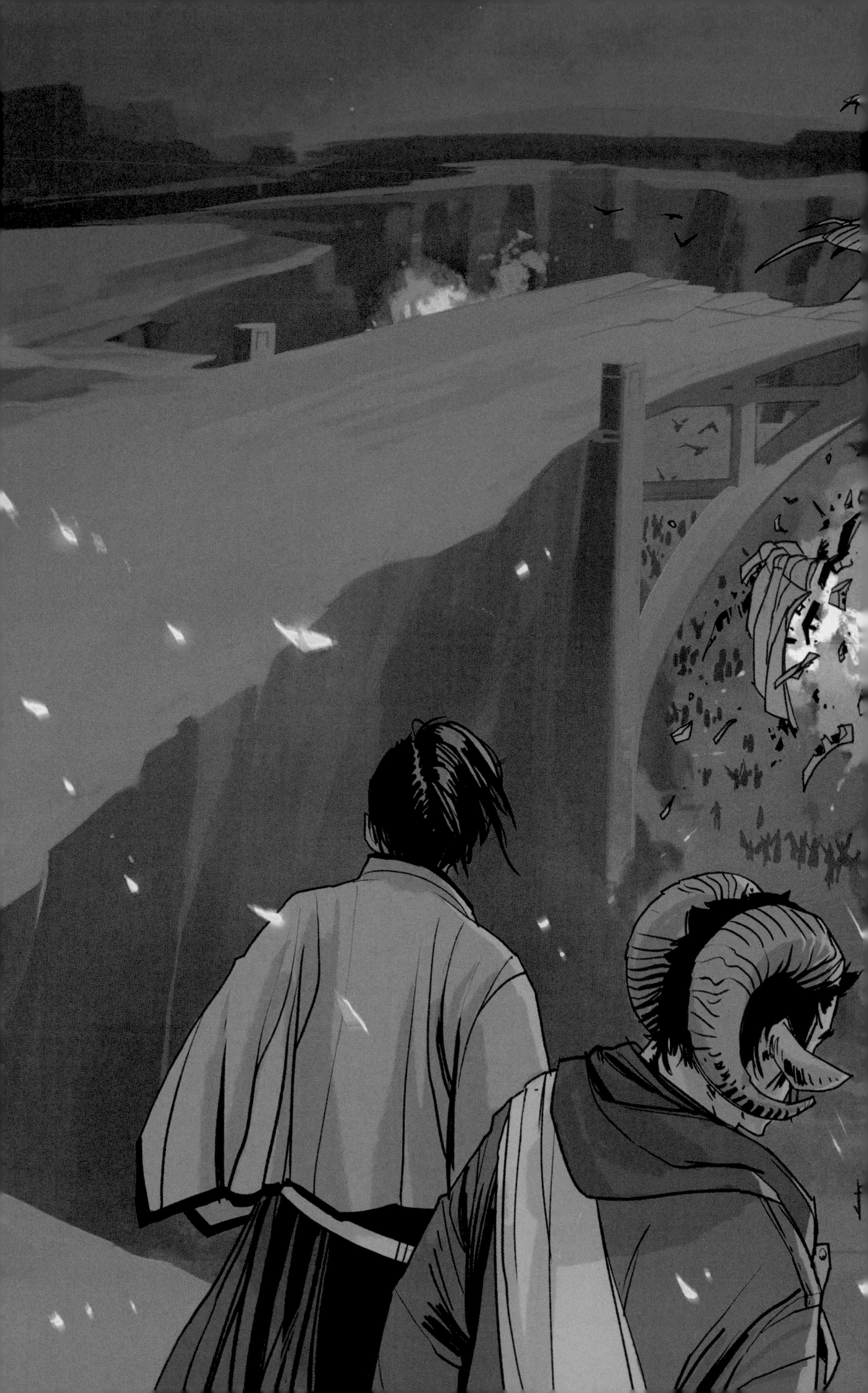

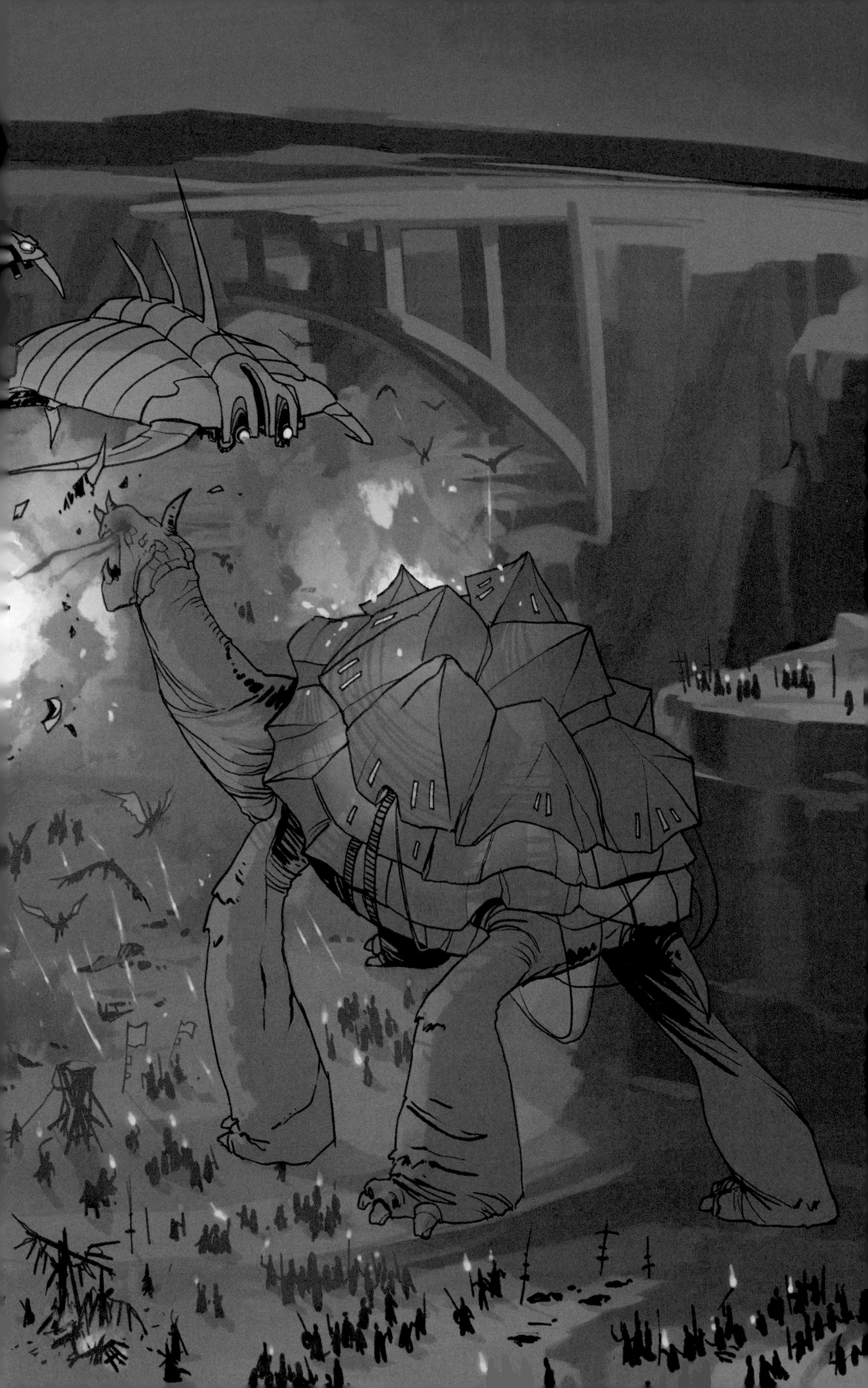

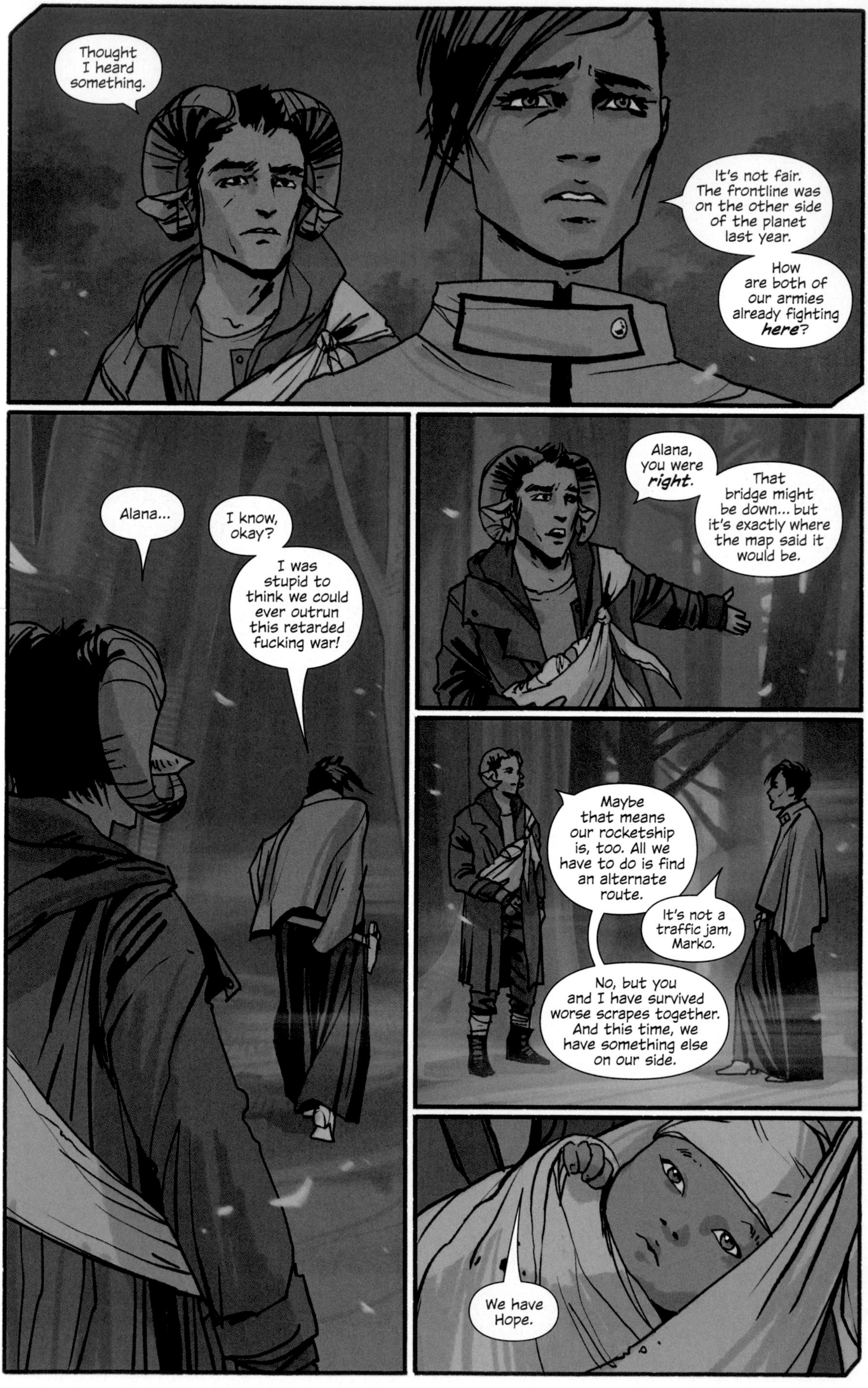
Thought I heard something.
It's not fair. The frontline was on the other side of the planet last year.
How are both of our armies already fighting *here*?
Alana...
I know, okay?
I was stupid to think we could ever outrun this retarded fucking war!
Alana, you were *right*.
That bridge might be down... but it's exactly where the map said it would be.
Maybe that means our rocketship is, too. All we have to do is find an alternate route.
It's not a traffic jam, Marko.
No, but you and I have survived worse scrapes together. And this time, we have something else on our side.
We have Hope.

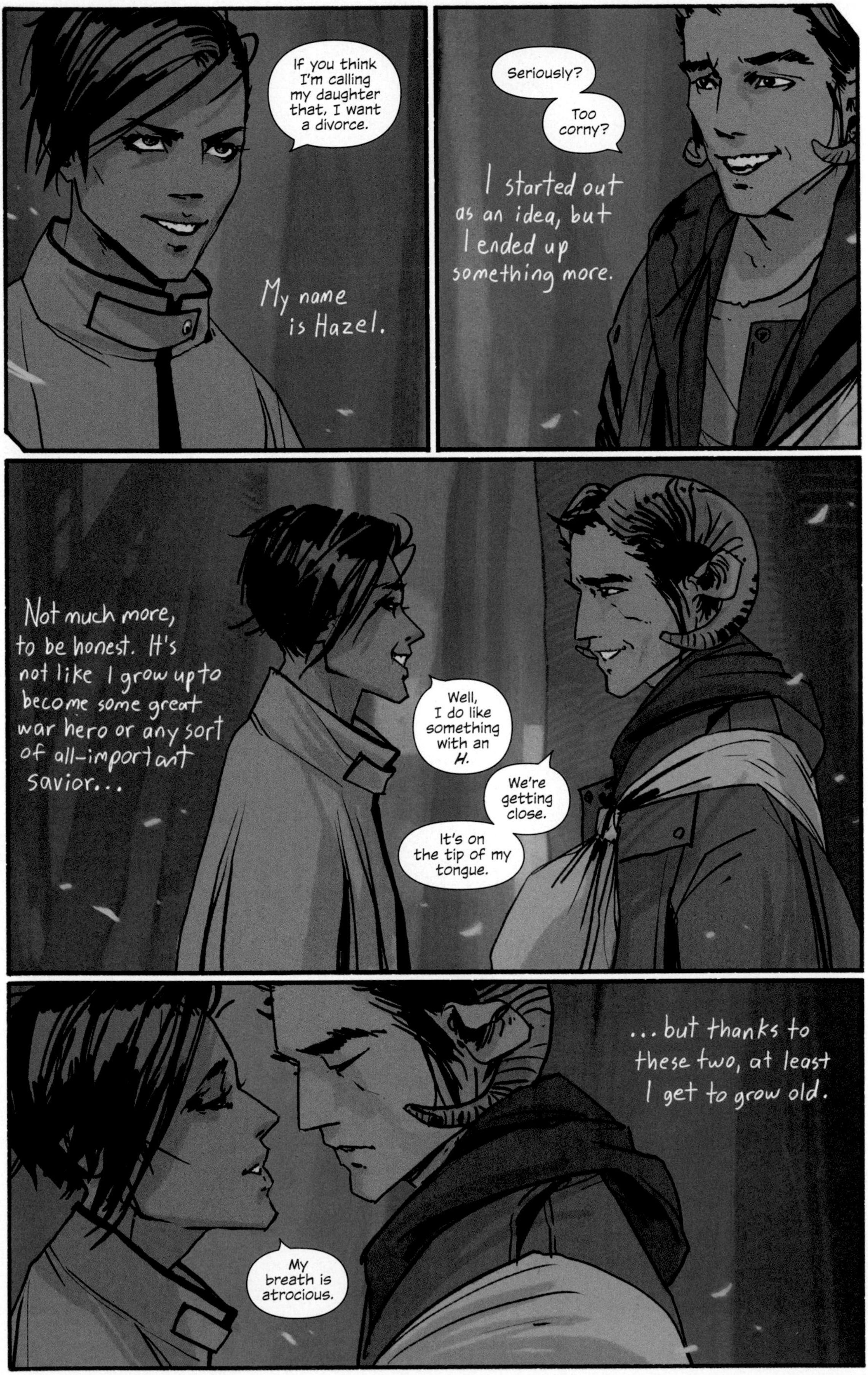
If you think I'm calling my daughter that, I want a divorce.
My name is Hazel.
Seriously?
Too corny?
I started out as an idea, but I ended up something more.
Not much more, to be honest. It's not like I grow up to become some great war hero or any sort of all-important savior...
Well, I do like something with an H.
We're getting close.
It's on the tip of my tongue.
...but thanks to these two, at least I get to grow old.
My breath is atrocious.

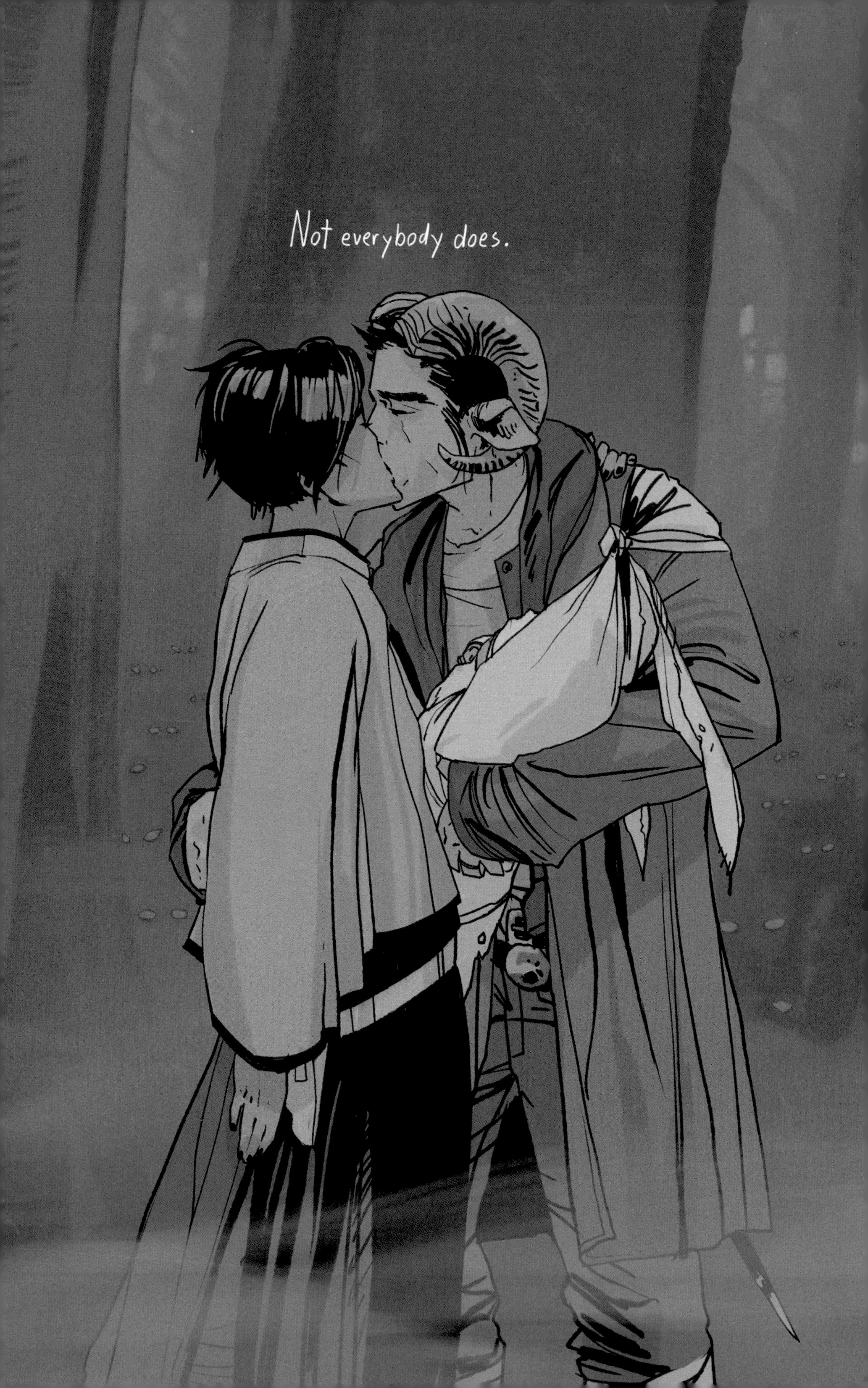
Not everybody does.

end chapter one

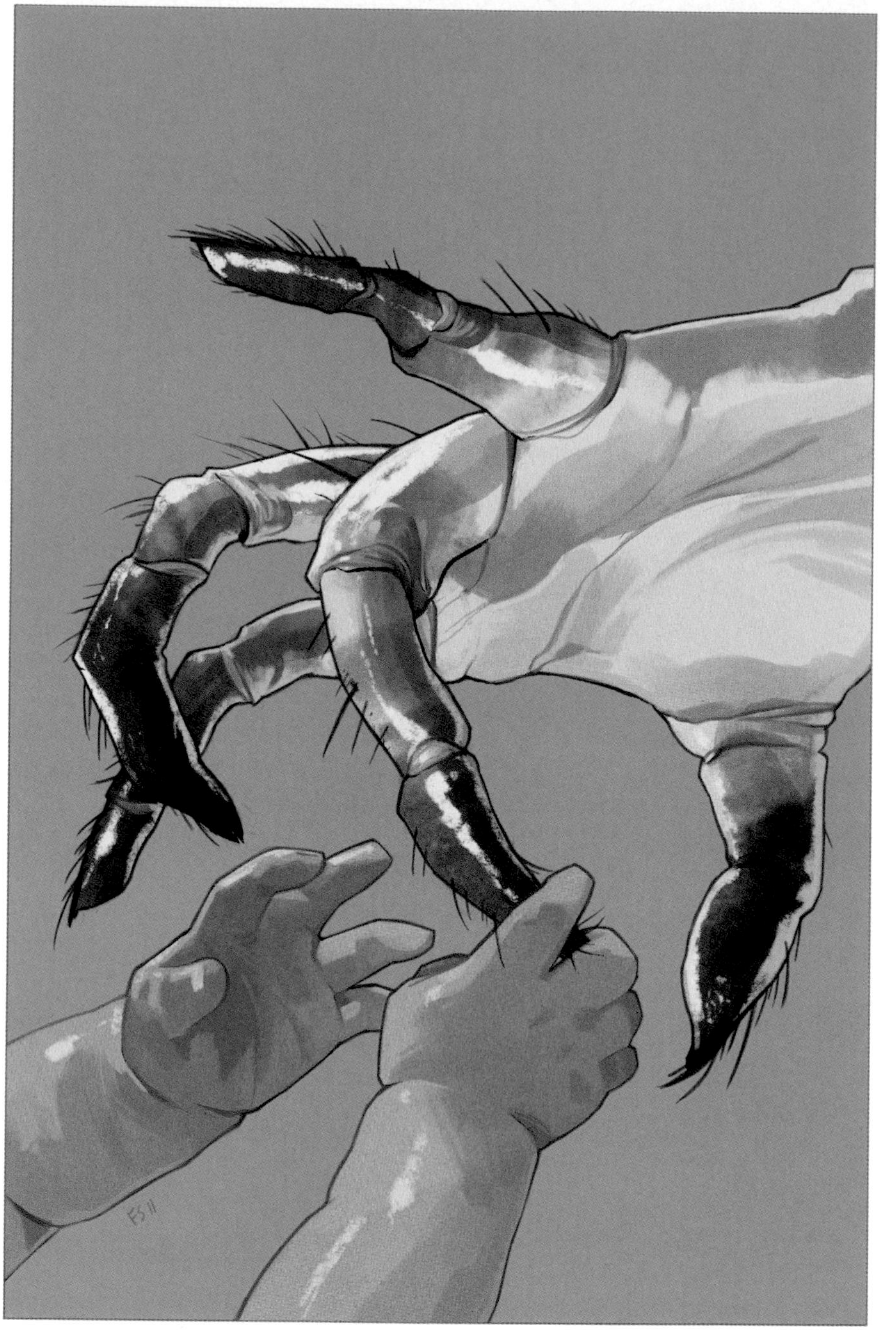
FS 11

CHAPTER
TWO

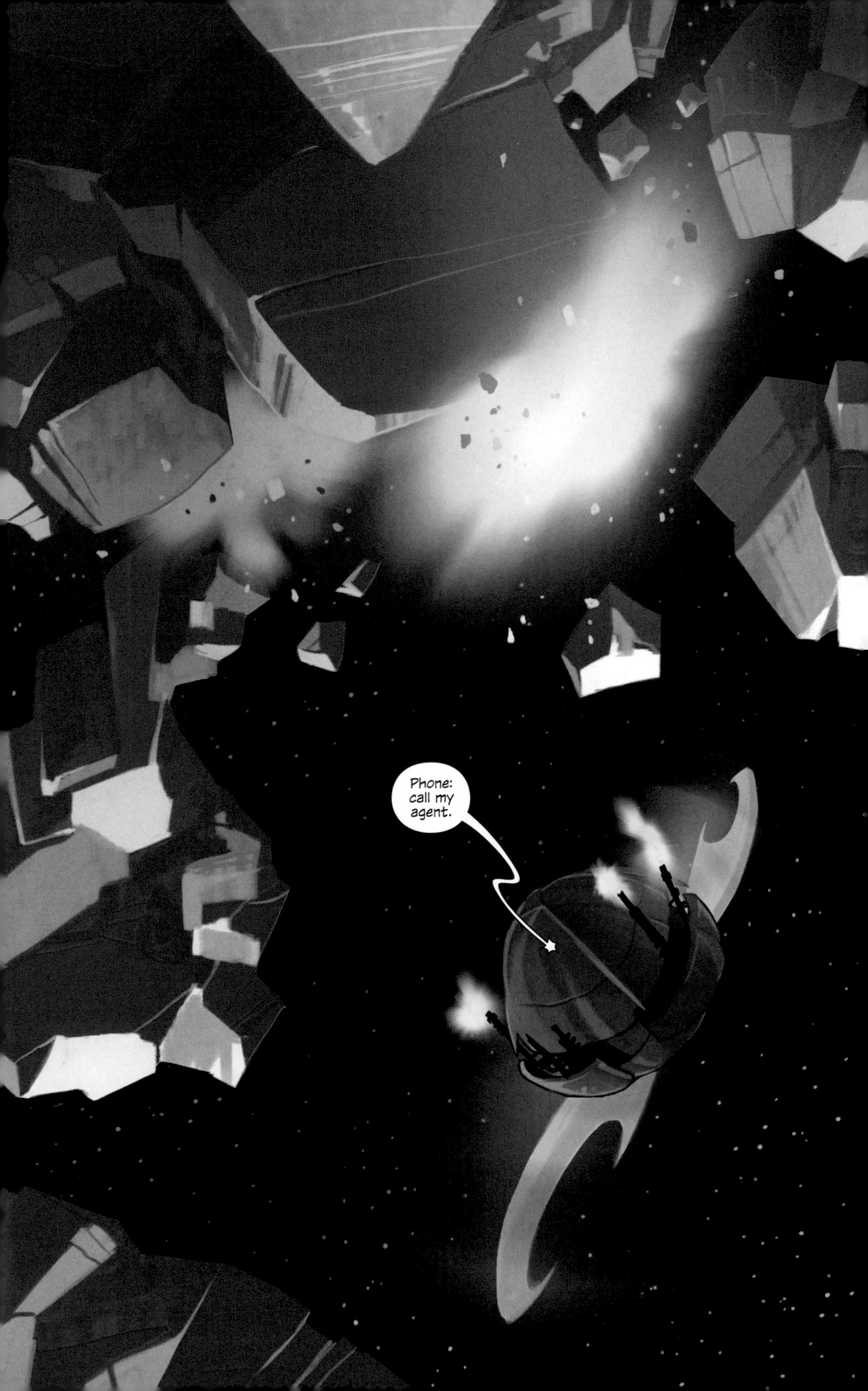
Phone: call my agent.

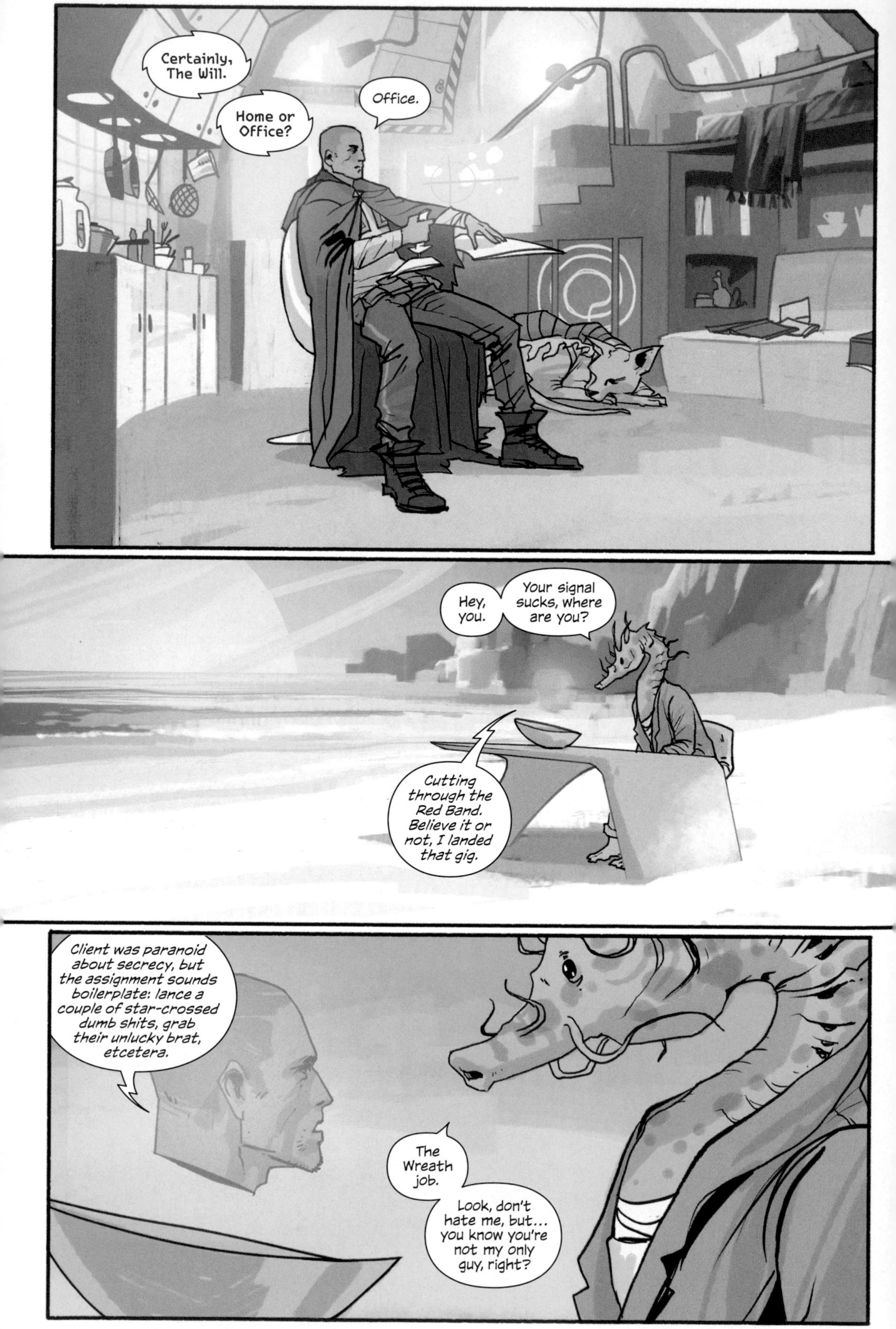
Certainly, The Will.
Home or Office?
Office.
Hey, you.
Your signal sucks, where are you?
Cutting through the Red Band. Believe it or not, I landed that gig.
Client was paranoid about secrecy, but the assignment sounds boilerplate: lance a couple of star-crossed dumb shits, grab their unlucky brat, etcetera.
The Wreath job.
Look, don't hate me, but... you know you're not my only guy, right?

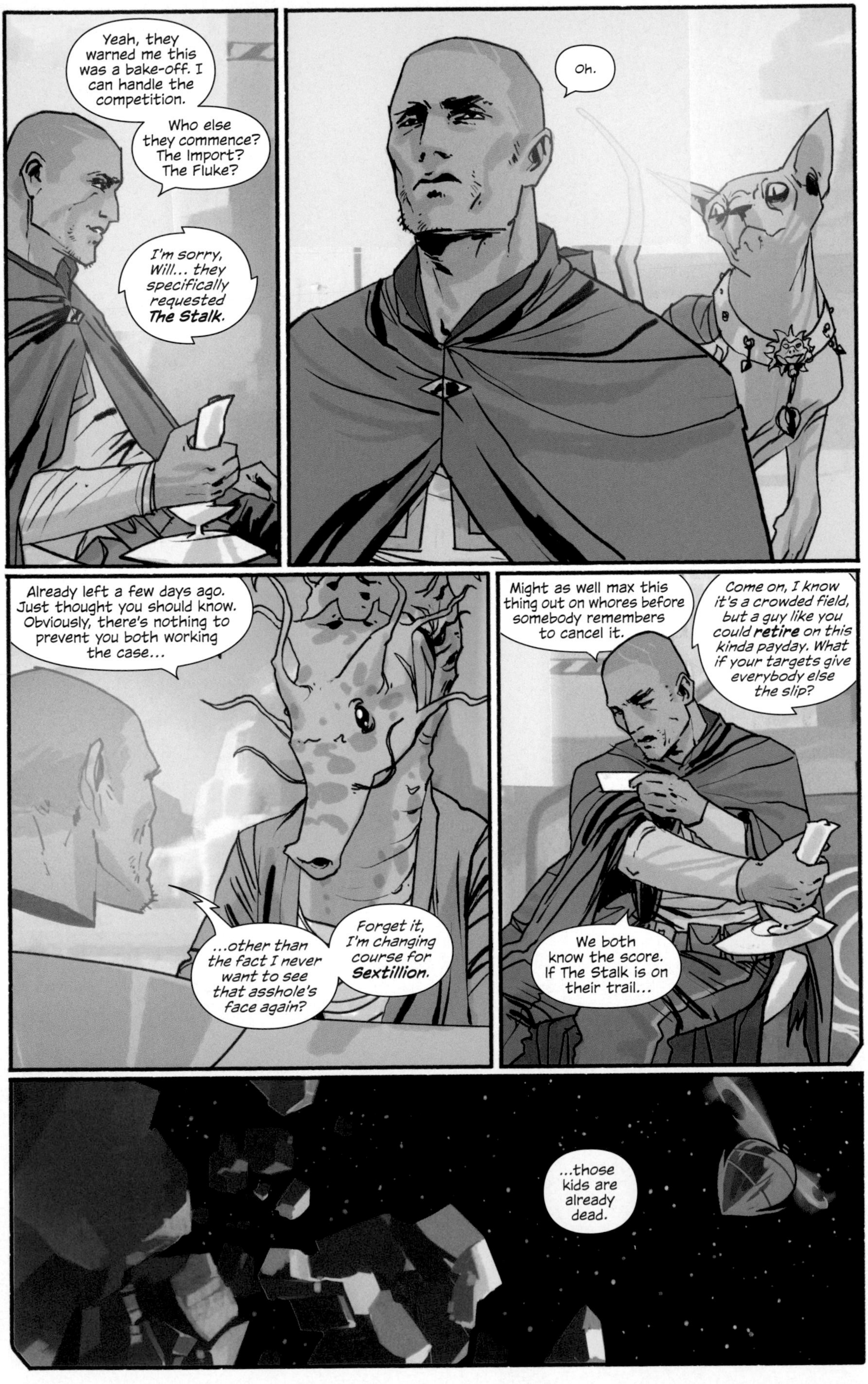
Yeah, they warned me this was a bake-off. I can handle the competition.
Who else they commence? The Import? The Fluke?
I'm sorry, Will... they specifically requested **The Stalk**.
Oh.
Already left a few days ago. Just thought you should know. Obviously, there's nothing to prevent you both working the case...
...other than the fact I never want to see that asshole's face again?
Forget it, I'm changing course for **Sextillion**.
Might as well max this thing out on whores before somebody remembers to cancel it.
Come on, I know it's a crowded field, but a guy like you could **retire** on this kinda payday. What if your targets give everybody else the slip?
We both know the score. If The Stalk is on their trail...
...those kids are already dead.

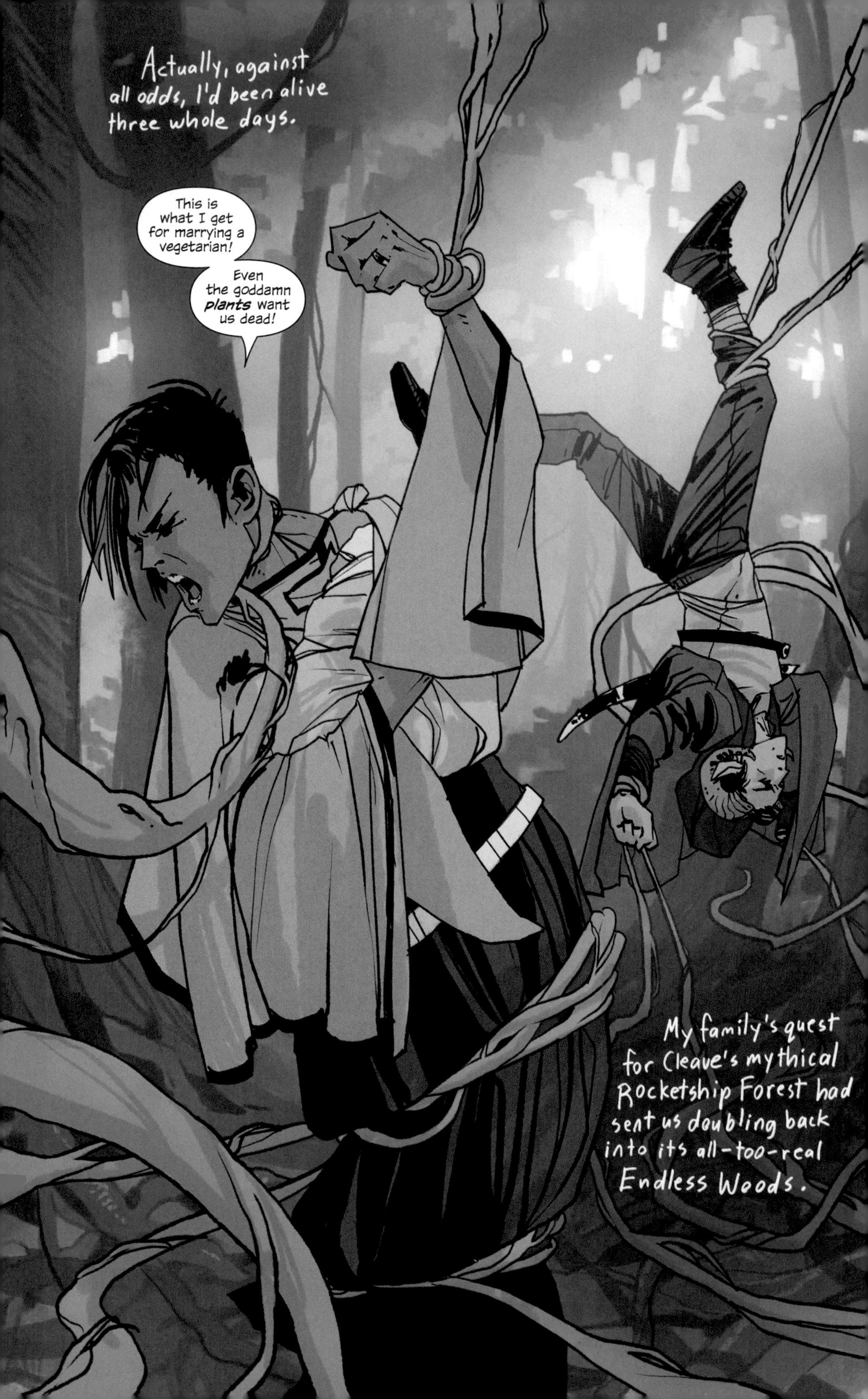
Actually, against all odds, I'd been alive three whole days.
This is what I get for marrying a vegetarian!
Even the goddamn *plants* want us dead!
My family's quest for Cleave's mythical Rocketship Forest had sent us doubling back into its all-too-real Endless Woods.

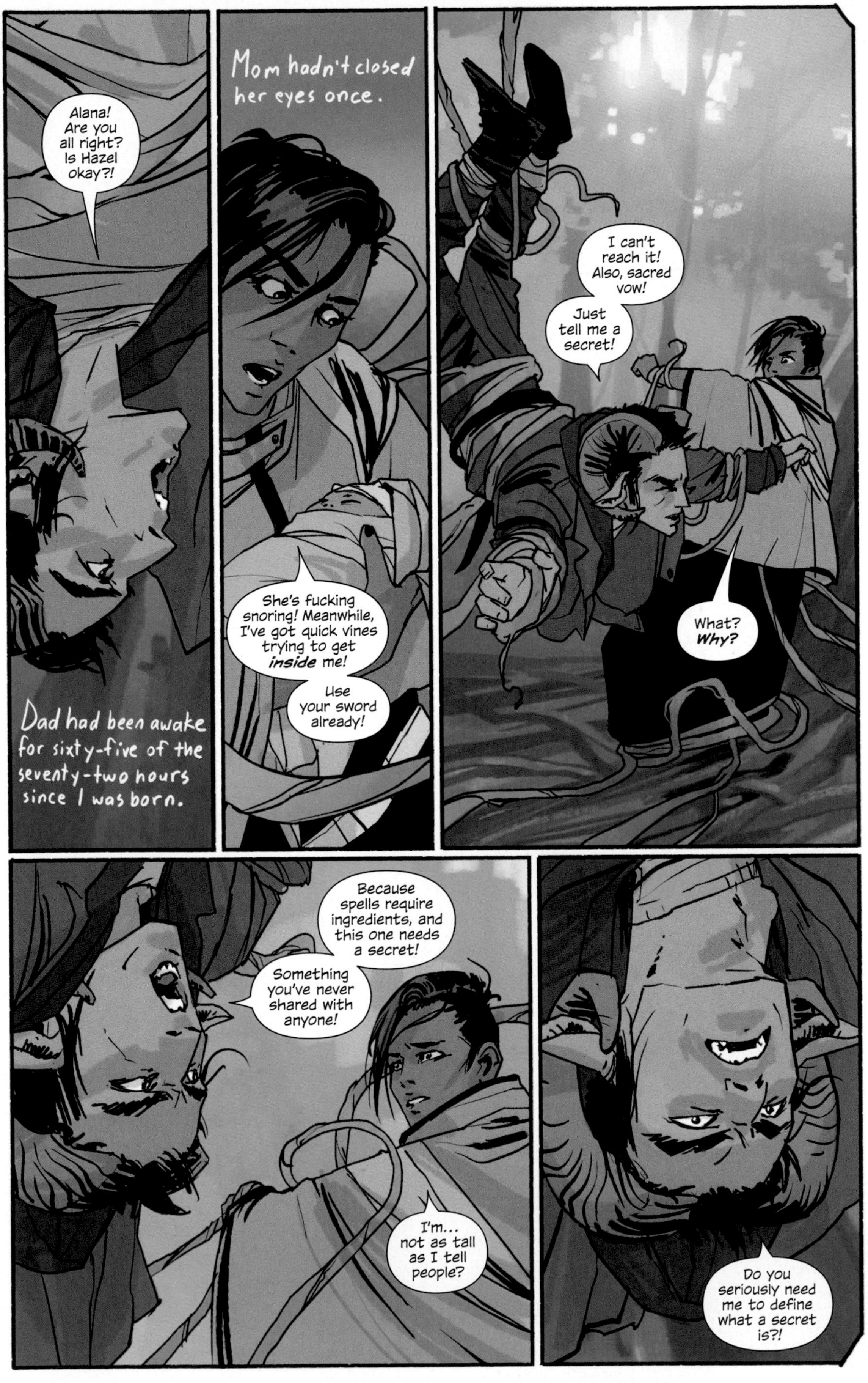
Alana! Are you all right? Is Hazel okay?!
Dad had been awake for sixty-five of the seventy-two hours since I was born.
Mom hadn't closed her eyes once.
She's fucking snoring! Meanwhile, I've got quick vines trying to get *inside* me!
Use your sword already!
I can't reach it! Also, sacred vow!
Just tell me a secret!
What? *Why?*
Because spells require ingredients, and this one needs a secret!
Something you've never shared with anyone!
I'm... not as tall as I tell people?
Do you seriously need me to define what a secret is?!

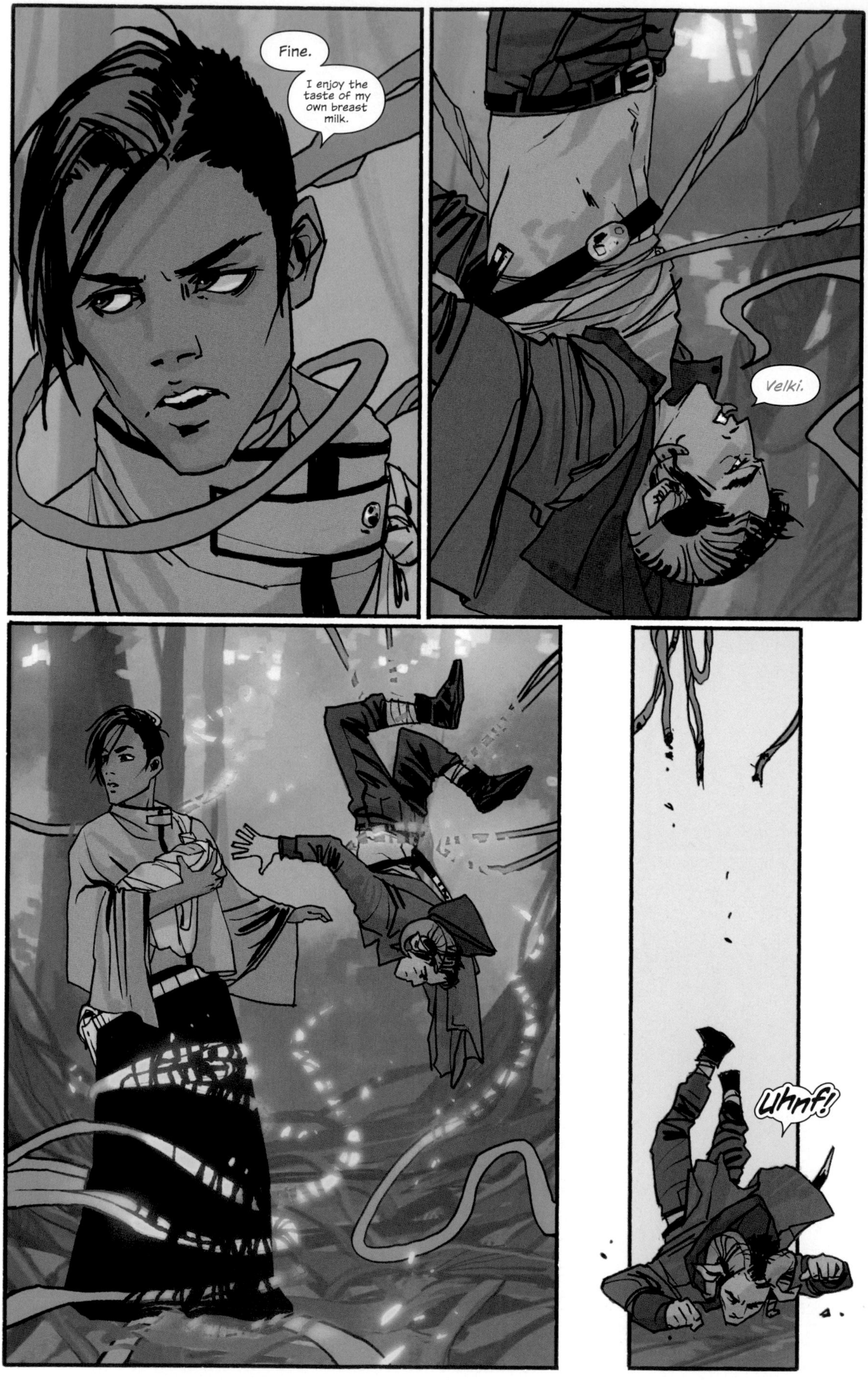
Fine.
I enjoy the taste of my own breast milk.
Velki.
Uhnf!

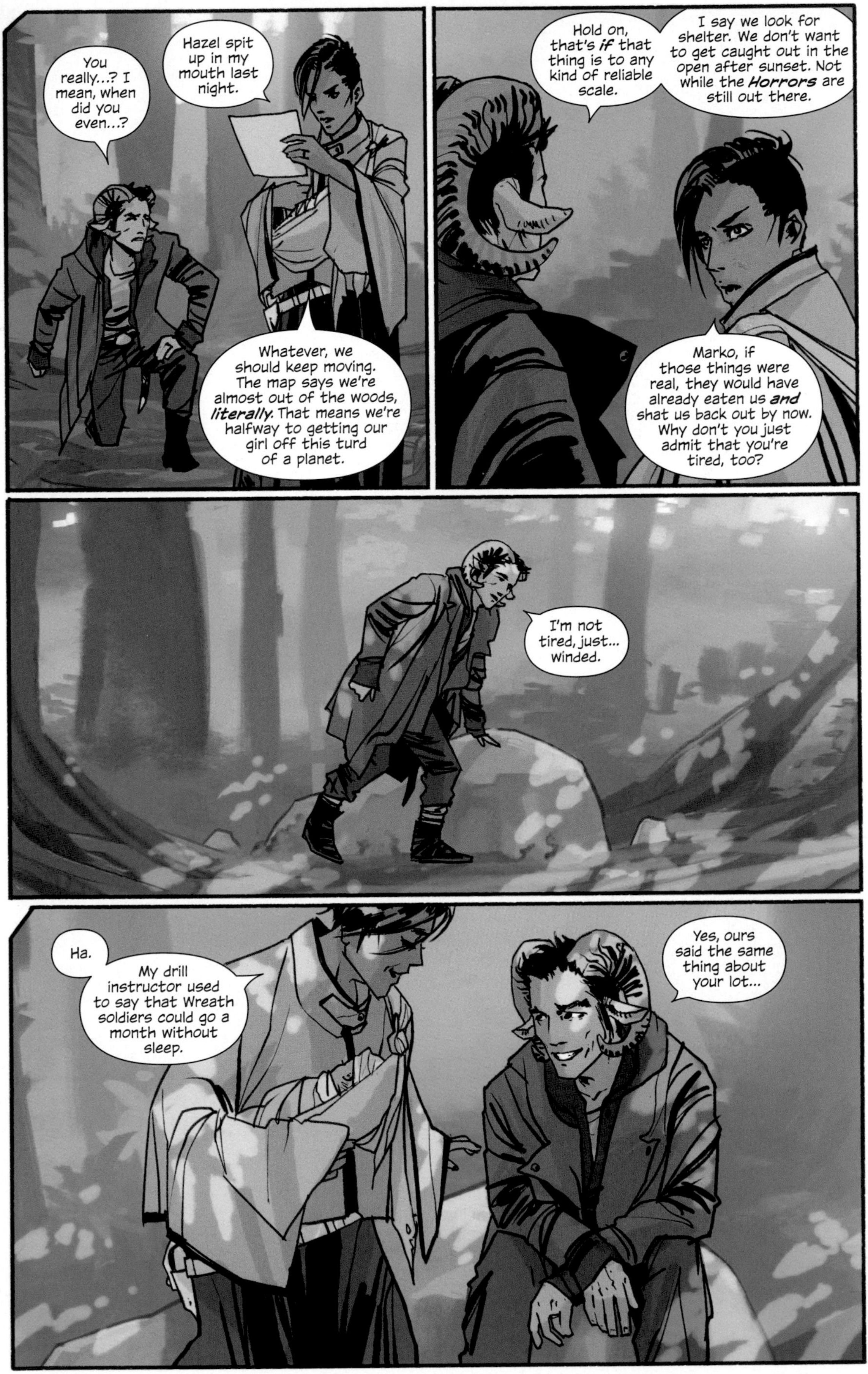
You really...? I mean, when did you even...?
Hazel spit up in my mouth last night.
Whatever, we should keep moving. The map says we're almost out of the woods, *literally.* That means we're halfway to getting our girl off this turd of a planet.
Hold on, that's ***if*** that thing is to any kind of reliable scale.
I say we look for shelter. We don't want to get caught out in the open after sunset. Not while the ***Horrors*** are still out there.
Marko, if those things were real, they would have already eaten us ***and*** shat us back out by now. Why don't you just admit that you're tired, too?
I'm not tired, just... winded.
Ha.
My drill instructor used to say that Wreath soldiers could go a month without sleep.
Yes, ours said the same thing about your lot...

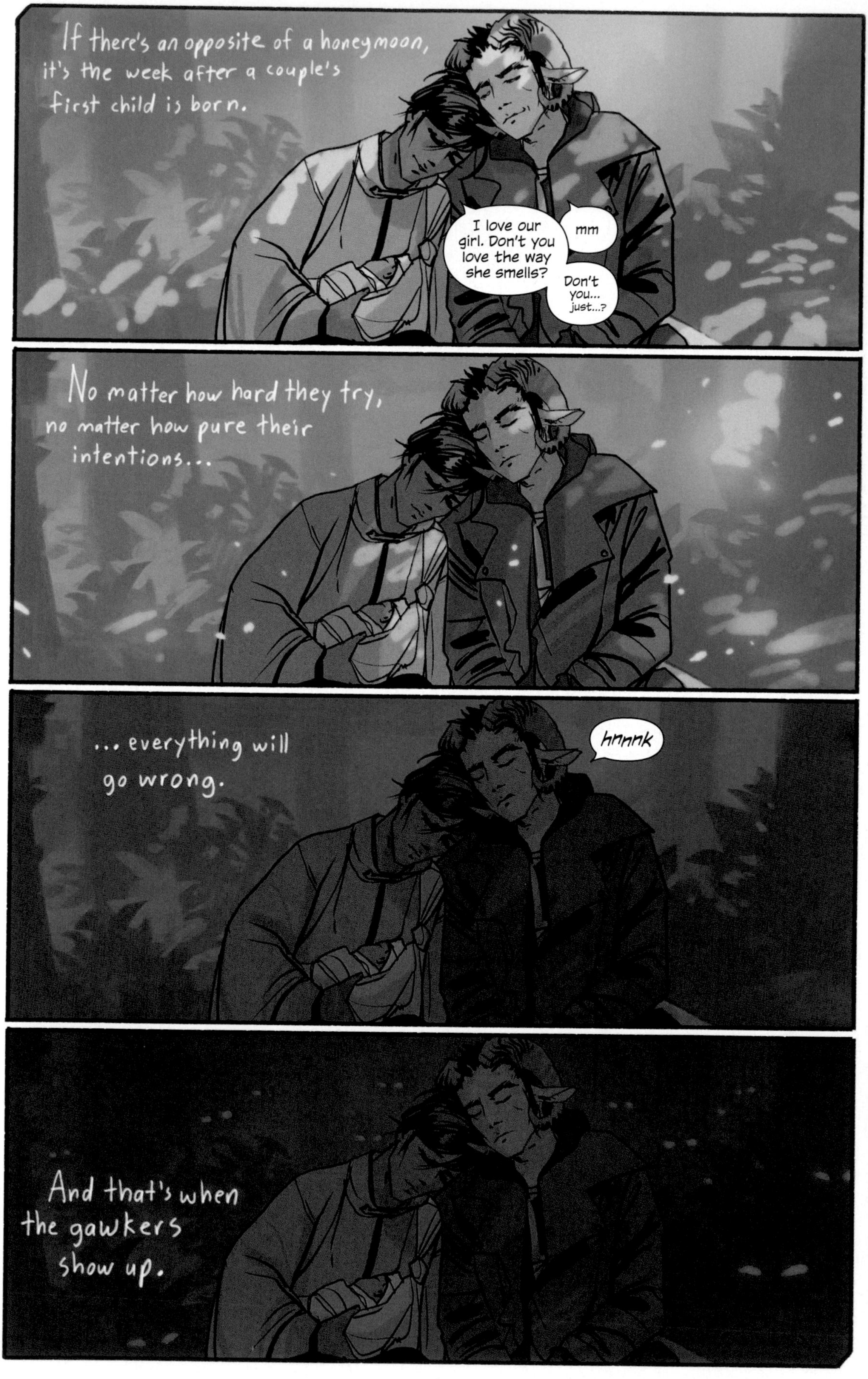
If there's an opposite of a honeymoon, it's the week after a couple's first child is born.
I love our girl. Don't you love the way she smells?
mm
Don't you... just...?
No matter how hard they try, no matter how pure their intentions...
...everything will go wrong.
hnnnk
And that's when the gawkers show up.

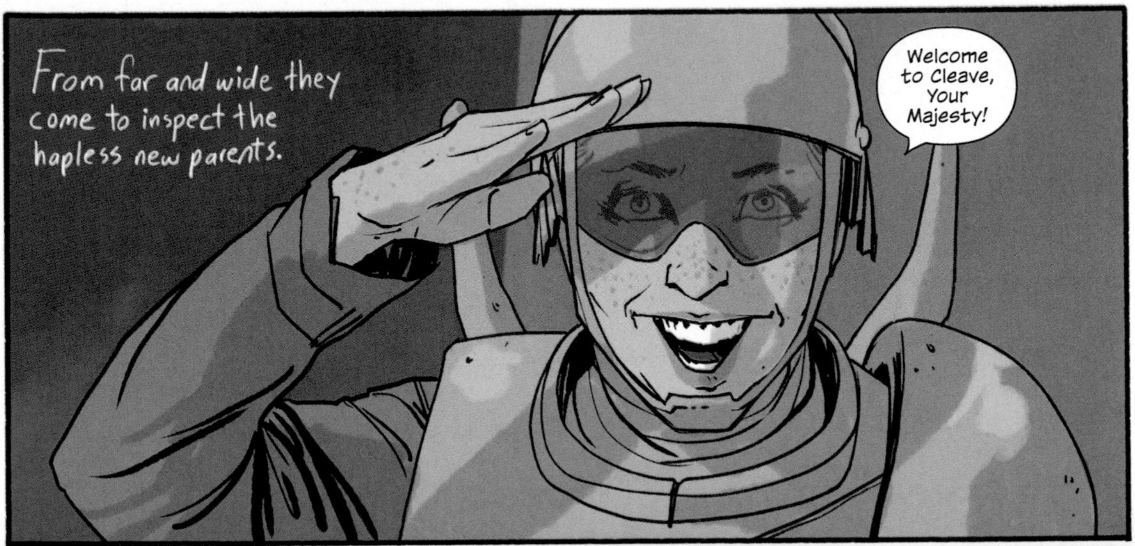
From far and wide they come to inspect the hapless new parents.
Welcome to Cleave, Your Majesty!

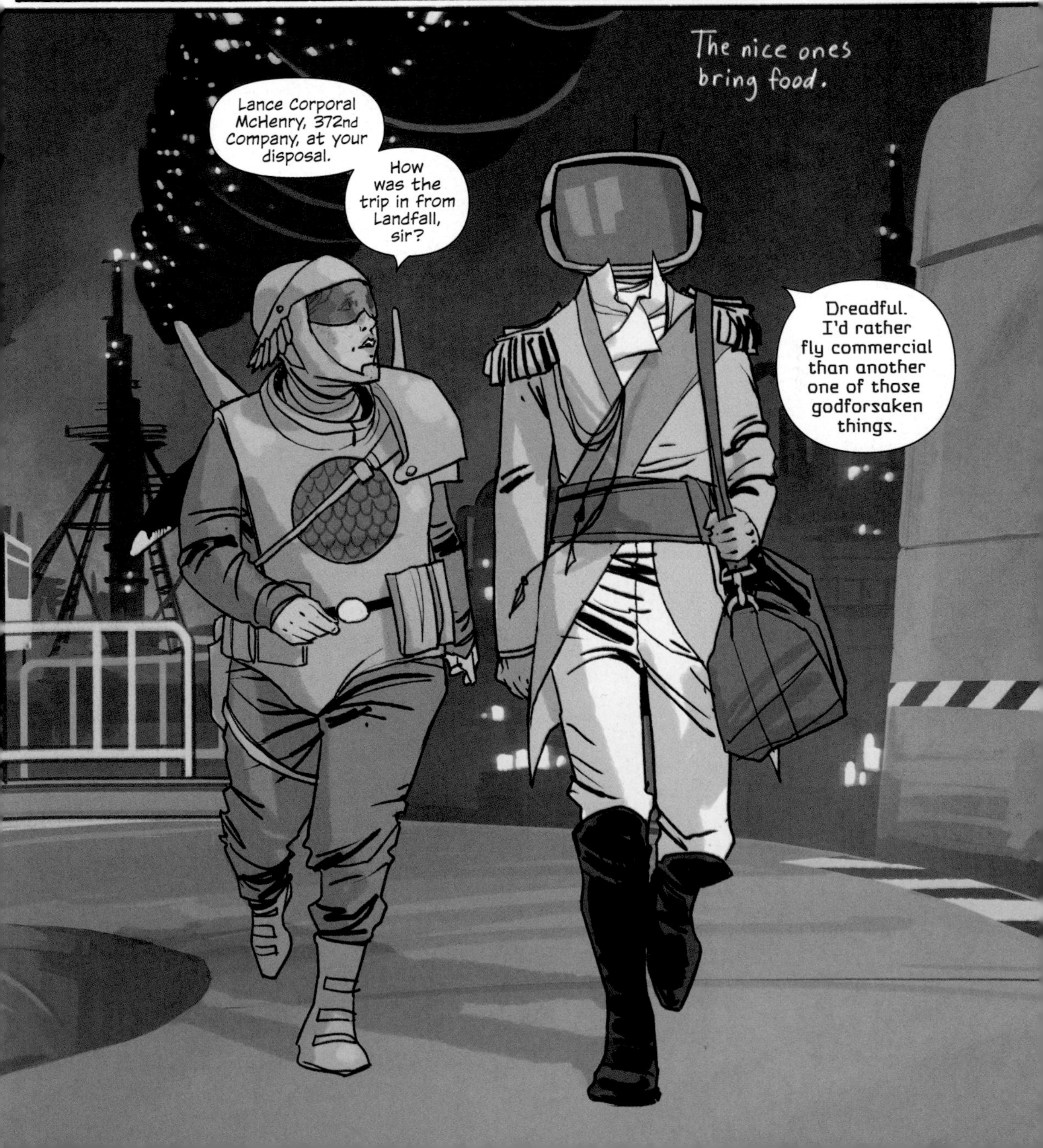
The nice ones bring food.
Lance Corporal McHenry, 372nd Company, at your disposal.
How was the trip in from Landfall, sir?
Dreadful. I'd rather fly commercial than another one of those godforsaken things.

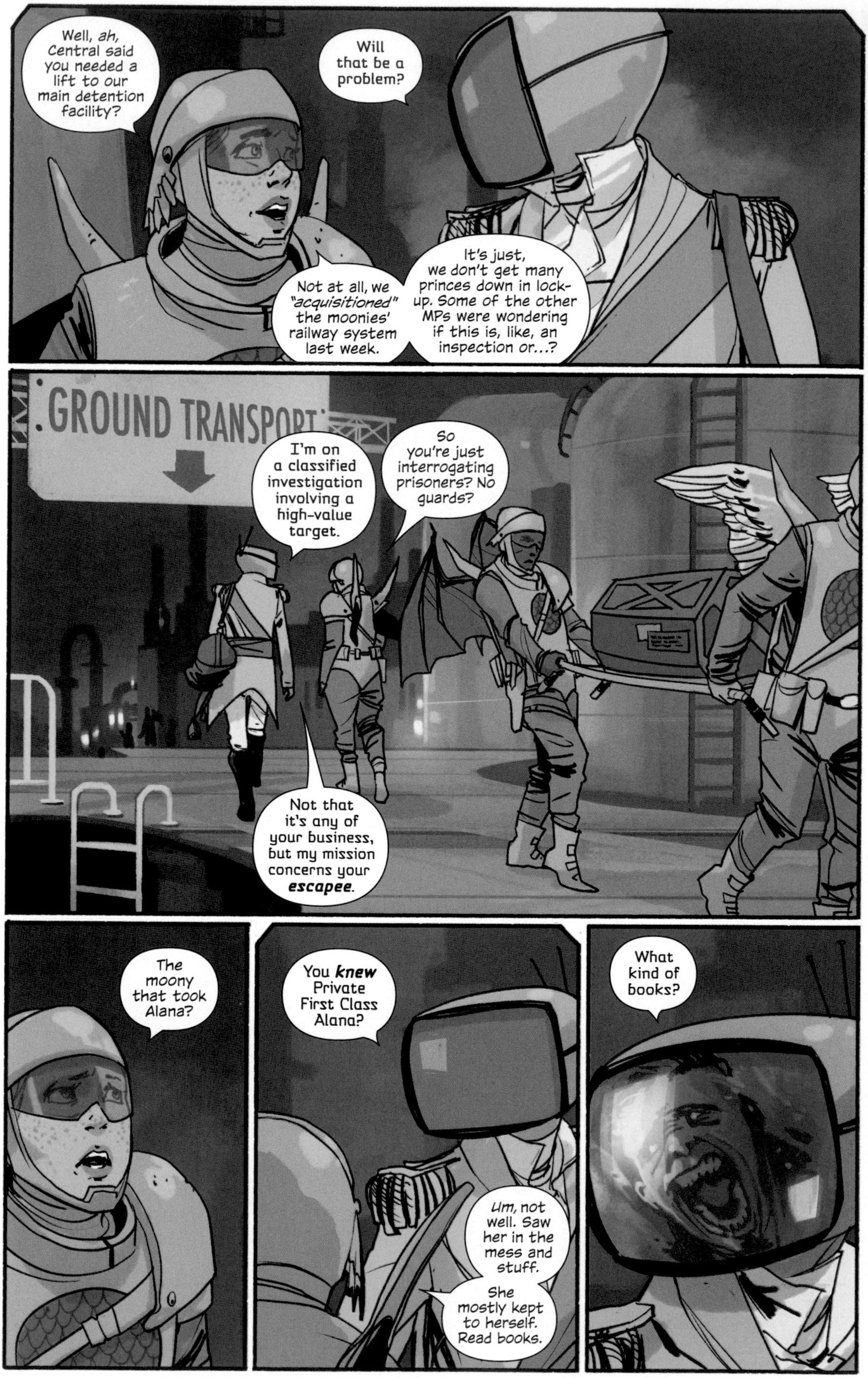
Well, *ah*, Central said you needed a lift to our main detention facility?
Will that be a problem?
Not at all, we *"acquisitioned"* the moonies' railway system last week.
It's just, we don't get many princes down in lock-up. Some of the other MPs were wondering if this is, like, an inspection or...?
GROUND TRANSPORT
So you're just interrogating prisoners? No guards?
I'm on a classified investigation involving a high-value target.
Not that it's any of your business, but my mission concerns your ***escapee***.
The moony that took Alana?
You ***knew*** Private First Class Alana?
Um, not well. Saw her in the mess and stuff.
She mostly kept to herself. Read books.
What kind of books?

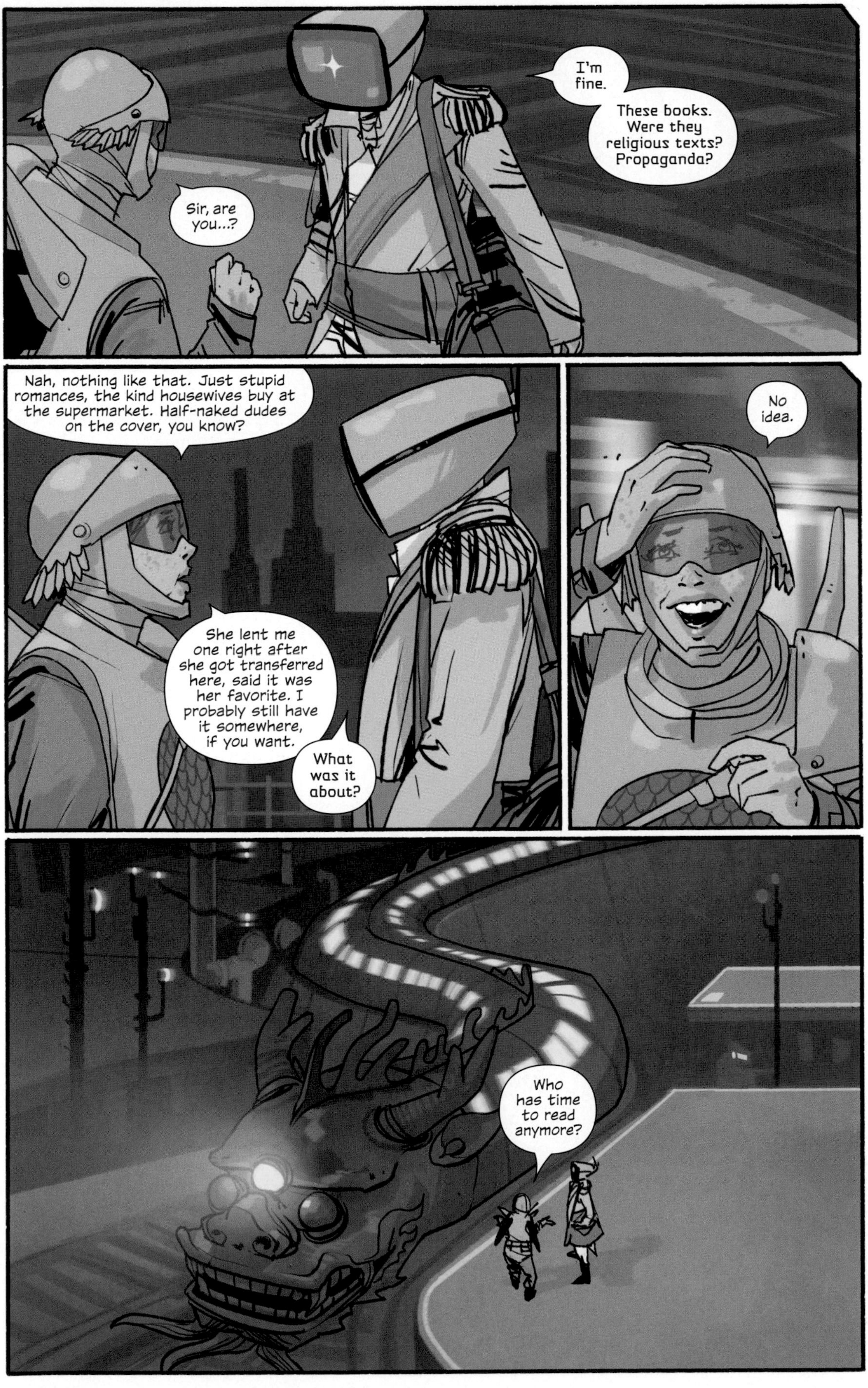
Sir, are you...?
I'm fine.
These books. Were they religious texts? Propaganda?
Nah, nothing like that. Just stupid romances, the kind housewives buy at the supermarket. Half-naked dudes on the cover, you know?
She lent me one right after she got transferred here, said it was her favorite. I probably still have it somewhere, if you want.
What was it about?
No idea.
Who has time to read anymore?

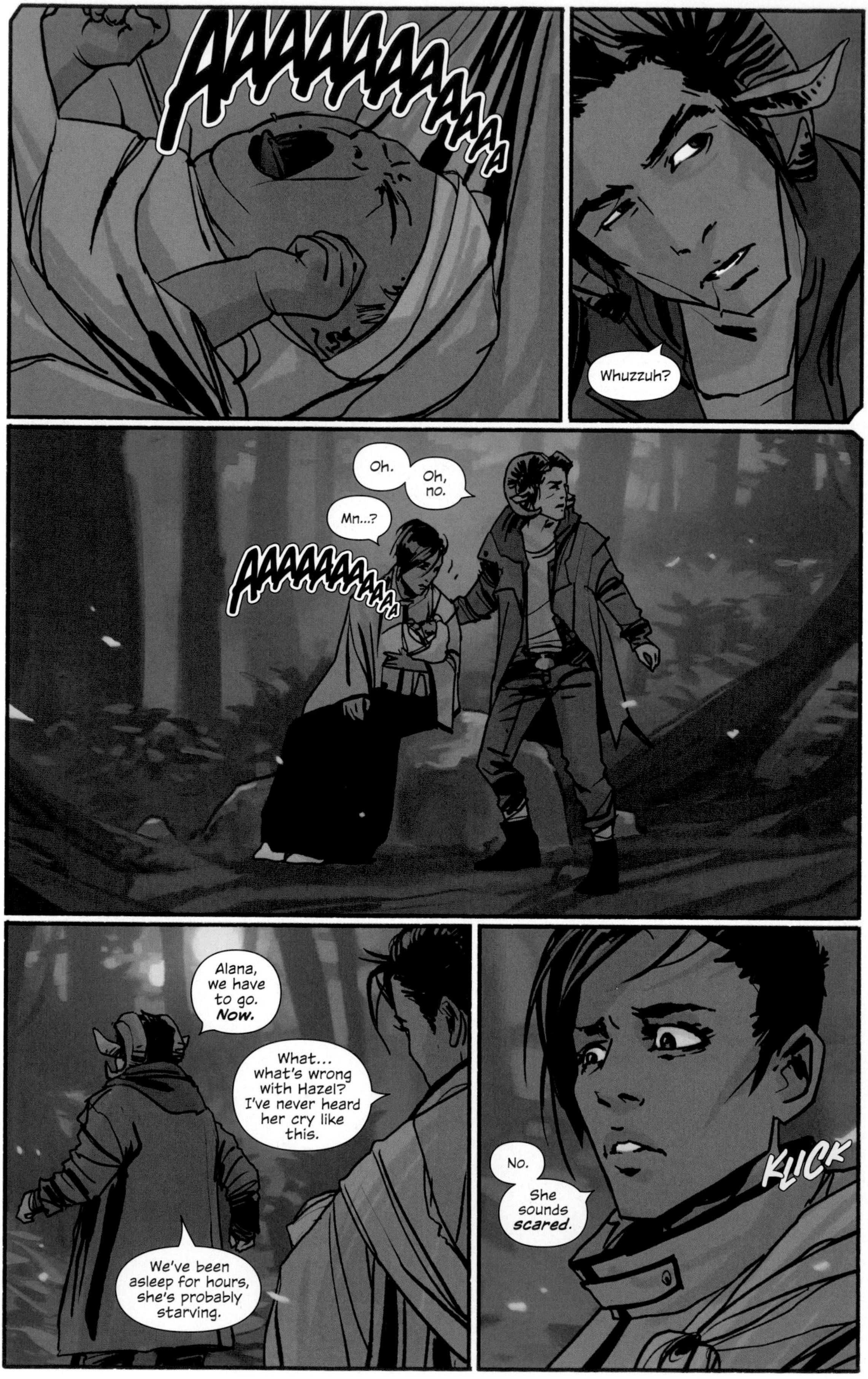
AAAAAAAAAAAAA
Whuzzuh?
Oh.
Oh, no.
Mn...?
AAAAAAAAAA
Alana, we have to go. **Now.**
What... what's wrong with Hazel? I've never heard her cry like this.
We've been asleep for hours, she's probably starving.
No.
She sounds *scared.*
KLICK

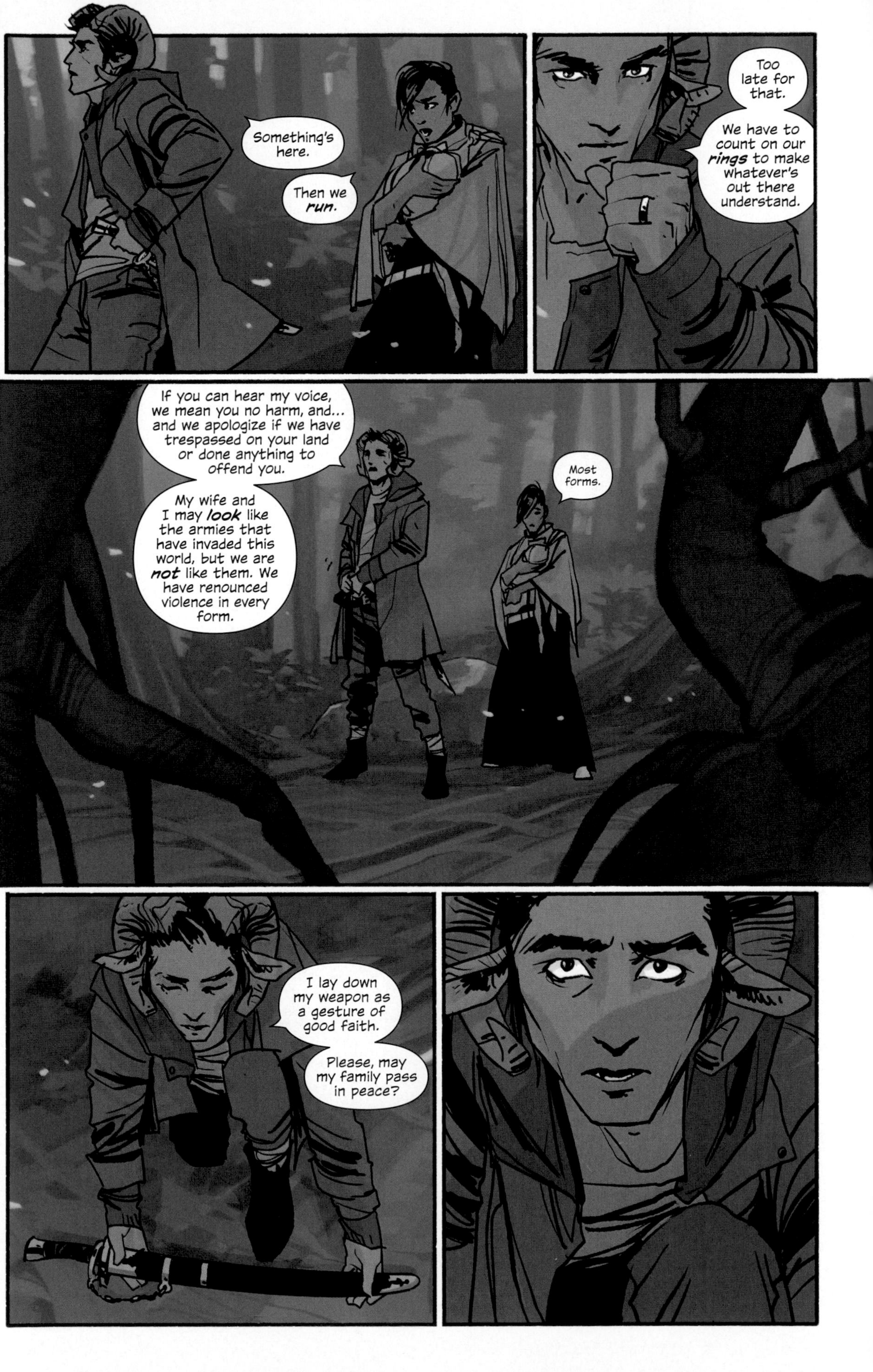
Something's here.
Then we *run*.
Too late for that.
We have to count on our *rings* to make whatever's out there understand.
If you can hear my voice, we mean you no harm, and... and we apologize if we have trespassed on your land or done anything to offend you.
My wife and I may *look* like the armies that have invaded this world, but we are *not* like them. We have renounced violence in every form.
Most forms.
I lay down my weapon as a gesture of good faith.
Please, may my family pass in peace?

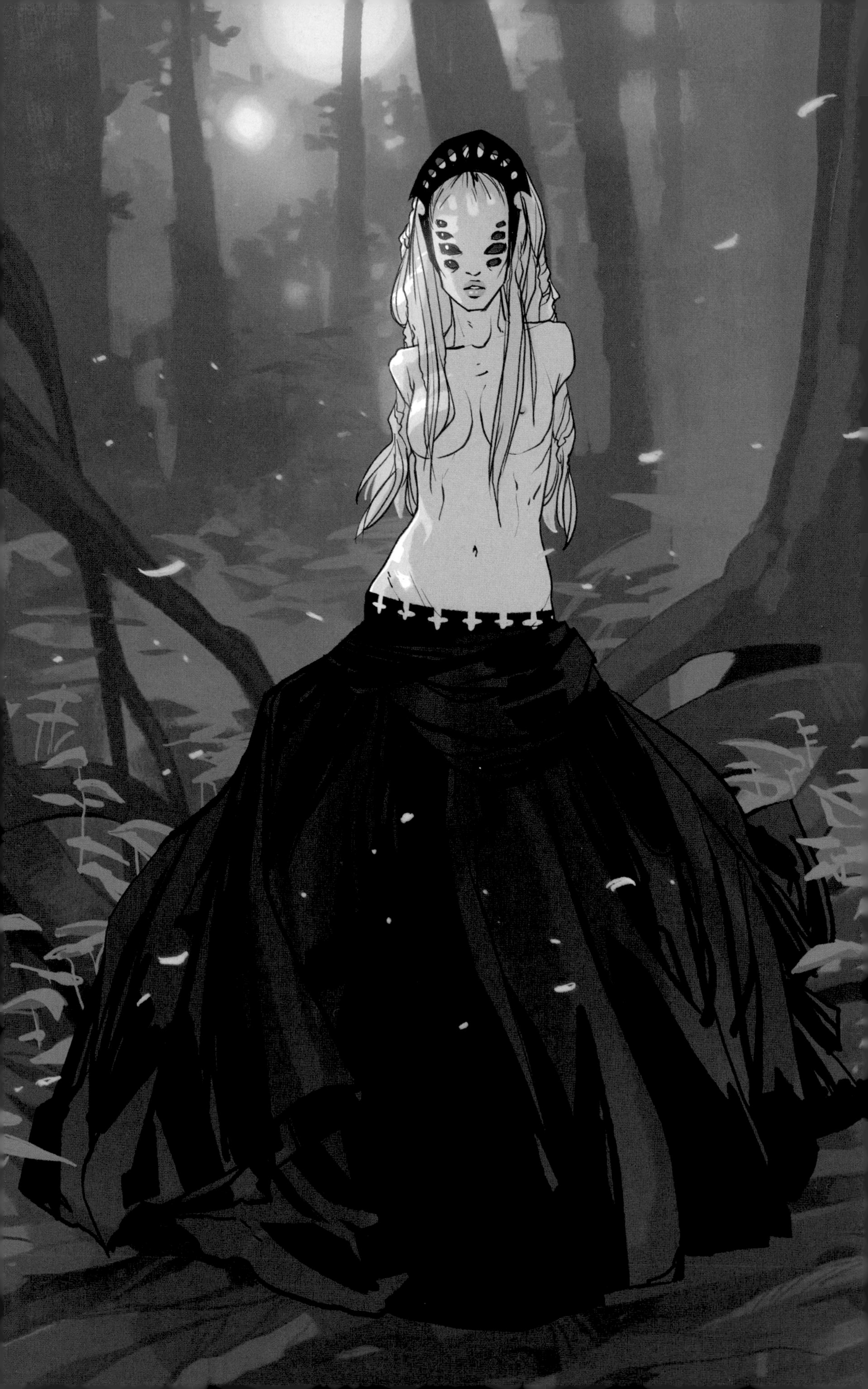

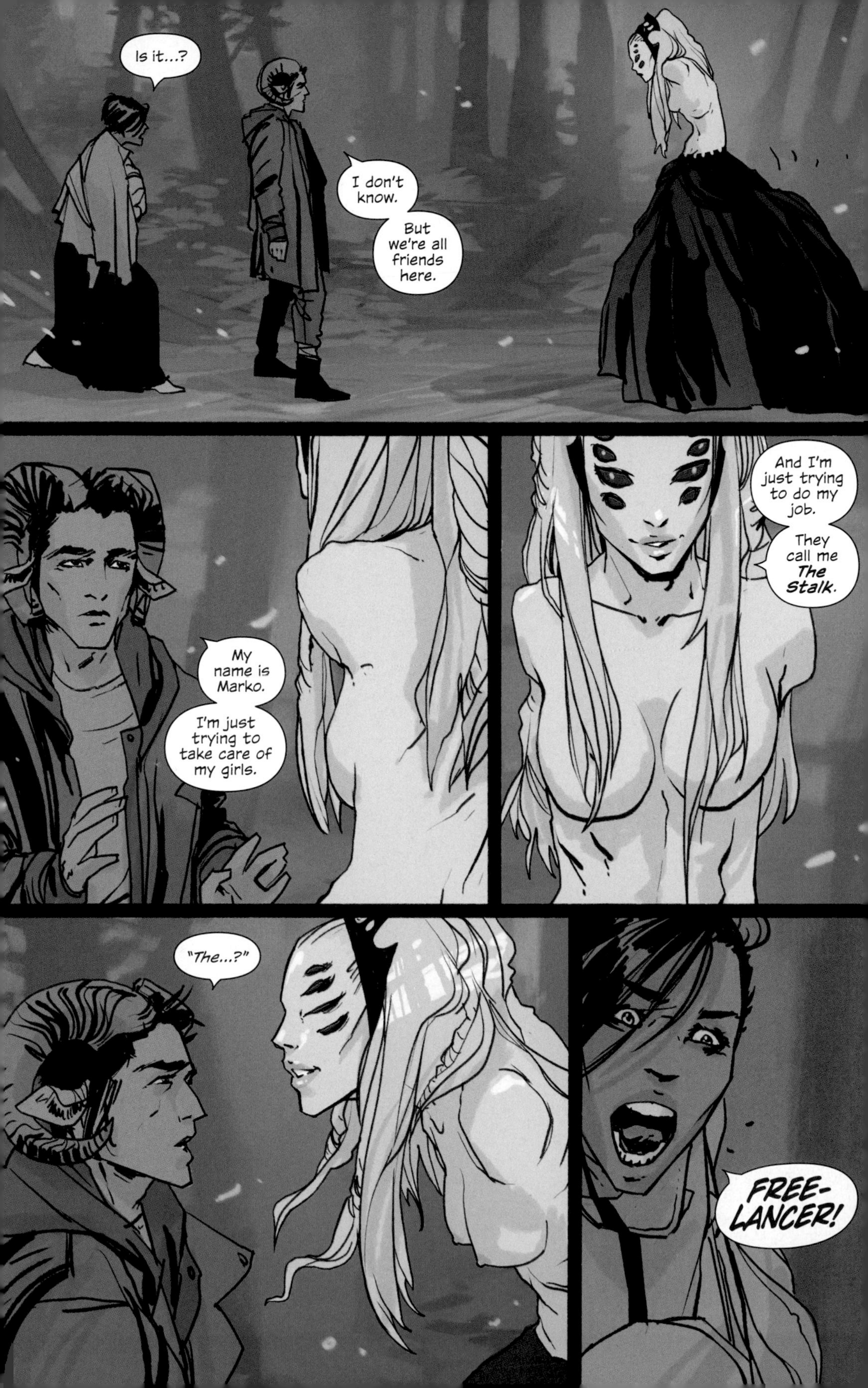
Is it...?
I don't know.
But we're all friends here.
My name is Marko.
I'm just trying to take care of my girls.
And I'm just trying to do my job.
They call me *The Stalk*.
"The...?"
FREE-LANCER!

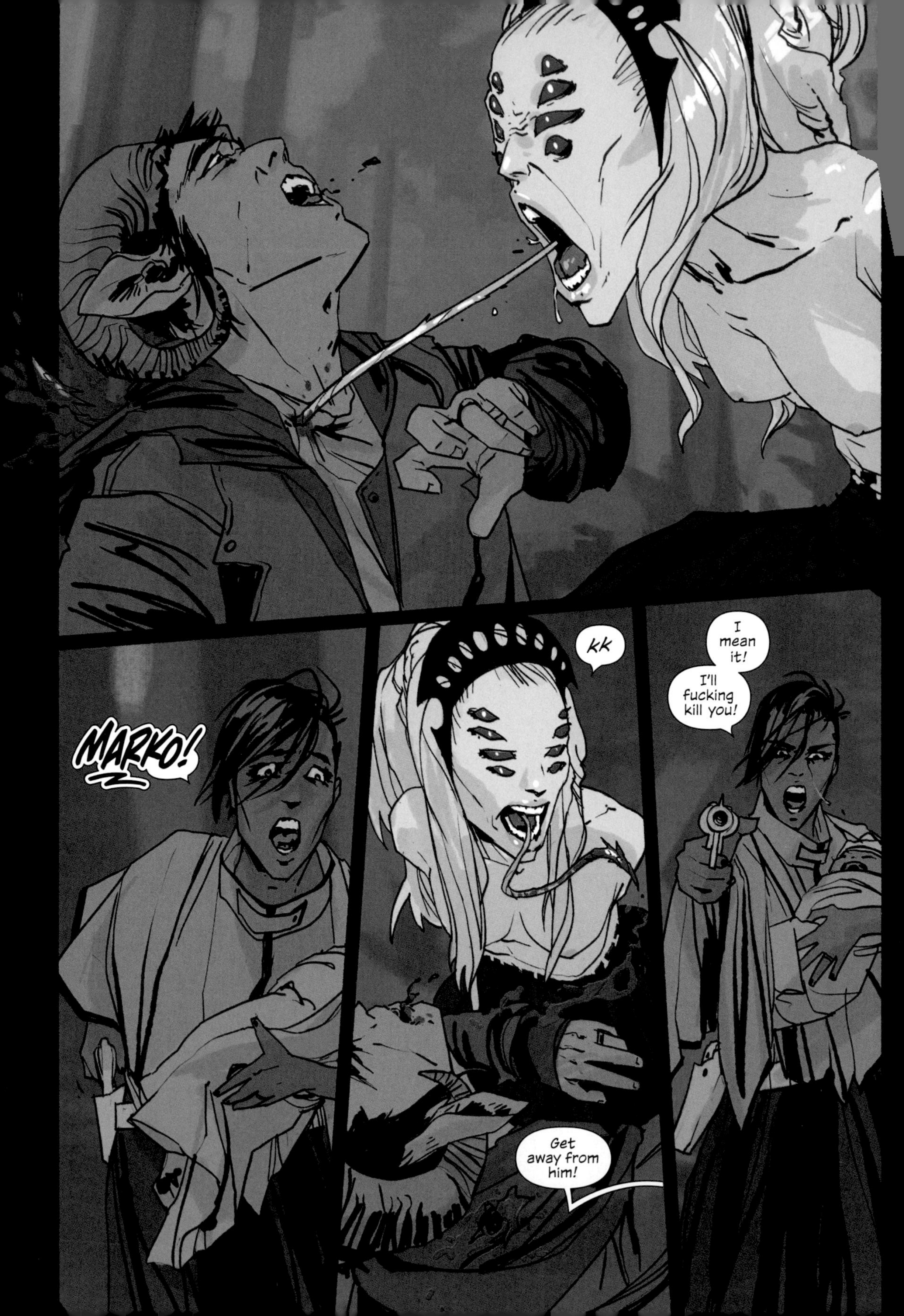
MARKO!
KK
Get away from him!
I mean it!
I'll fucking kill you!

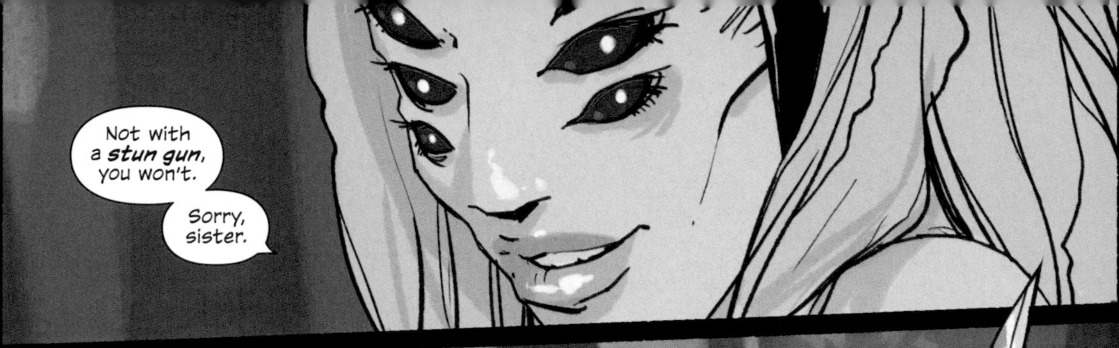
Not with a **stun gun**, you won't.
Sorry, sister.
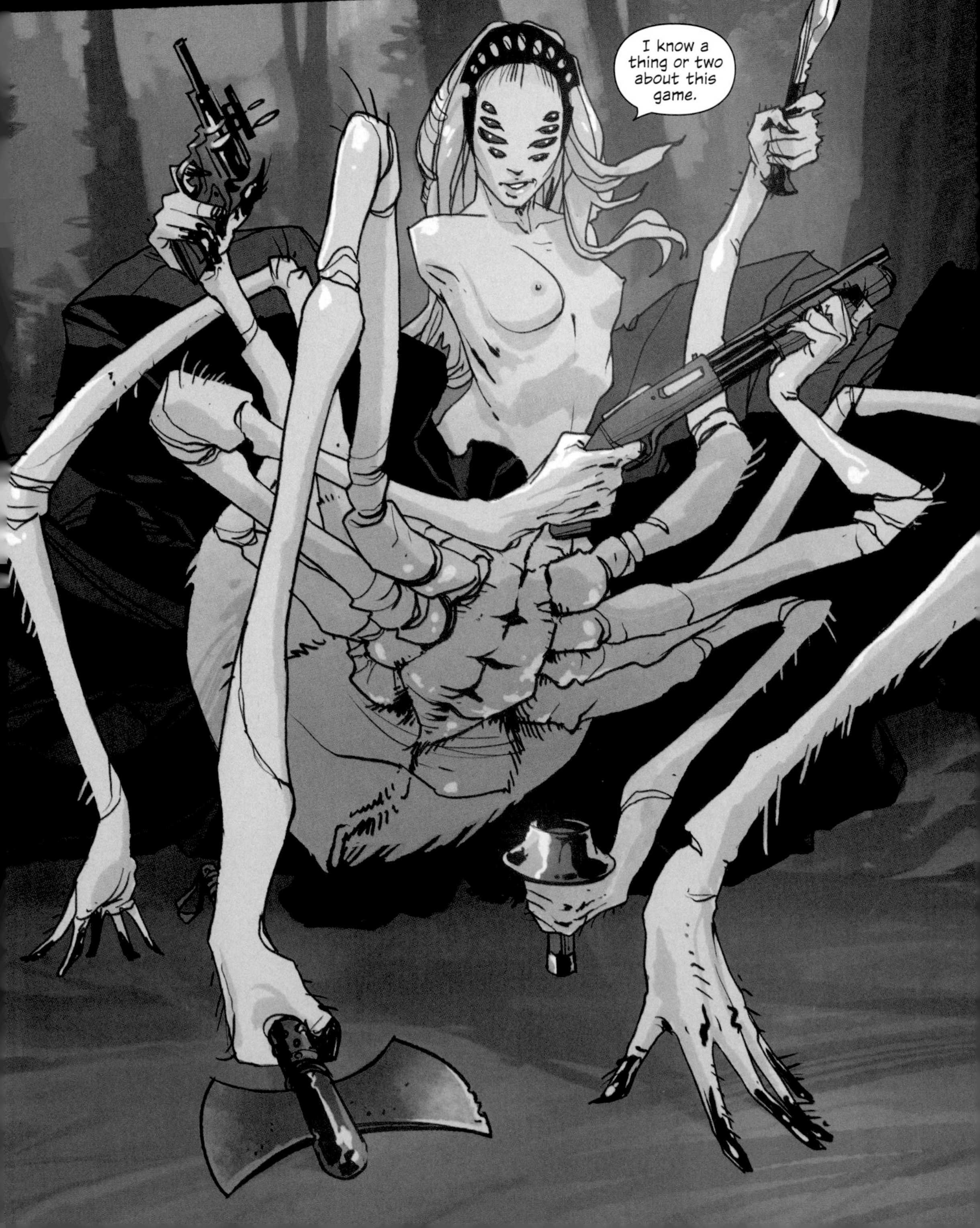
I know a thing or two about this game.

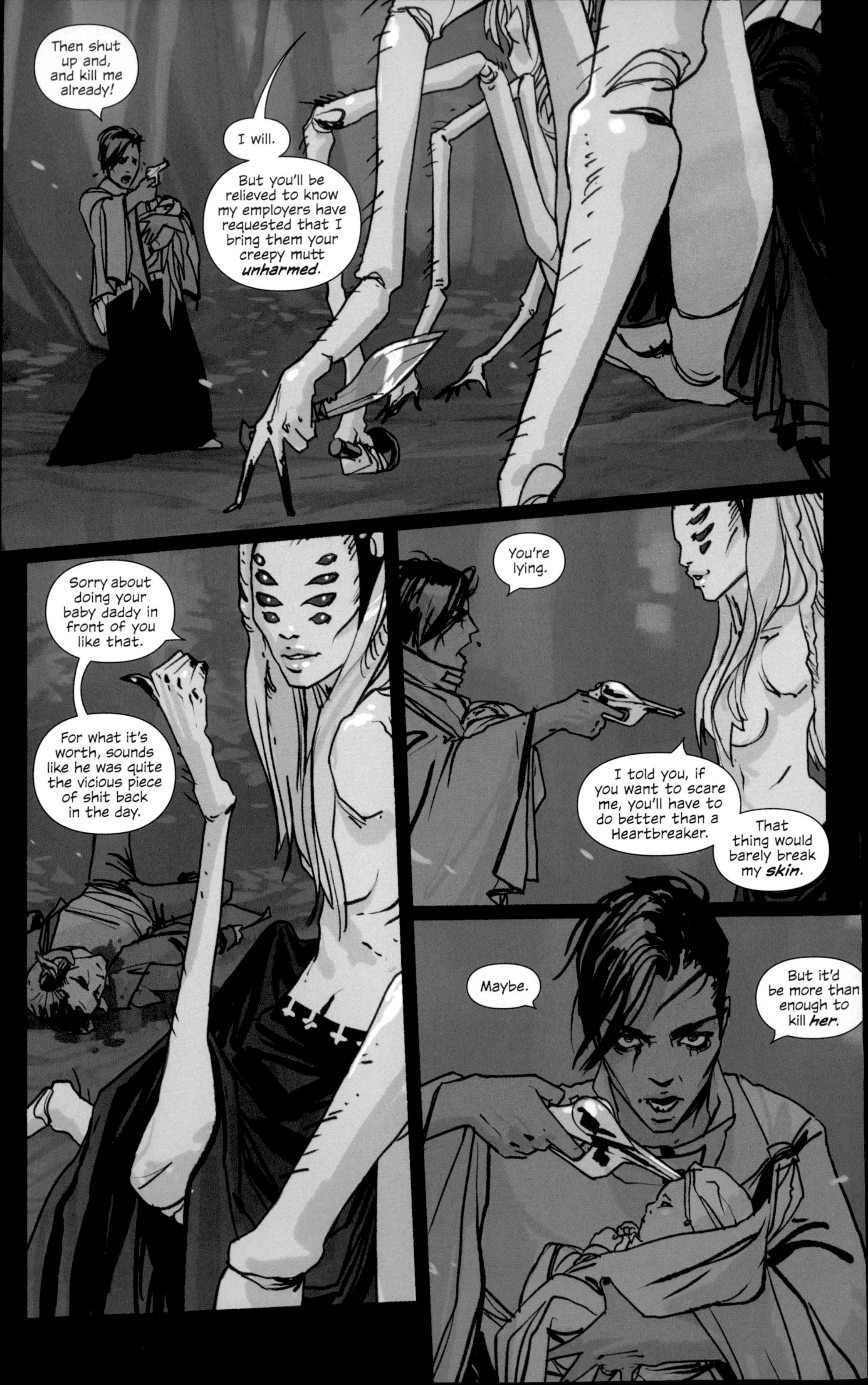
Then shut up and, and kill me already!
I will.
But you'll be relieved to know my employers have requested that I bring them your creepy mutt *unharmed*.
Sorry about doing your baby daddy in front of you like that.
For what it's worth, sounds like he was quite the vicious piece of shit back in the day.
You're lying.
I told you, if you want to scare me, you'll have to do better than a Heartbreaker.
That thing would barely break my *skin*.
Maybe.
But it'd be more than enough to kill *her*.

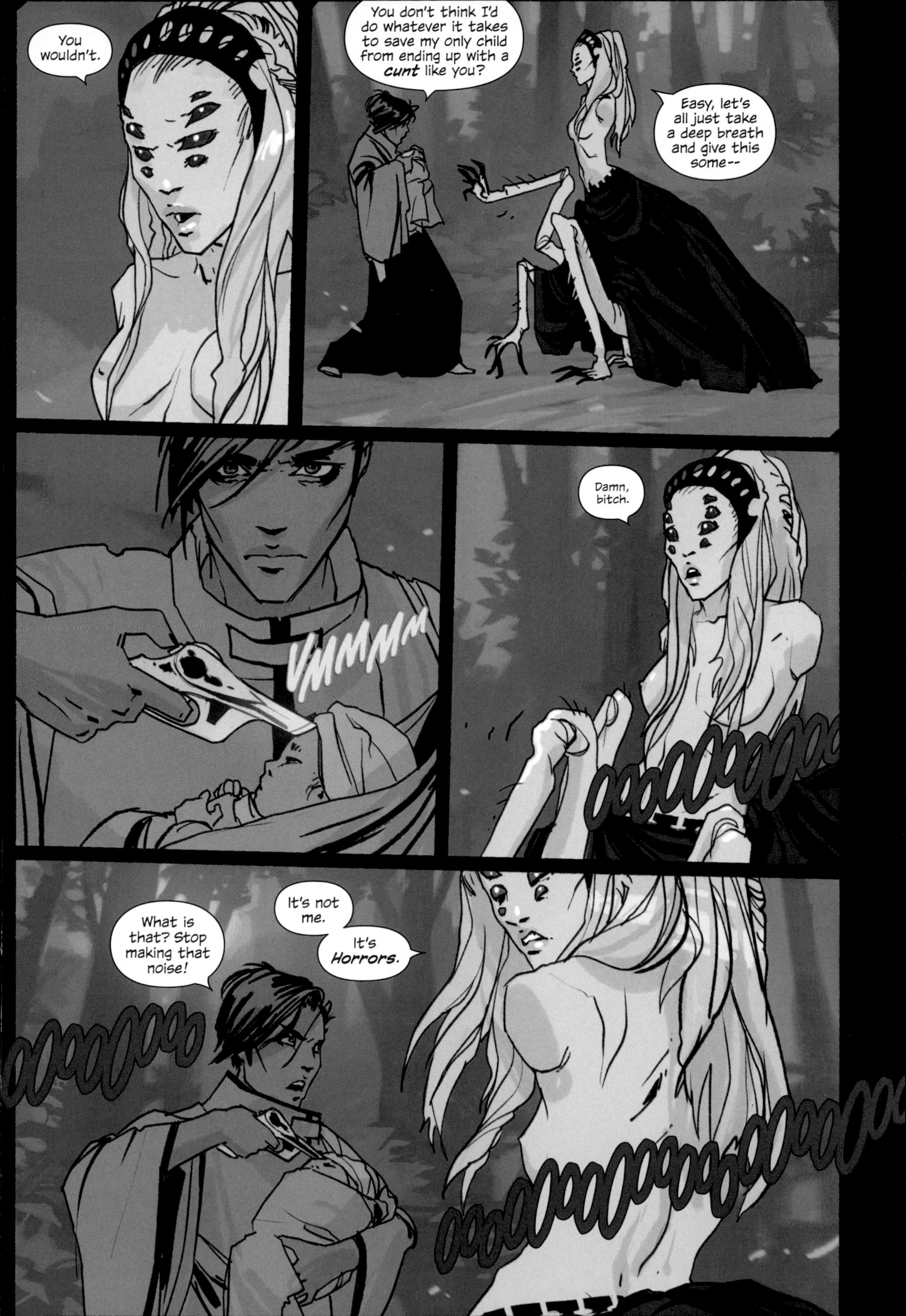

You wouldn't.
You don't think I'd do whatever it takes to save my only child from ending up with a cunt like you?
Easy, let's all just take a deep breath and give this some--
VMMMM
Damn, bitch.
What is that? Stop making that noise!
It's not me.
It's Horrors.

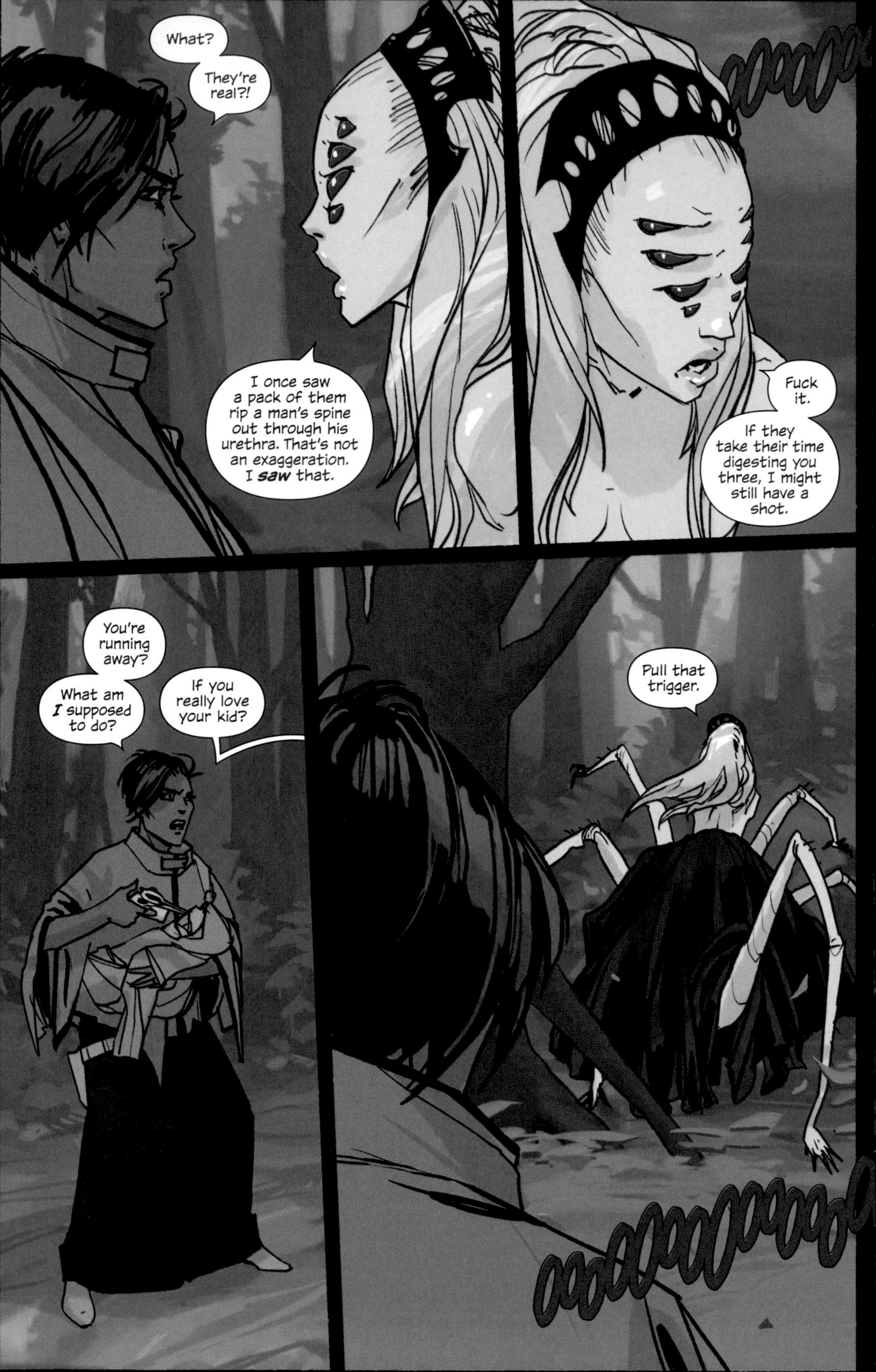
What?
They're real?!
I once saw a pack of them rip a man's spine out through his urethra. That's not an exaggeration. I **saw** that.
Fuck it.
If they take their time digesting you three, I might still have a shot.
You're running away?
What am *I* supposed to do?
If you really love your kid?
Pull that trigger.

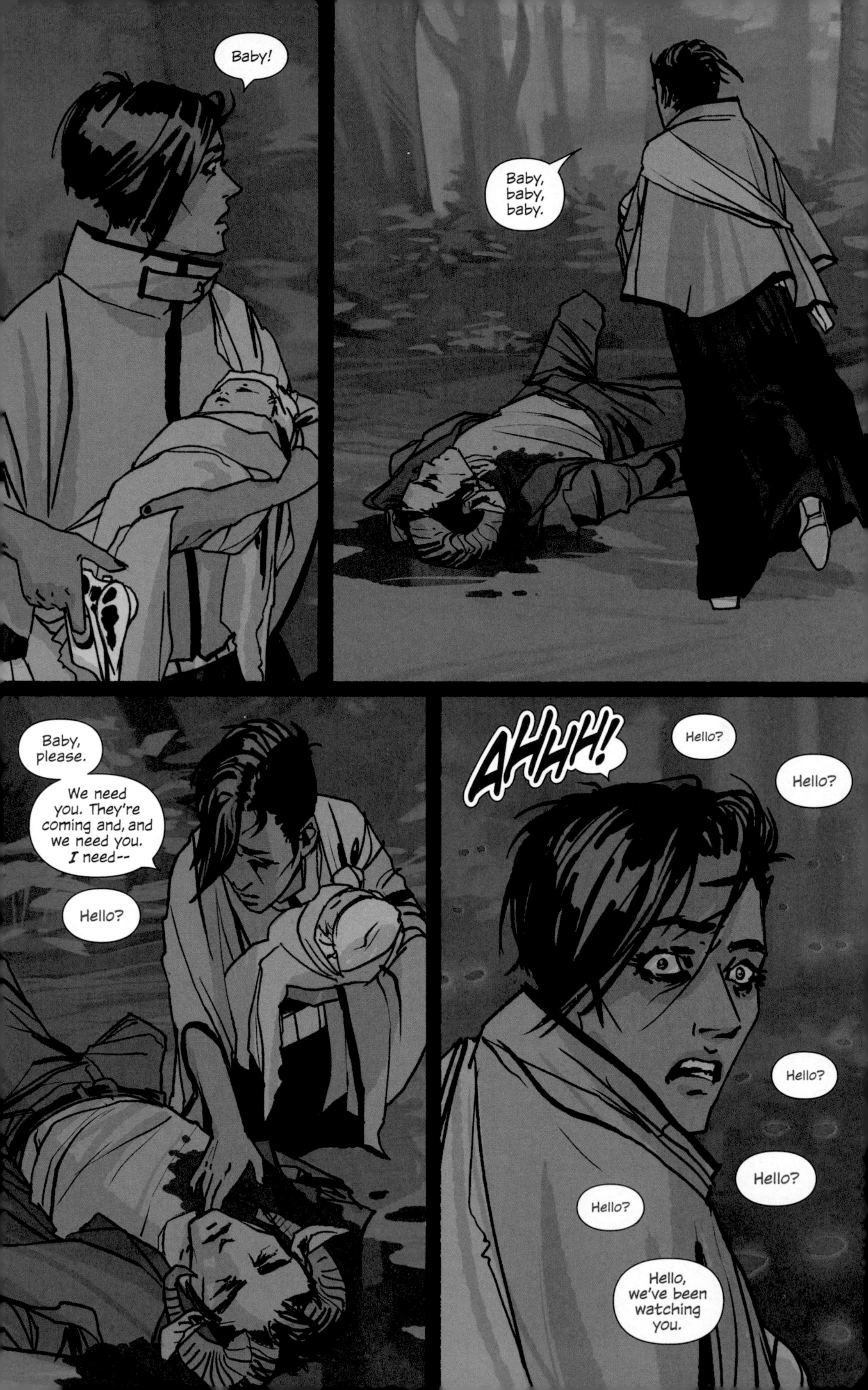
Baby!
Baby, baby, baby.
Baby, please.
We need you. They're coming and, and we need you. I need--
Hello?
AHHH!
Hello?
Hello?
Hello?
Hello?
Hello?
Hello, we've been watching you.

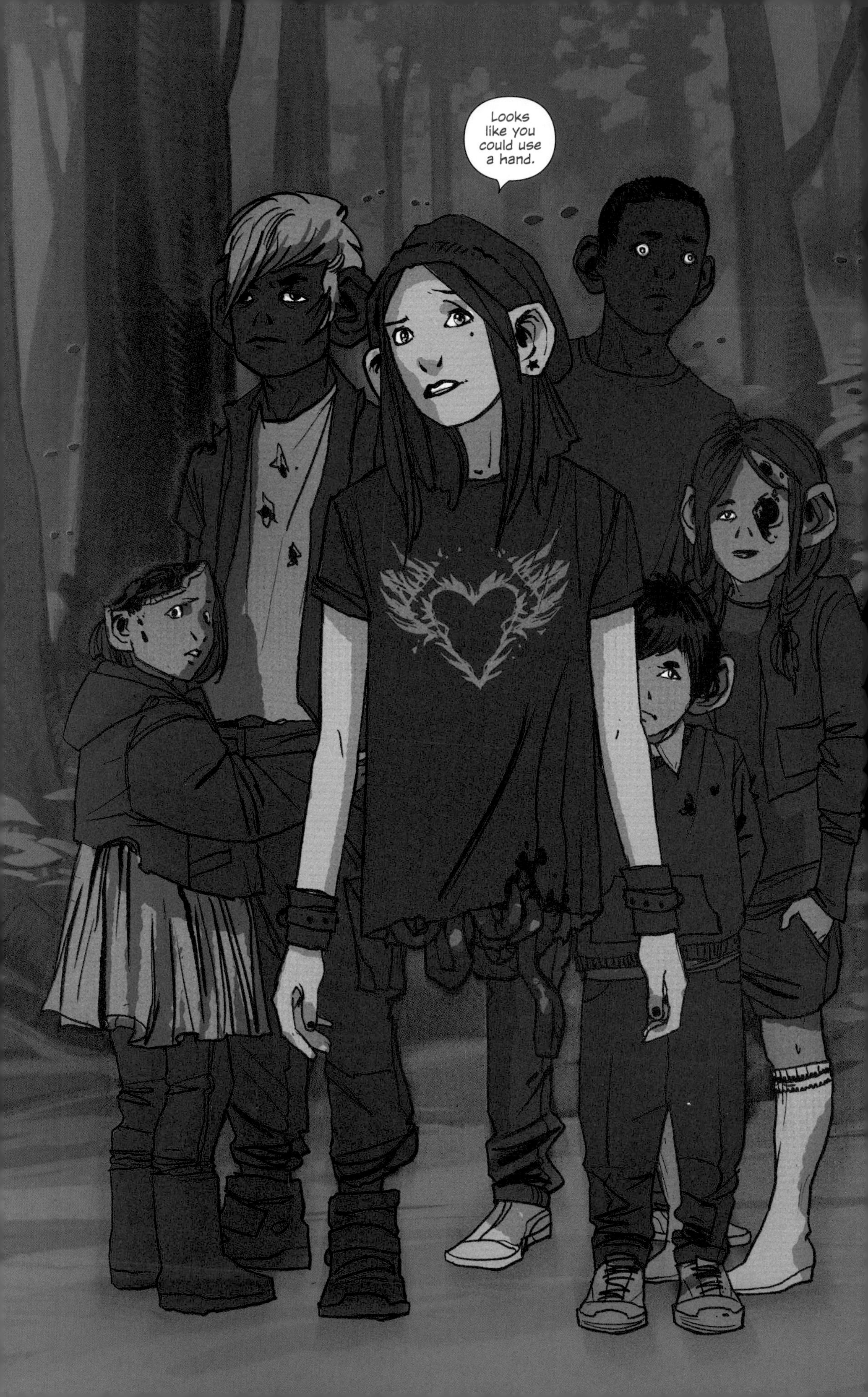
Looks like you could use a hand.

end chapter two

CHAPTER
THREE

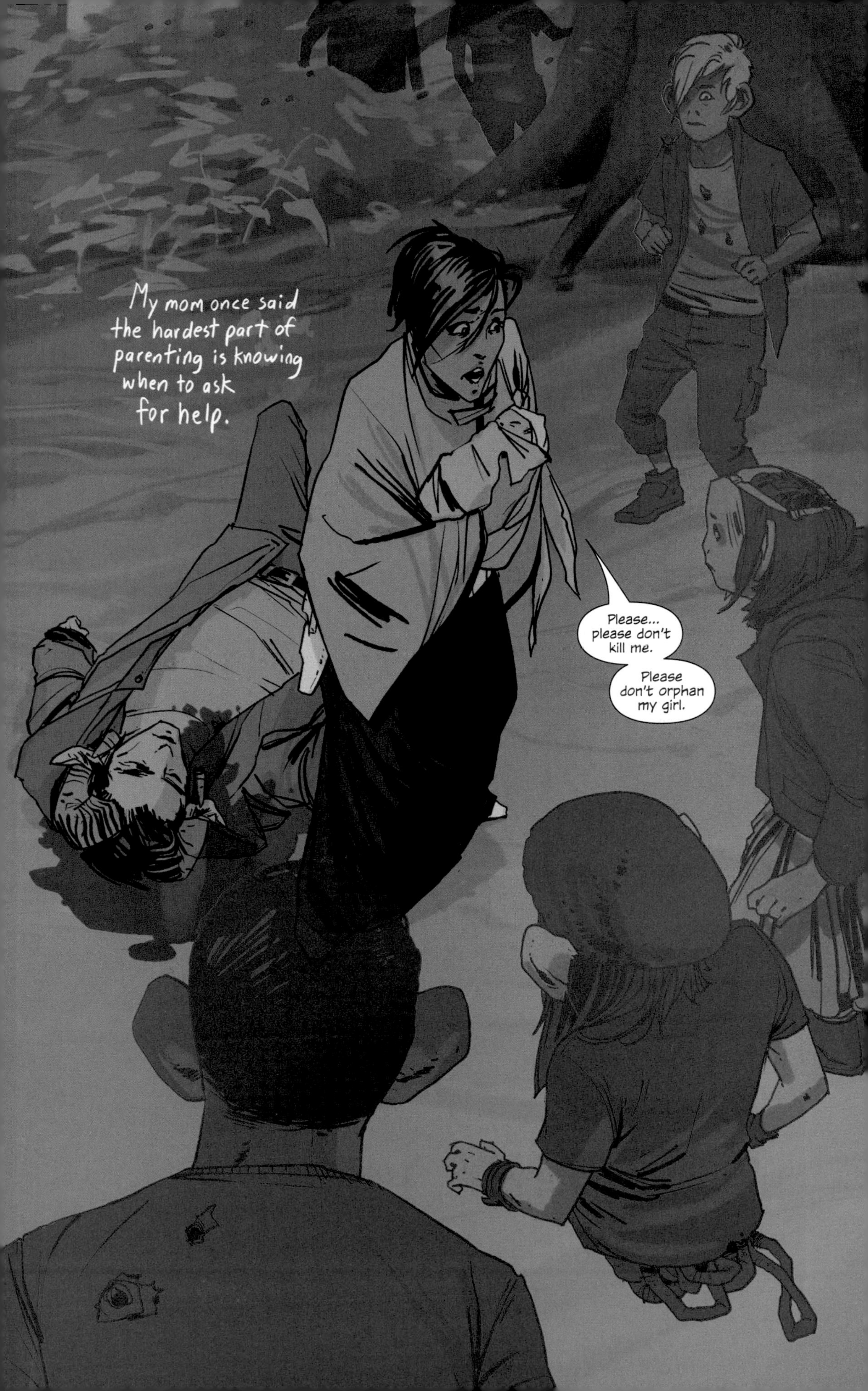
My mom once said the hardest part of parenting is knowing when to ask for help.
Please... please don't kill me.
Please don't orphan my girl.

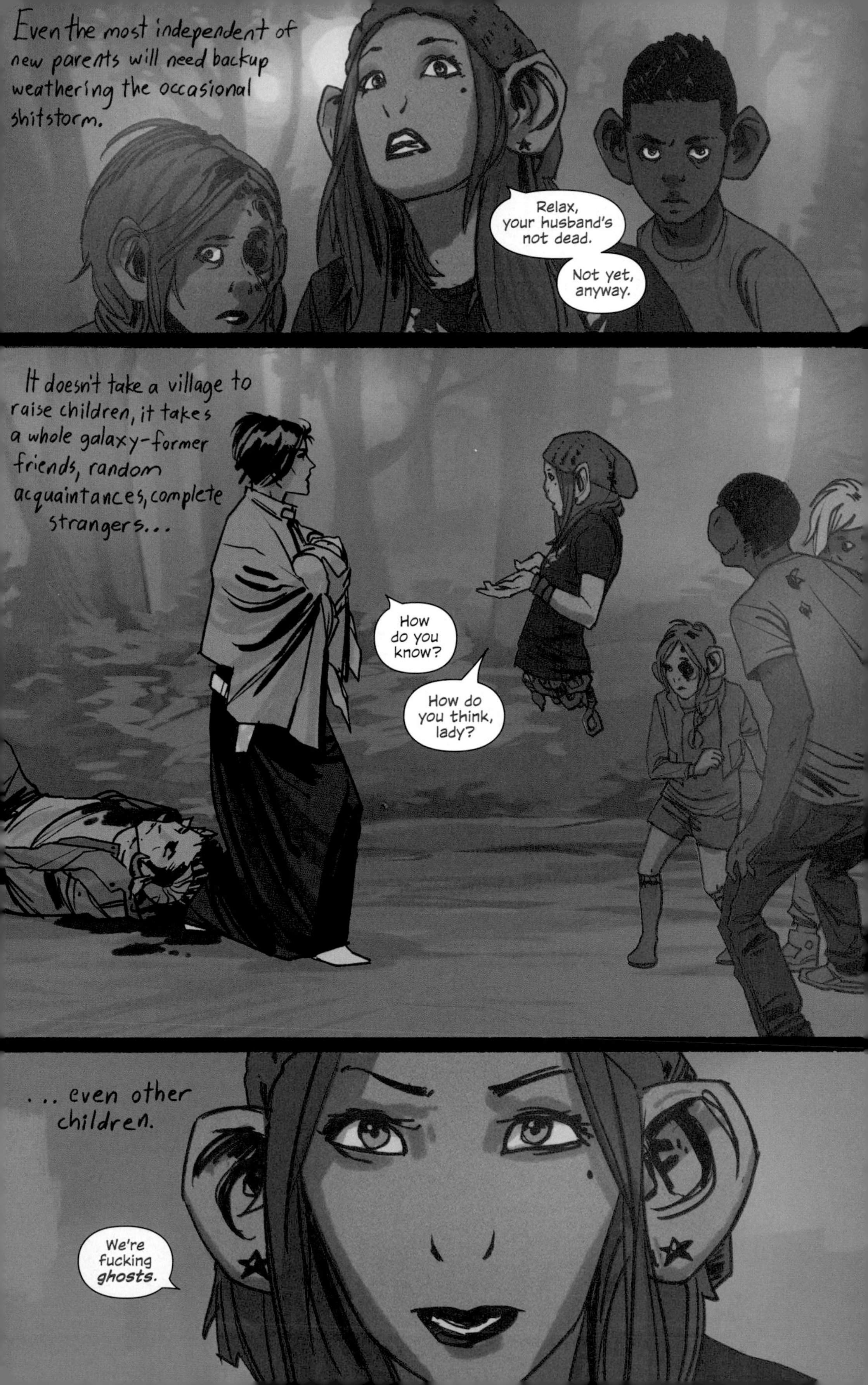
Even the most independent of new parents will need backup weathering the occasional shitstorm.
Relax, your husband's not dead.
Not yet, anyway.
It doesn't take a village to raise children, it takes a whole galaxy-former friends, random acquaintances, complete strangers...
How do you know?
How do you think, lady?
...even other children.
We're fucking ghosts.

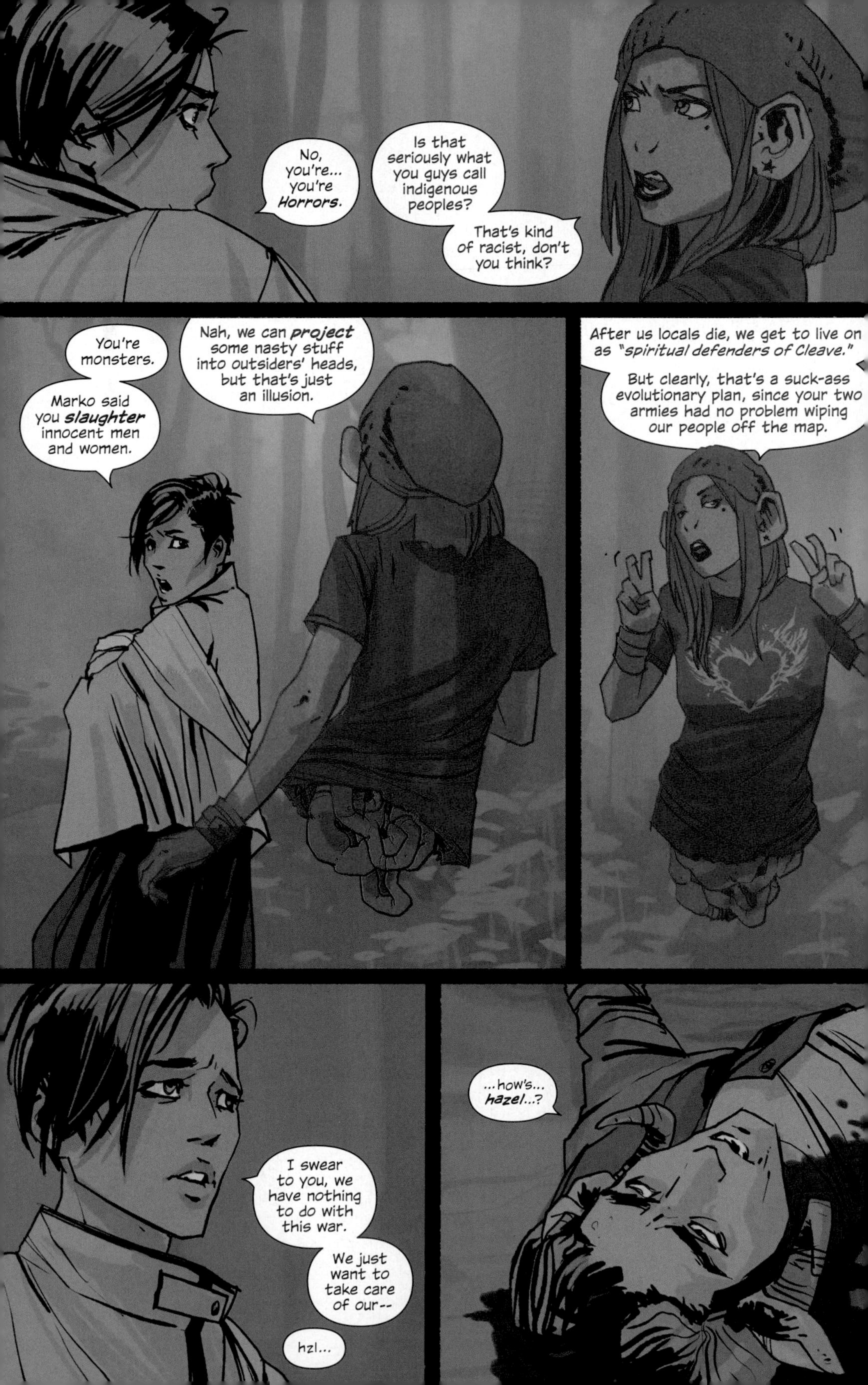
No, you're... you're **Horrors**.
Is that seriously what you guys call indigenous peoples?
That's kind of racist, don't you think?
You're monsters.
Marko said you **slaughter** innocent men and women.
Nah, we can **project** some nasty stuff into outsiders' heads, but that's just an illusion.
After us locals die, we get to live on as *"spiritual defenders of Cleave."*
But clearly, that's a suck-ass evolutionary plan, since your two armies had no problem wiping our people off the map.
I swear to you, we have nothing to do with this war.
We just want to take care of our--
hzl...
...how's... **hazel**...?

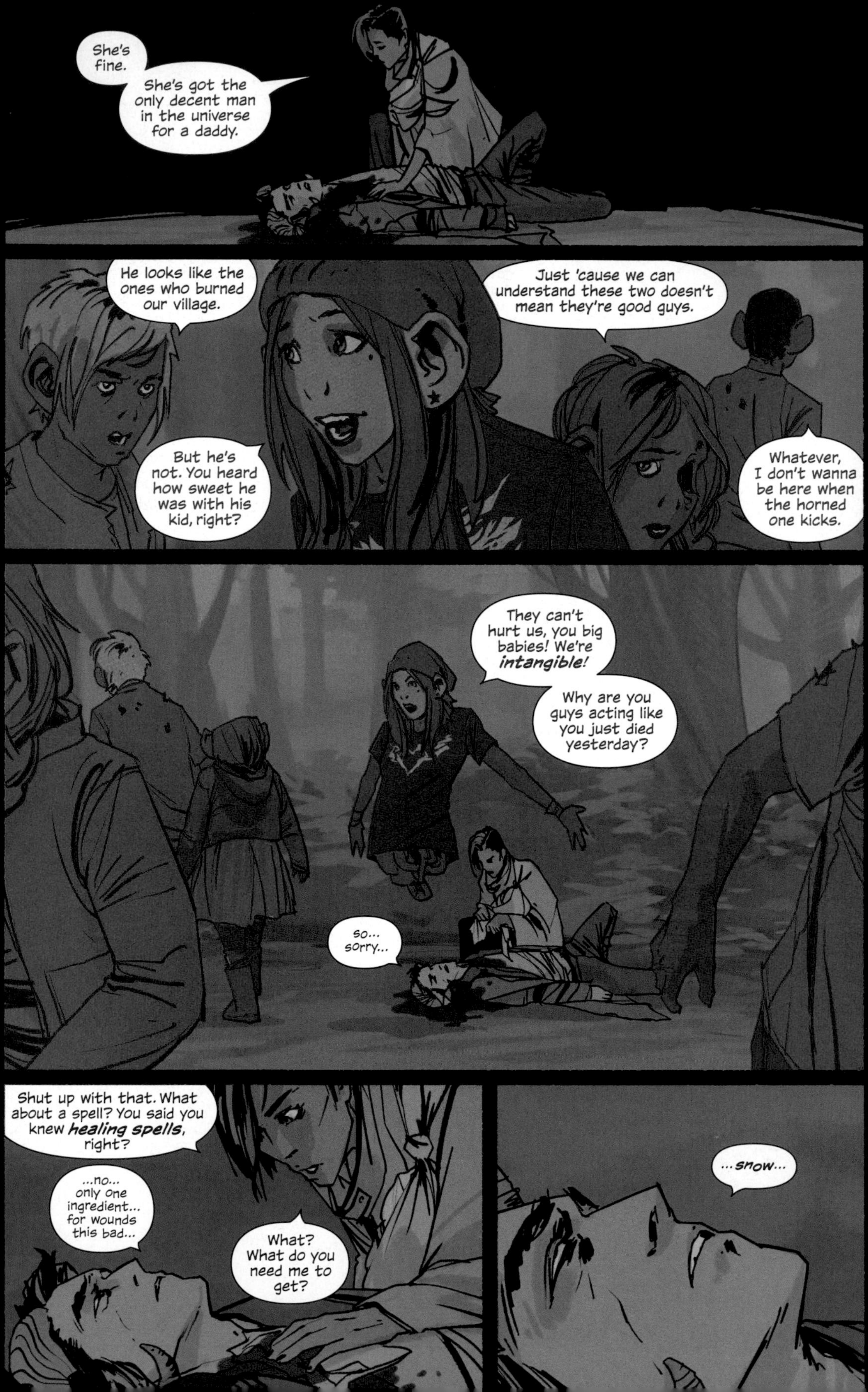
She's fine.
She's got the only decent man in the universe for a daddy.
He looks like the ones who burned our village.
Just 'cause we can understand these two doesn't mean they're good guys.
But he's not. You heard how sweet he was with his kid, right?
Whatever, I don't wanna be here when the horned one kicks.
They can't hurt us, you big babies! We're *intangible!*
Why are you guys acting like you just died yesterday?
so... sorry...
Shut up with that. What about a spell? You said you knew *healing spells*, right?
...no... only one ingredient... for wounds this bad...
What? What do you need me to get?
...snow...

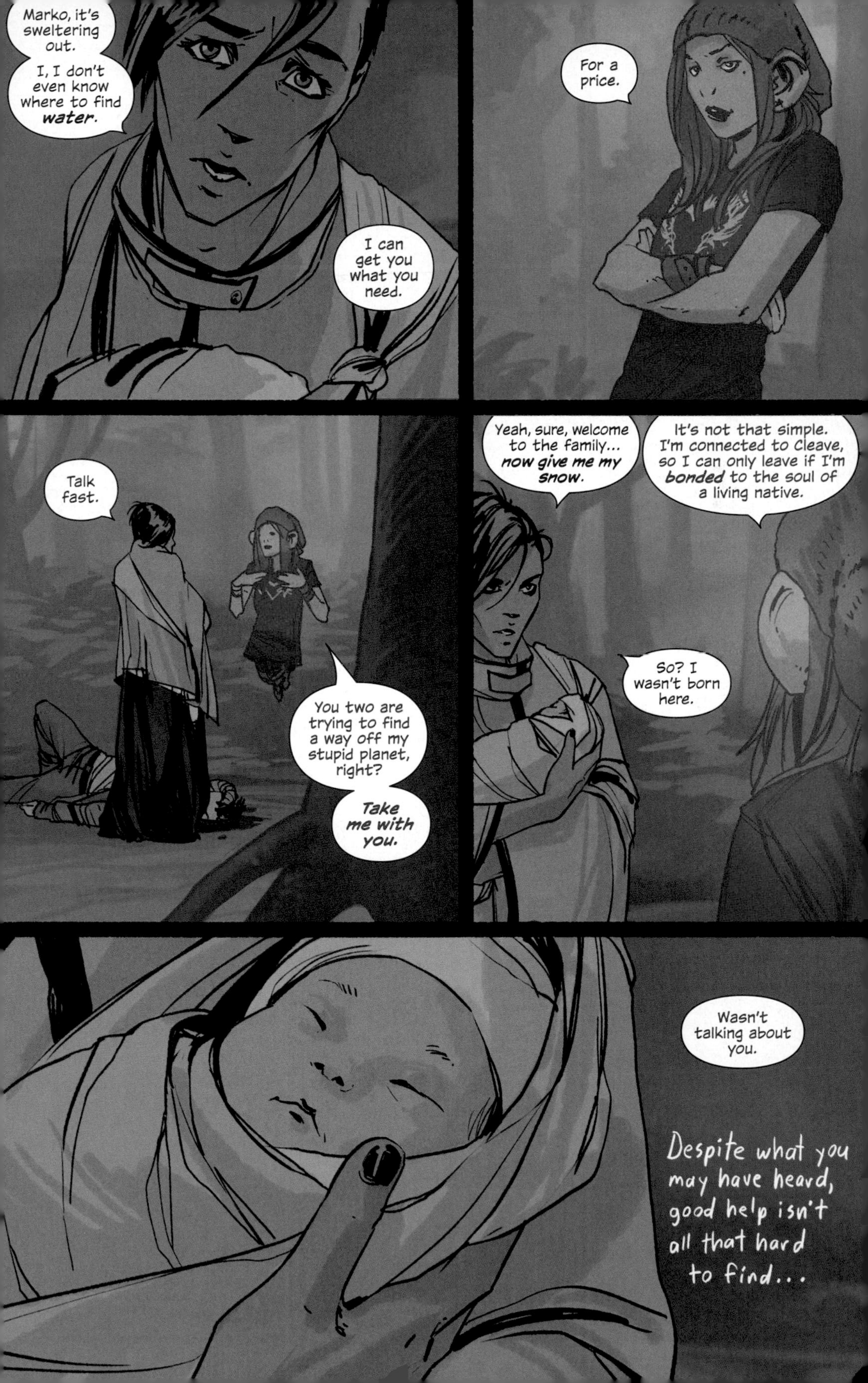

Marko, it's sweltering out.
I, I don't even know where to find **water**.
For a price.
I can get you what you need.
Talk fast.
You two are trying to find a way off my stupid planet, right?
Take me with you.
Yeah, sure, welcome to the family... ***now give me my snow.***
It's not that simple. I'm connected to Cleave, so I can only leave if I'm ***bonded*** to the soul of a living native.
So? I wasn't born here.
Wasn't talking about you.
Despite what you may have heard, good help isn't all that hard to find...

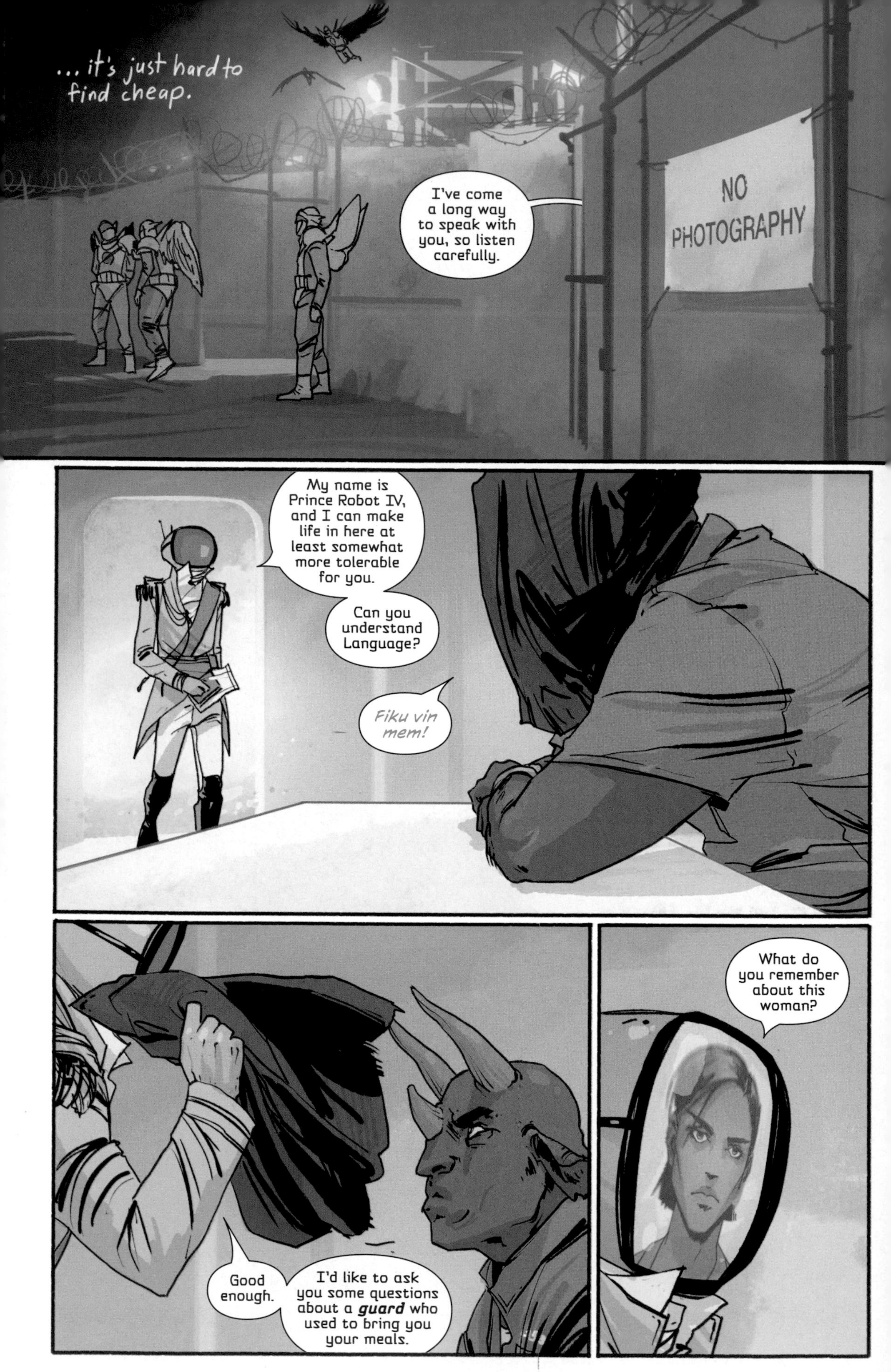

... it's just hard to find cheap.
I've come a long way to speak with you, so listen carefully.
NO PHOTOGRAPHY
My name is Prince Robot IV, and I can make life in here at least somewhat more tolerable for you.
Can you understand Language?
Fiku vin mem!
Good enough.
I'd like to ask you some questions about a guard who used to bring you your meals.
What do you remember about this woman?

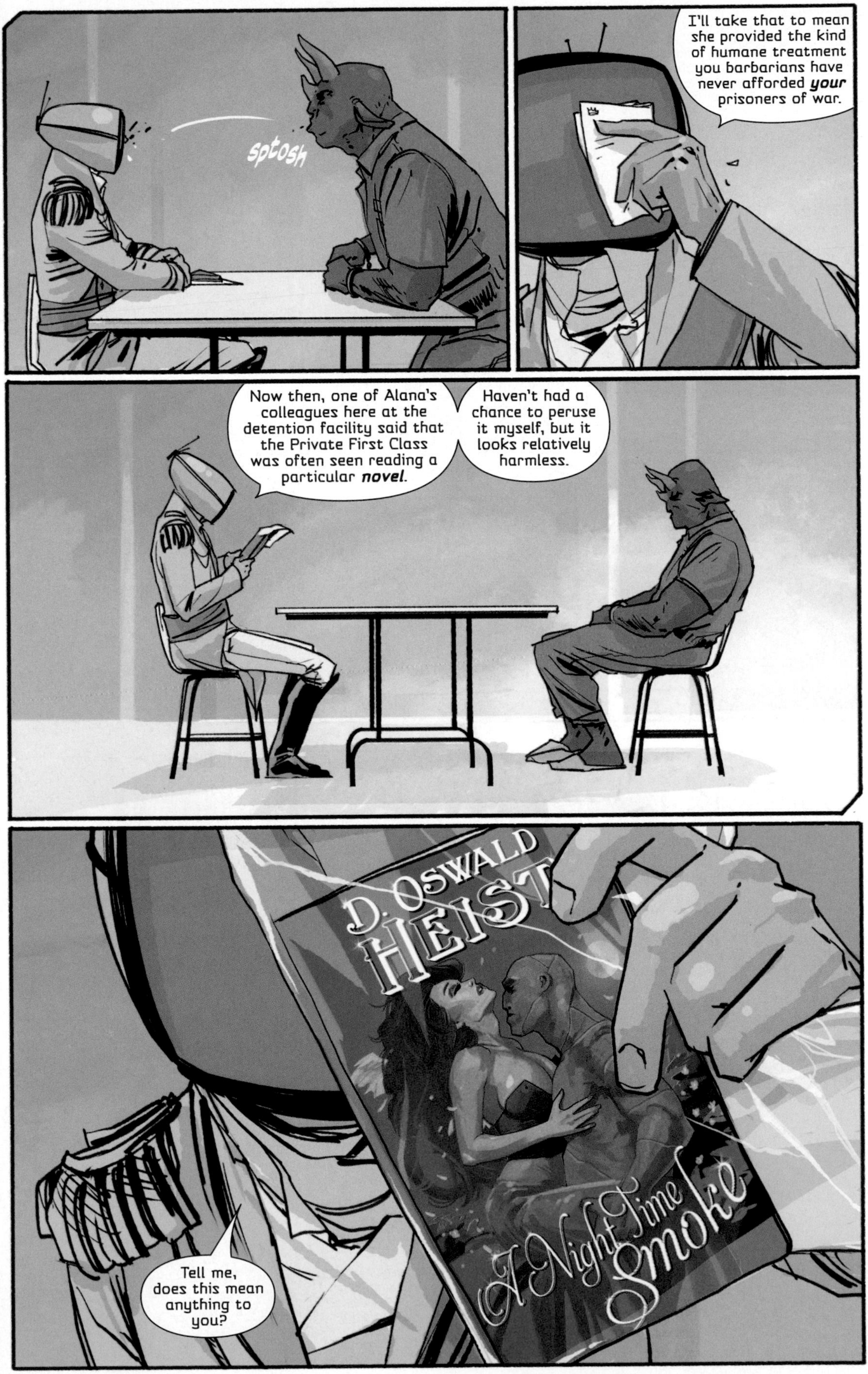
sptosh
I'll take that to mean she provided the kind of humane treatment you barbarians have never afforded ***your*** prisoners of war.
Now then, one of Alana's colleagues here at the detention facility said that the Private First Class was often seen reading a particular ***novel***.
Haven't had a chance to peruse it myself, but it looks relatively harmless.
D. OSWALD HEIST
A Night Time Smoke
Tell me, does this mean anything to you?

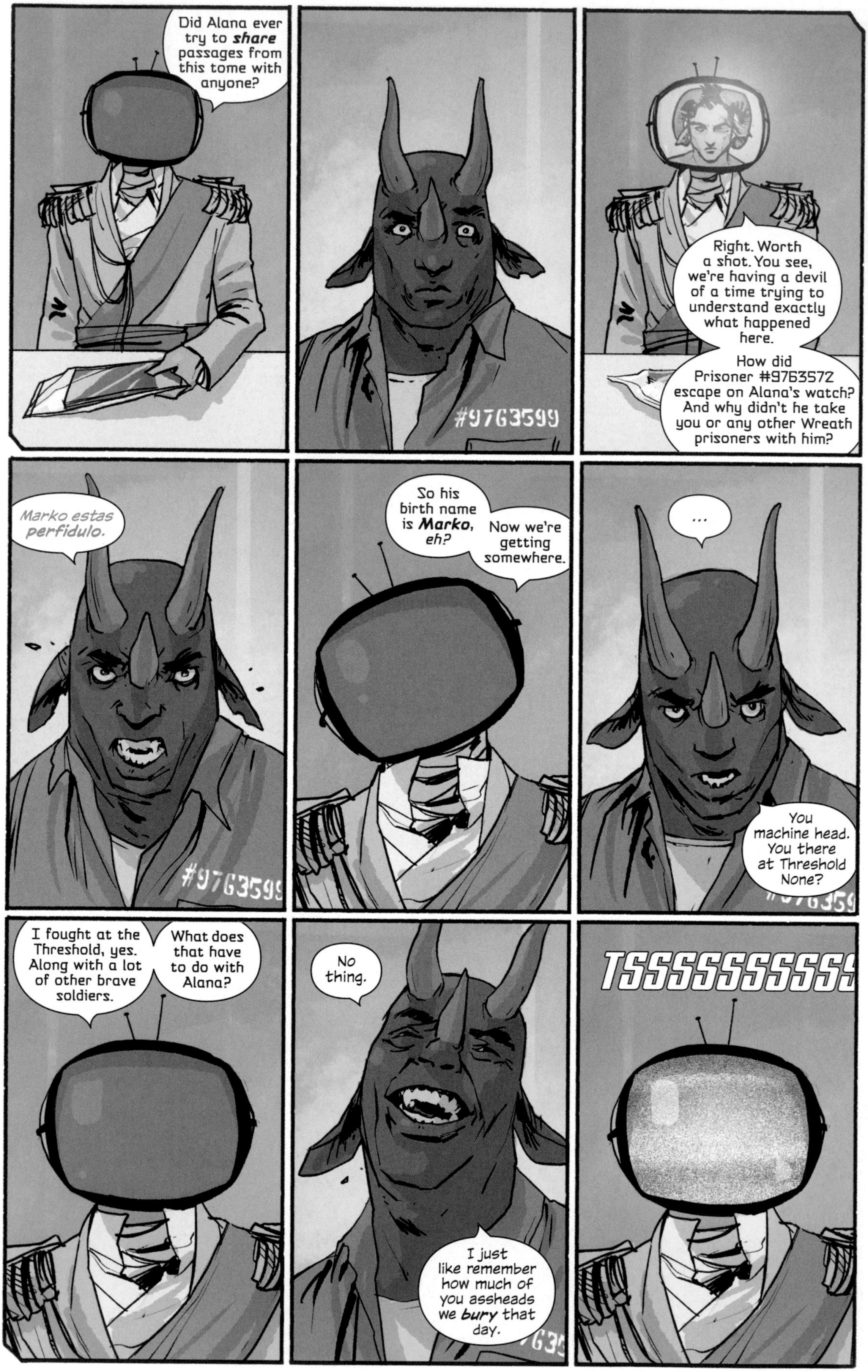

Did Alana ever try to *share* passages from this tome with anyone?
#9763599
Right. Worth a shot. You see, we're having a devil of a time trying to understand exactly what happened here.
How did Prisoner #9763572 escape on Alana's watch? And why didn't he take you or any other Wreath prisoners with him?
Marko estas perfidulo.
#9763599
So his birth name is ***Marko****, eh?*
Now we're getting somewhere.
...
You machine head. You there at Threshold None?
I fought at the Threshold, yes. Along with a lot of other brave soldiers.
What does that have to do with Alana?
No thing.
I just like remember how much of you assheads we ***bury*** that day.
TSSSSSSSSSS

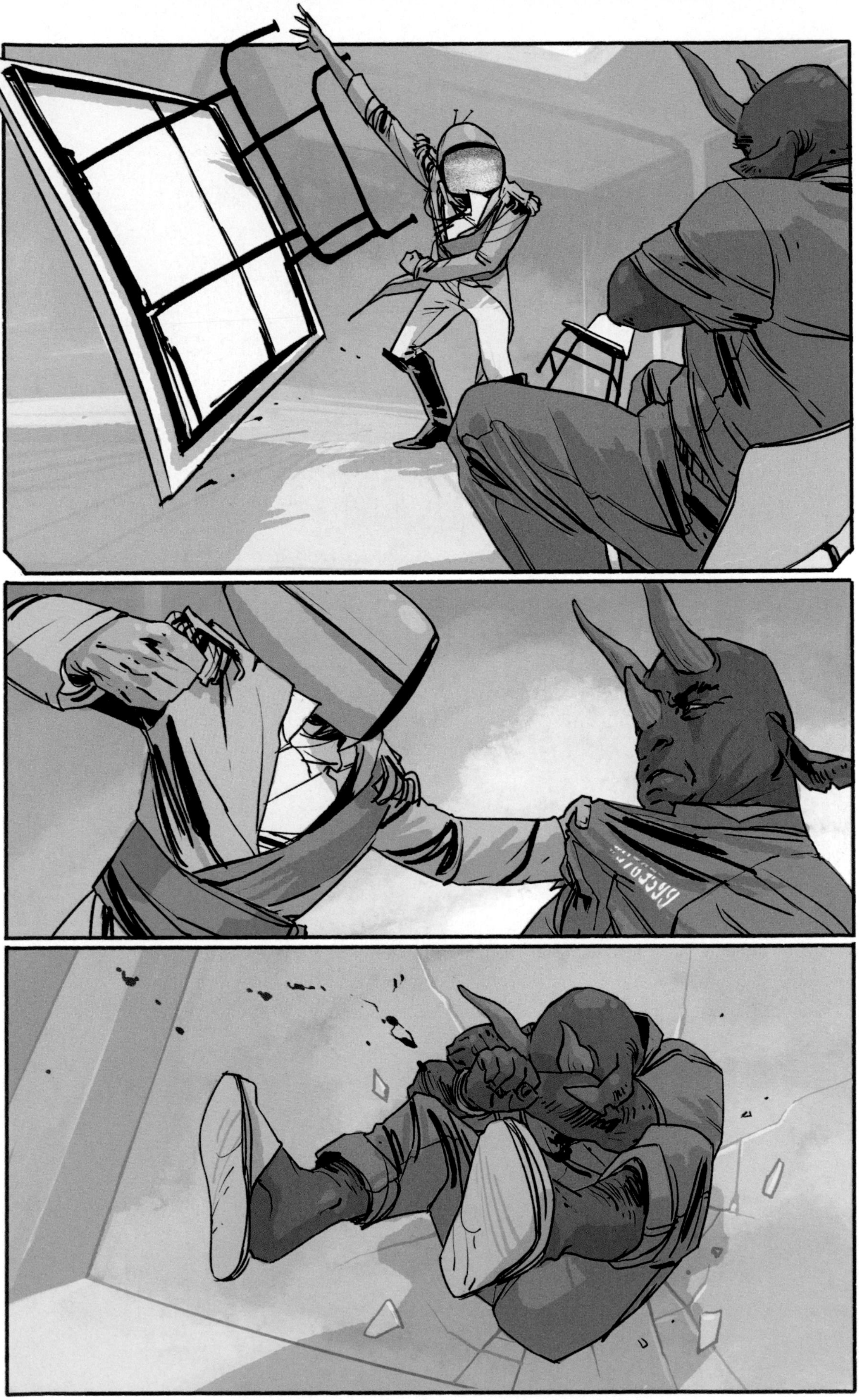

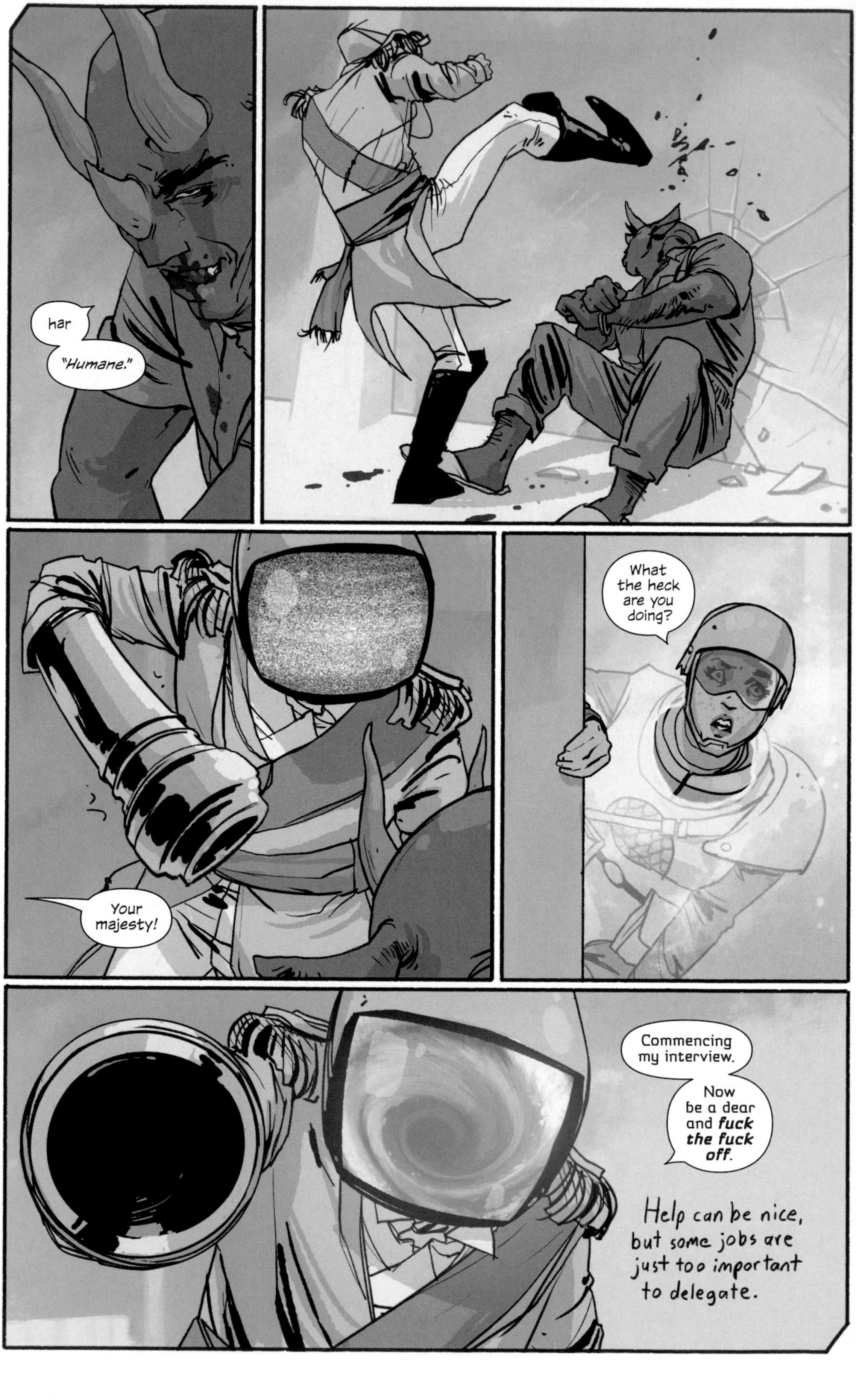
har
"Humane."
Your majesty!
What the heck are you doing?
Commencing my interview.
Now be a dear and **fuck the fuck off**.
Help can be nice, but some jobs are just too important to delegate.

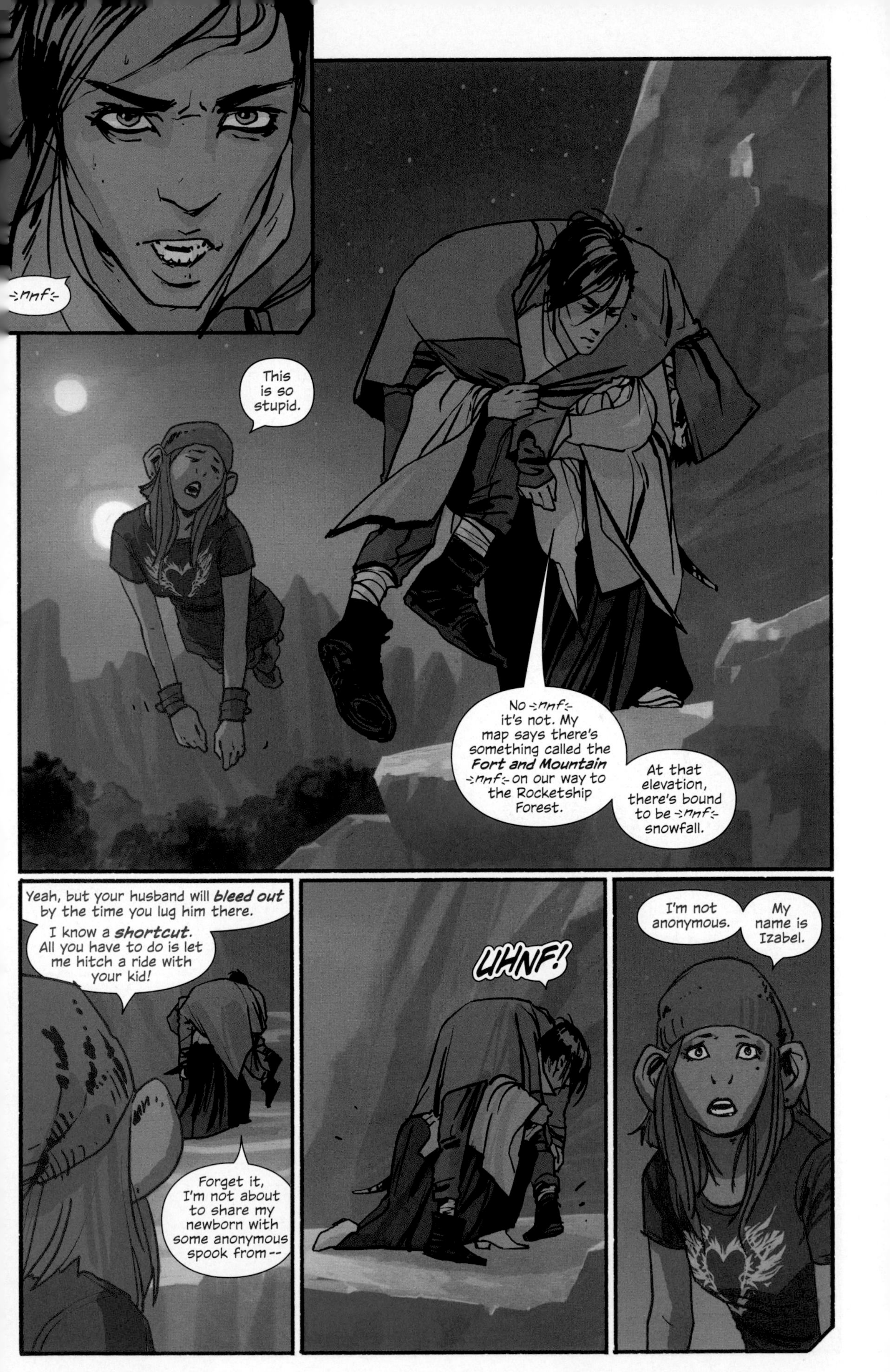

-mnf-
This is so stupid.
No -mnf- it's not. My map says there's something called the **Fort and Mountain** -mnf- on our way to the Rocketship Forest.
At that elevation, there's bound to be -mnf- snowfall.
Yeah, but your husband will ***bleed out*** by the time you lug him there.
I know a ***shortcut***. All you have to do is let me hitch a ride with your kid!
Forget it, I'm not about to share my newborn with some anonymous spook from --
UHNF!
I'm not anonymous.
My name is Izabel.

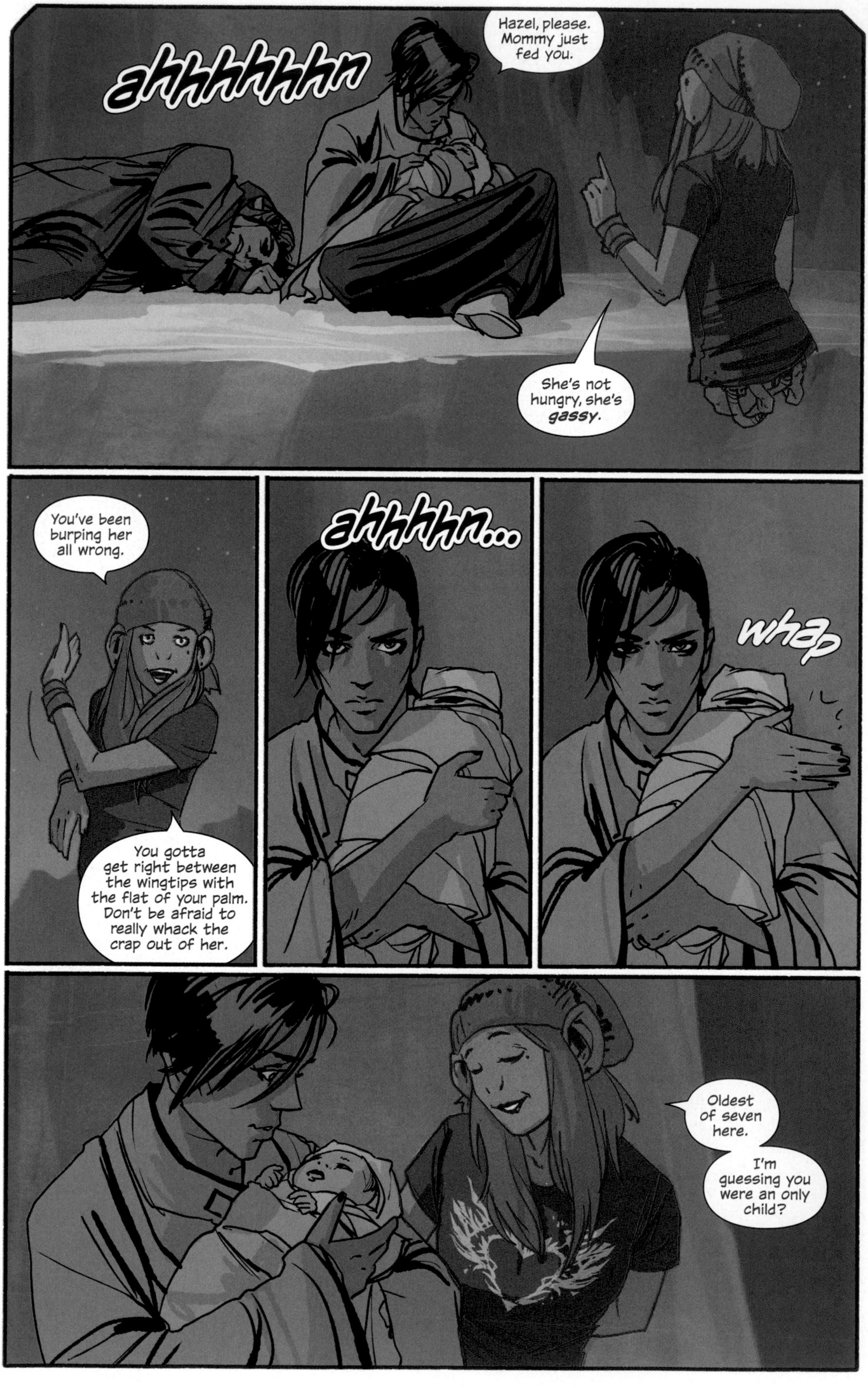
ahhhhhhhn
Hazel, please. Mommy just fed you.
She's not hungry, she's *gassy*.
You've been burping her all wrong.
You gotta get right between the wingtips with the flat of your palm. Don't be afraid to really whack the crap out of her.
ahhhhhn...
whap
Oldest of seven here.
I'm guessing you were an only child?

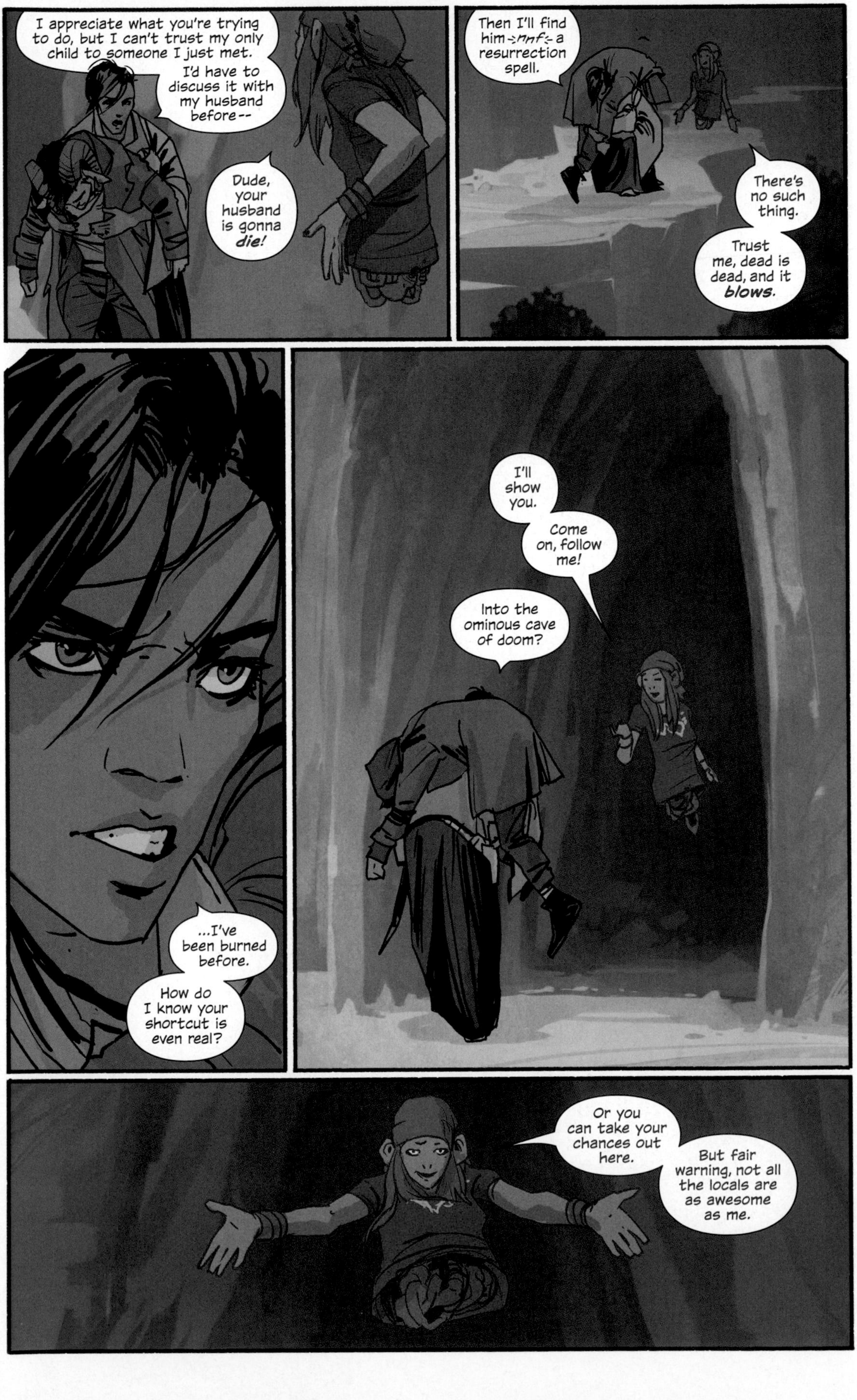
I appreciate what you're trying to do, but I can't trust my only child to someone I just met.
I'd have to discuss it with my husband before--
Dude, your husband is gonna *die!*
Then I'll find him -nnf- a resurrection spell.
There's no such thing.
Trust me, dead is dead, and it ***blows.***
...I've been burned before.
How do I know your shortcut is even real?
I'll show you.
Come on, follow me!
Into the ominous cave of doom?
Or you can take your chances out here.
But fair warning, not all the locals are as awesome as me.

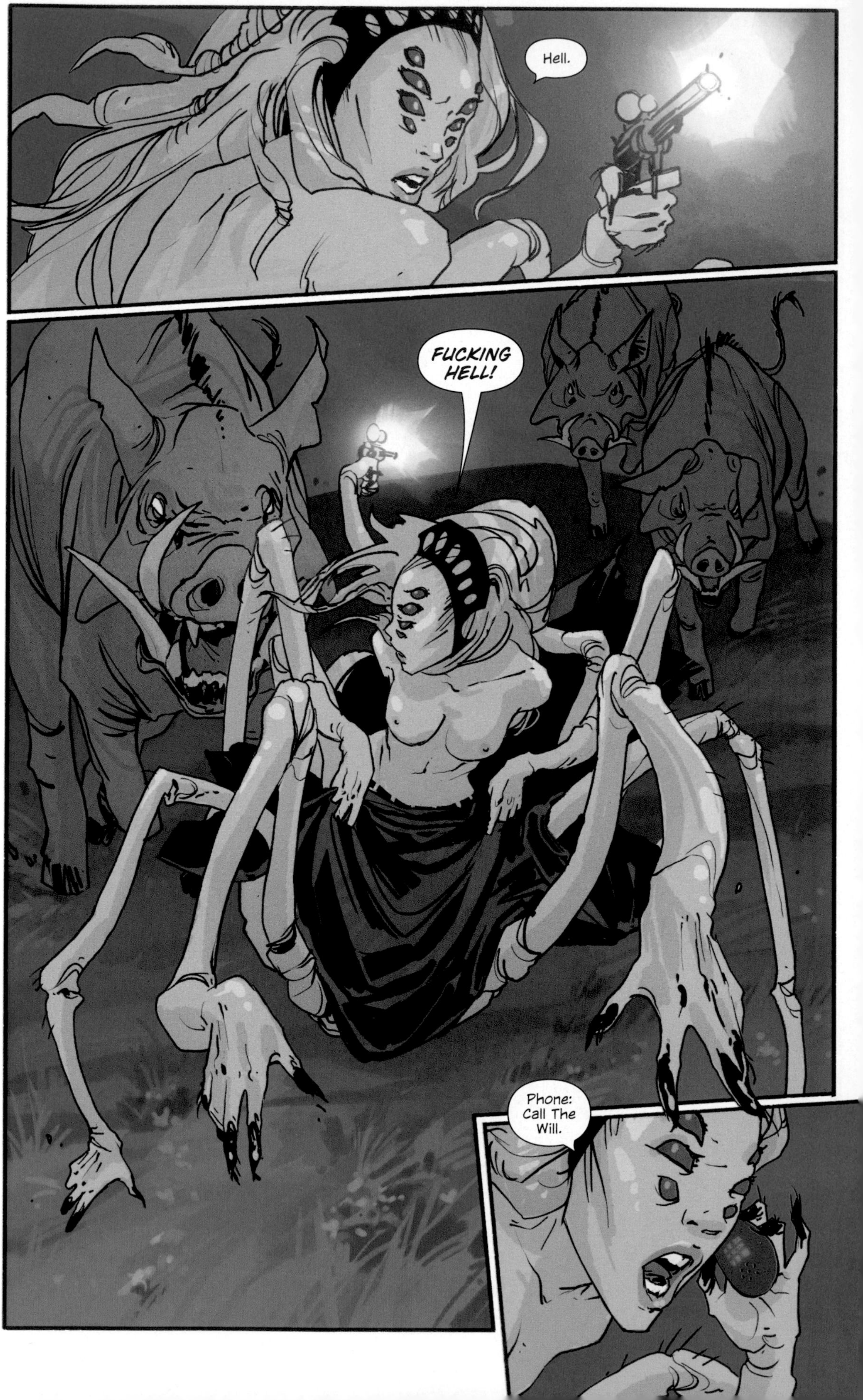
Hell.
FUCKING HELL!
Phone: Call The Will.

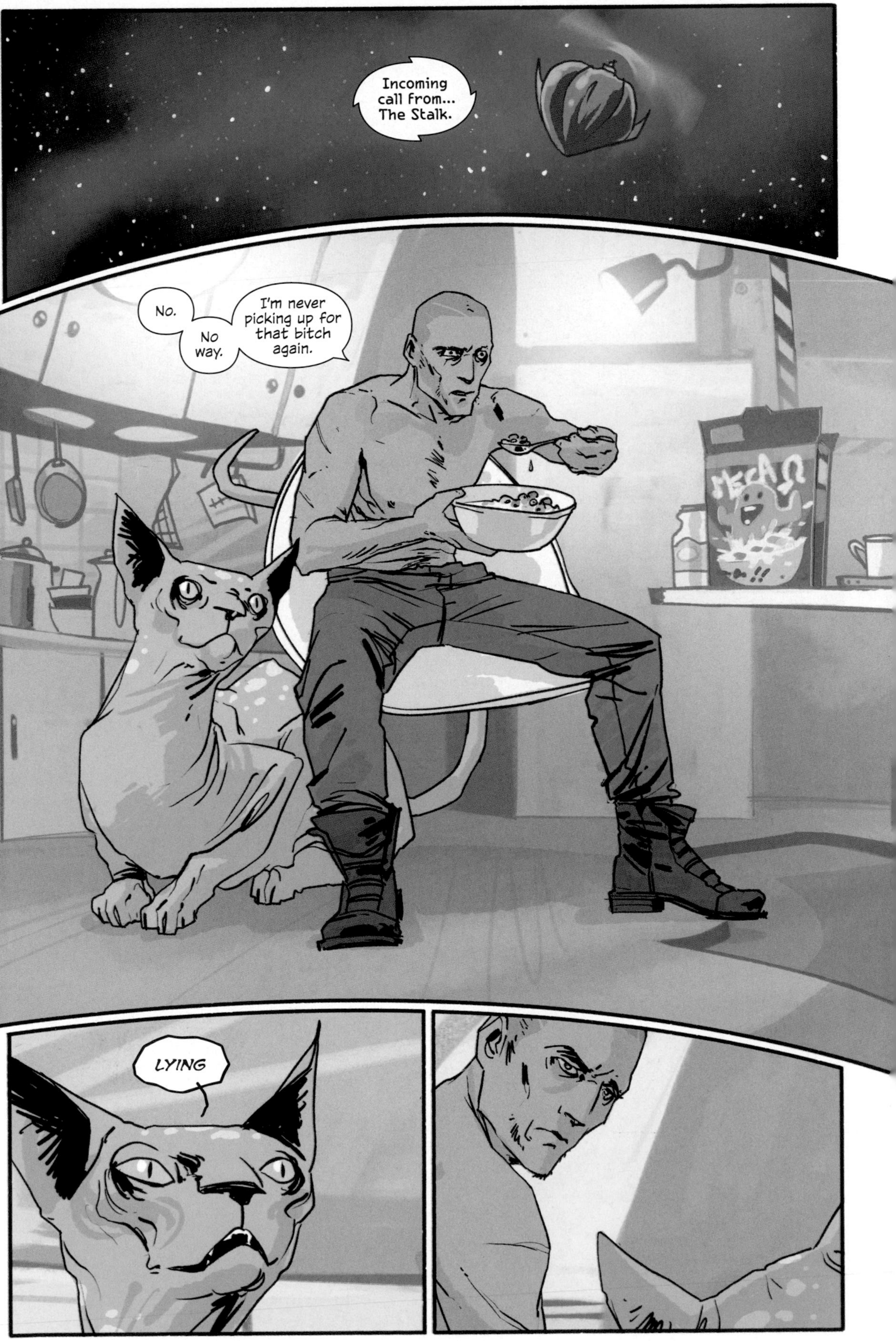
Incoming call from... The Stalk.
No.
No way.
I'm never picking up for that bitch again.
LYING

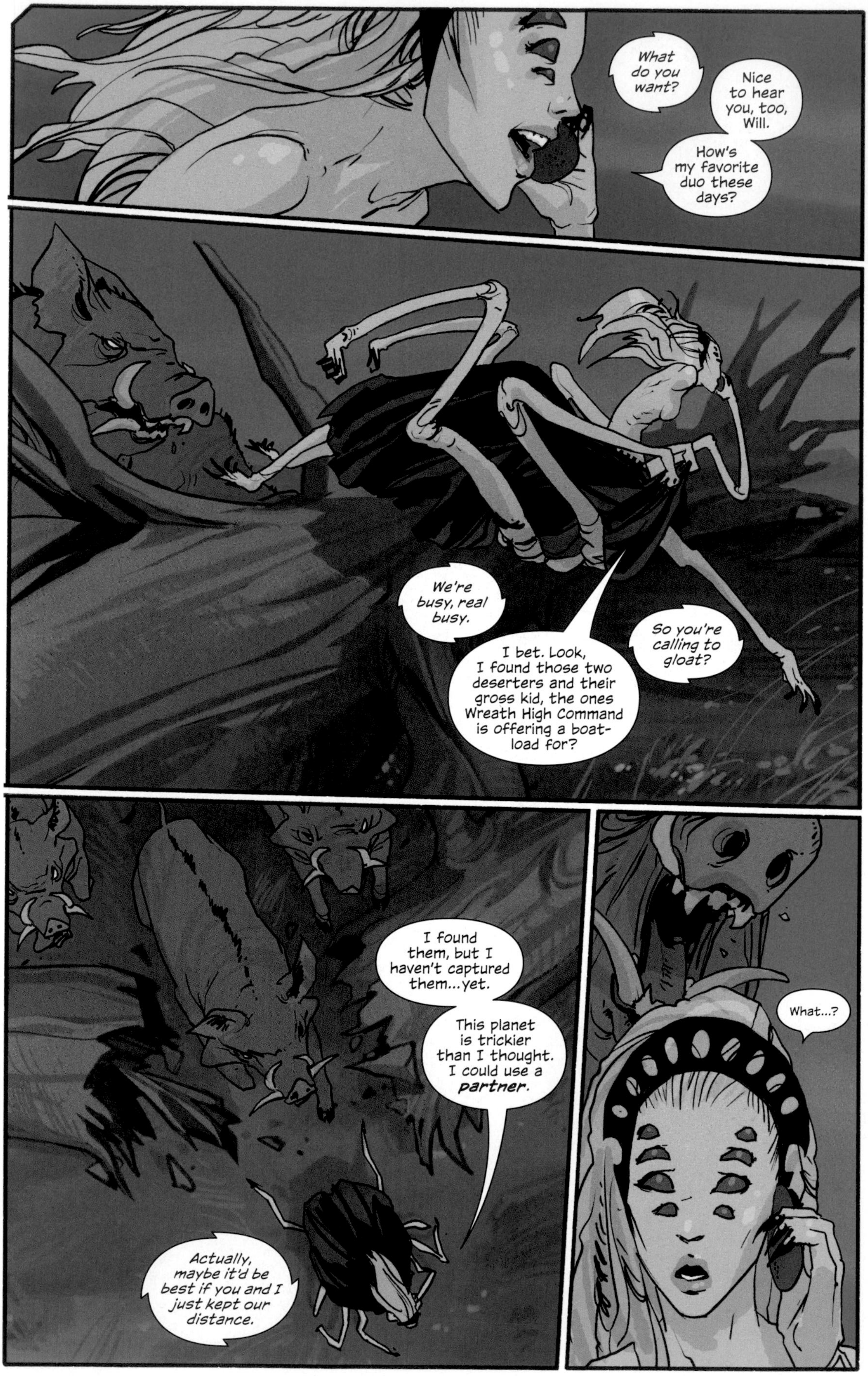
What do you want?
Nice to hear you, too, Will.
How's my favorite duo these days?
We're busy, real busy.
I bet. Look, I found those two deserters and their gross kid, the ones Wreath High Command is offering a boat-load for?
So you're calling to gloat?
I found them, but I haven't captured them...yet.
This planet is trickier than I thought. I could use a **partner**.
Actually, maybe it'd be best if you and I just kept our distance.
What...?

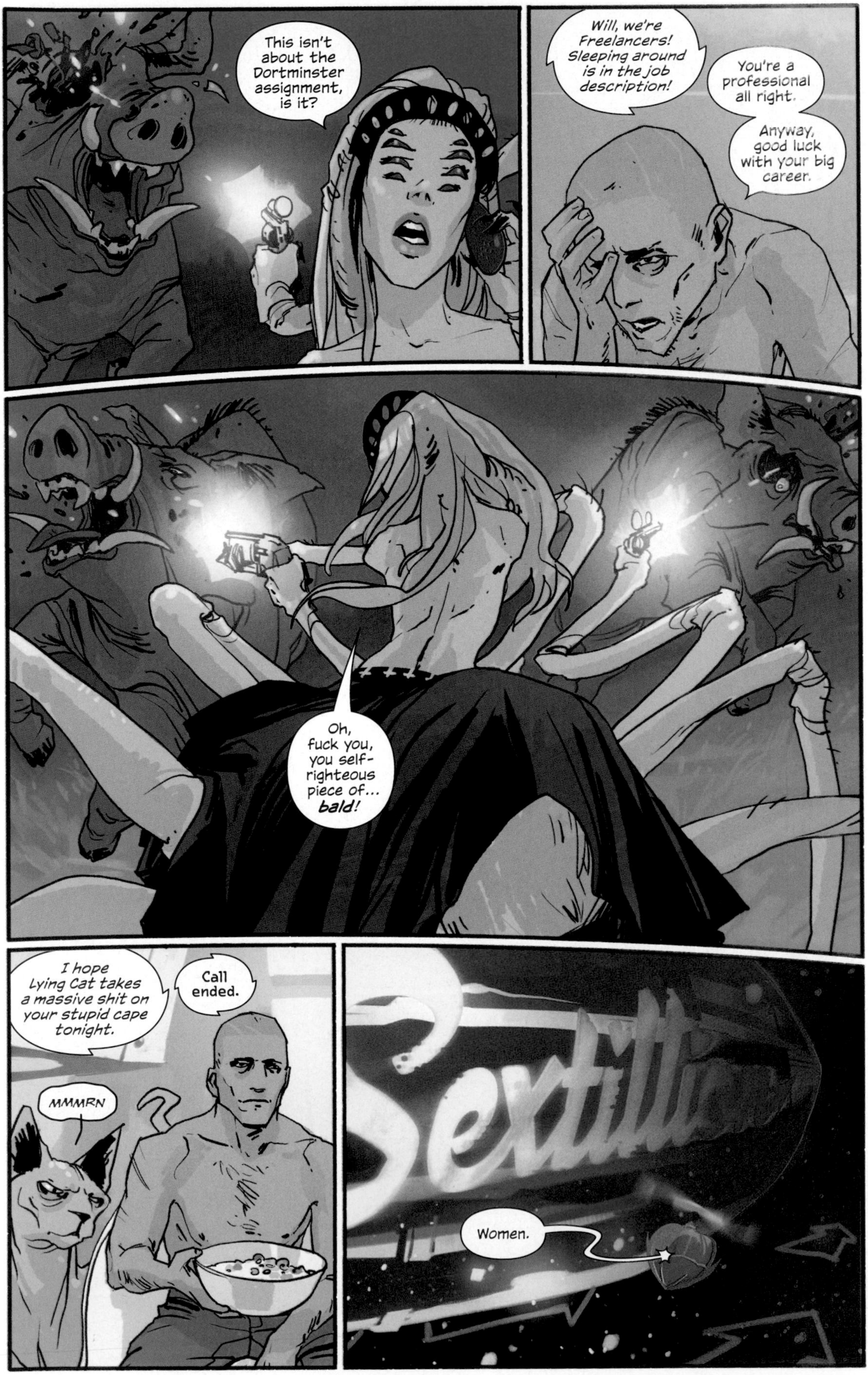
This isn't about the Dortminster assignment, is it?
Will, we're Freelancers! Sleeping around is in the job description!
You're a professional all right.
Anyway, good luck with your big career.
Oh, fuck you, you self-righteous piece of... **bald**!
I hope Lying Cat takes a massive shit on your stupid cape tonight.
Call ended.
MMMRN
Women.

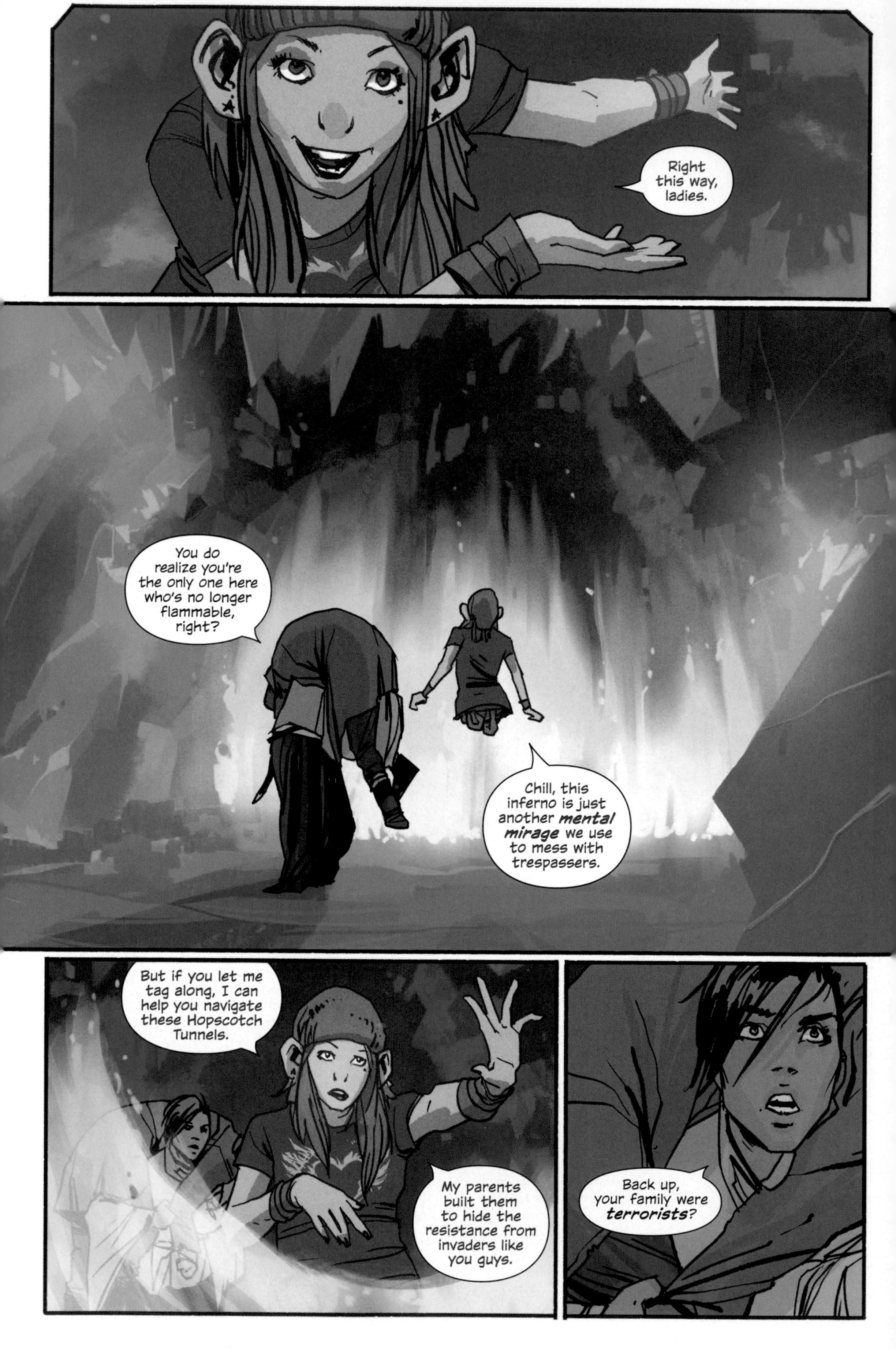
Right this way, ladies.
You do realize you're the only one here who's no longer flammable, right?
Chill, this inferno is just another *mental mirage* we use to mess with trespassers.
But if you let me tag along, I can help you navigate these Hopscotch Tunnels.
My parents built them to hide the resistance from invaders like you guys.
Back up, your family were *terrorists*?

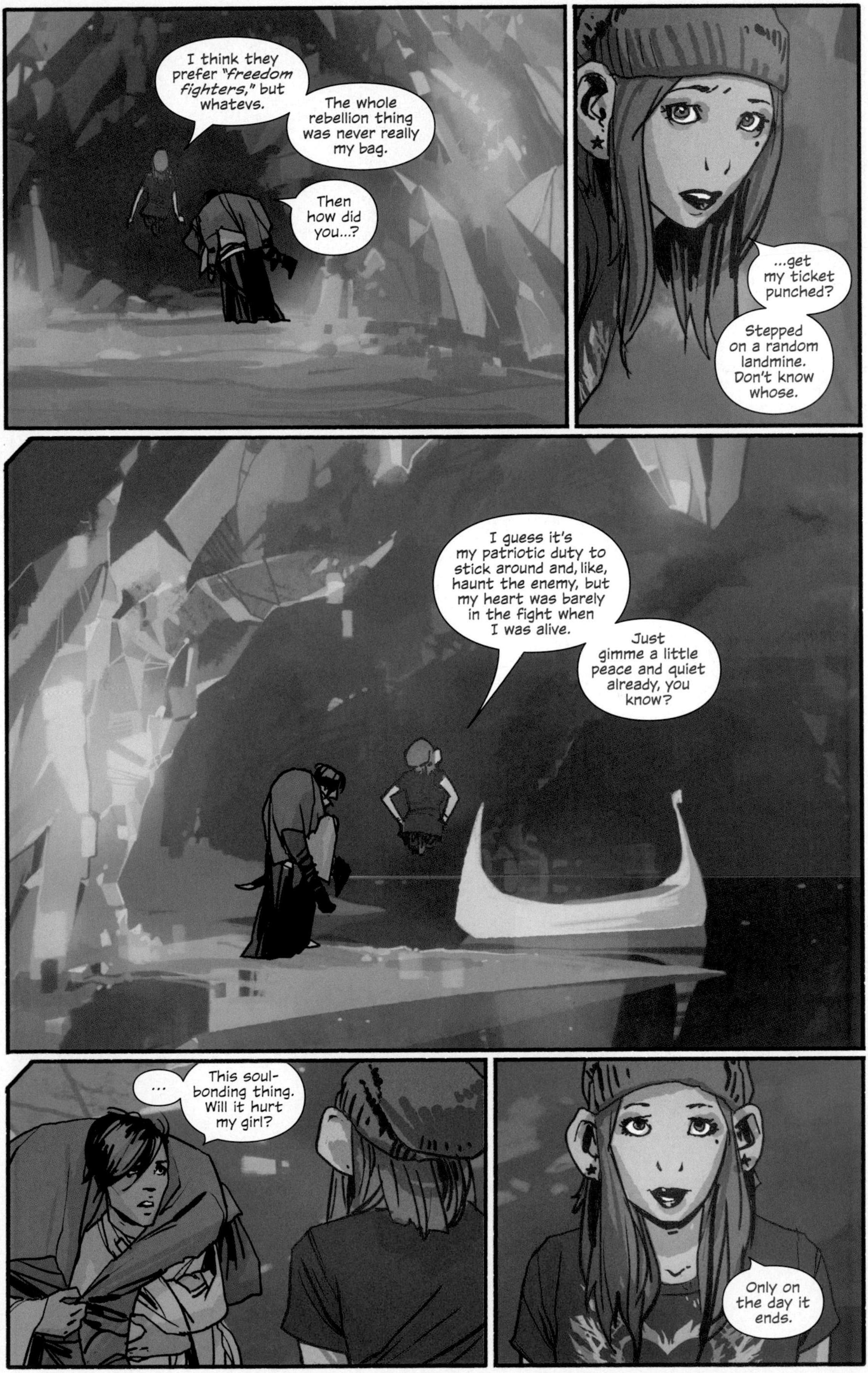
I think they prefer "freedom fighters," but whatevs.
The whole rebellion thing was never really my bag.
Then how did you...?
...get my ticket punched?
Stepped on a random landmine. Don't know whose.
I guess it's my patriotic duty to stick around and, like, haunt the enemy, but my heart was barely in the fight when I was alive.
Just gimme a little peace and quiet already, you know?
...
This soul-bonding thing. Will it hurt my girl?
Only on the day it ends.

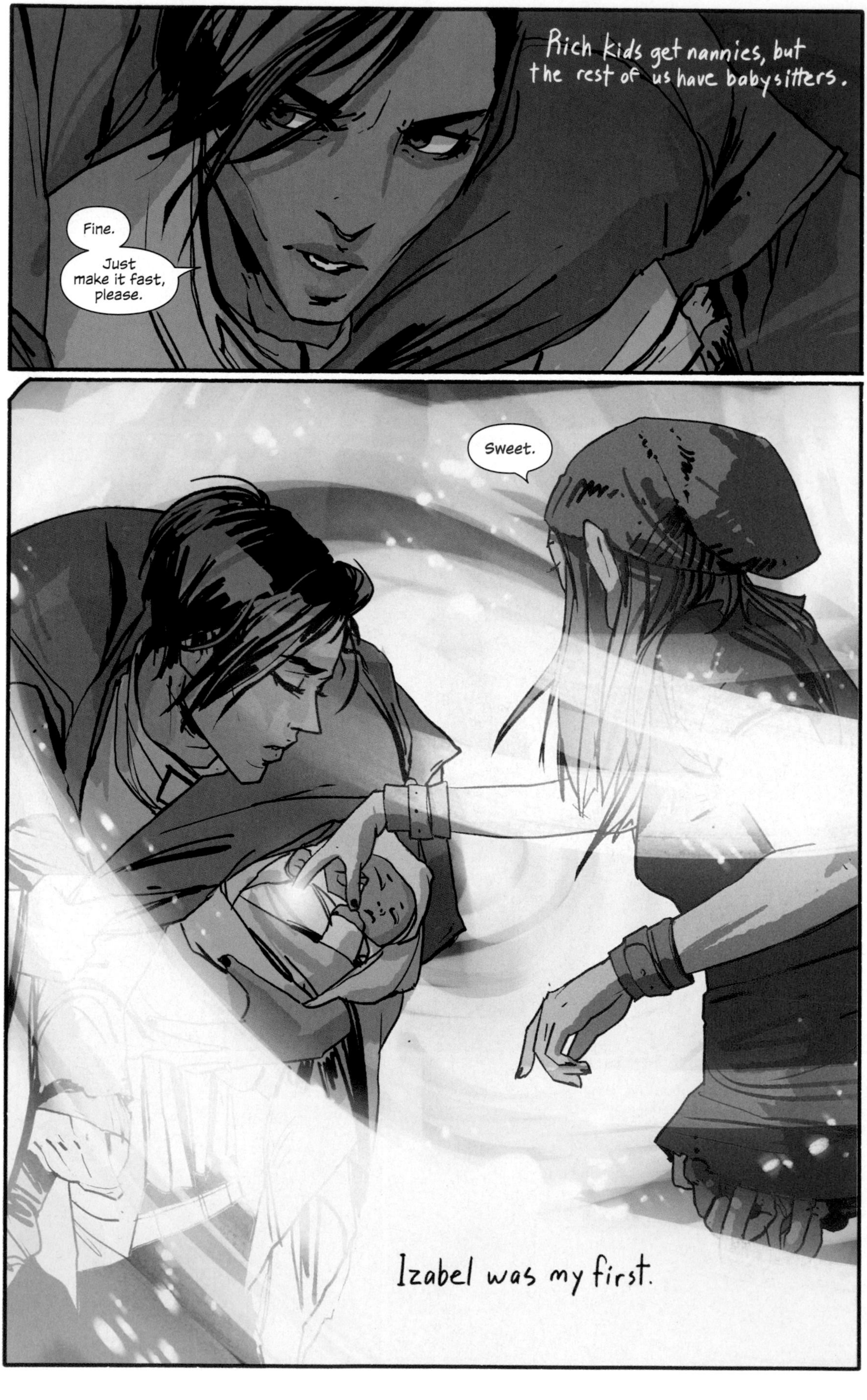
Rich kids get nannies, but the rest of us have babysitters.
Fine.
Just make it fast, please.
Sweet.
Izabel was my first.

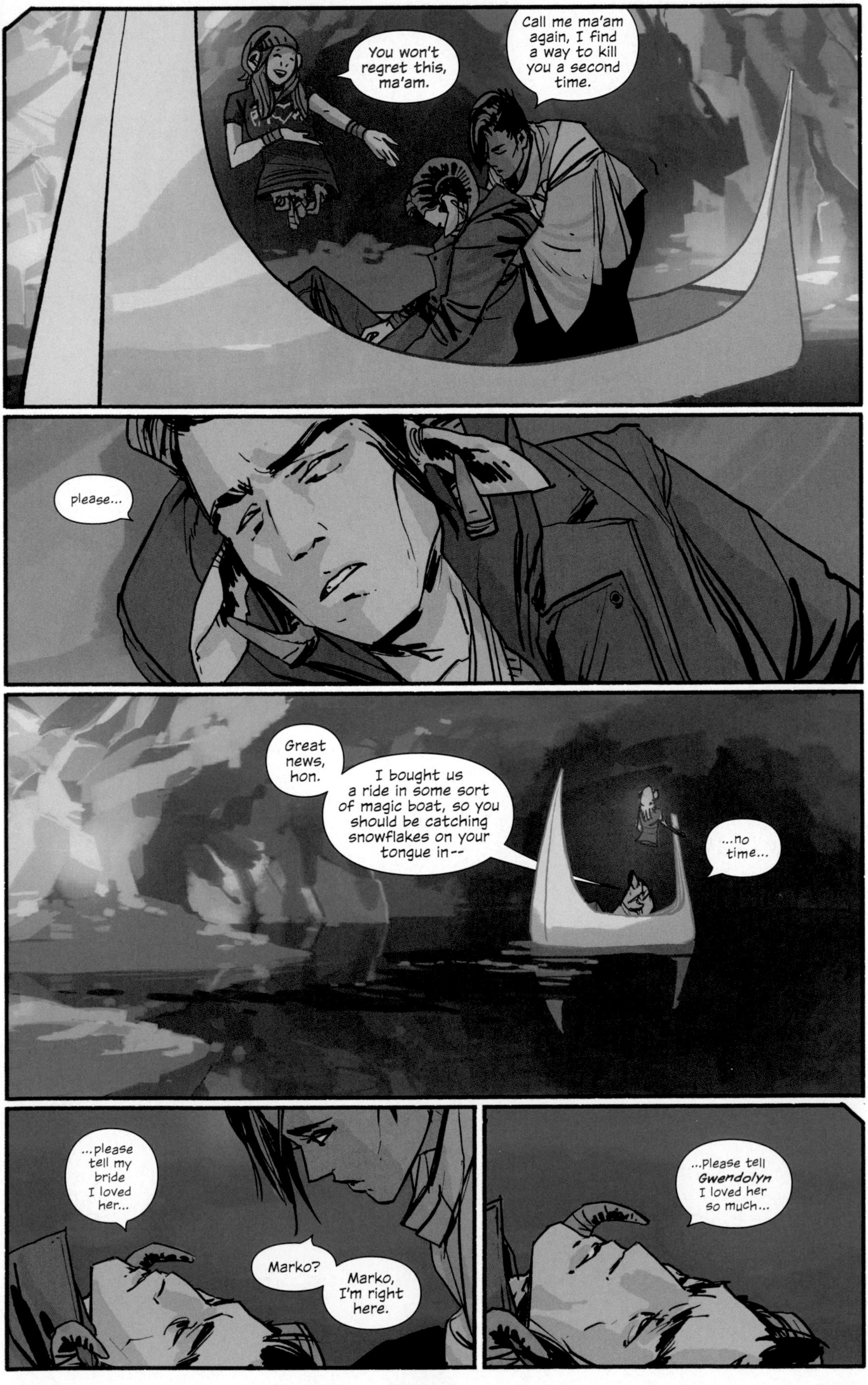
You won't regret this, ma'am.
Call me ma'am again, I find a way to kill you a second time.
please...
Great news, hon.
I bought us a ride in some sort of magic boat, so you should be catching snowflakes on your tongue in--
...no time...
...please tell my bride I loved her...
Marko?
Marko, I'm right here.
...Please tell Gwendolyn I loved her so much...

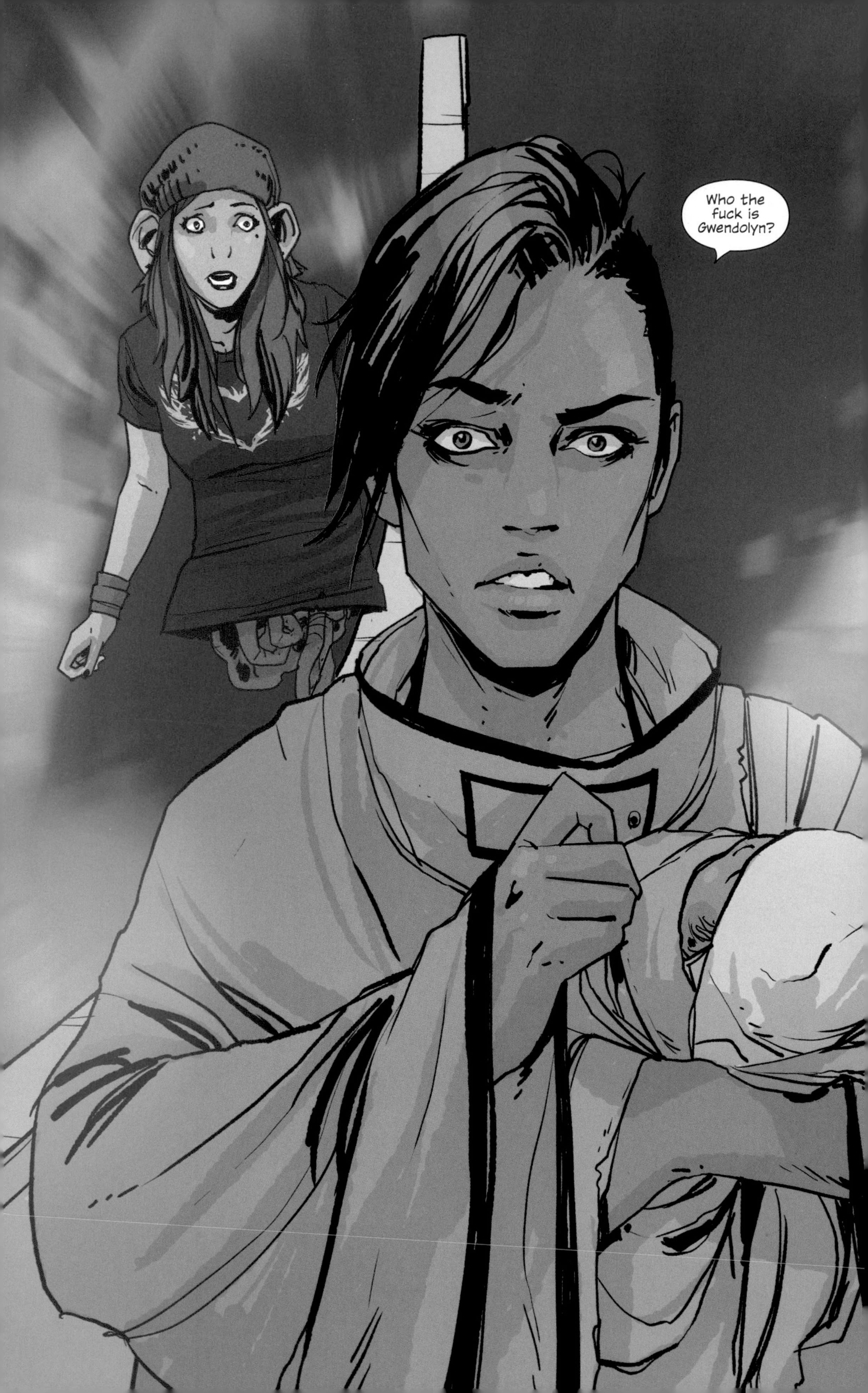
Who the fuck is Gwendolyn?

end chapter three

FS'12

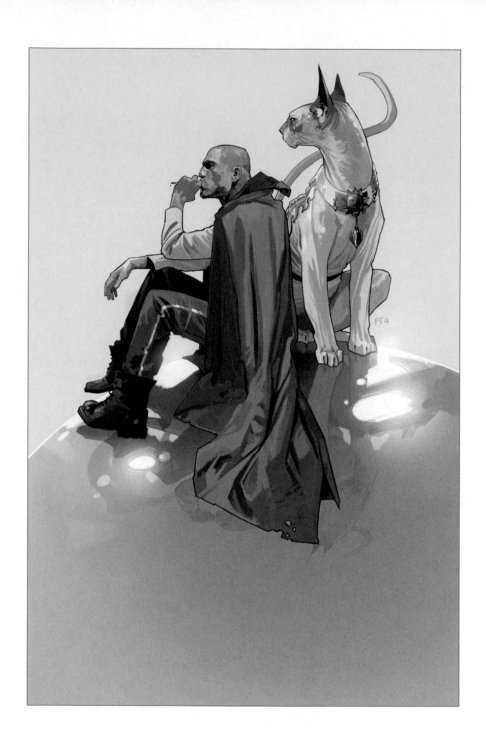

CHAPTER
FOUR

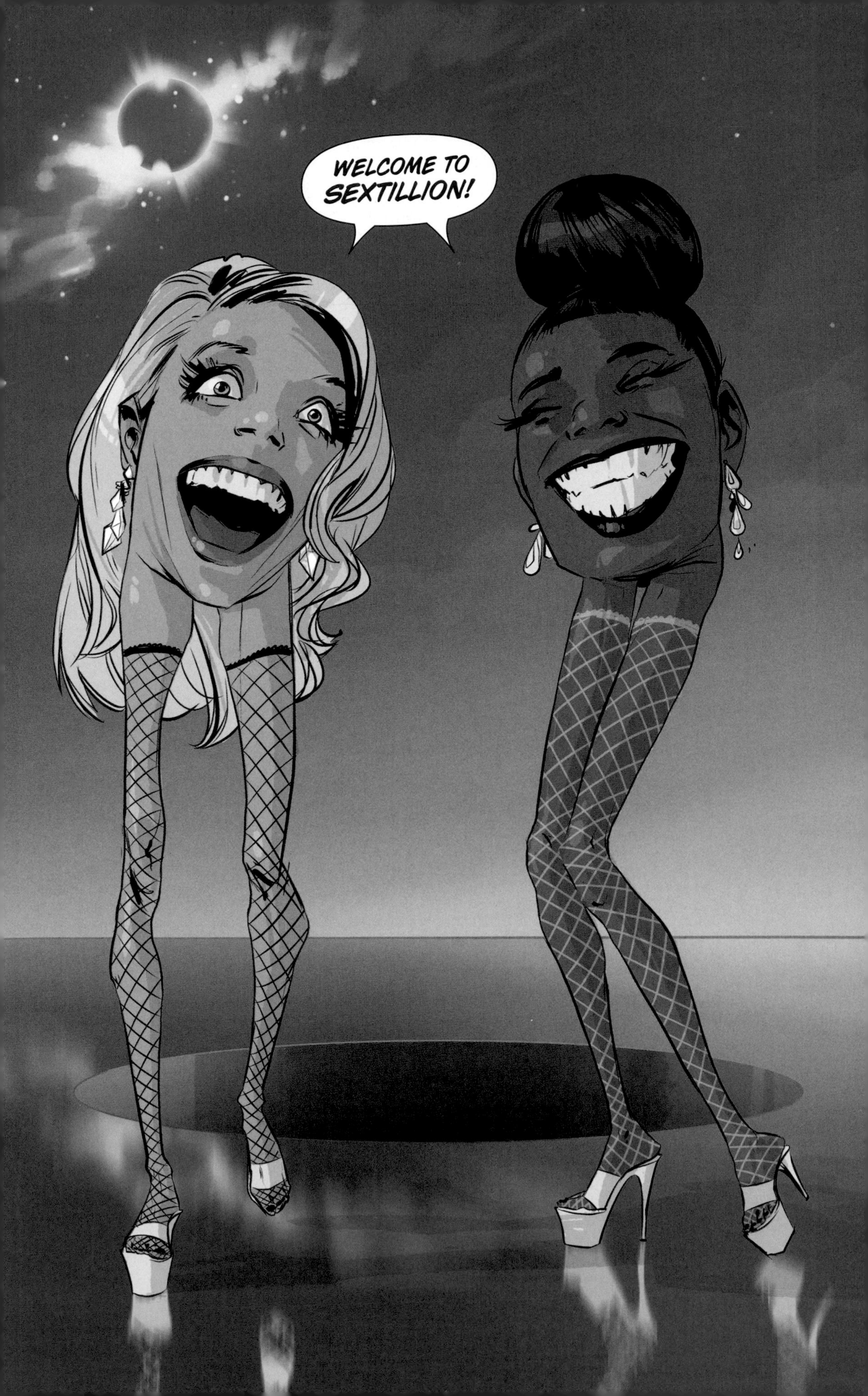
WELCOME TO SEXTILLION!

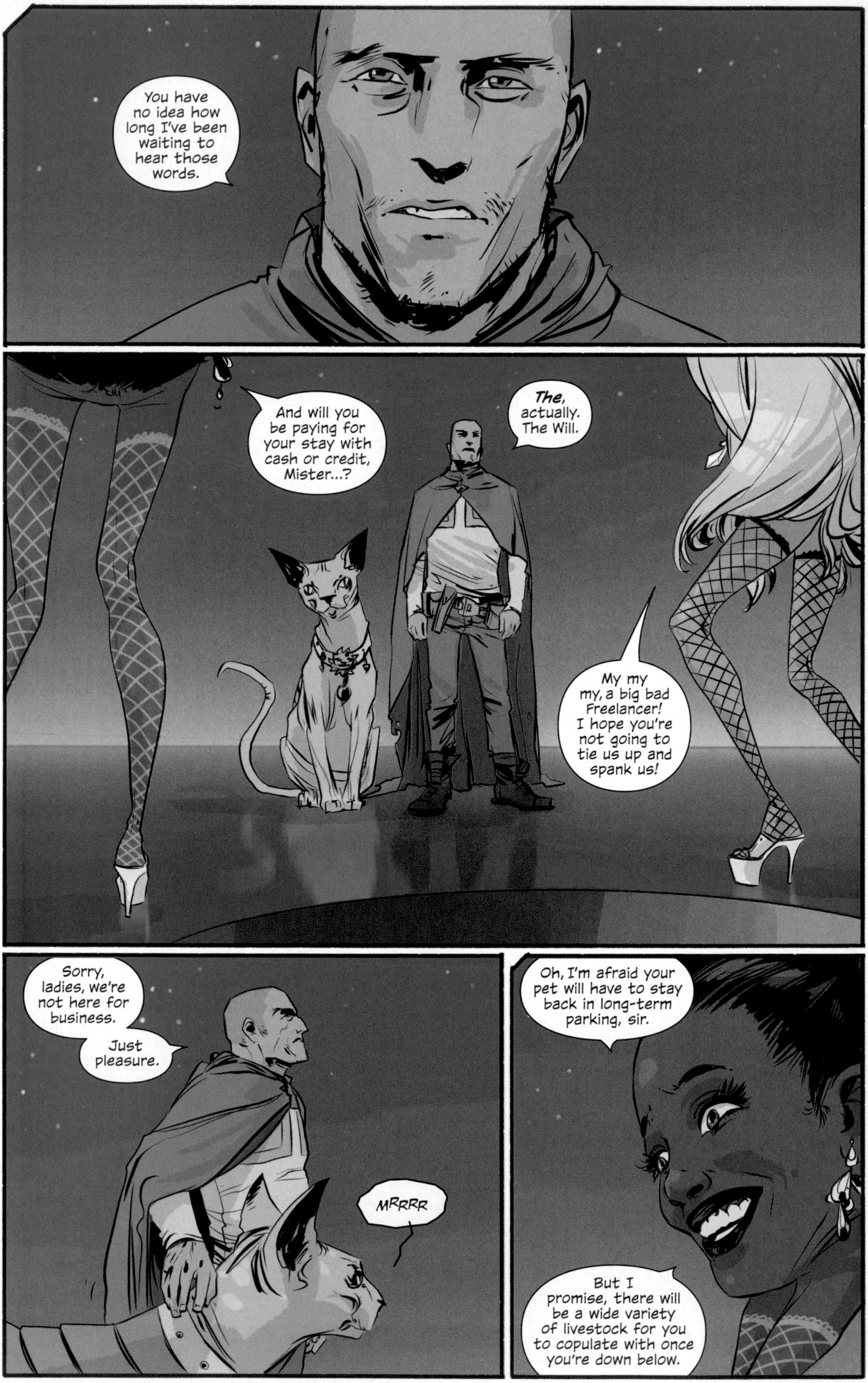
You have no idea how long I've been waiting to hear those words.
And will you be paying for your stay with cash or credit, Mister...?
The, actually. The Will.
My my my, a big bad Freelancer! I hope you're not going to tie us up and spank us!
Sorry, ladies, we're not here for business.
Just pleasure.
MRRRR
Oh, I'm afraid your pet will have to stay back in long-term parking, sir.
But I promise, there will be a wide variety of livestock for you to copulate with once you're down below.

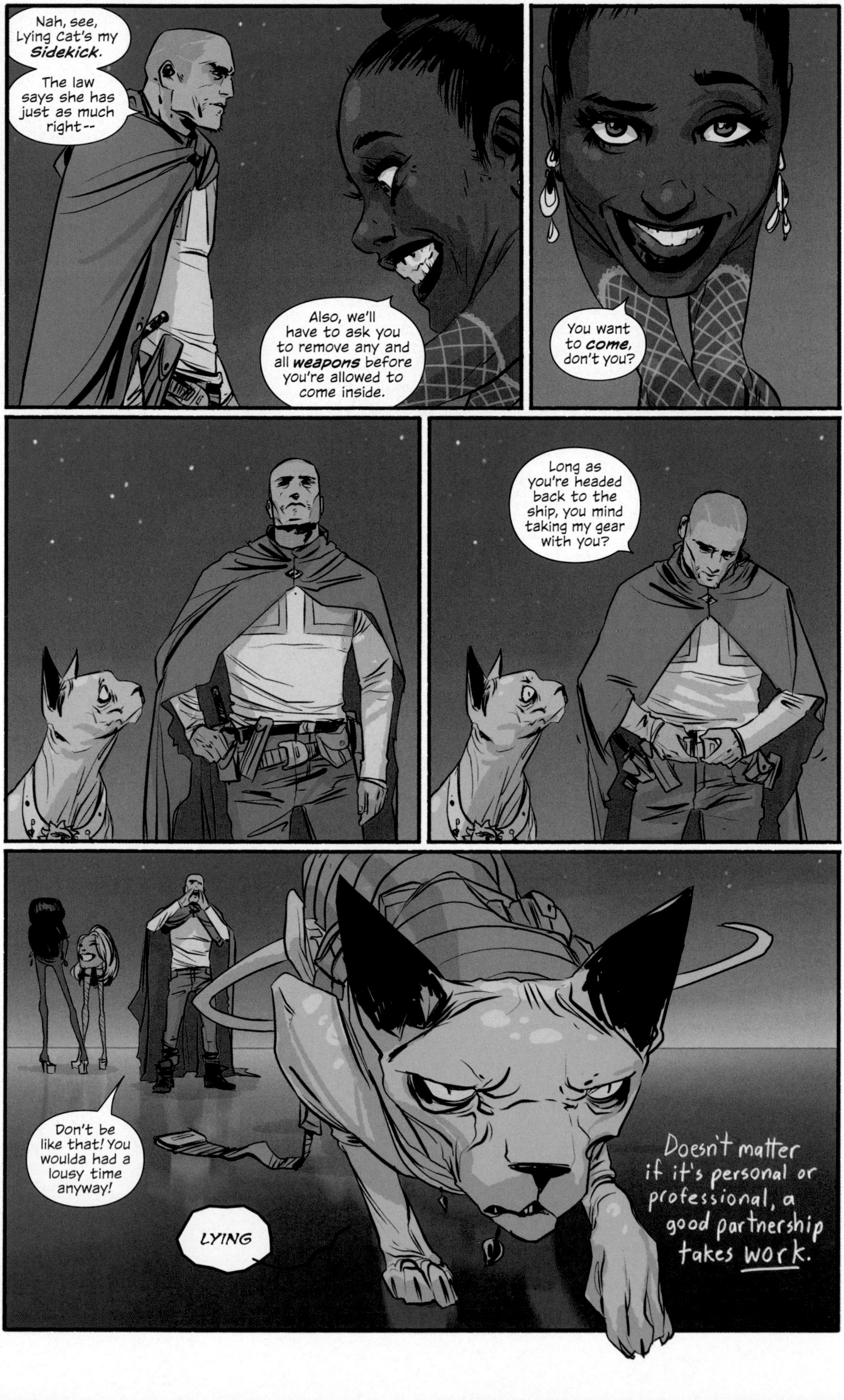

Nah, see, Lying Cat's my Sidekick.
The law says she has just as much right--
Also, we'll have to ask you to remove any and all weapons before you're allowed to come inside.
You want to come, don't you?
Long as you're headed back to the ship, you mind taking my gear with you?
Don't be like that! You woulda had a lousy time anyway!
LYING
Doesn't matter if it's personal or professional, a good partnership takes work.

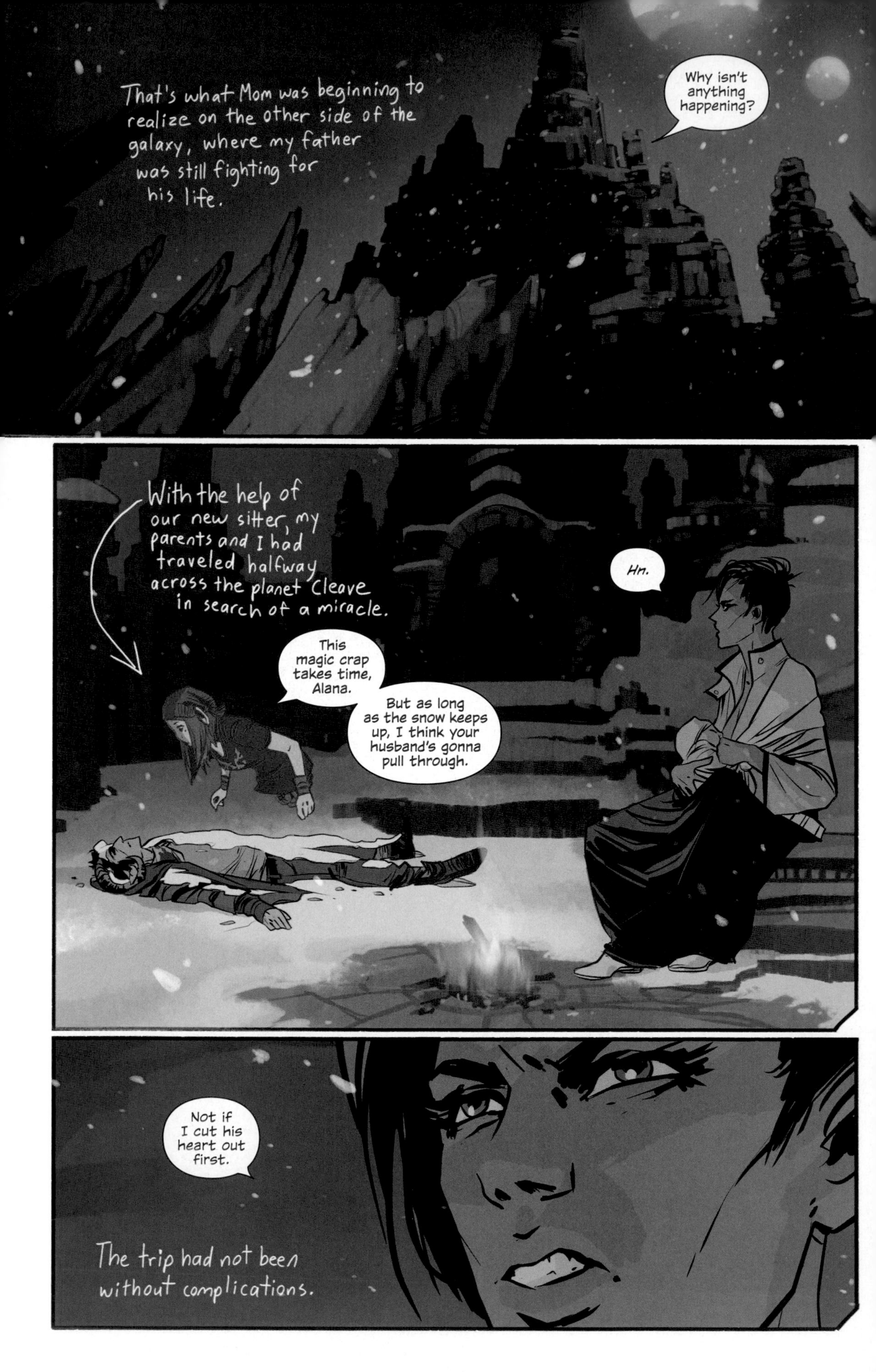
That's what Mom was beginning to realize on the other side of the galaxy, where my father was still fighting for his life.
Why isn't anything happening?
With the help of our new sitter, my parents and I had traveled halfway across the planet Cleave in search of a miracle.
Hn.
This magic crap takes time, Alana.
But as long as the snow keeps up, I think your husband's gonna pull through.
Not if I cut his heart out first.
The trip had not been without complications.

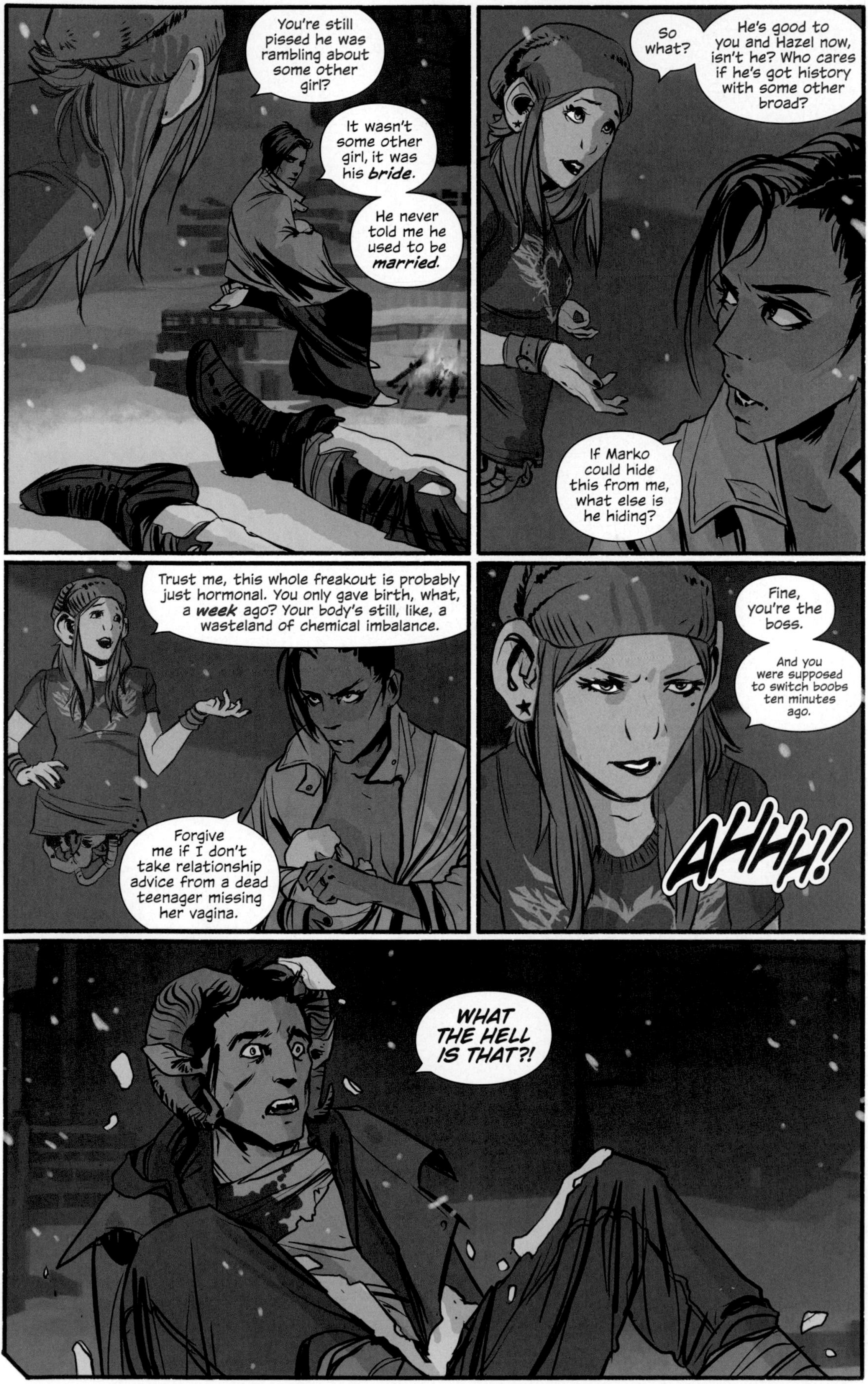

You're still pissed he was rambling about some other girl?
It wasn't some other girl, it was his **bride**.
He never told me he used to be **married**.
So what?
He's good to you and Hazel now, isn't he? Who cares if he's got history with some other broad?
If Marko could hide this from me, what else is he hiding?
Trust me, this whole freakout is probably just hormonal. You only gave birth, what, a **week** ago? Your body's still, like, a wasteland of chemical imbalance.
Forgive me if I don't take relationship advice from a dead teenager missing her vagina.
Fine, you're the boss.
And you were supposed to switch boobs ten minutes ago.
AHHH!
WHAT THE HELL IS THAT?!

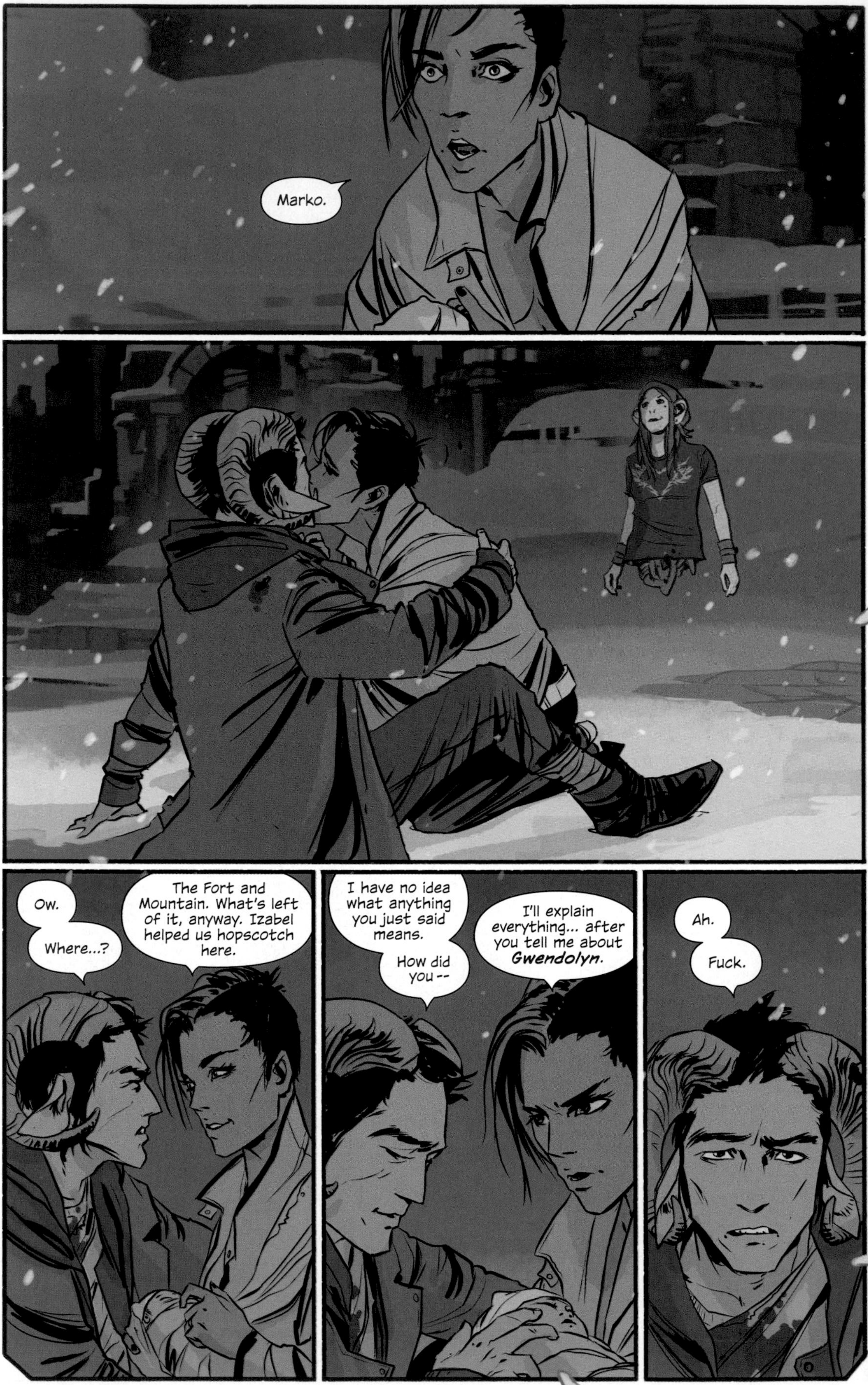
Marko.
Ow.
Where...?
The Fort and Mountain. What's left of it, anyway. Izabel helped us hopscotch here.
I have no idea what anything you just said means.
How did you --
I'll explain everything... after you tell me about **Gwendolyn**.
Ah.
Fuck.

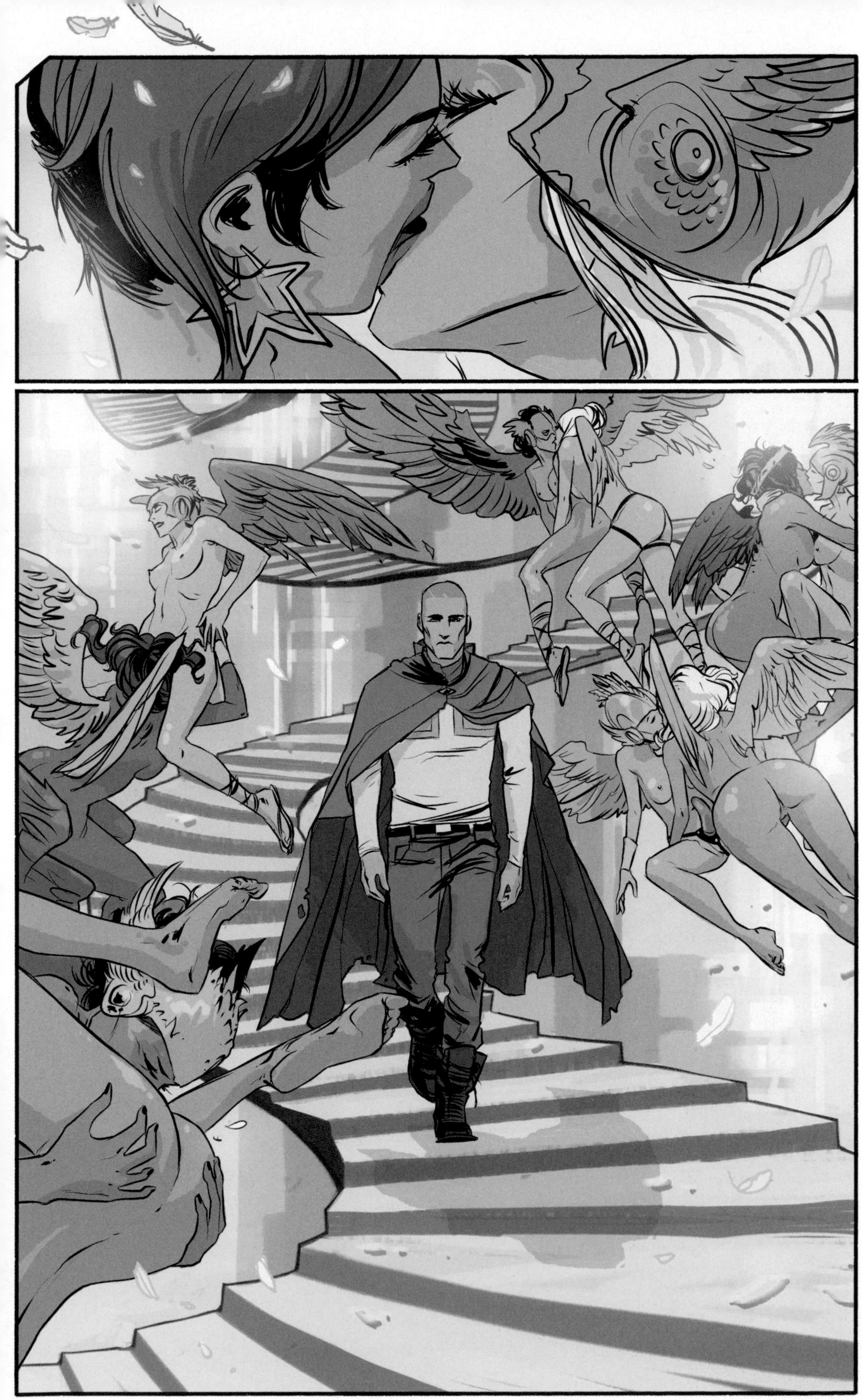

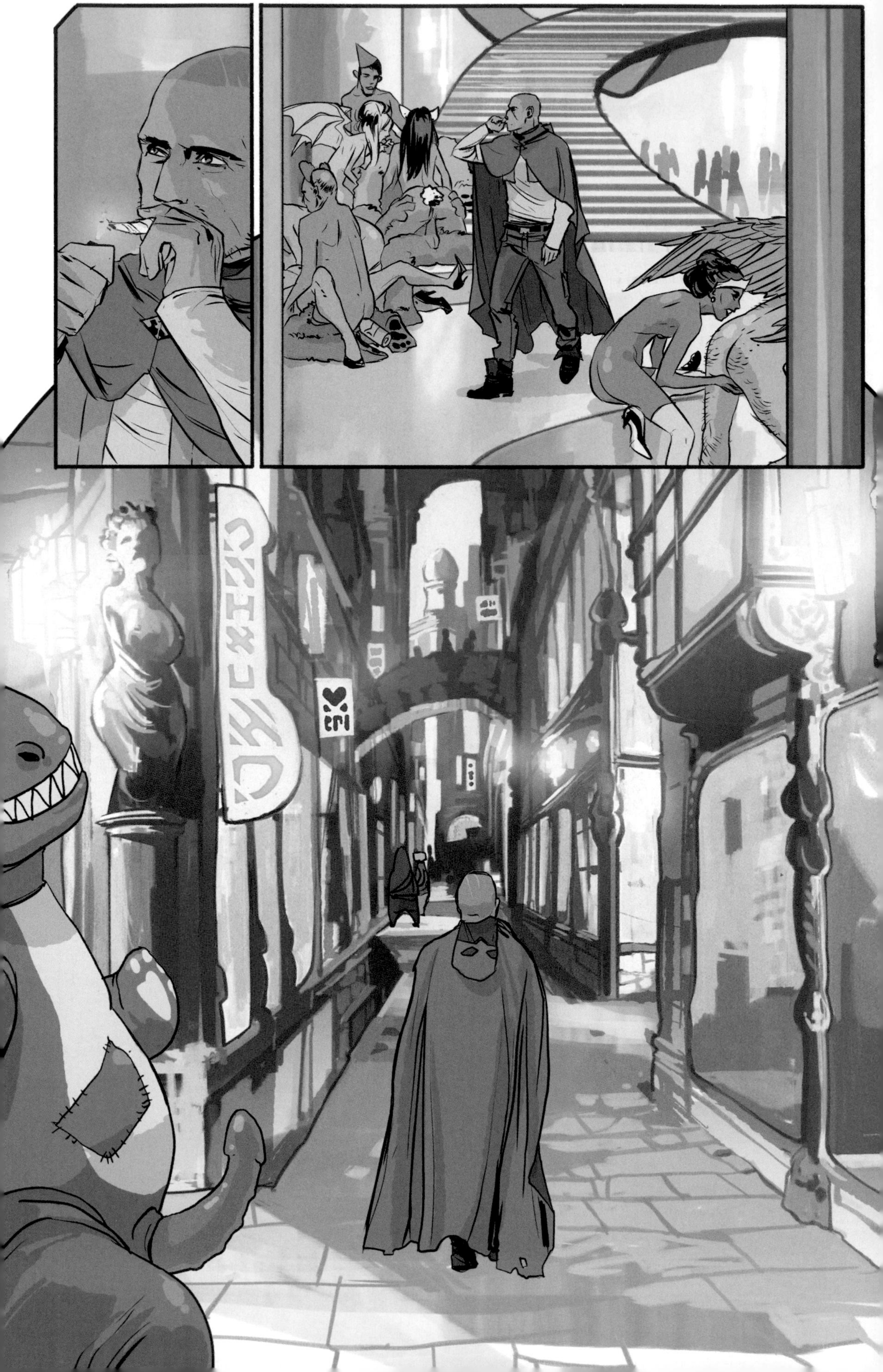

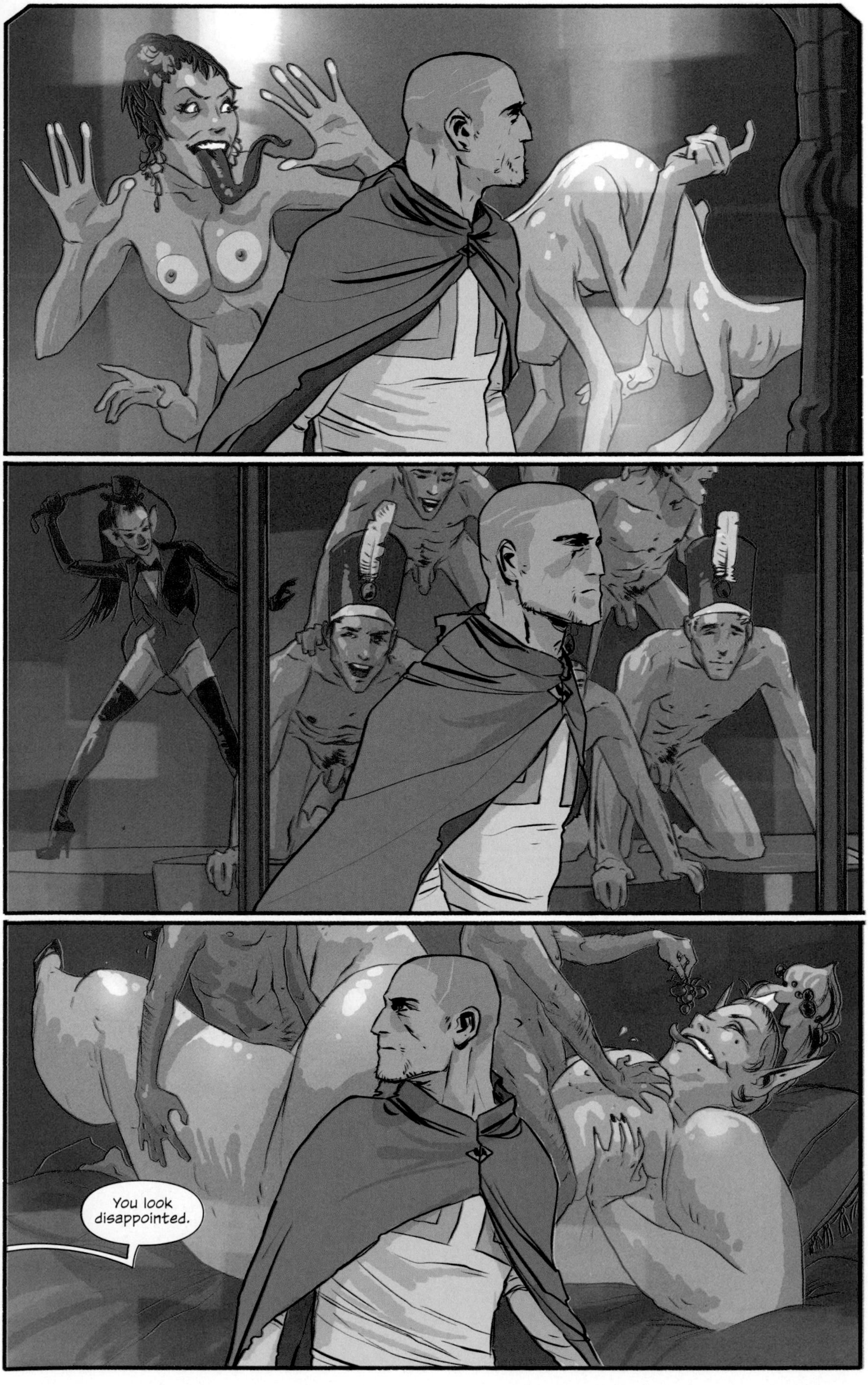
You look disappointed.

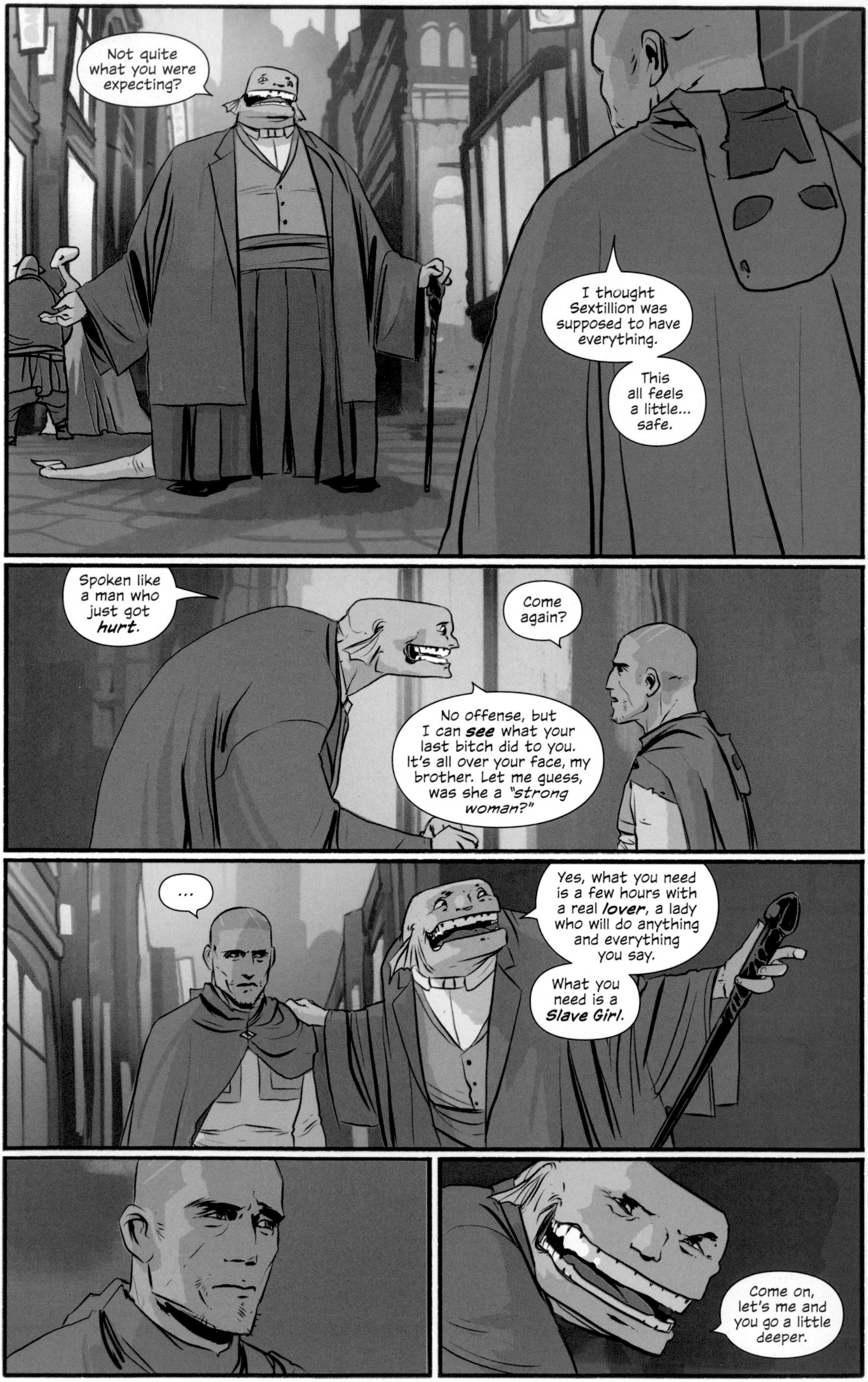
Not quite what you were expecting?
I thought Sextillion was supposed to have everything.
This all feels a little... safe.
Spoken like a man who just got *hurt*.
Come again?
No offense, but I can *see* what your last bitch did to you. It's all over your face, my brother. Let me guess, was she a *"strong woman?"*
...
Yes, what you need is a few hours with a real *lover*, a lady who will do anything and everything you say.
What you need is a *Slave Girl*.
Come on, let's me and you go a little deeper.

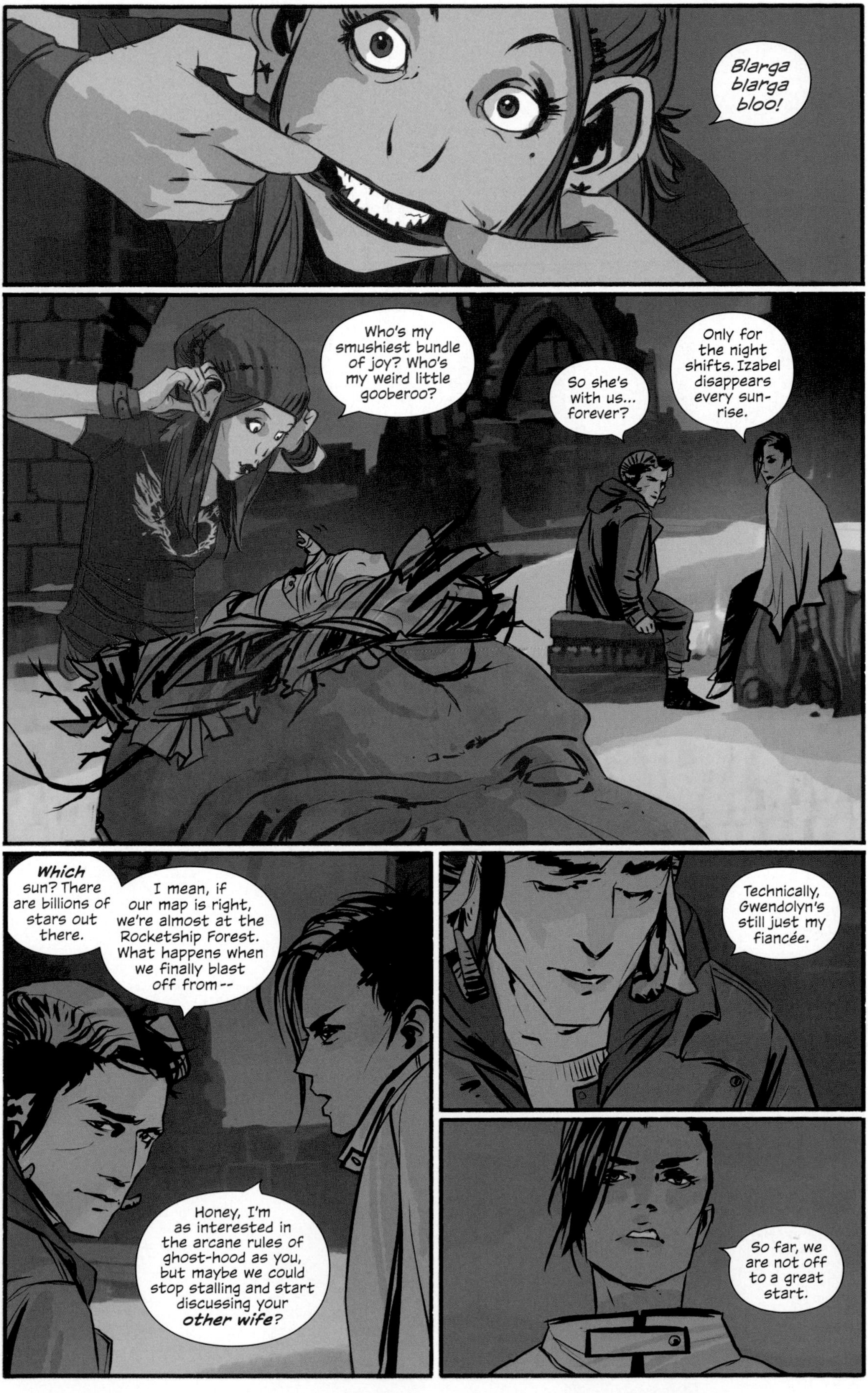
Blarga blarga bloo!
Who's my smushiest bundle of joy? Who's my weird little gooberoo?
So she's with us... forever?
Only for the night shifts. Izabel disappears every sun-rise.
Which sun? There are billions of stars out there.
I mean, if our map is right, we're almost at the Rocketship Forest. What happens when we finally blast off from--
Honey, I'm as interested in the arcane rules of ghost-hood as you, but maybe we could stop stalling and start discussing your *other wife*?
Technically, Gwendolyn's still just my fiancée.
So far, we are not off to a great start.

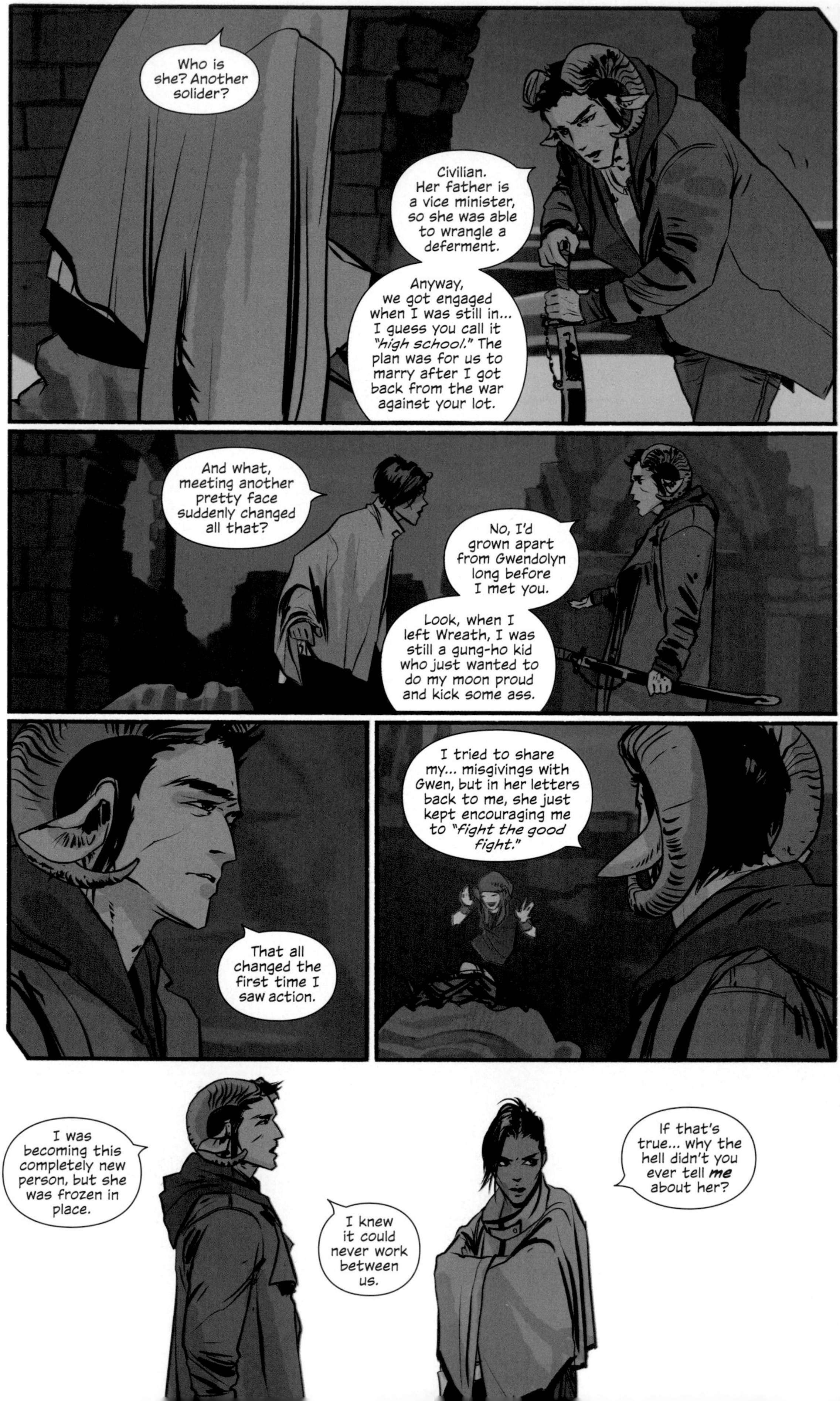
Who is she? Another solider?
Civilian. Her father is a vice minister, so she was able to wrangle a deferment.
Anyway, we got engaged when I was still in... I guess you call it *"high school."* The plan was for us to marry after I got back from the war against your lot.
And what, meeting another pretty face suddenly changed all that?
No, I'd grown apart from Gwendolyn long before I met you.
Look, when I left Wreath, I was still a gung-ho kid who just wanted to do my moon proud and kick some ass.
That all changed the first time I saw action.
I tried to share my... misgivings with Gwen, but in her letters back to me, she just kept encouraging me to *"fight the good fight."*
I was becoming this completely new person, but she was frozen in place.
I knew it could never work between us.
If that's true... why the hell didn't you ever tell ***me*** about her?

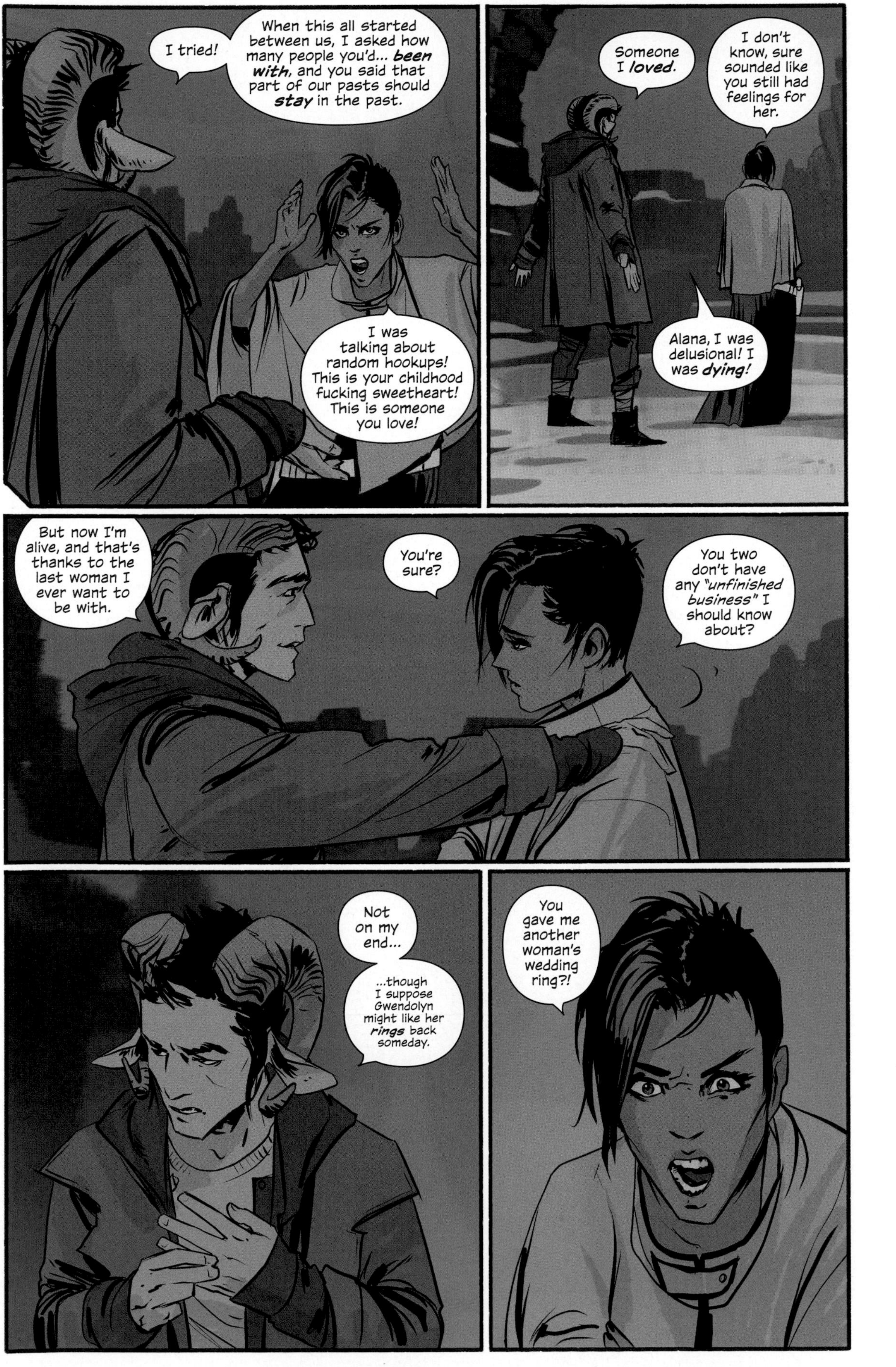
I tried!
When this all started between us, I asked how many people you'd... **been with**, and you said that part of our pasts should **stay** in the past.
I was talking about random hookups! This is your childhood fucking sweetheart! This is someone you love!
Someone I *loved*.
I don't know, sure sounded like you still had feelings for her.
Alana, I was delusional! I was **dying**!
But now I'm alive, and that's thanks to the last woman I ever want to be with.
You're sure?
You two don't have any *"unfinished business"* I should know about?
Not on my end...
...though I suppose Gwendolyn might like her **rings** back someday.
You gave me another woman's wedding ring?!

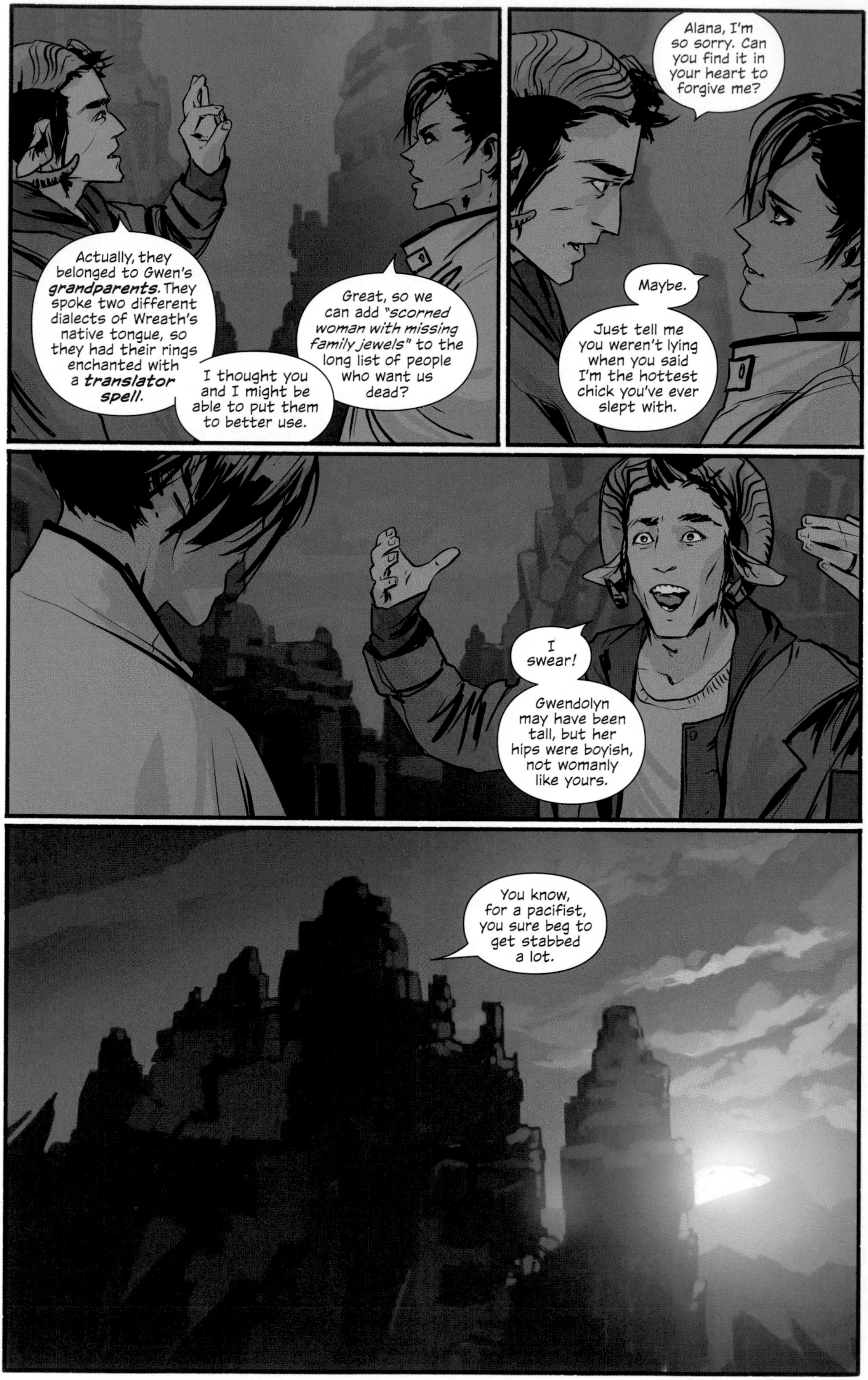

Actually, they belonged to Gwen's **grandparents**. They spoke two different dialects of Wreath's native tongue, so they had their rings enchanted with a **translator spell**.
I thought you and I might be able to put them to better use.
Great, so we can add *"scorned woman with missing family jewels"* to the long list of people who want us dead?
Alana, I'm so sorry. Can you find it in your heart to forgive me?
Maybe.
Just tell me you weren't lying when you said I'm the hottest chick you've ever slept with.
I swear!
Gwendolyn may have been tall, but her hips were boyish, not womanly like yours.
You know, for a pacifist, you sure beg to get stabbed a lot.

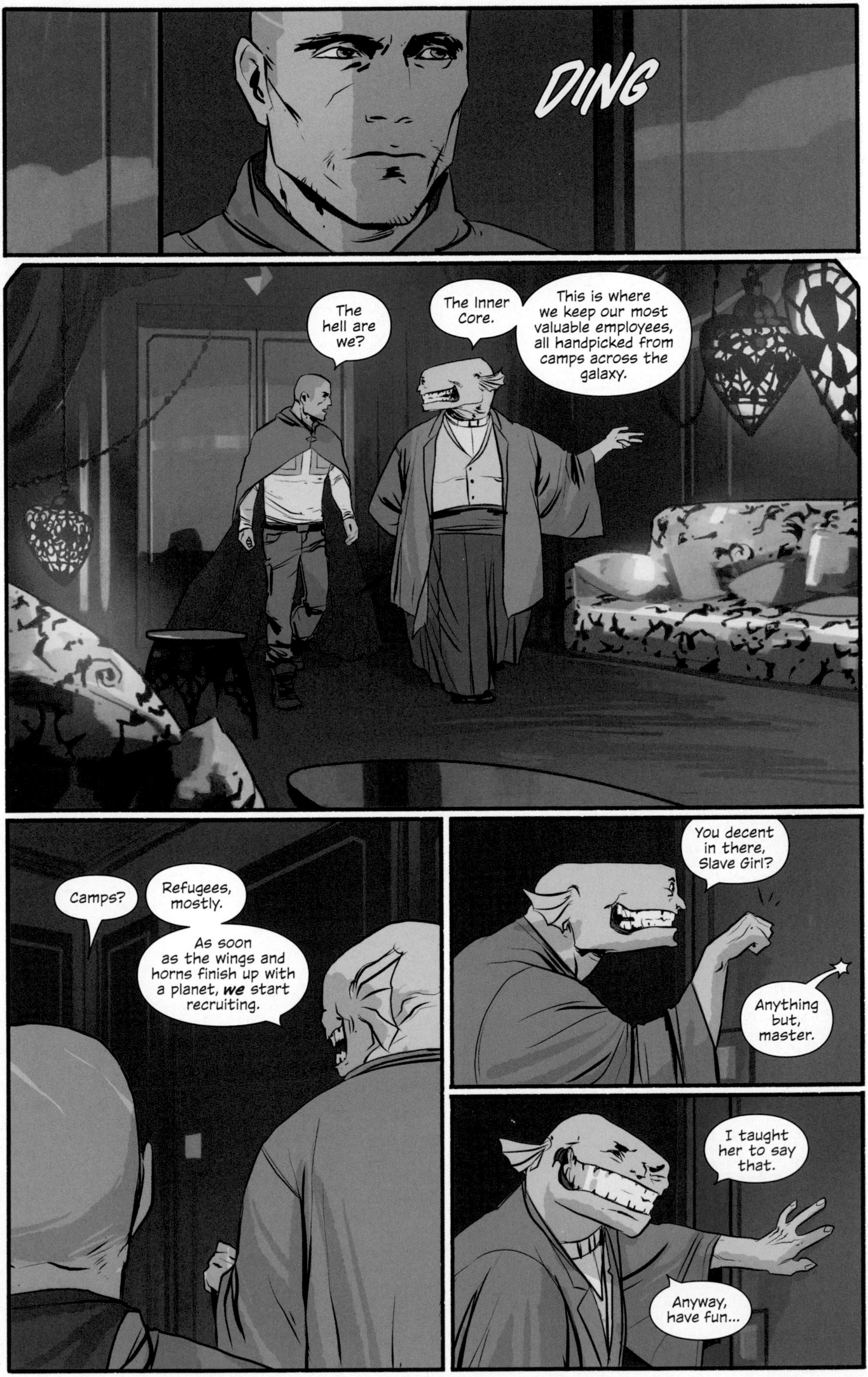
DING
The hell are we?
The Inner Core.
This is where we keep our most valuable employees, all handpicked from camps across the galaxy.
Camps?
Refugees, mostly.
As soon as the wings and horns finish up with a planet, *we* start recruiting.
You decent in there, Slave Girl?
Anything but, master.
I taught her to say that.
Anyway, have fun...

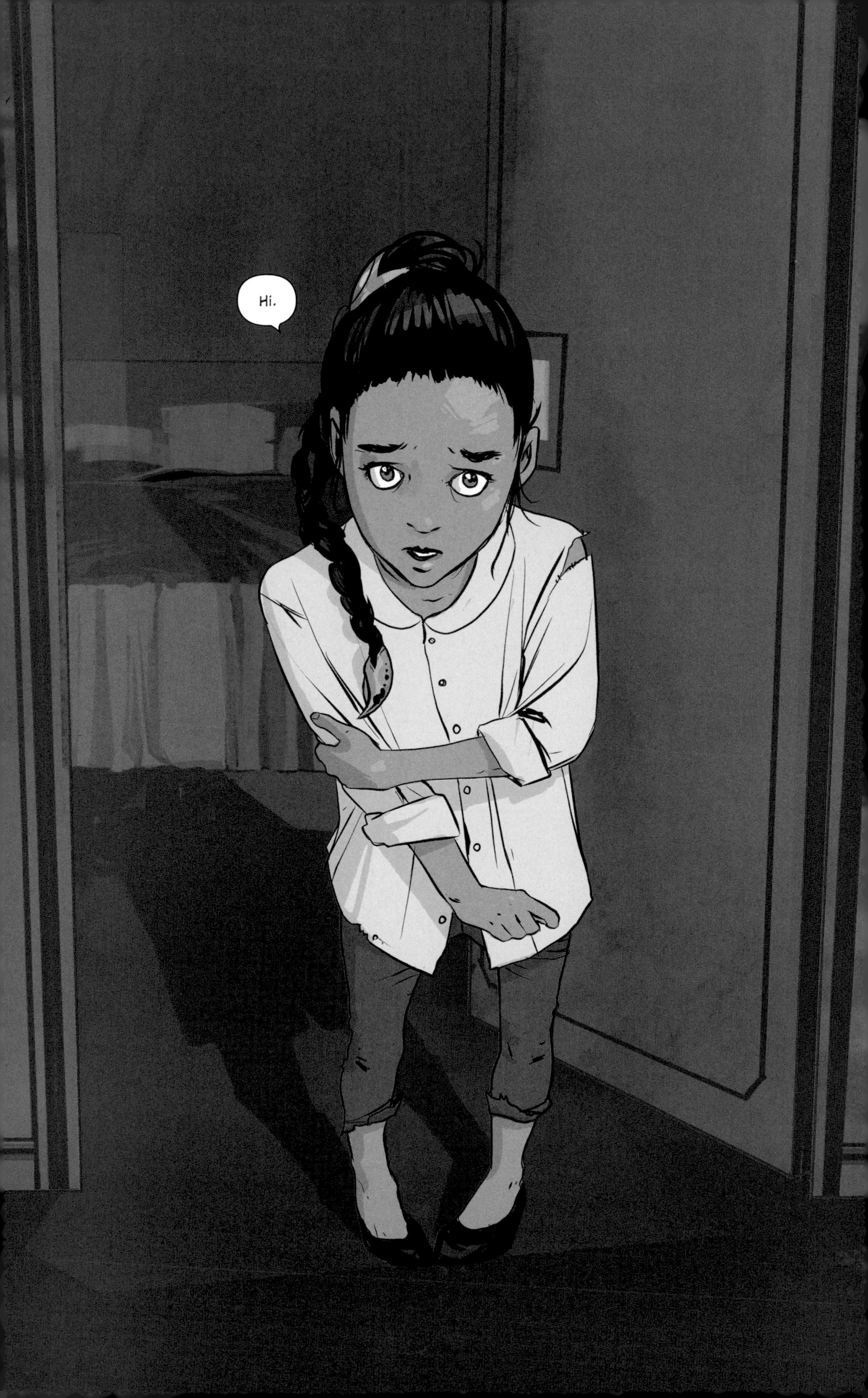
Hi.

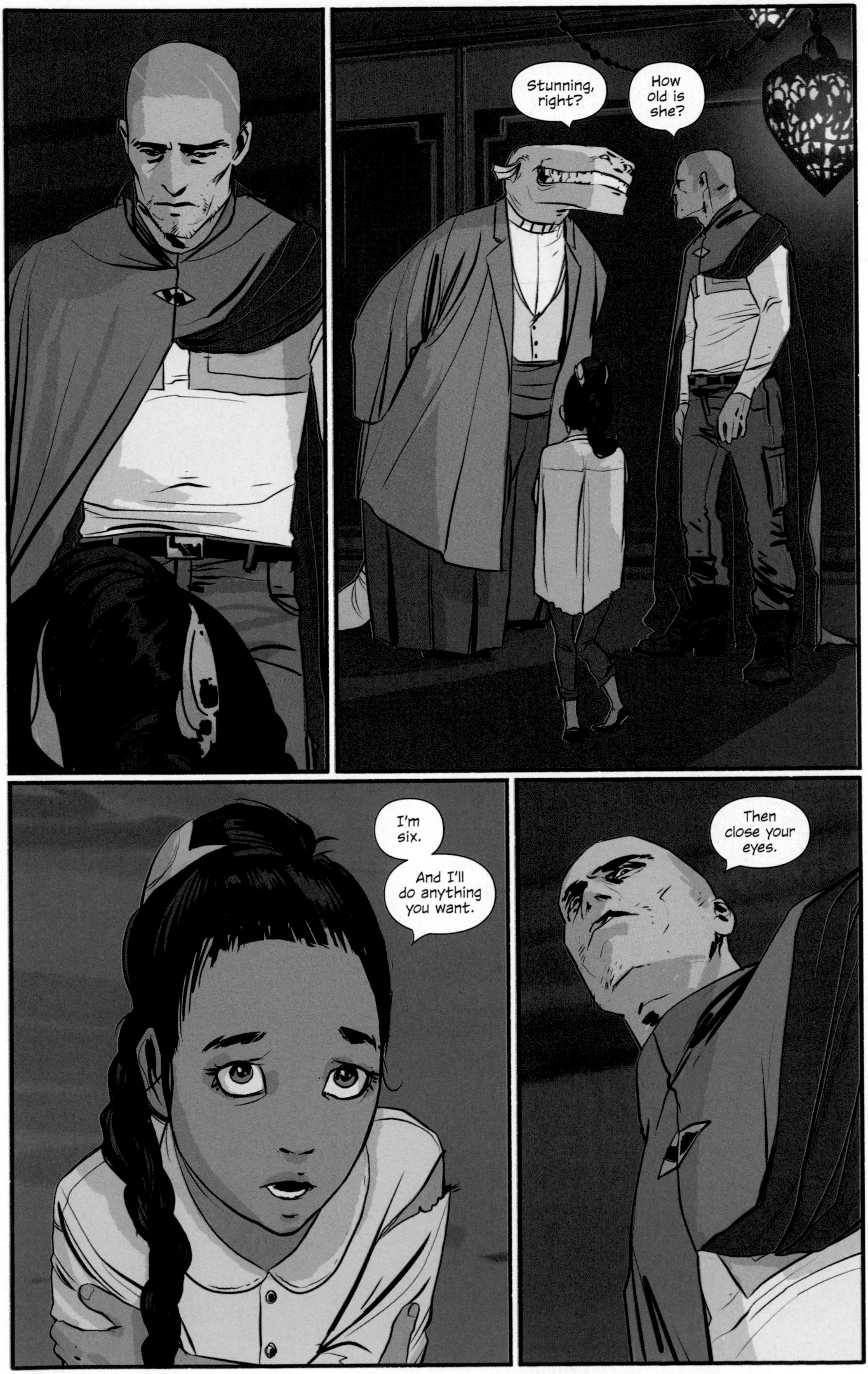
Stunning, right?
How old is she?
I'm six.
And I'll do anything you want.
Then close your eyes.

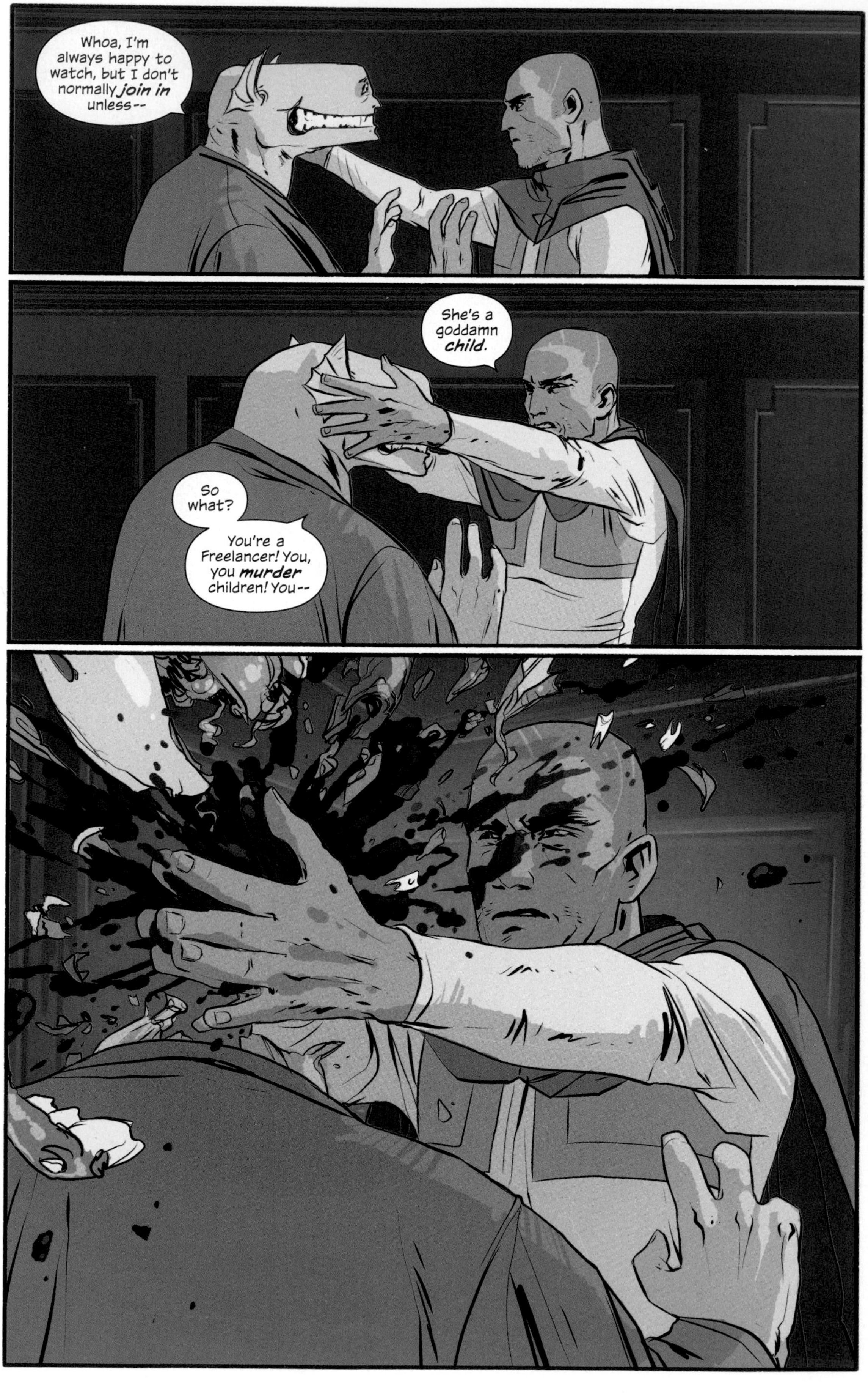
Whoa, I'm always happy to watch, but I don't normally *join in* unless--
She's a goddamn *child*.
So what?
You're a Freelancer! You, you *murder* children! You--

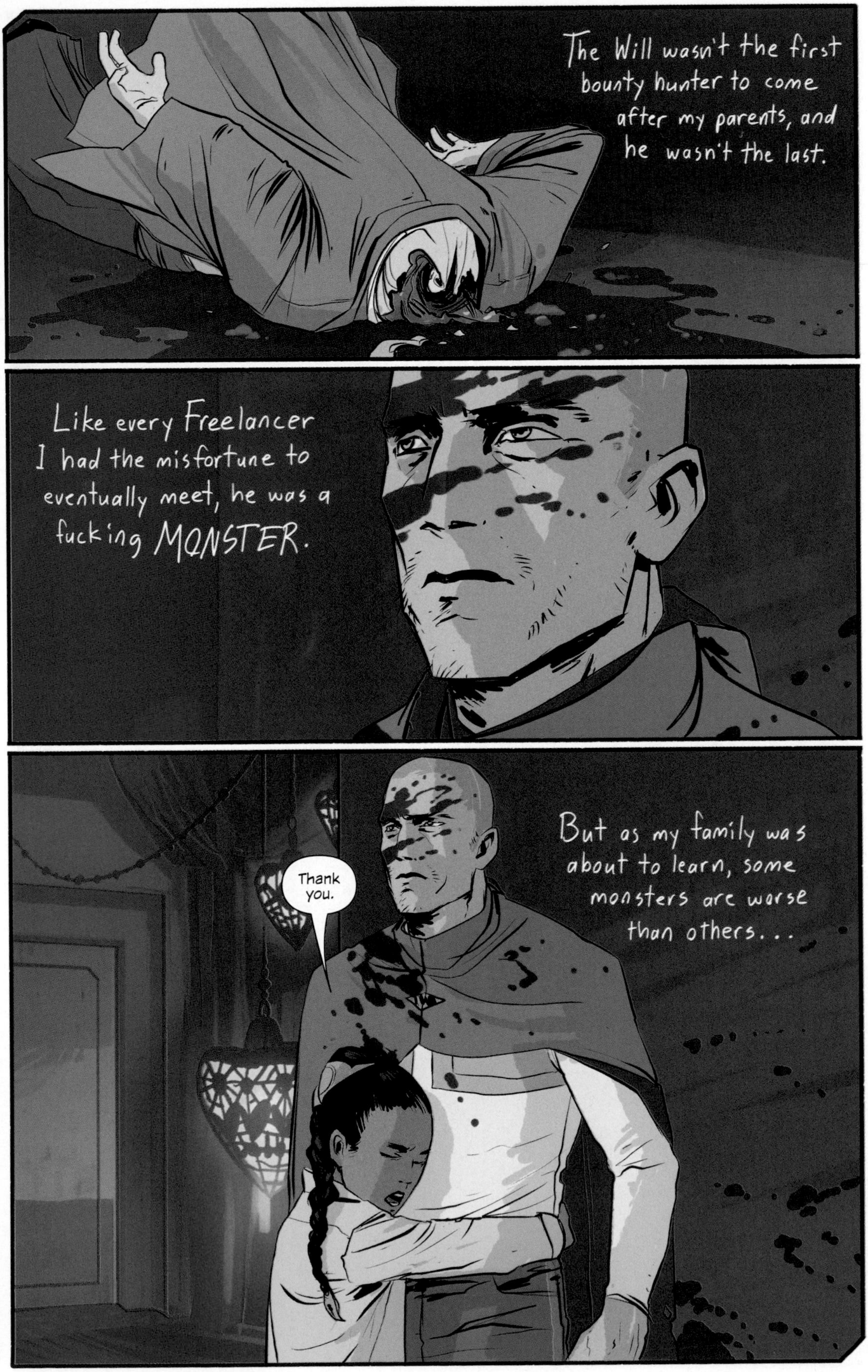
The Will wasn't the first bounty hunter to come after my parents, and he wasn't the last.
Like every Freelancer I had the misfortune to eventually meet, he was a fucking MONSTER.
Thank you.
But as my family was about to learn, some monsters are worse than others...

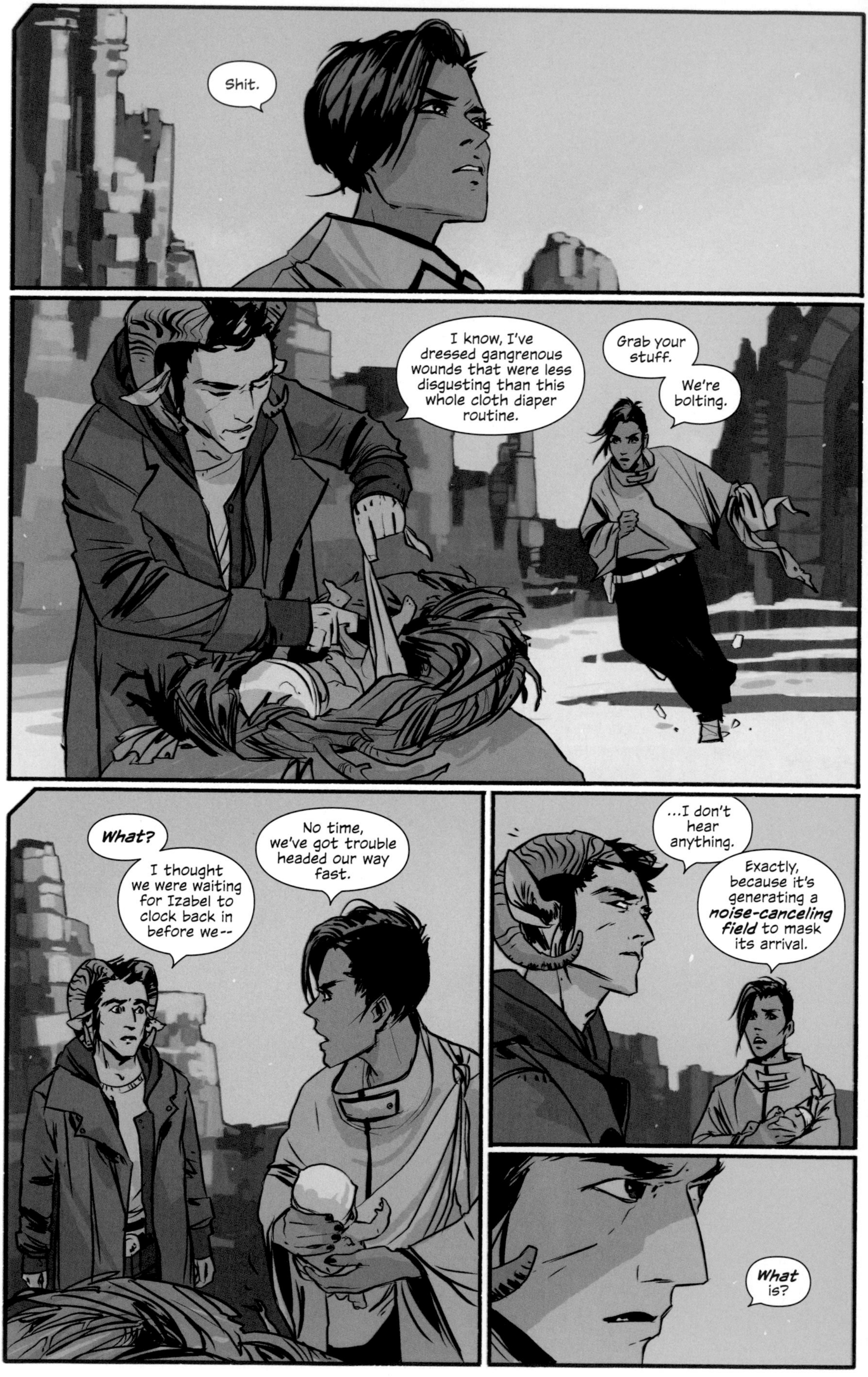

Shit.
I know, I've dressed gangrenous wounds that were less disgusting than this whole cloth diaper routine.
Grab your stuff.
We're bolting.
What?
I thought we were waiting for Izabel to clock back in before we--
No time, we've got trouble headed our way fast.
...I don't hear anything.
Exactly, because it's generating a noise-canceling field to mask its arrival.
What is?

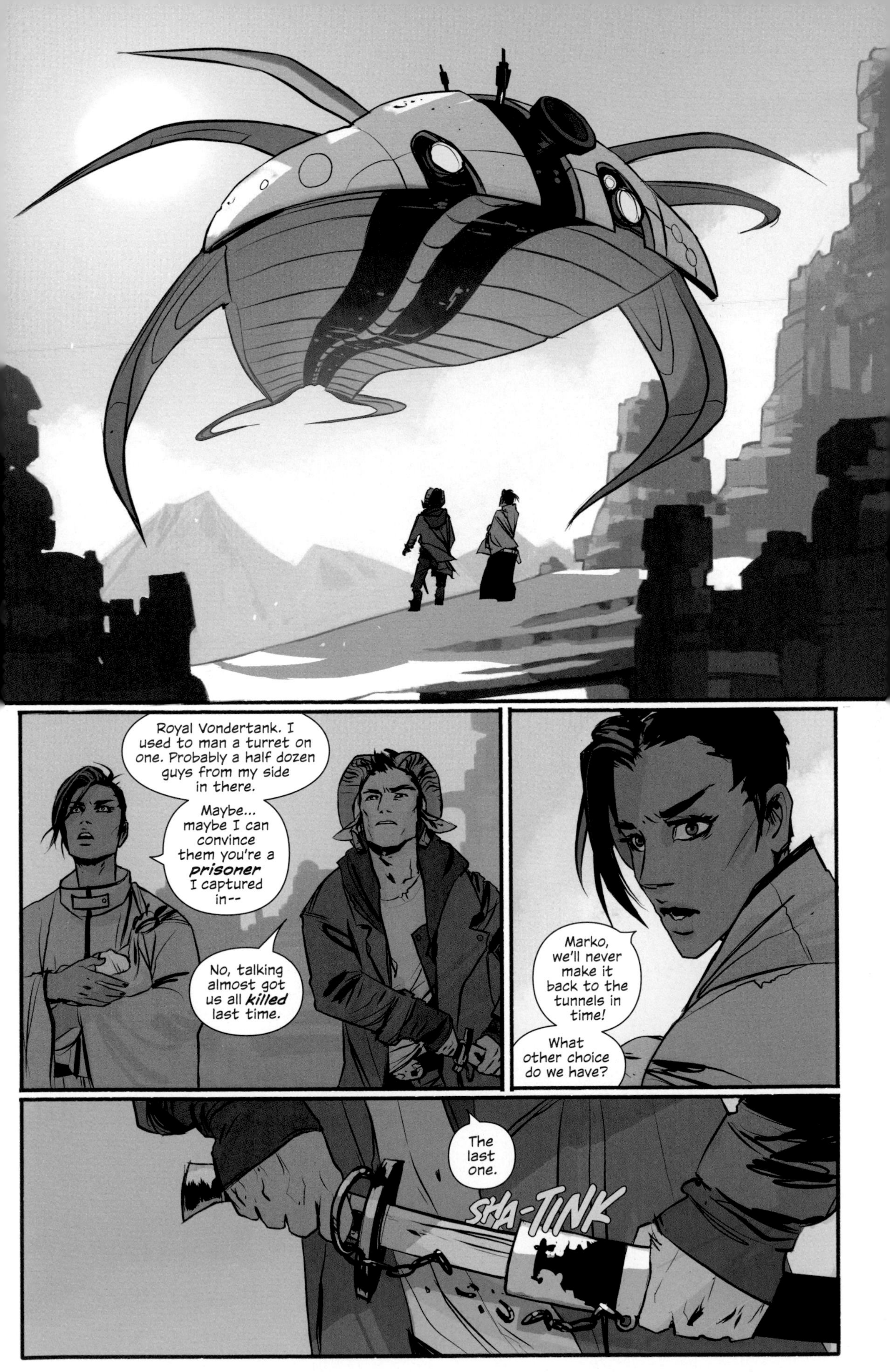
Royal Vondertank. I used to man a turret on one. Probably a half dozen guys from my side in there.
Maybe... maybe I can convince them you're a *prisoner* I captured in--
No, talking almost got us all *killed* last time.
Marko, we'll never make it back to the tunnels in time!
What other choice do we have?
The last one.
SHA-TINK

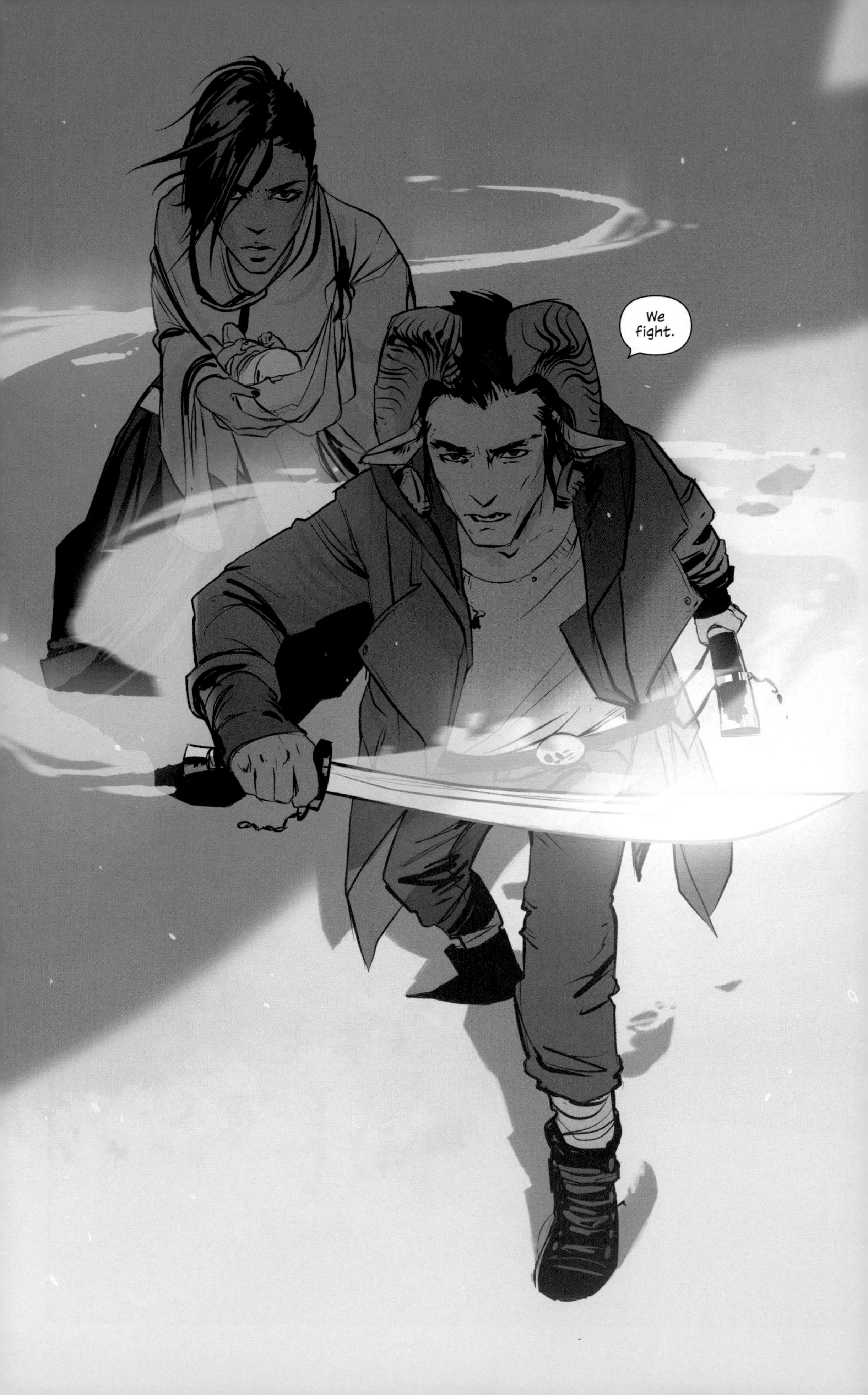
We fight.

end chapter four

CHAPTER
FIVE

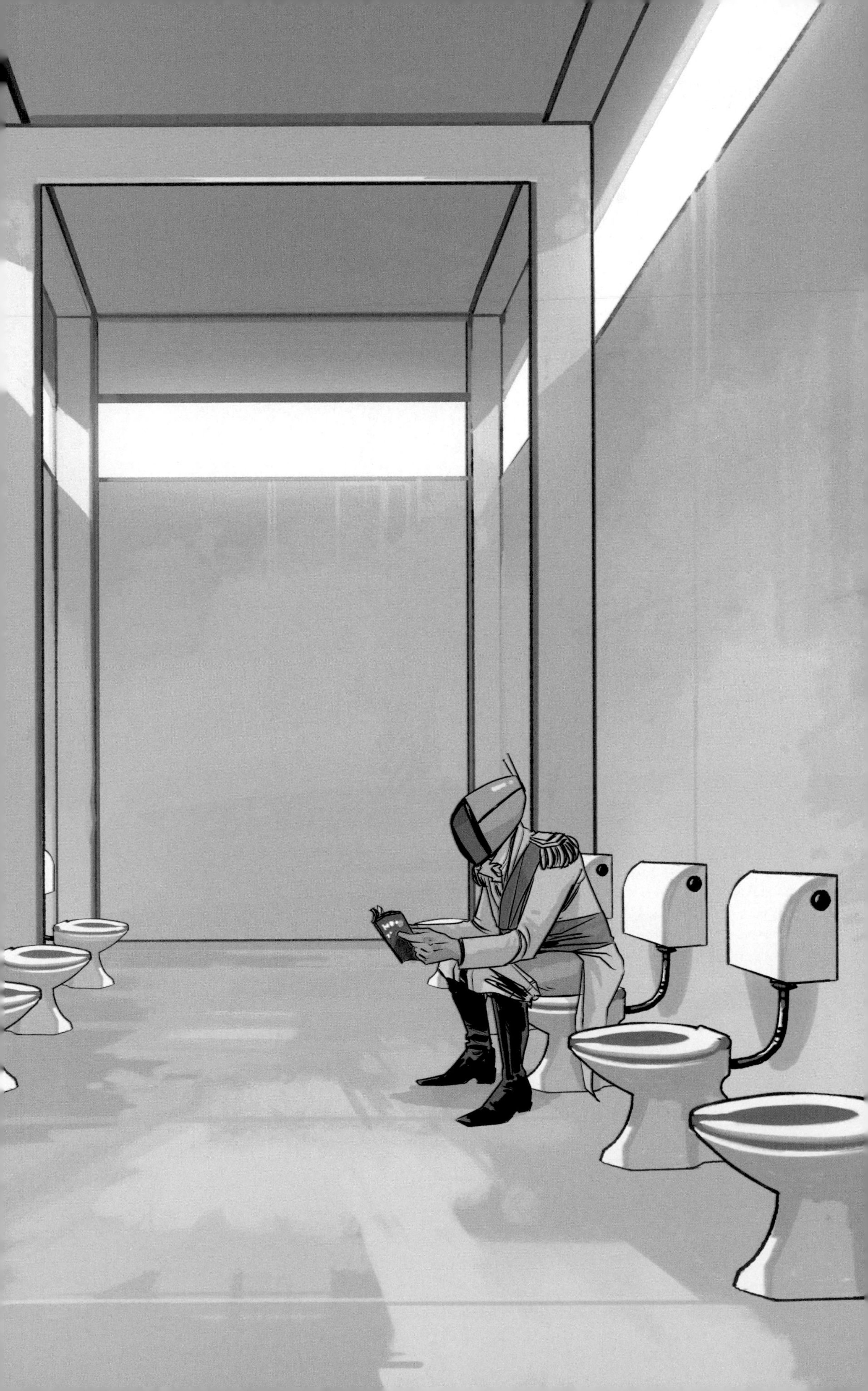

Incoming priority transmission from the Robot Kingdom.

Hm. I'll accept.

IV, sweetheart, can you hear me?

Princess? They don't really like us using the royal channel for personal conversations.

Lovely to hear your voice, as well.

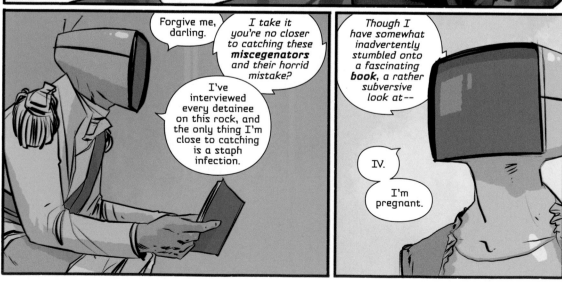

Forgive me, darling.

I take it you're no closer to catching these *miscegenators* and their horrid mistake?

I've interviewed every detainee on this rock, and the only thing I'm close to catching is a staph infection.

Though I have somewhat inadvertently stumbled onto a fascinating *book*, a rather subversive look at--

IV.

I'm pregnant.

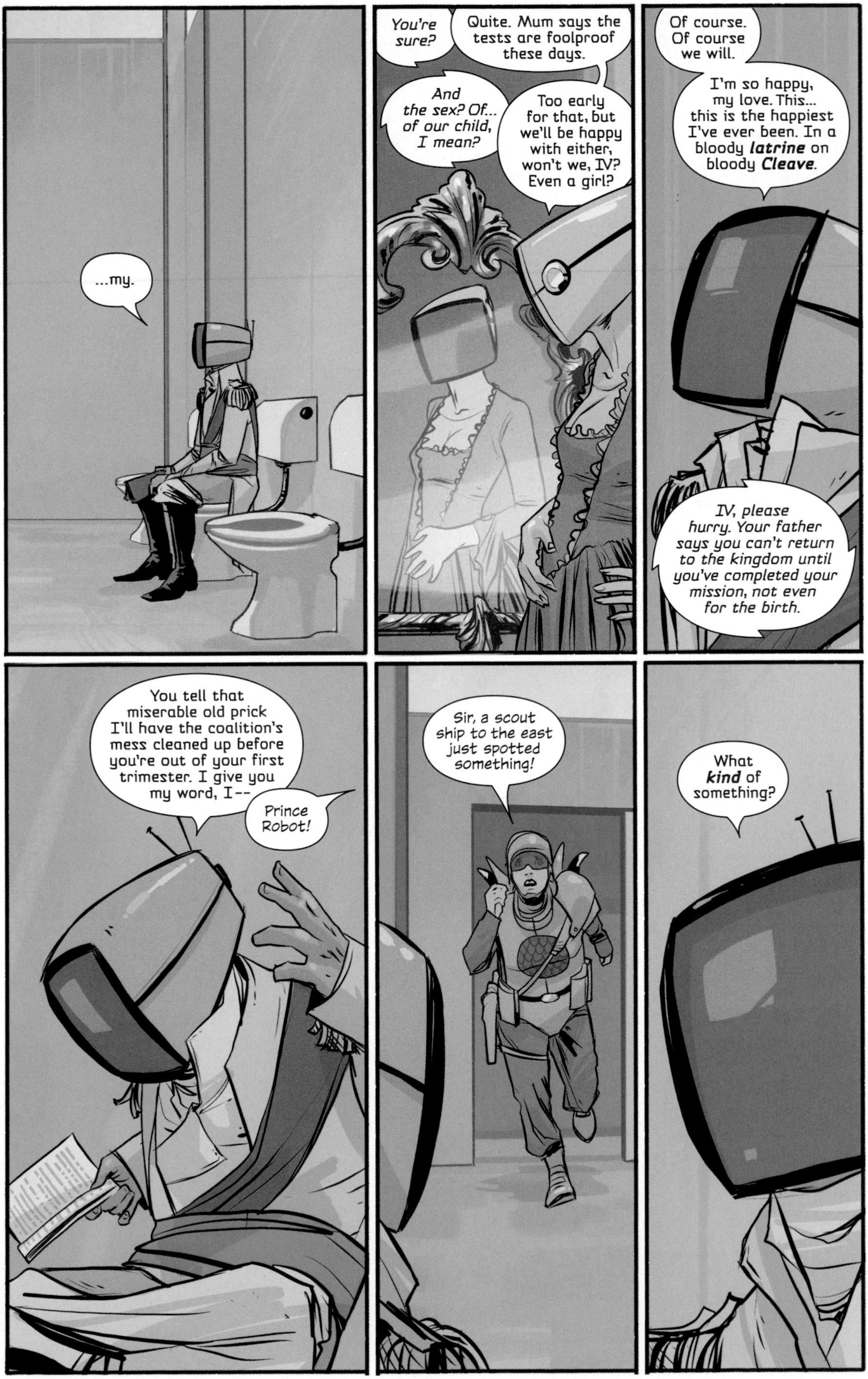
...my.
You're sure?
Quite. Mum says the tests are foolproof these days.
And the sex? Of... of our child, I mean?
Too early for that, but we'll be happy with either, won't we, IV? Even a girl?
Of course. Of course we will.
I'm so happy, my love. This... this is the happiest I've ever been. In a bloody *latrine* on bloody *Cleave*.
IV, please hurry. Your father says you can't return to the kingdom until you've completed your mission, not even for the birth.
You tell that miserable old prick I'll have the coalition's mess cleaned up before you're out of your first trimester. I give you my word, I--
Prince Robot!
Sir, a scout ship to the east just spotted something!
What *kind* of something?

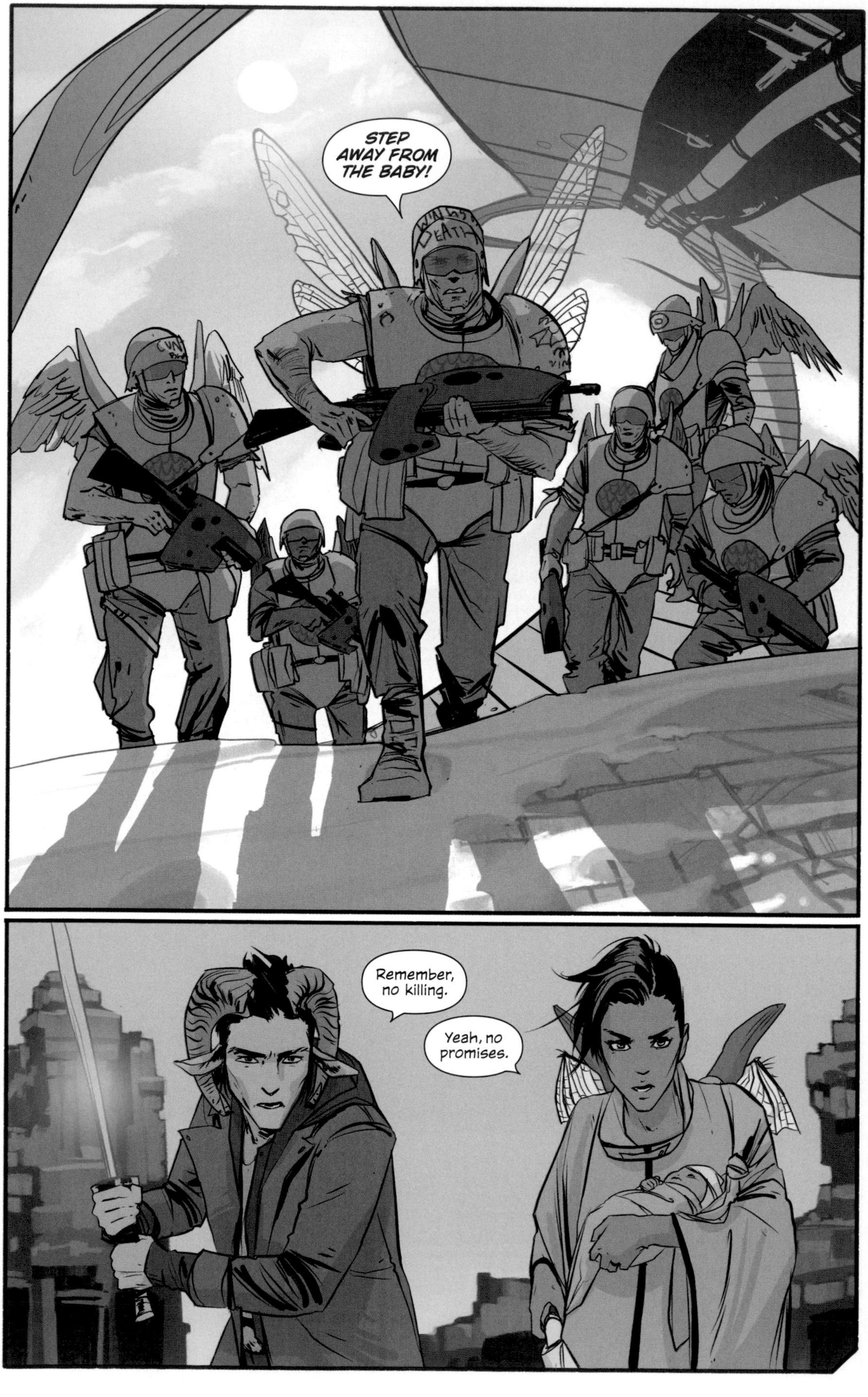
STEP AWAY FROM THE BABY!
Remember, no killing.
Yeah, no promises.

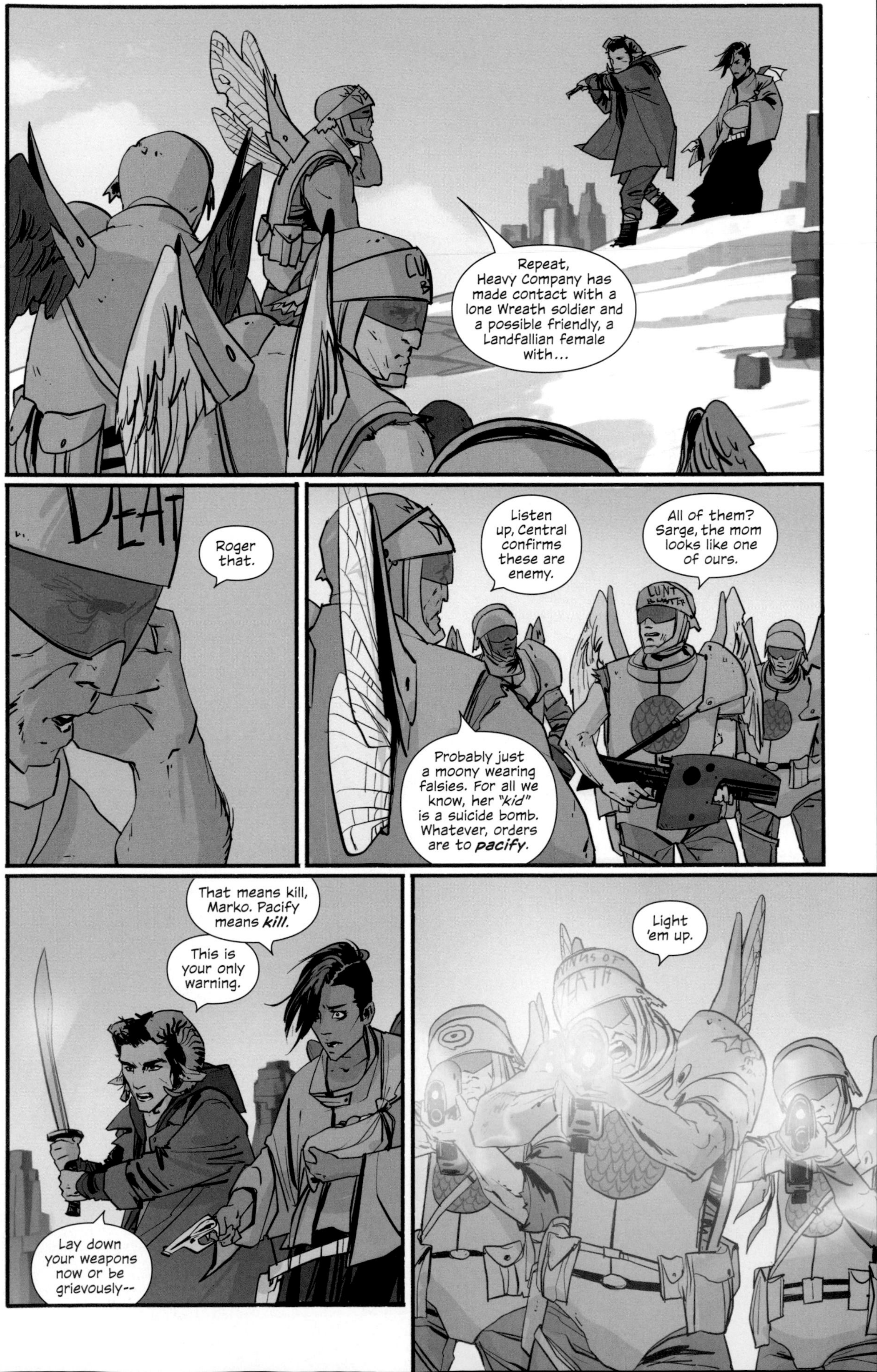

Repeat, Heavy Company has made contact with a lone Wreath soldier and a possible friendly, a Landfallian female with...
Roger that.
Listen up, Central confirms these are enemy.
All of them? Sarge, the mom looks like one of ours.
Probably just a moony wearing falsies. For all we know, her "*kid*" is a suicide bomb. Whatever, orders are to ***pacify***.
That means kill, Marko. Pacify means ***kill***.
This is your only warning.
Lay down your weapons now or be grievously--
Light 'em up.

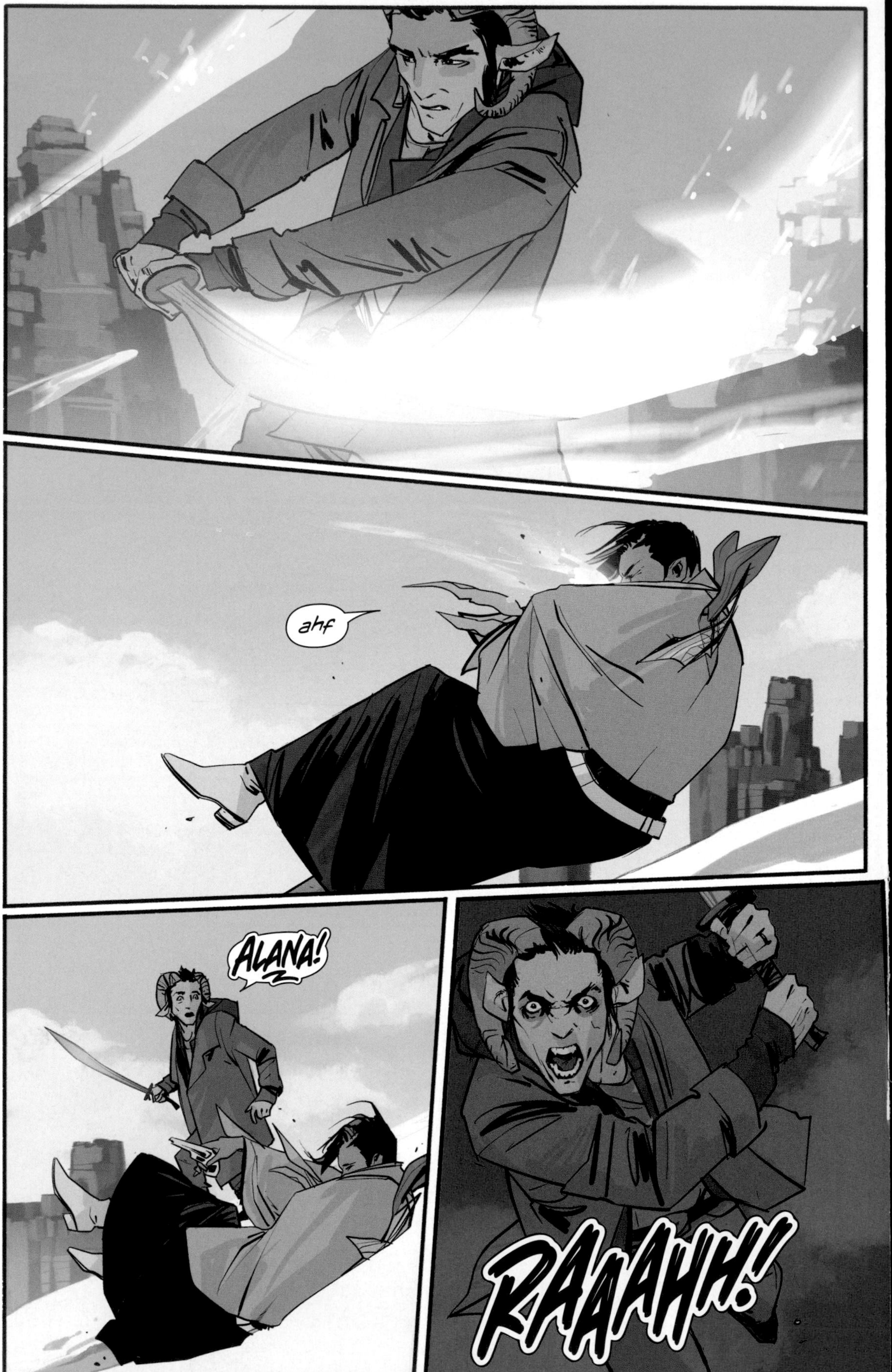

ahf
ALANA!
RAAAHH!

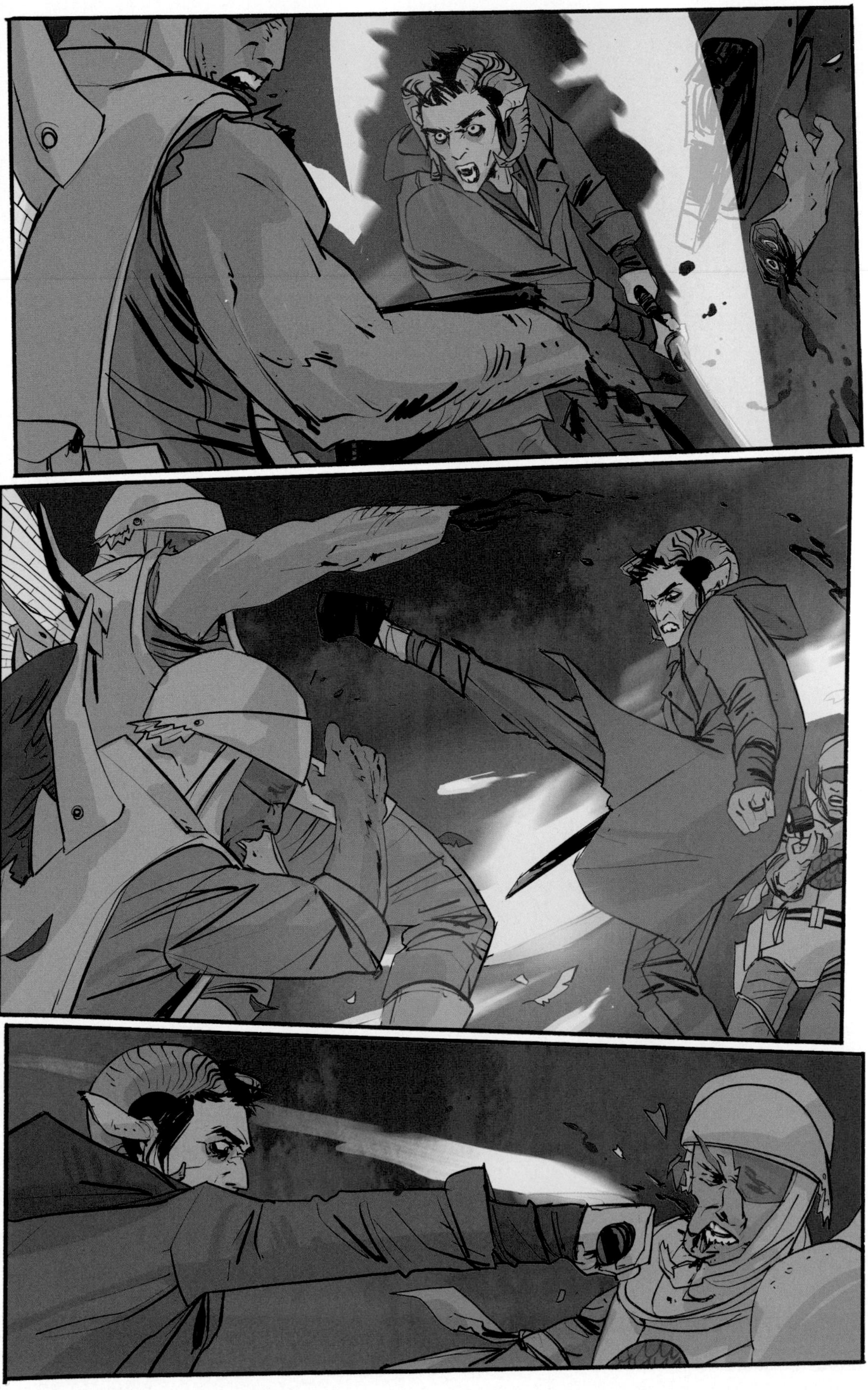

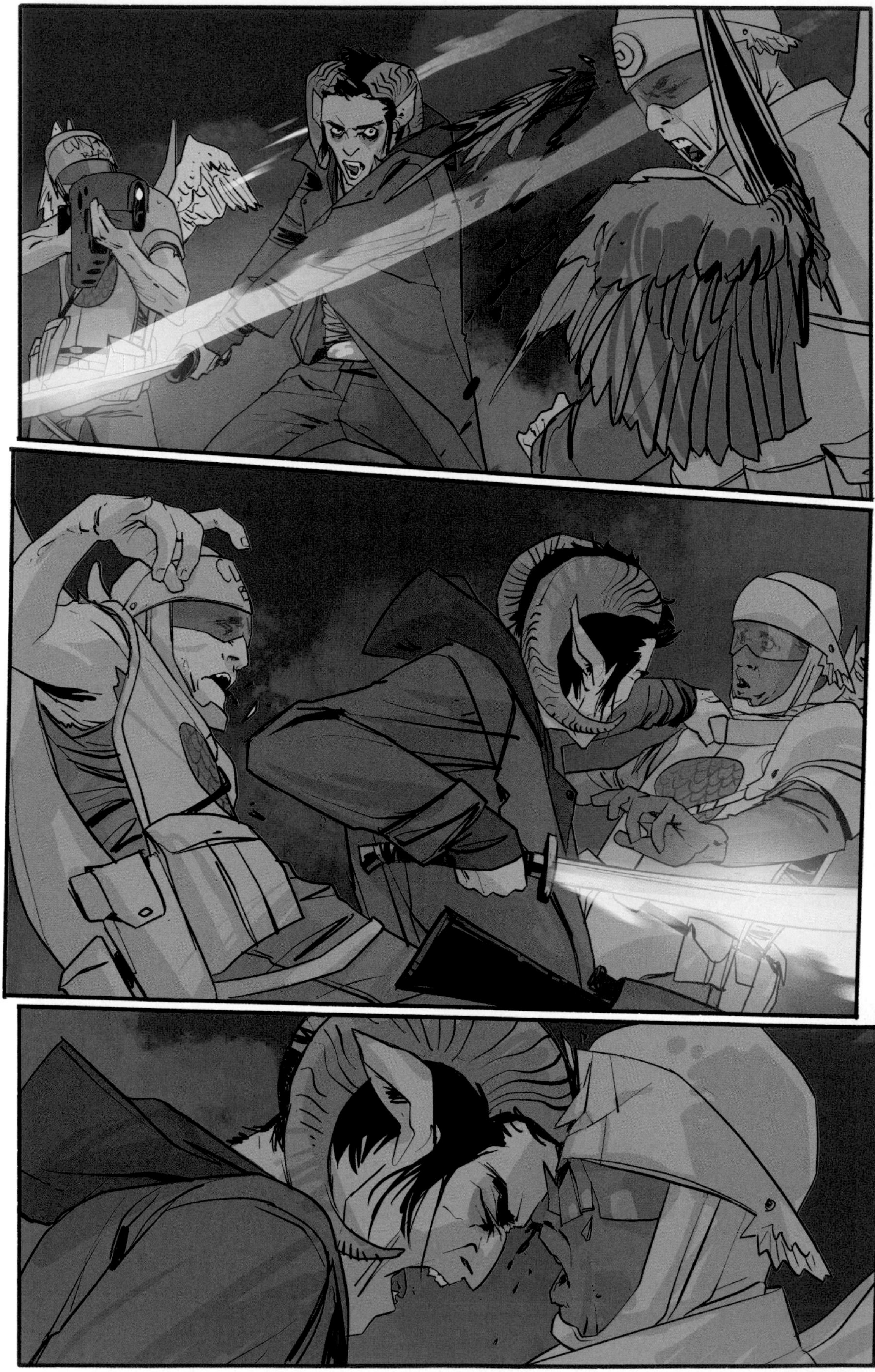

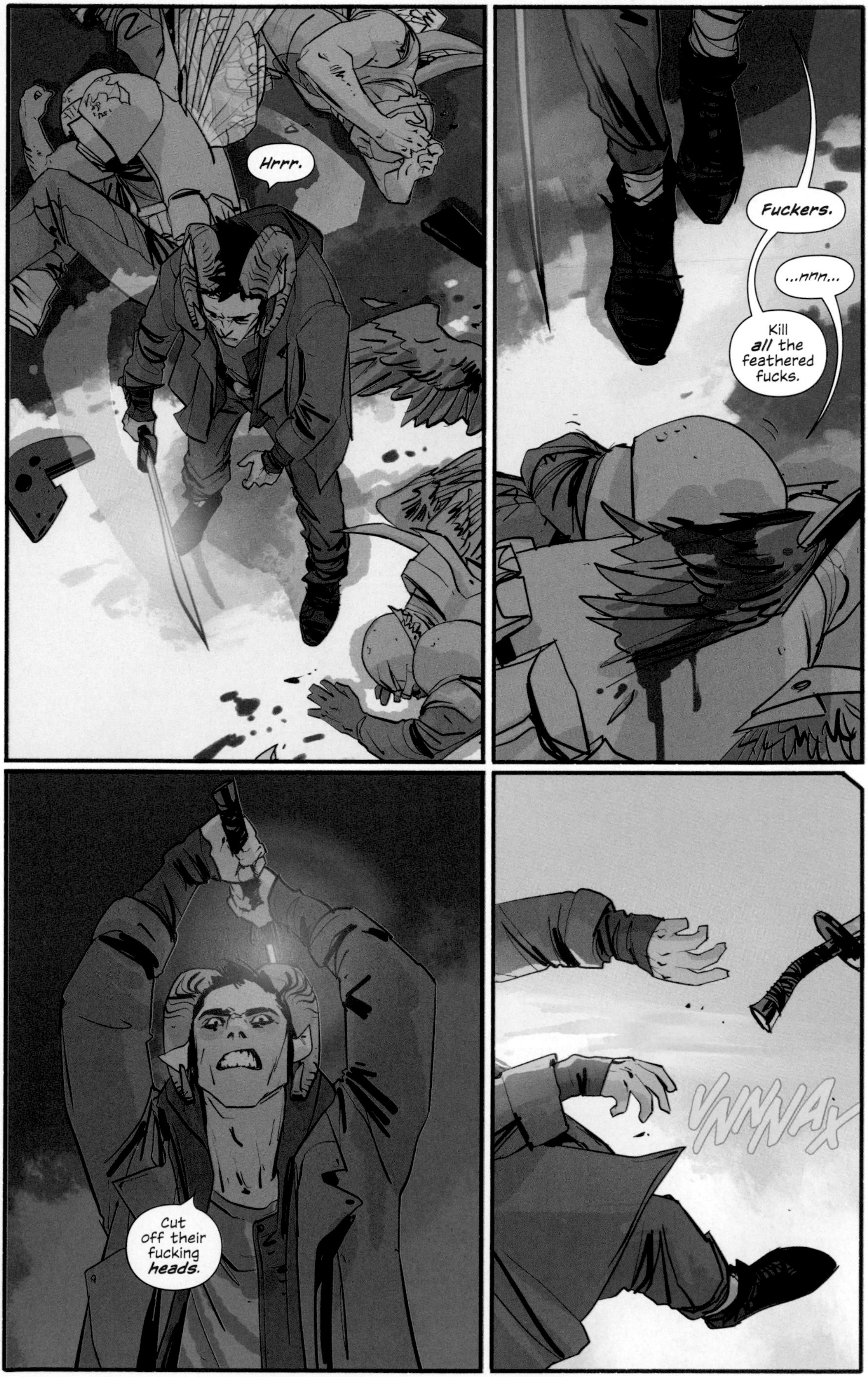
Hrrr.
Fuckers.
...nnn...
Kill all the feathered fucks.
Cut off their fucking heads.
VNNNAX

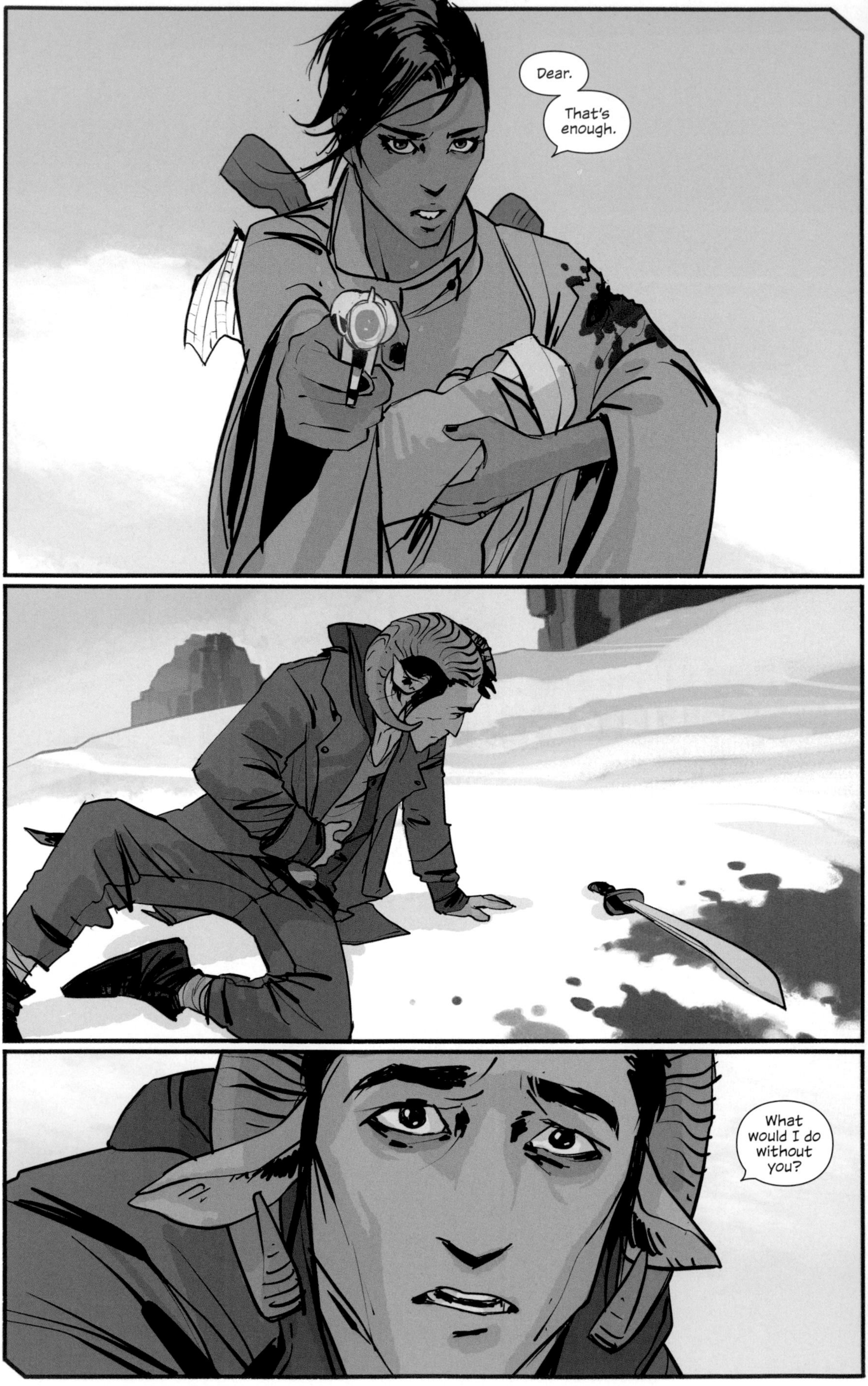
Dear.
That's enough.
What would I do without you?

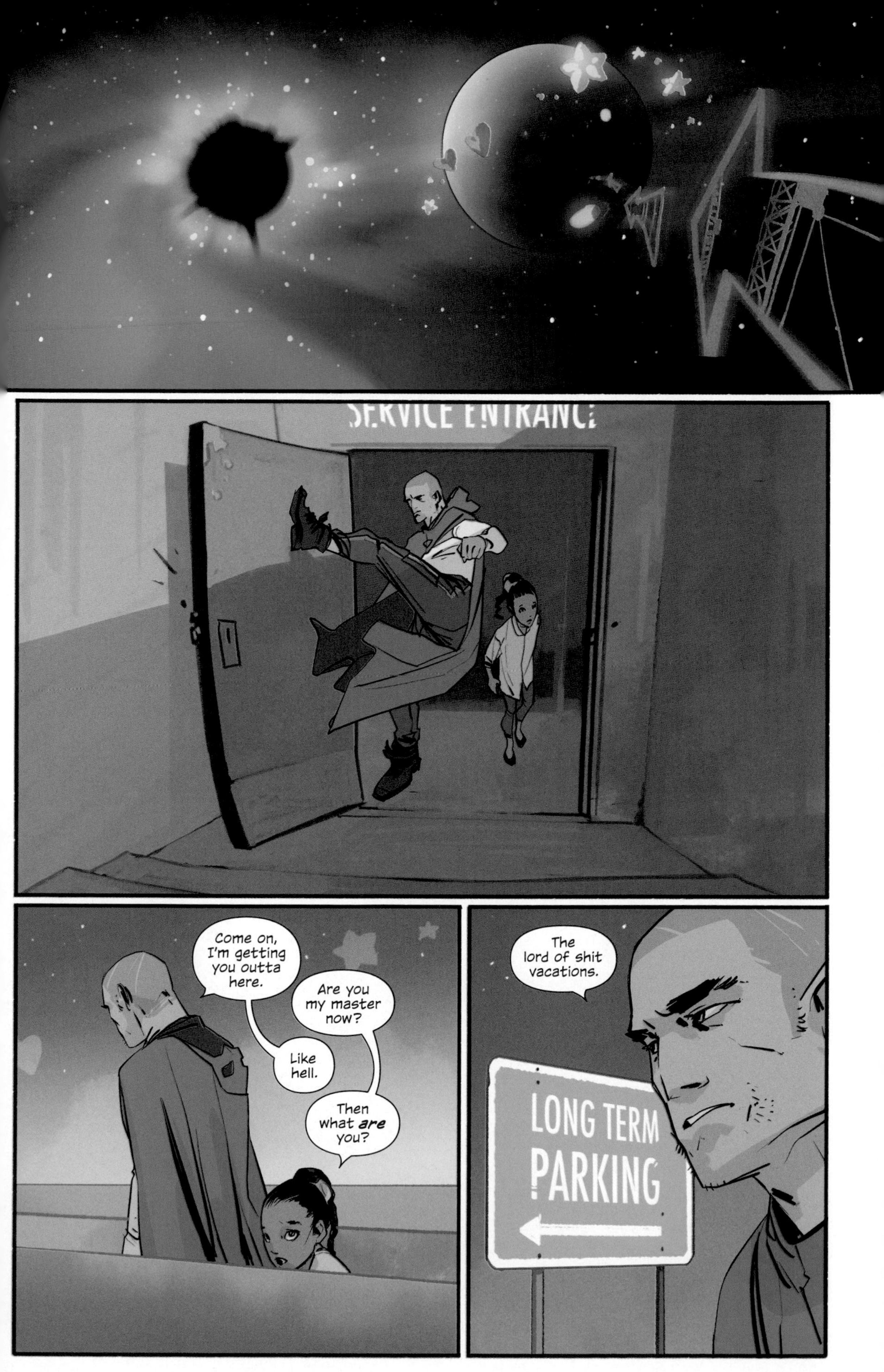
SERVICE ENTRANCE
Come on, I'm getting you outta here.
Are you my master now?
Like hell.
Then what *are* you?
The lord of shit vacations.
LONG TERM PARKING

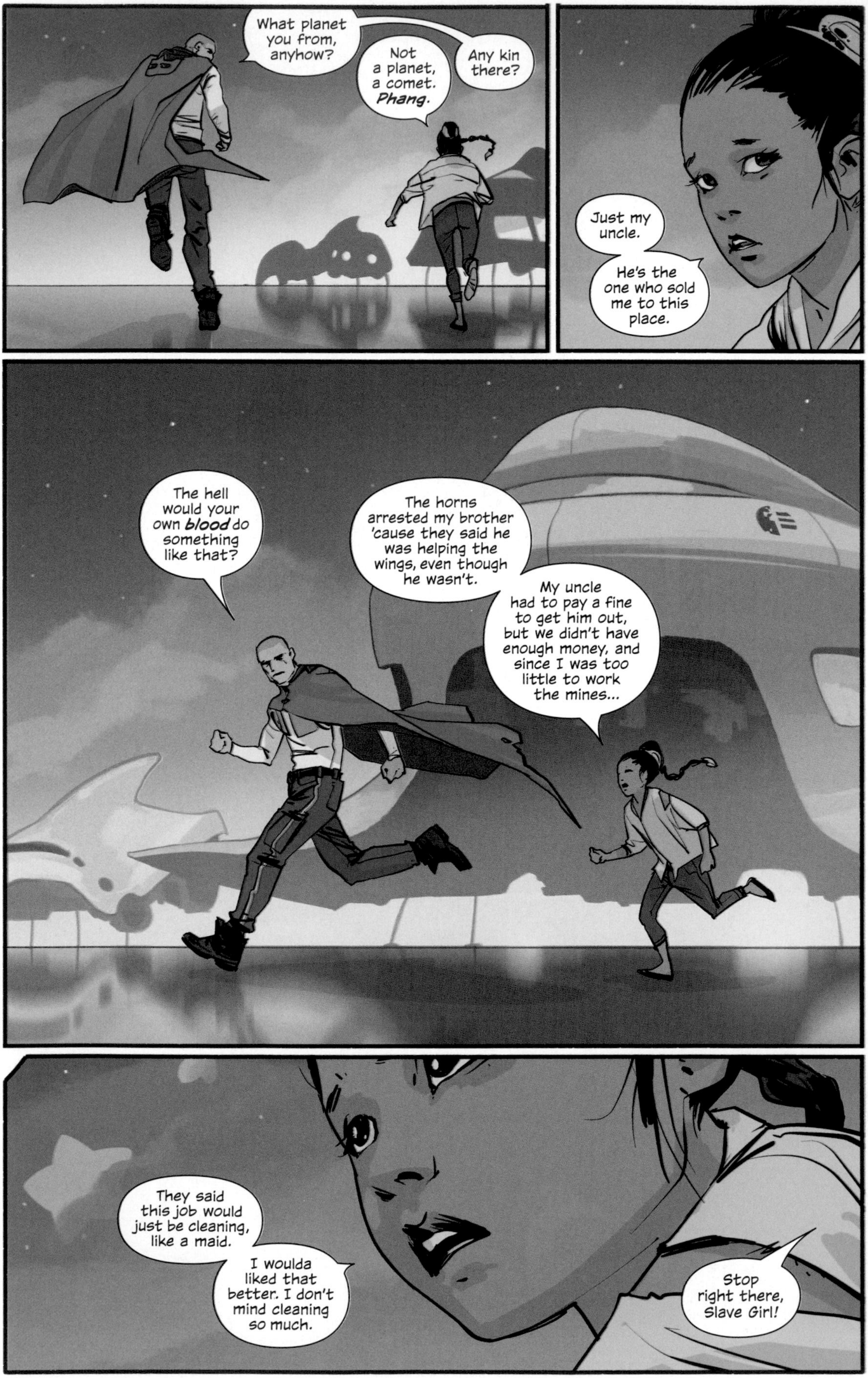

What planet you from, anyhow?
Not a planet, a comet. *Phang*.
Any kin there?
Just my uncle.
He's the one who sold me to this place.
The hell would your own *blood* do something like that?
The horns arrested my brother 'cause they said he was helping the wings, even though he wasn't.
My uncle had to pay a fine to get him out, but we didn't have enough money, and since I was too little to work the mines...
They said this job would just be cleaning, like a maid.
I woulda liked that better. I don't mind cleaning so much.
Stop right there, Slave Girl!

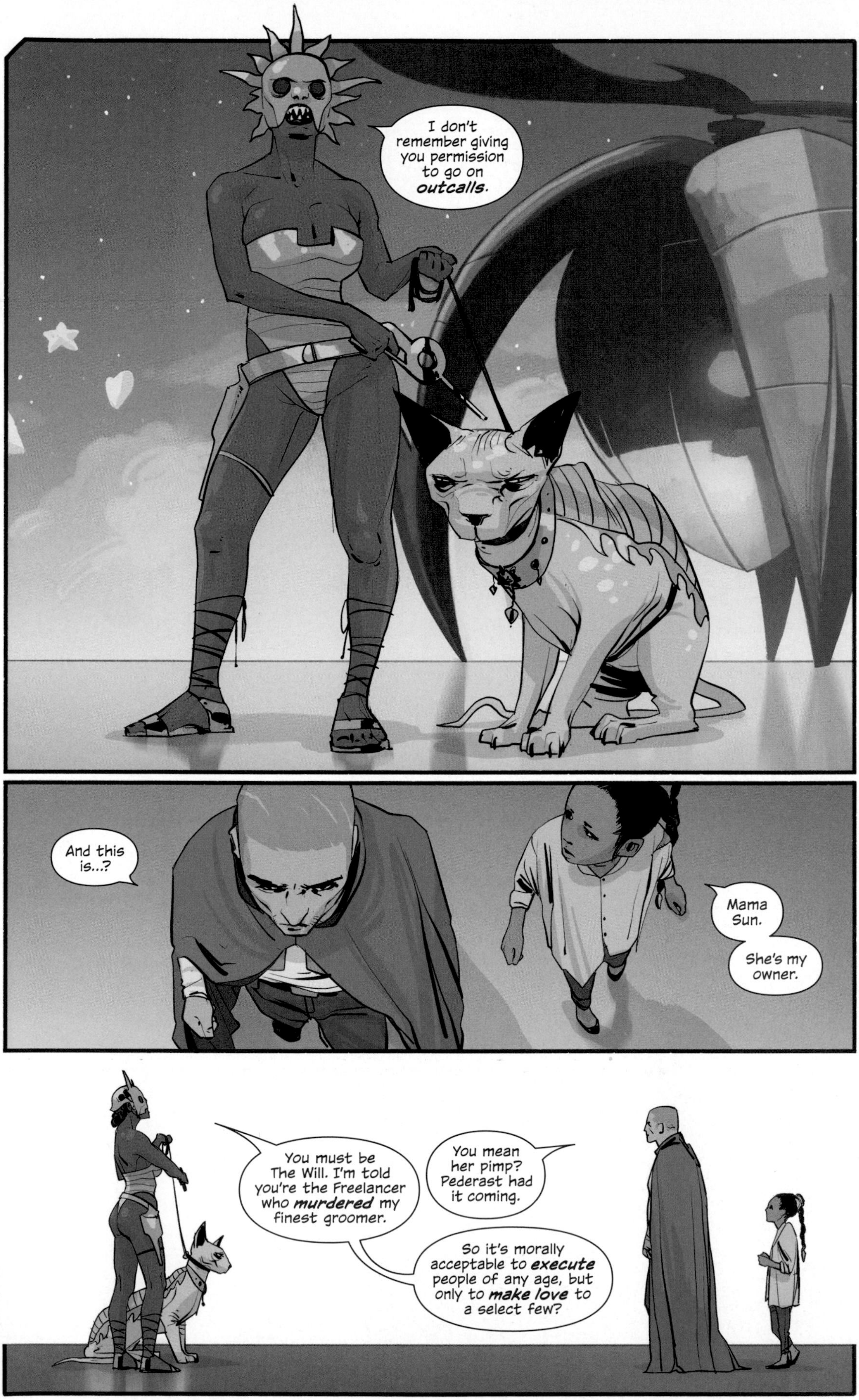
I don't remember giving you permission to go on *outcalls*.
And this is...?
Mama Sun.
She's my owner.
You must be The Will. I'm told you're the Freelancer who *murdered* my finest groomer.
You mean her pimp? Pederast had it coming.
So it's morally acceptable to *execute* people of any age, but only to *make love* to a select few?

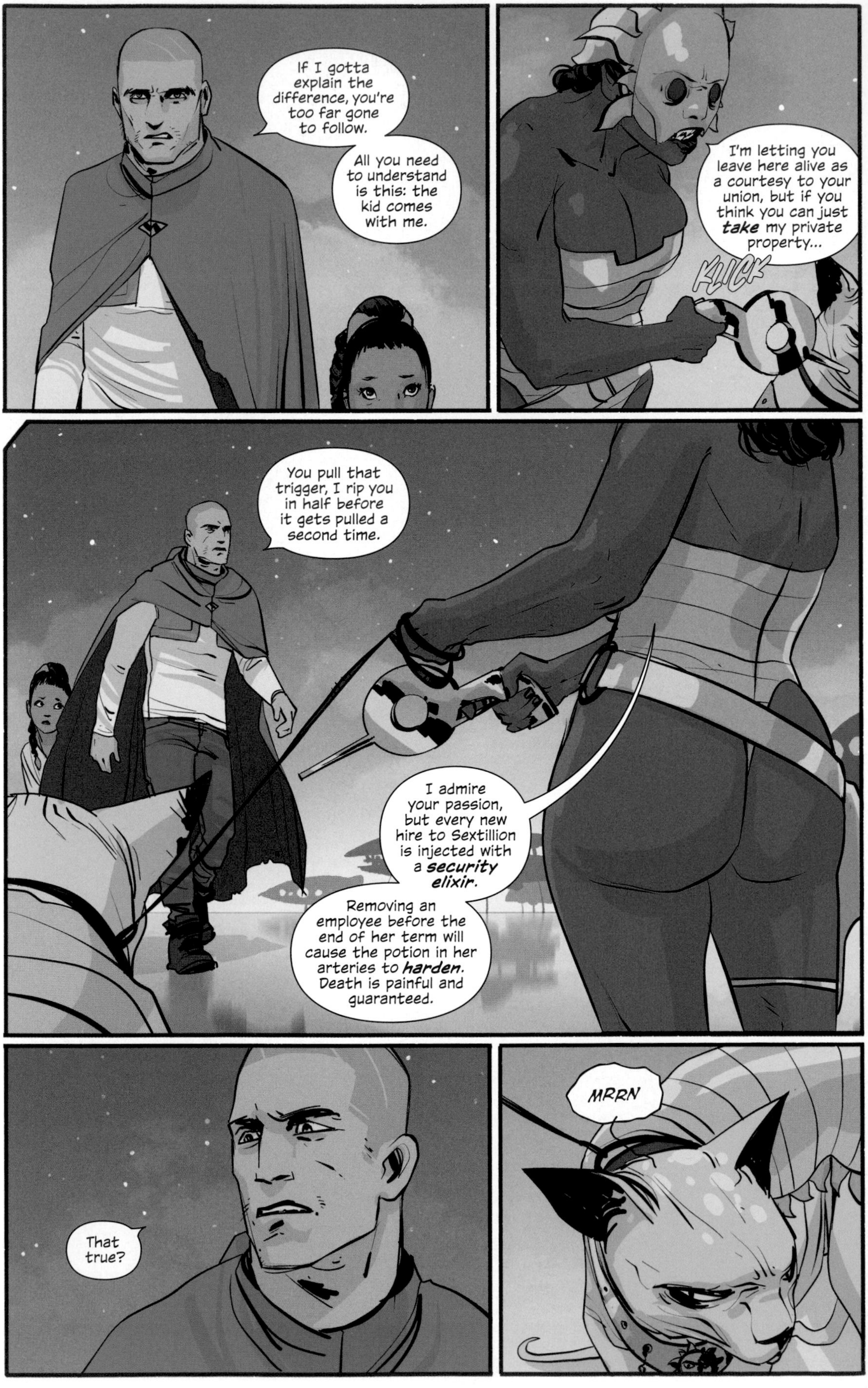

If I gotta explain the difference, you're too far gone to follow.
All you need to understand is this: the kid comes with me.
I'm letting you leave here alive as a courtesy to your union, but if you think you can just *take* my private property...
KLICK
You pull that trigger, I rip you in half before it gets pulled a second time.
I admire your passion, but every new hire to Sextillion is injected with a *security elixir*.
Removing an employee before the end of her term will cause the potion in her arteries to *harden*. Death is painful and guaranteed.
That true?
MRRN

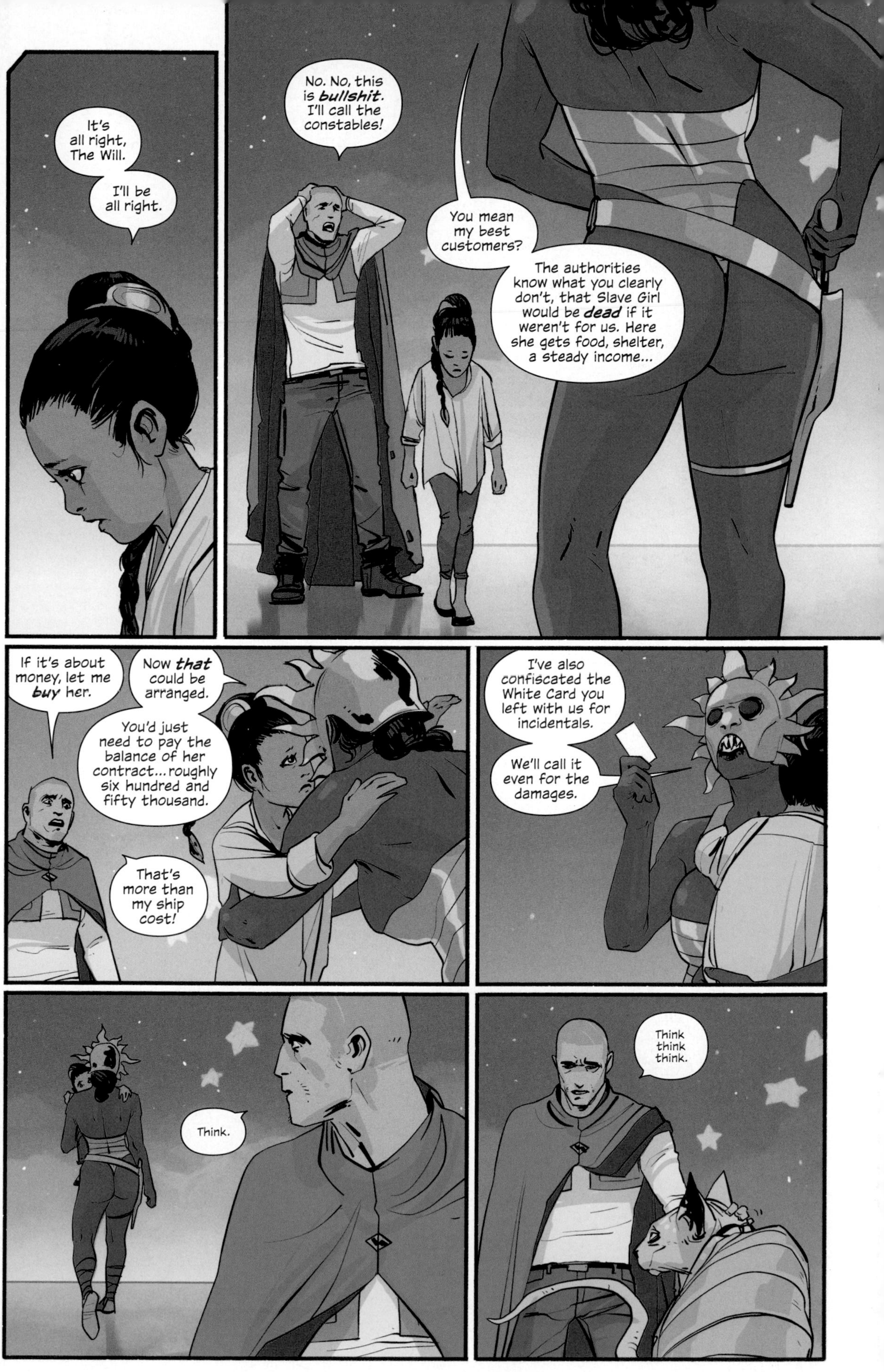
It's all right, The Will.
I'll be all right.
No. No, this is bullshit. I'll call the constables!
You mean my best customers?
The authorities know what you clearly don't, that Slave Girl would be dead if it weren't for us. Here she gets food, shelter, a steady income...
If it's about money, let me buy her.
Now that could be arranged.
You'd just need to pay the balance of her contract... roughly six hundred and fifty thousand.
That's more than my ship cost!
I've also confiscated the White Card you left with us for incidentals.
We'll call it even for the damages.
Think.
Think think think.

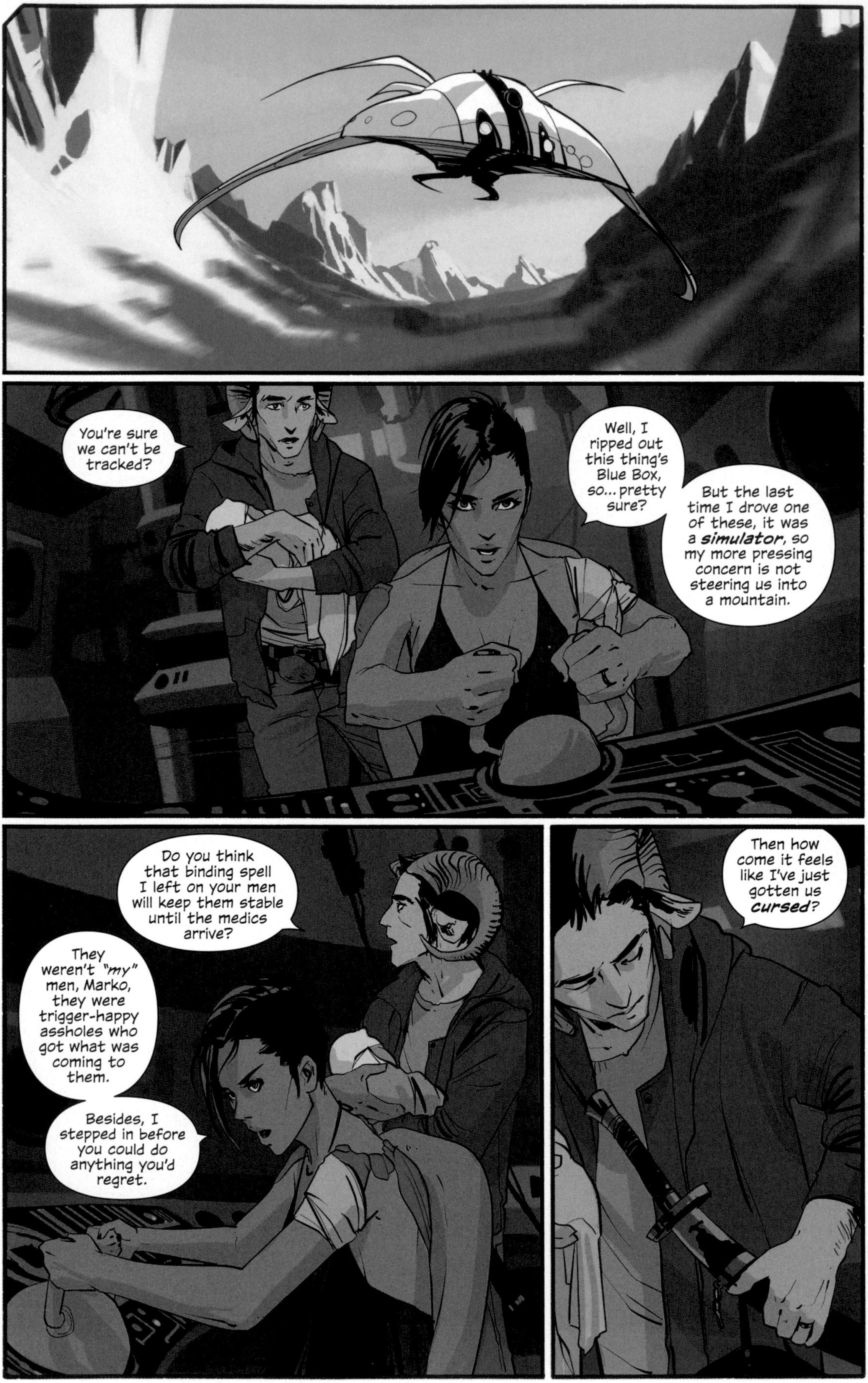
You're sure we can't be tracked?
Well, I ripped out this thing's Blue Box, so... pretty sure?
But the last time I drove one of these, it was a ***simulator***, so my more pressing concern is not steering us into a mountain.
Do you think that binding spell I left on your men will keep them stable until the medics arrive?
They weren't *"my"* men, Marko, they were trigger-happy assholes who got what was coming to them.
Besides, I stepped in before you could do anything you'd regret.
Then how come it feels like I've just gotten us ***cursed***?

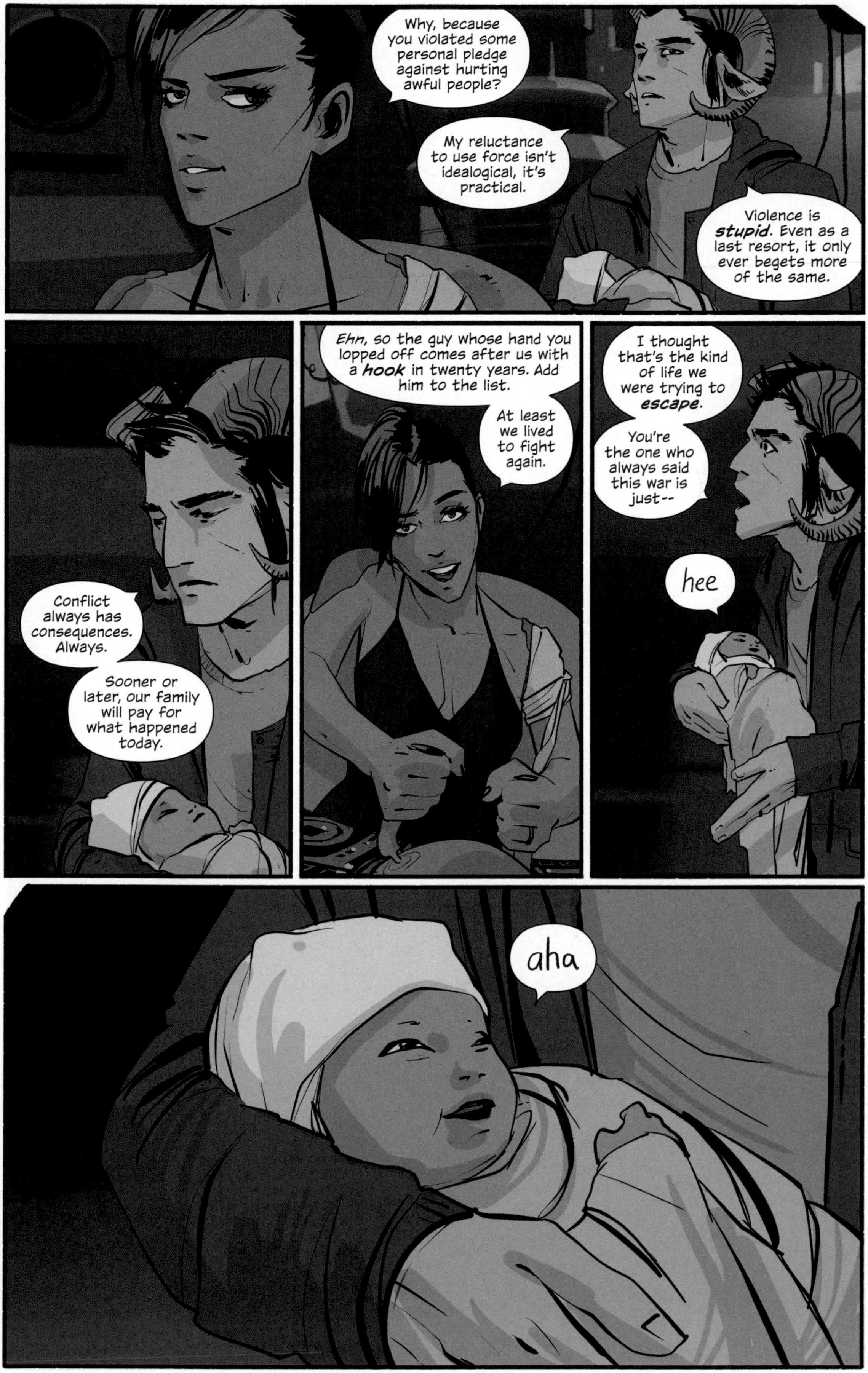

Why, because you violated some personal pledge against hurting awful people?
My reluctance to use force isn't idealogical, it's practical.
Violence is **stupid**. Even as a last resort, it only ever begets more of the same.
Conflict always has consequences. Always.
Sooner or later, our family will pay for what happened today.
Ehn, so the guy whose hand you lopped off comes after us with a **hook** in twenty years. Add him to the list.
At least we lived to fight again.
I thought that's the kind of life we were trying to **escape**.
You're the one who always said this war is just--
hee
aha

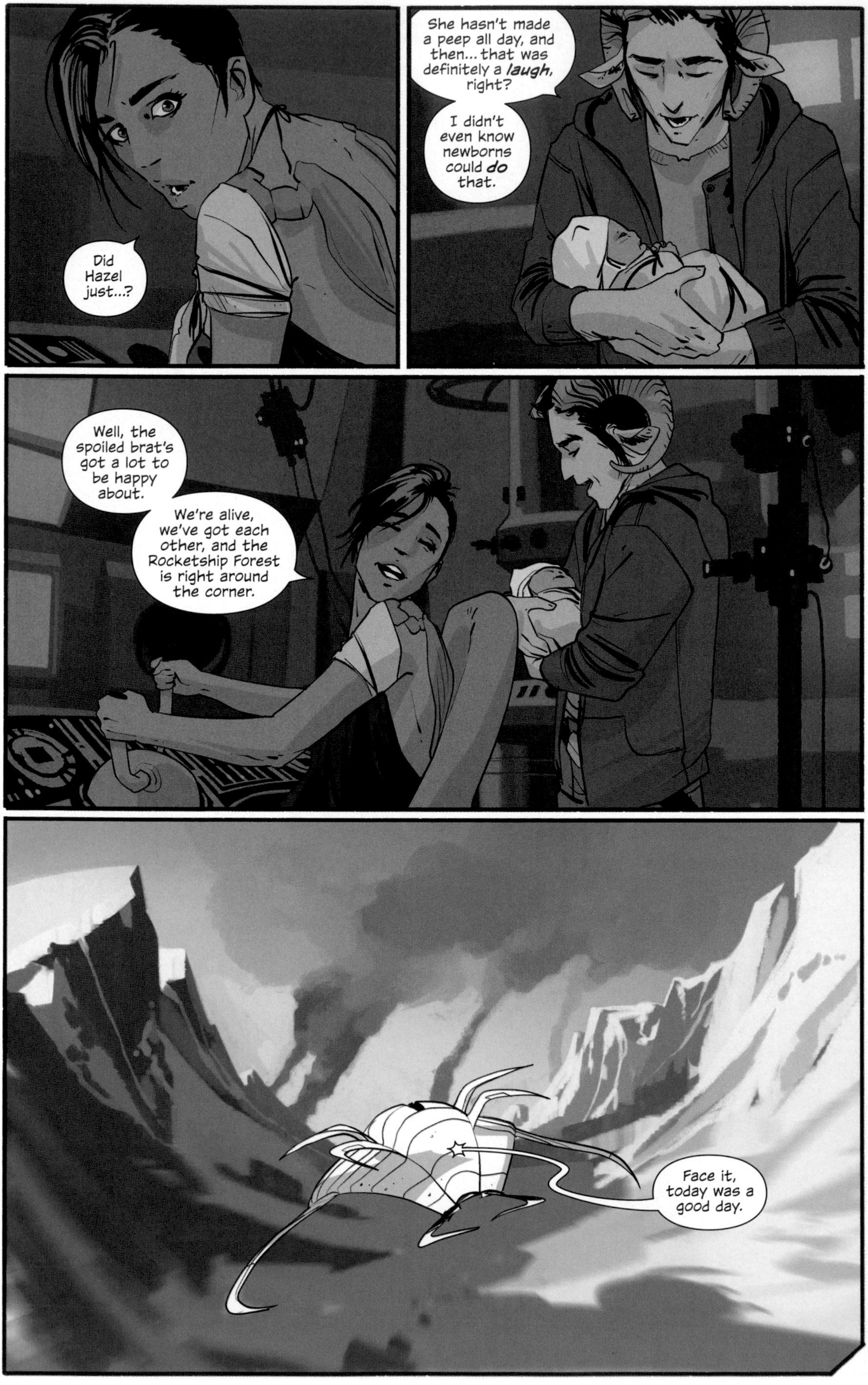
Did Hazel just...?
She hasn't made a peep all day, and then... that was definitely a *laugh*, right?
I didn't even know newborns could *do* that.
Well, the spoiled brat's got a lot to be happy about.
We're alive, we've got each other, and the Rocketship Forest is right around the corner.
Face it, today was a good day.

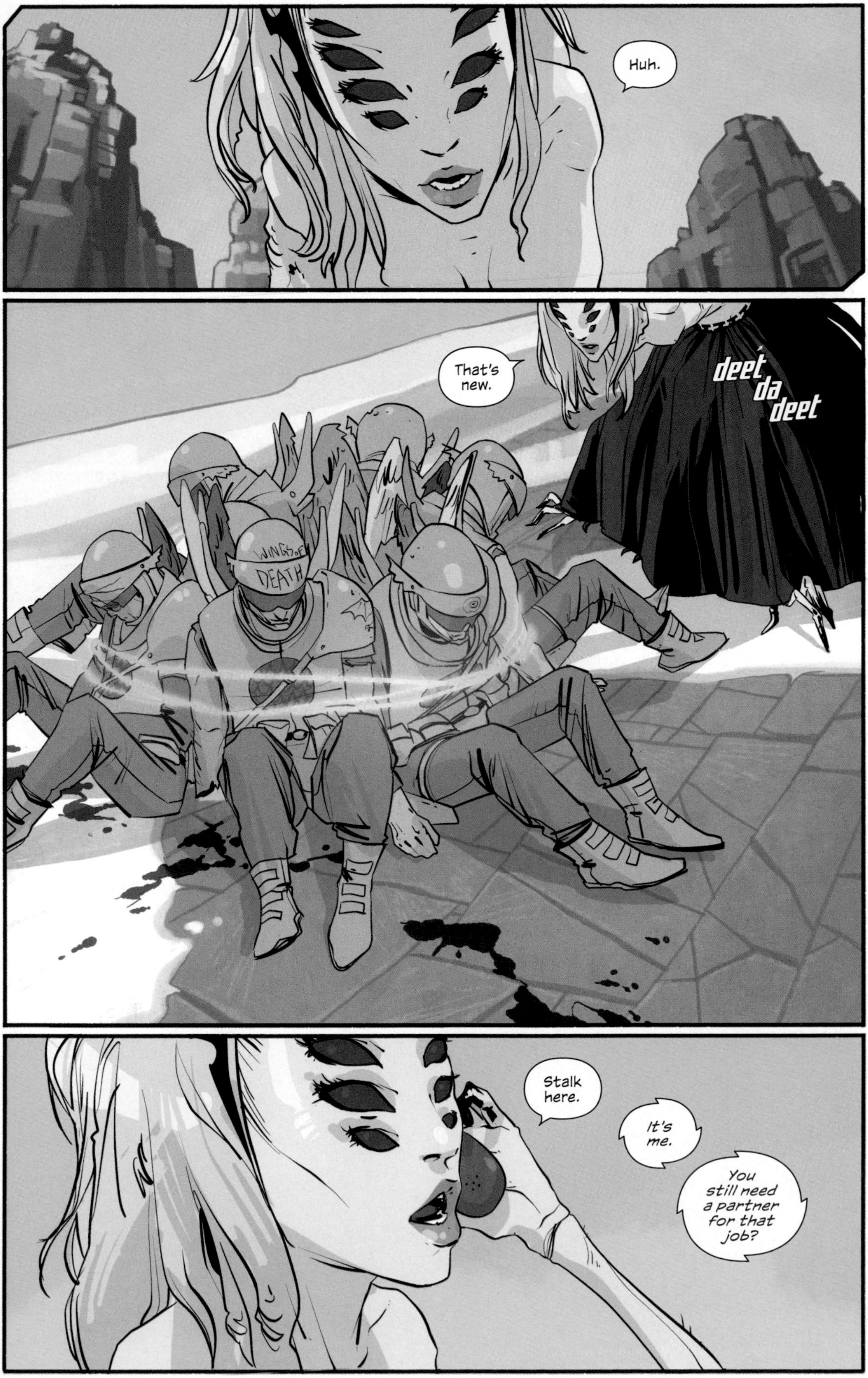
Huh.
That's new.
deet da deet
WINGS OF DEATH
Stalk here.
It's me.
You still need a partner for that job?

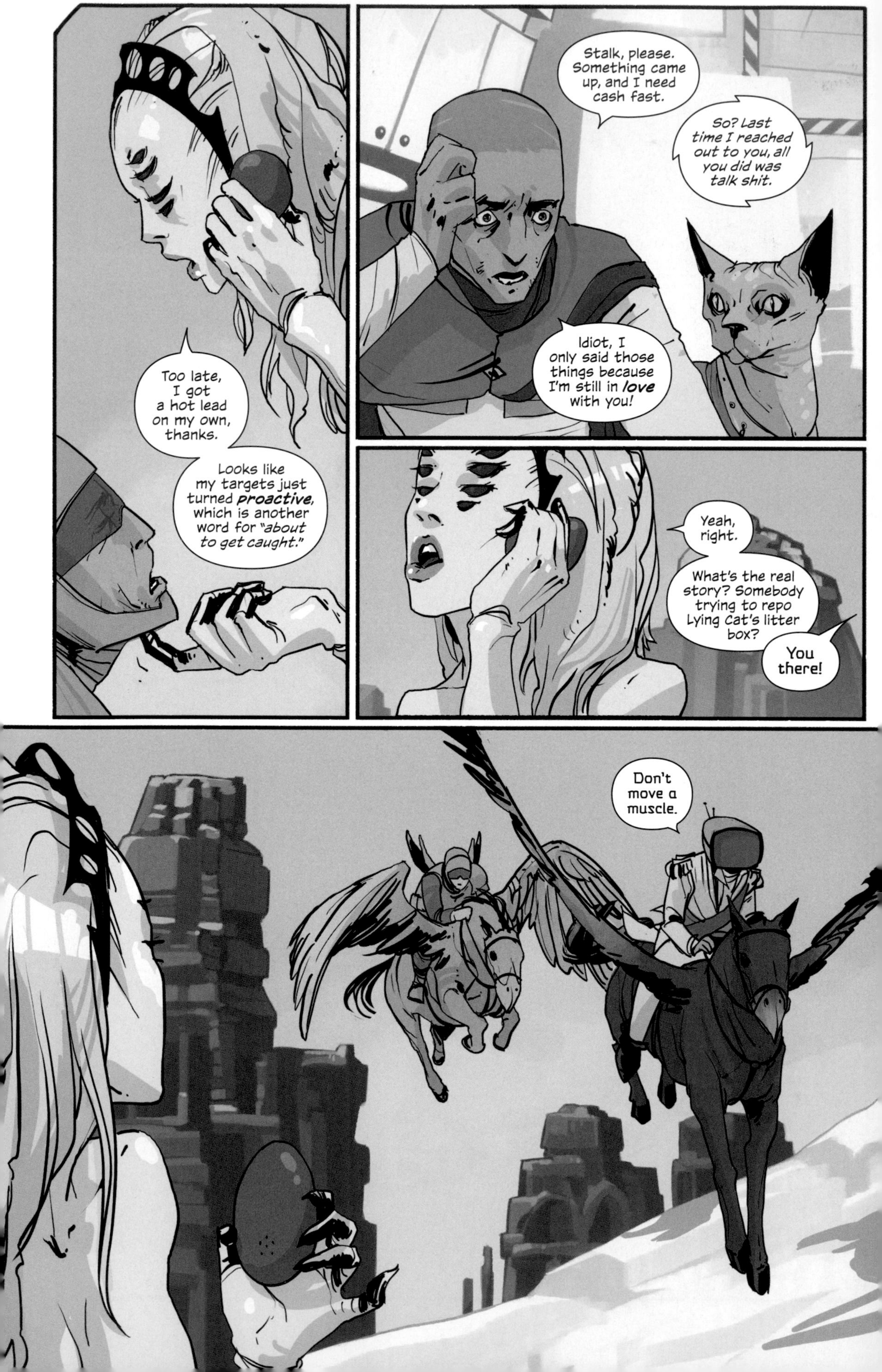
Stalk, please. Something came up, and I need cash fast.
So? Last time I reached out to you, all you did was talk shit.
Idiot, I only said those things because I'm still in *love* with you!
Too late, I got a hot lead on my own, thanks.
Looks like my targets just turned **proactive**, which is another word for "*about to get caught.*"
Yeah, right.
What's the real story? Somebody trying to repo Lying Cat's litter box?
You there!
Don't move a muscle.

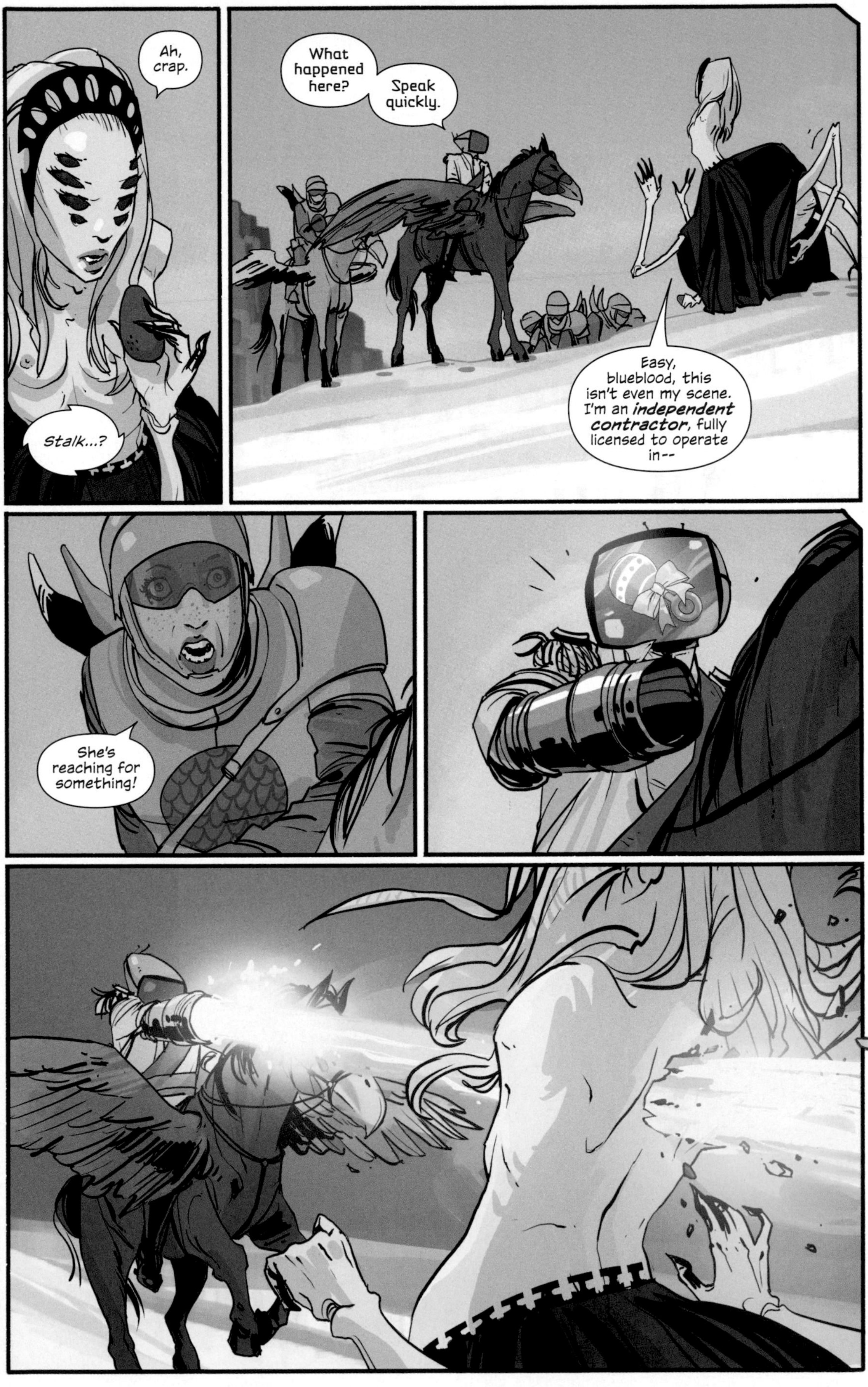

Ah, crap.
Stalk...?
What happened here?
Speak quickly.
Easy, blueblood, this isn't even my scene. I'm an ***independent contractor***, fully licensed to operate in--
She's reaching for something!

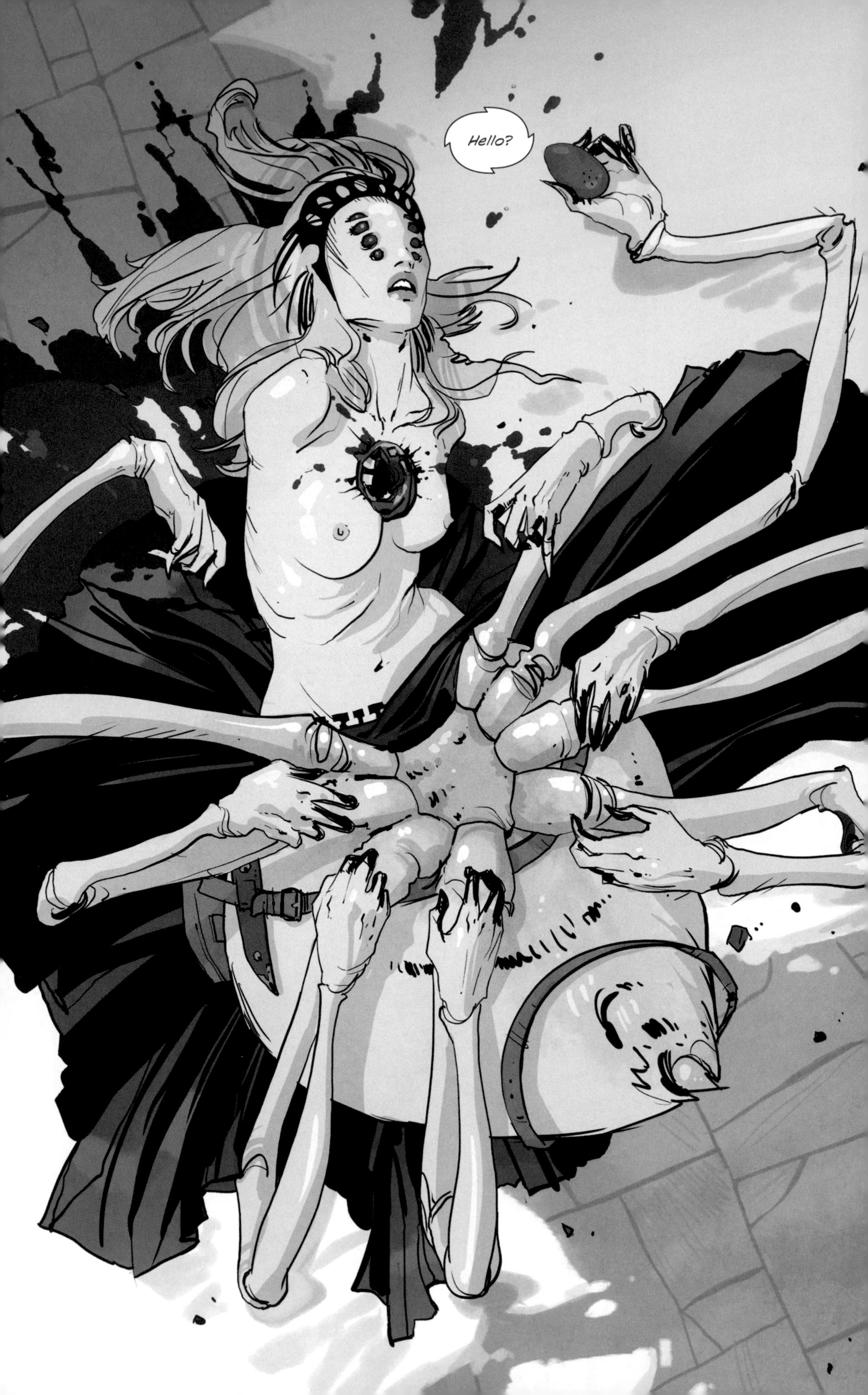
Hello?

end chapter five

CHAPTER
SIX

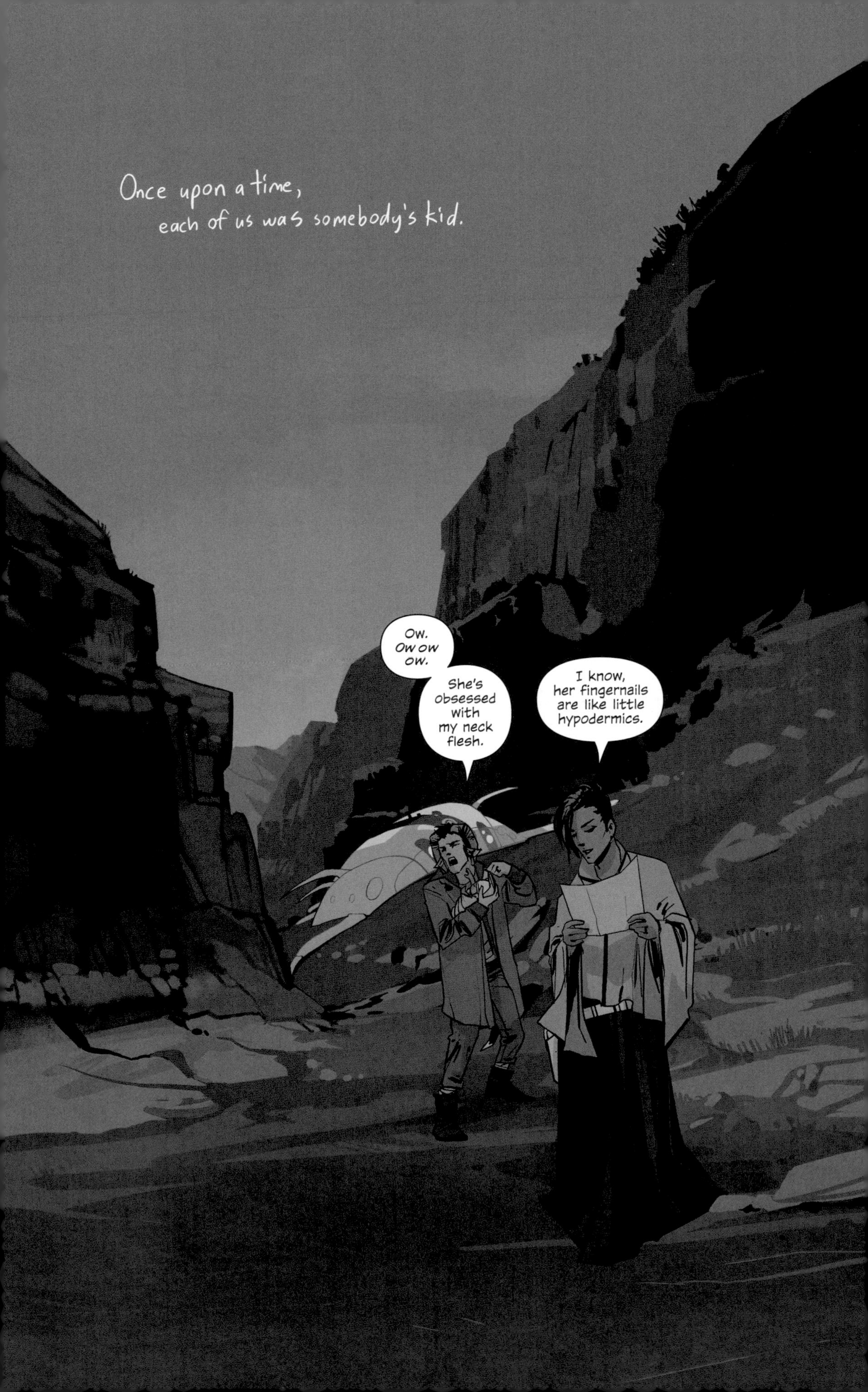
Once upon a time,
each of us was somebody's kid.
Ow. Ow ow ow.
She's obsessed with my neck flesh.
I know, her fingernails are like little hypodermics.

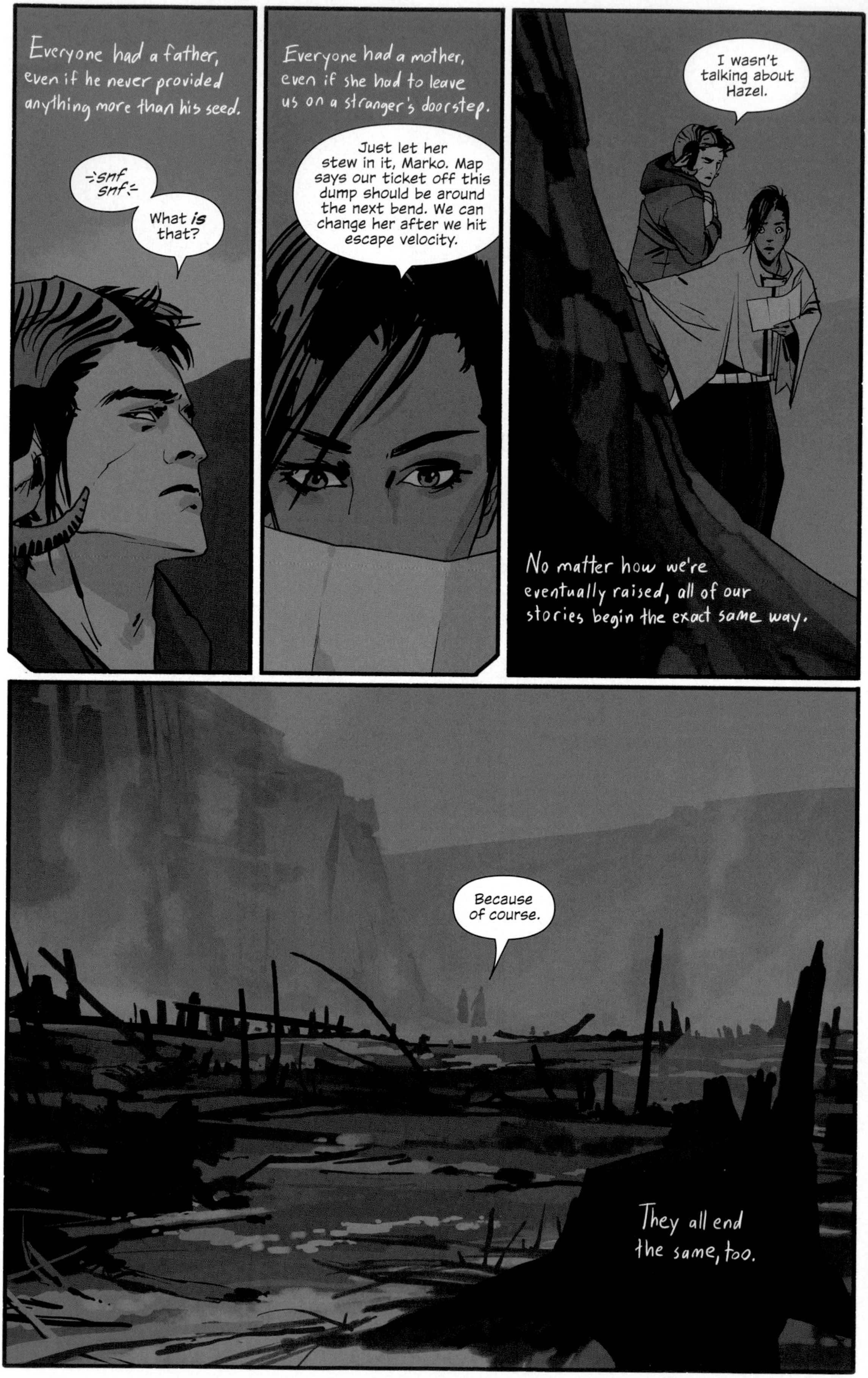
Everyone had a father, even if he never provided anything more than his seed.
=snf snf=
What *is* that?
Everyone had a mother, even if she had to leave us on a stranger's doorstep.
Just let her stew in it, Marko. Map says our ticket off this dump should be around the next bend. We can change her after we hit escape velocity.
I wasn't talking about Hazel.
No matter how we're eventually raised, all of our stories begin the exact same way.
Because of course.
They all end the same, too.

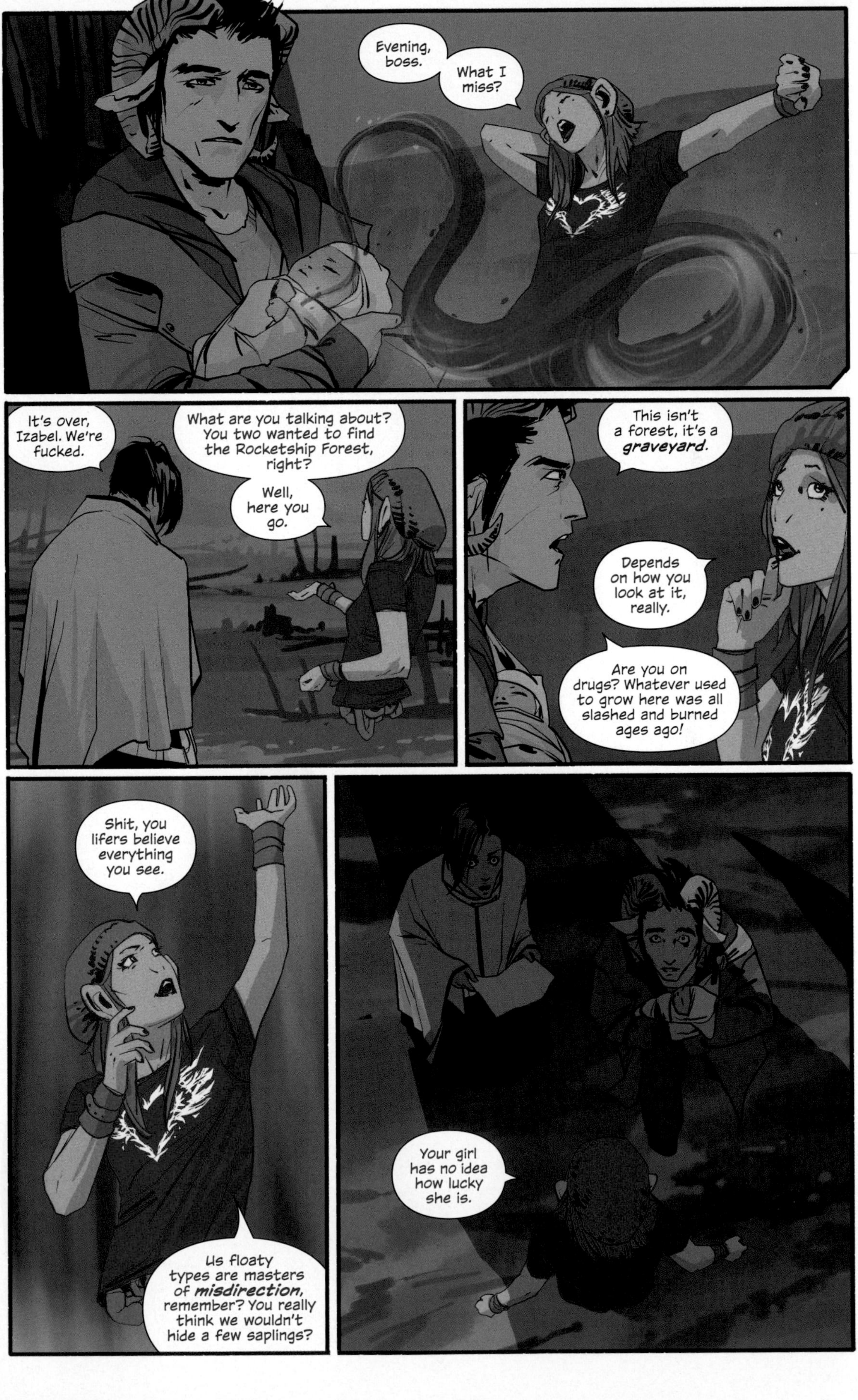
Evening, boss.
What I miss?
It's over, Izabel. We're fucked.
What are you talking about? You two wanted to find the Rocketship Forest, right?
Well, here you go.
This isn't a forest, it's a ***graveyard***.
Depends on how you look at it, really.
Are you on drugs? Whatever used to grow here was all slashed and burned ages ago!
Shit, you lifers believe everything you see.
Us floaty types are masters of ***misdirection***, remember? You really think we wouldn't hide a few saplings?
Your girl has no idea how lucky she is.

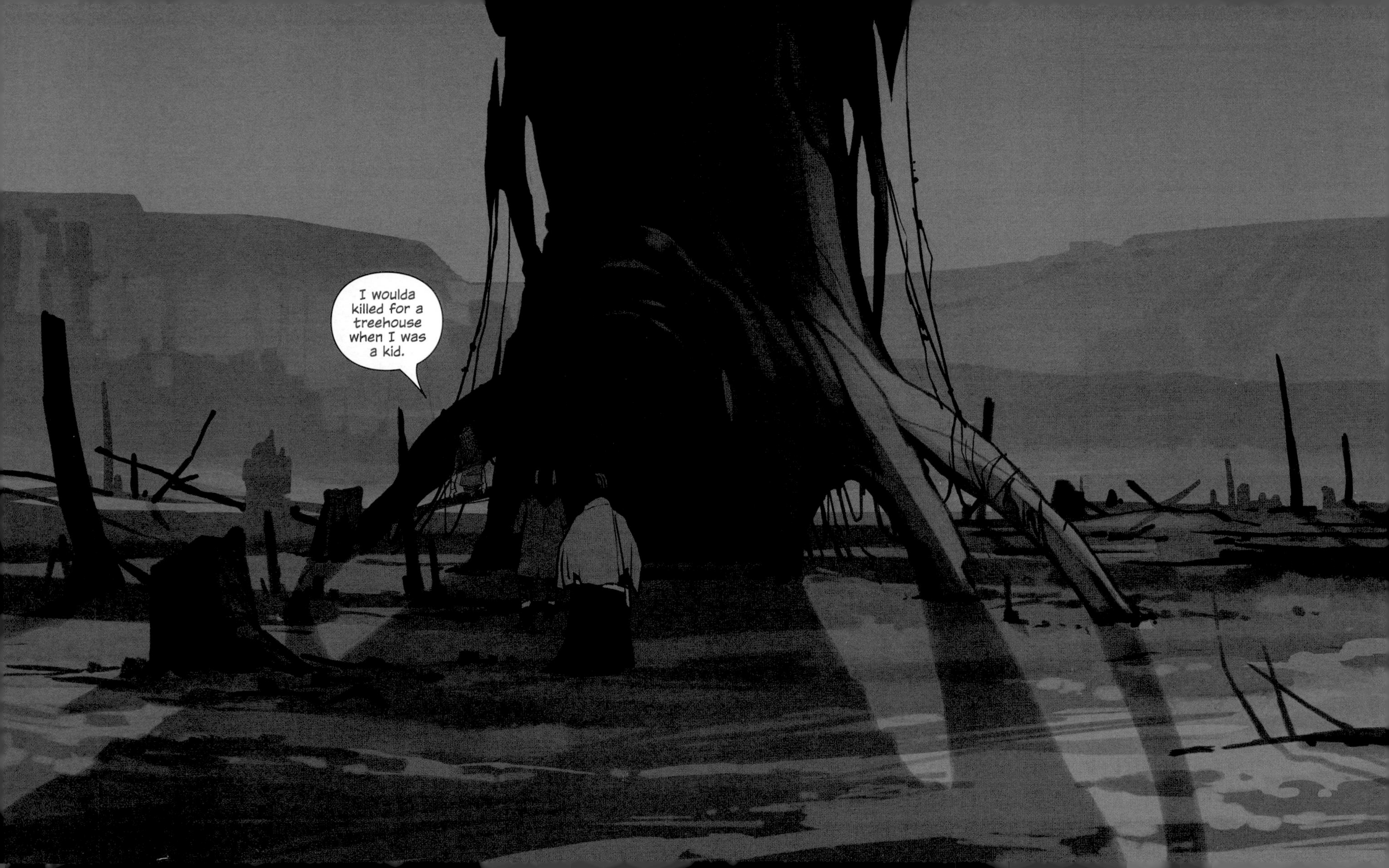
I woulda killed for a treehouse when I was a kid.

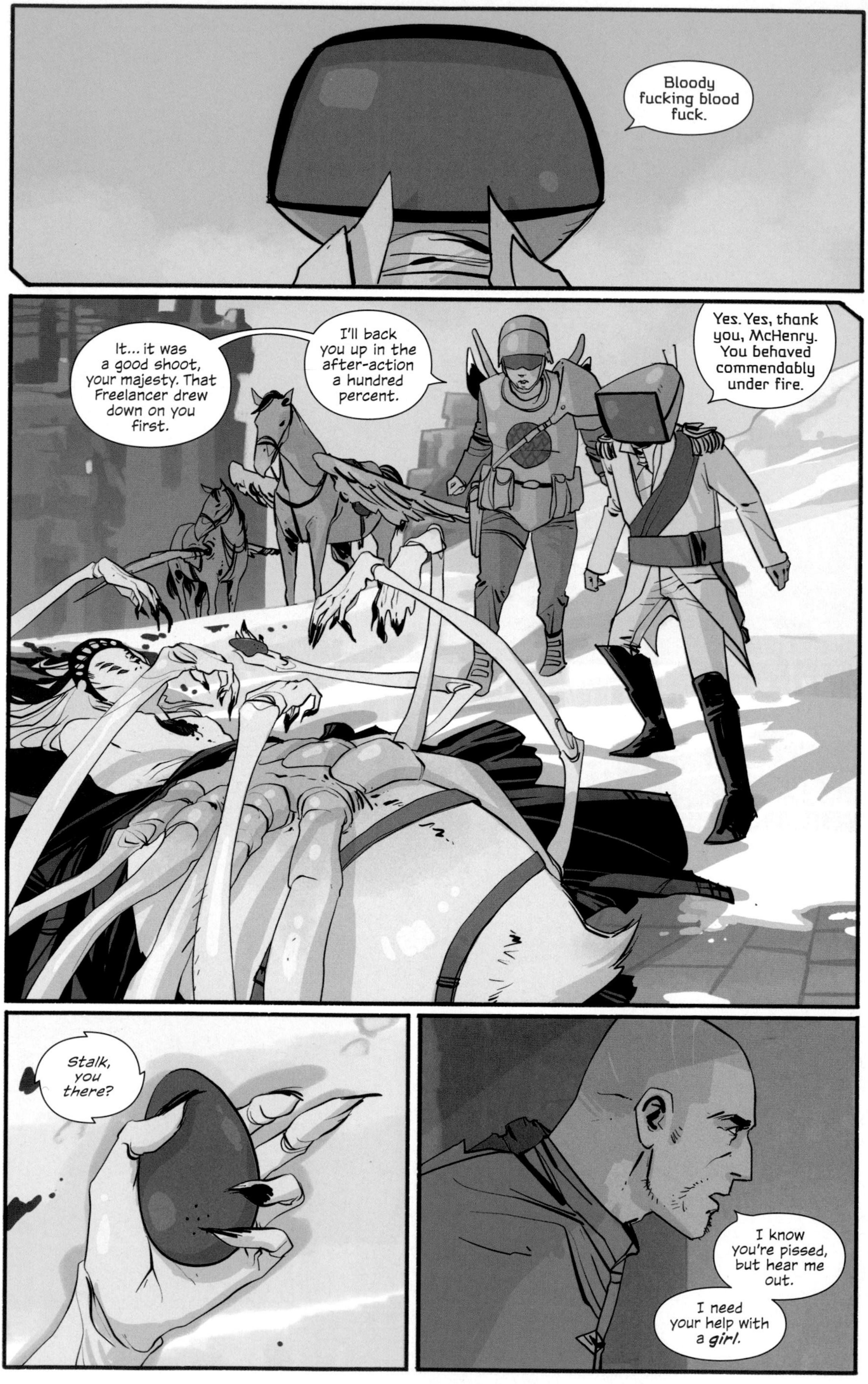
Bloody fucking blood fuck.
It... it was a good shoot, your majesty. That Freelancer drew down on you first.
I'll back you up in the after-action a hundred percent.
Yes. Yes, thank you, McHenry. You behaved commendably under fire.
Stalk, you there?
I know you're pissed, but hear me out.
I need your help with a girl.

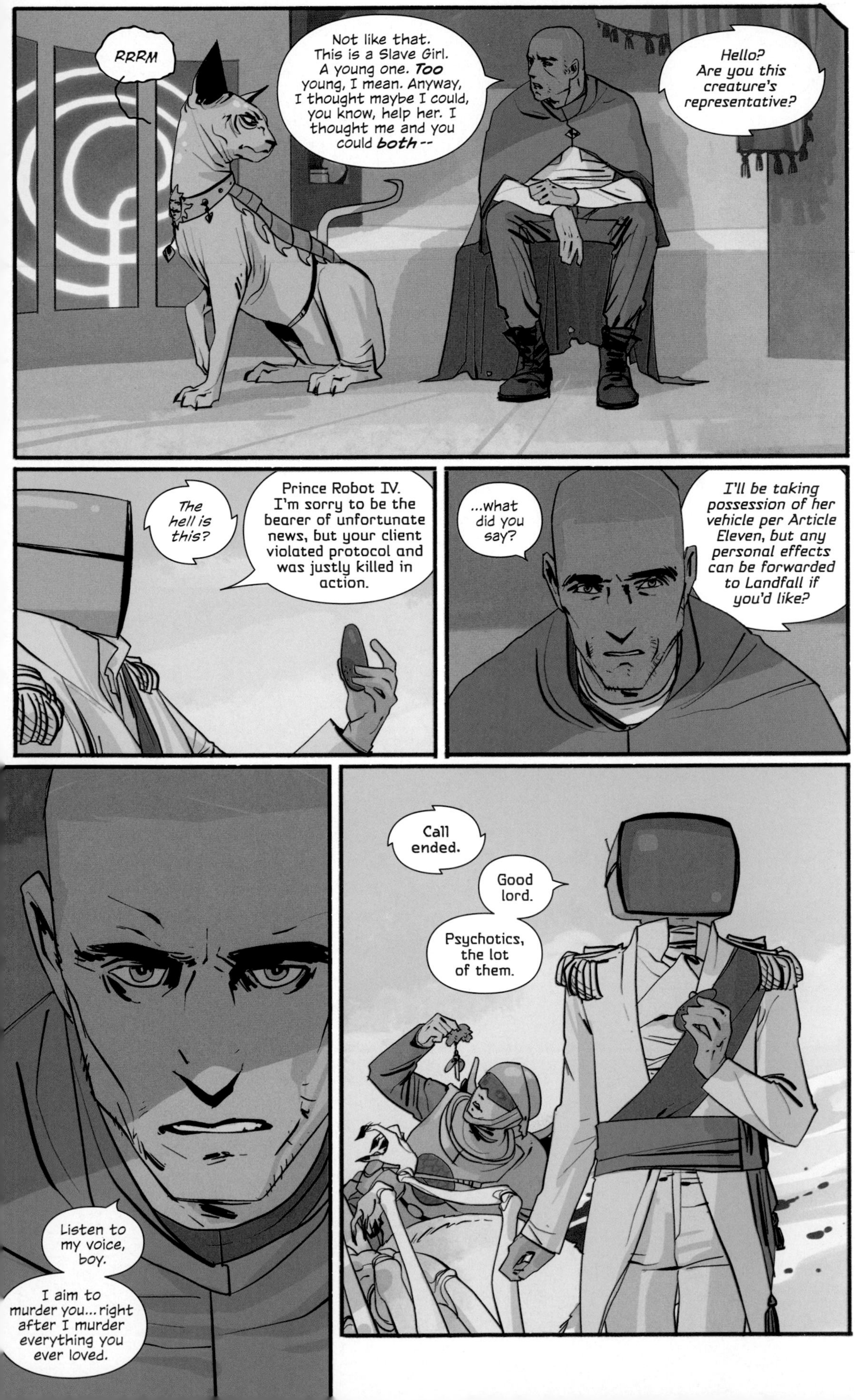
RRRM
Not like that. This is a Slave Girl. A young one. Too young, I mean. Anyway, I thought maybe I could, you know, help her. I thought me and you could both--
Hello? Are you this creature's representative?
The hell is this?
Prince Robot IV. I'm sorry to be the bearer of unfortunate news, but your client violated protocol and was justly killed in action.
...what did you say?
I'll be taking possession of her vehicle per Article Eleven, but any personal effects can be forwarded to Landfall if you'd like?
Listen to my voice, boy.
I aim to murder you... right after I murder everything you ever loved.
Call ended.
Good lord.
Psychotics, the lot of them.

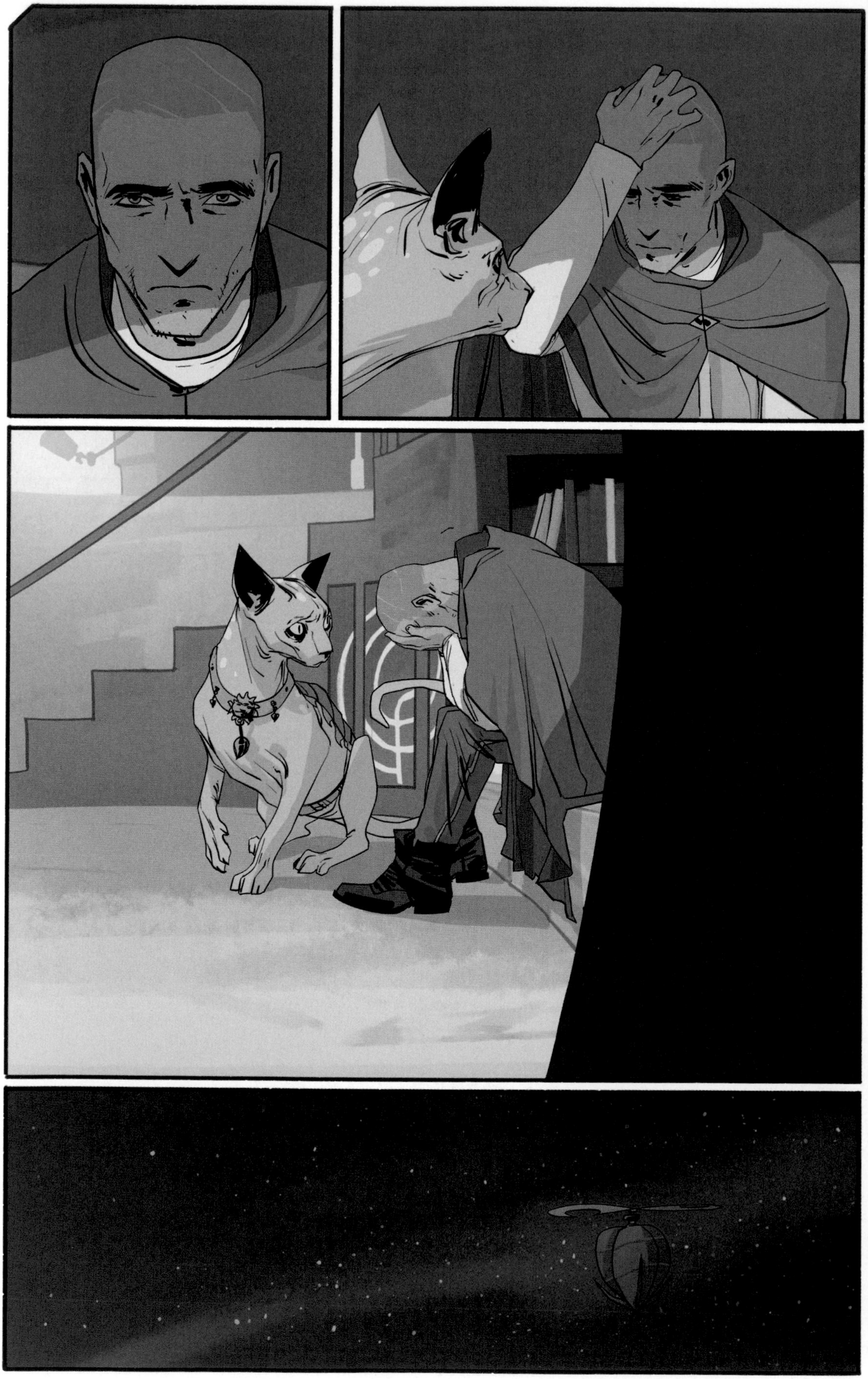

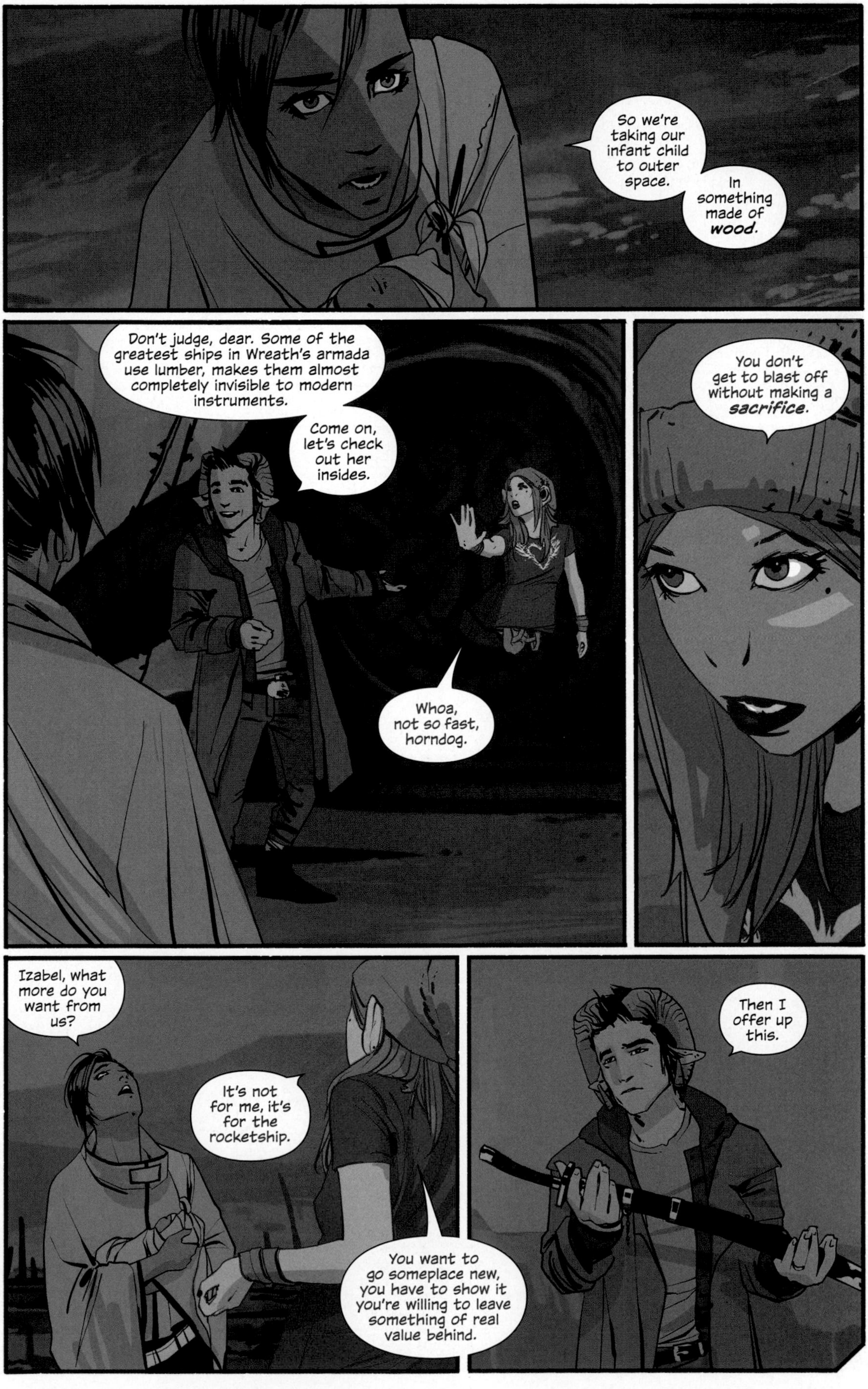
So we're taking our infant child to outer space.
In something made of *wood*.
Don't judge, dear. Some of the greatest ships in Wreath's armada use lumber, makes them almost completely invisible to modern instruments.
Come on, let's check out her insides.
Whoa, not so fast, horndog.
You don't get to blast off without making a *sacrifice*.
Izabel, what more do you want from us?
It's not for me, it's for the rocketship.
You want to go someplace new, you have to show it you're willing to leave something of real value behind.
Then I offer up this.

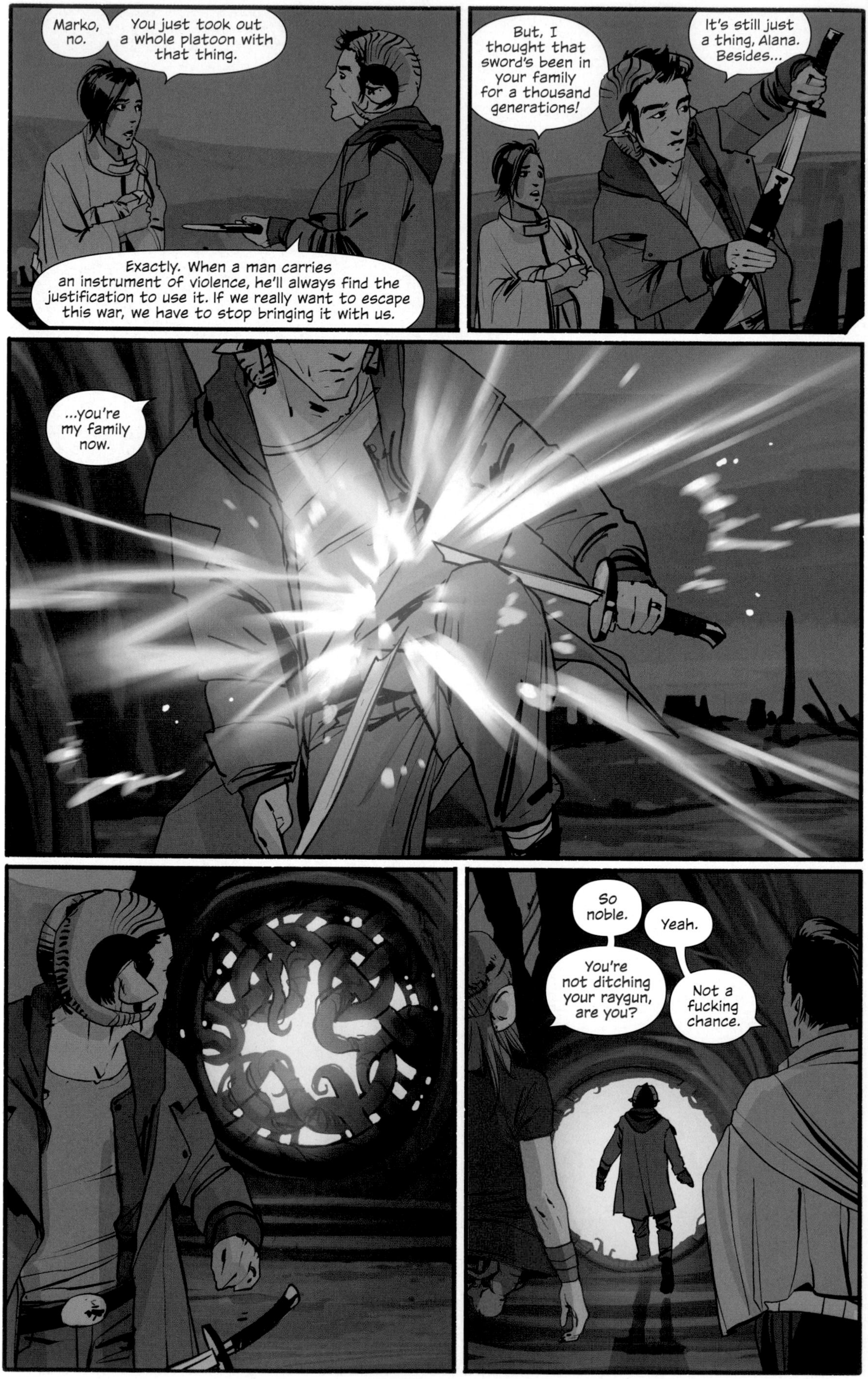
Marko, no.
You just took out a whole platoon with that thing.
Exactly. When a man carries an instrument of violence, he'll always find the justification to use it. If we really want to escape this war, we have to stop bringing it with us.
But, I thought that sword's been in your family for a thousand generations!
It's still just a thing, Alana. Besides...
...you're my family now.
So noble.
You're not ditching your raygun, are you?
Yeah.
Not a fucking chance.

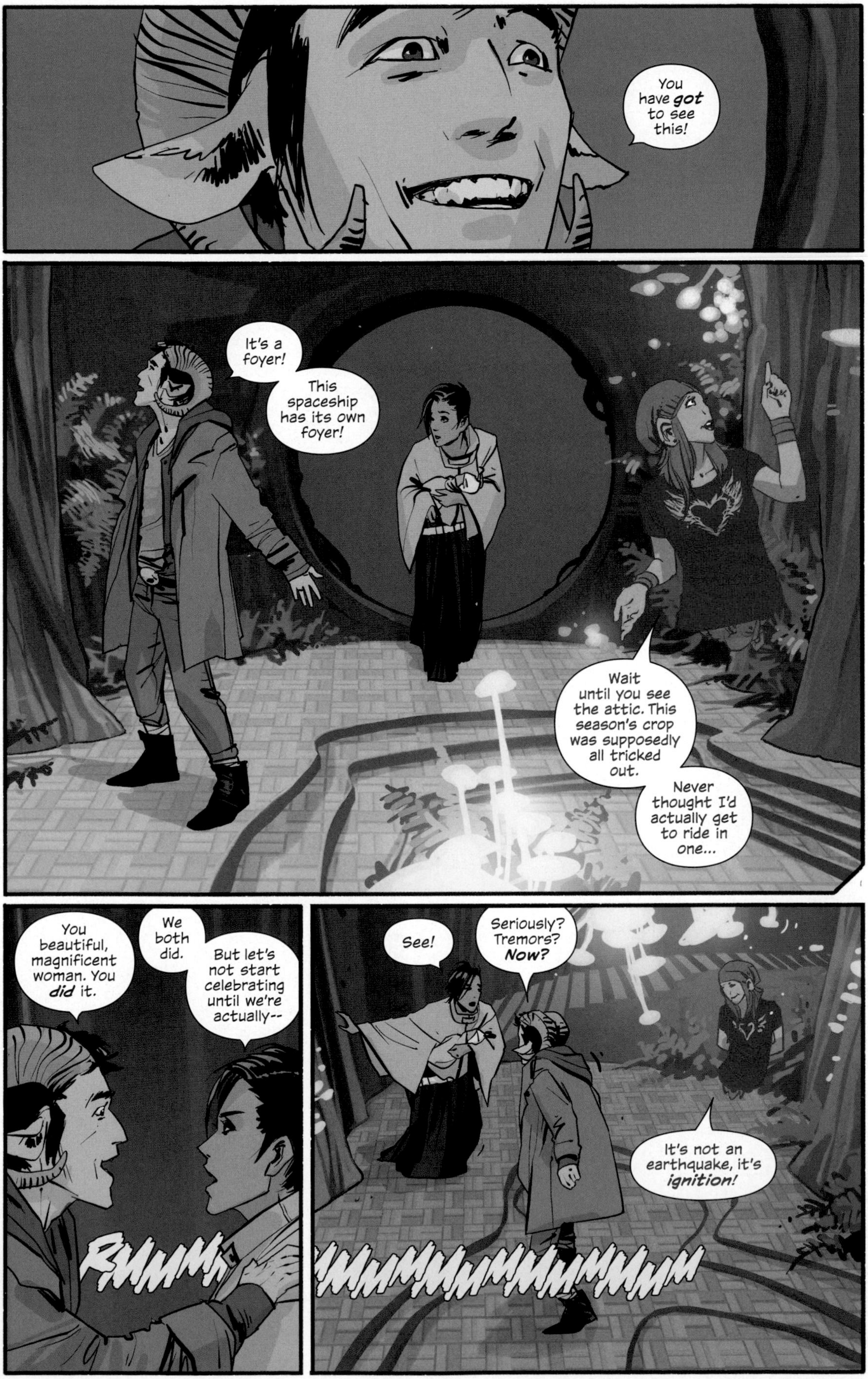
You have *got* to see this!
It's a foyer!
This spaceship has its own foyer!
Wait until you see the attic. This season's crop was supposedly all tricked out.
Never thought I'd actually get to ride in one...
You beautiful, magnificent woman. You *did* it.
We both did.
But let's not start celebrating until we're actually--
See!
Seriously? Tremors? *Now?*
It's not an earthquake, it's *ignition!*
RUMMMMMMMMMMMMMMMMMMMMMMM

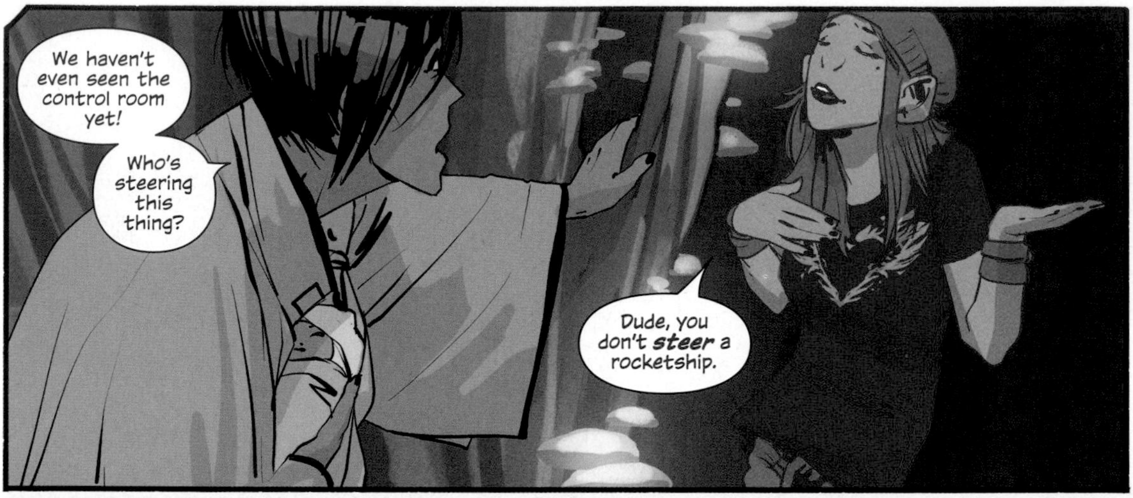
We haven't even seen the control room yet!
Who's steering this thing?
Dude, you don't **steer** a rocketship.
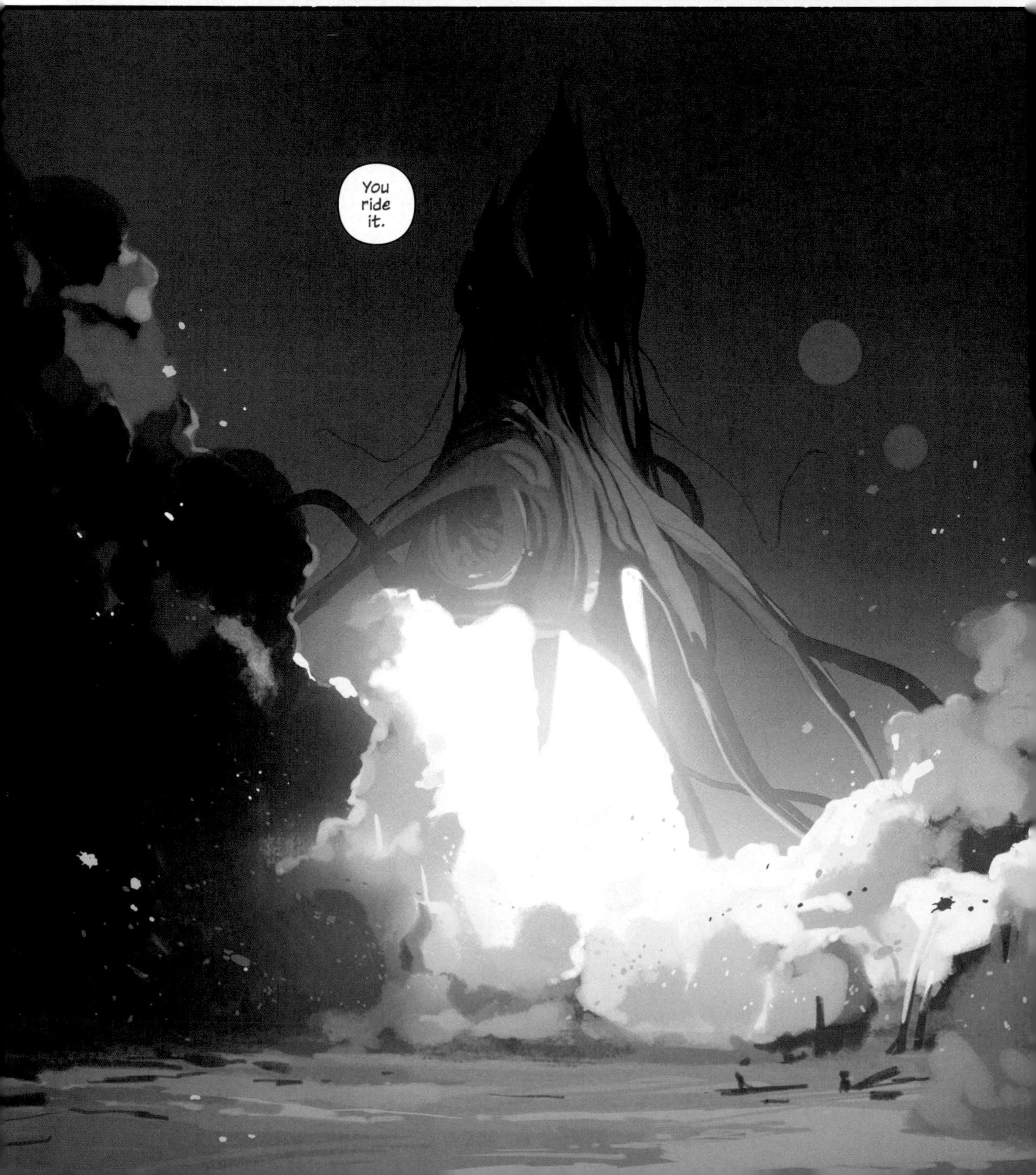
You ride it.

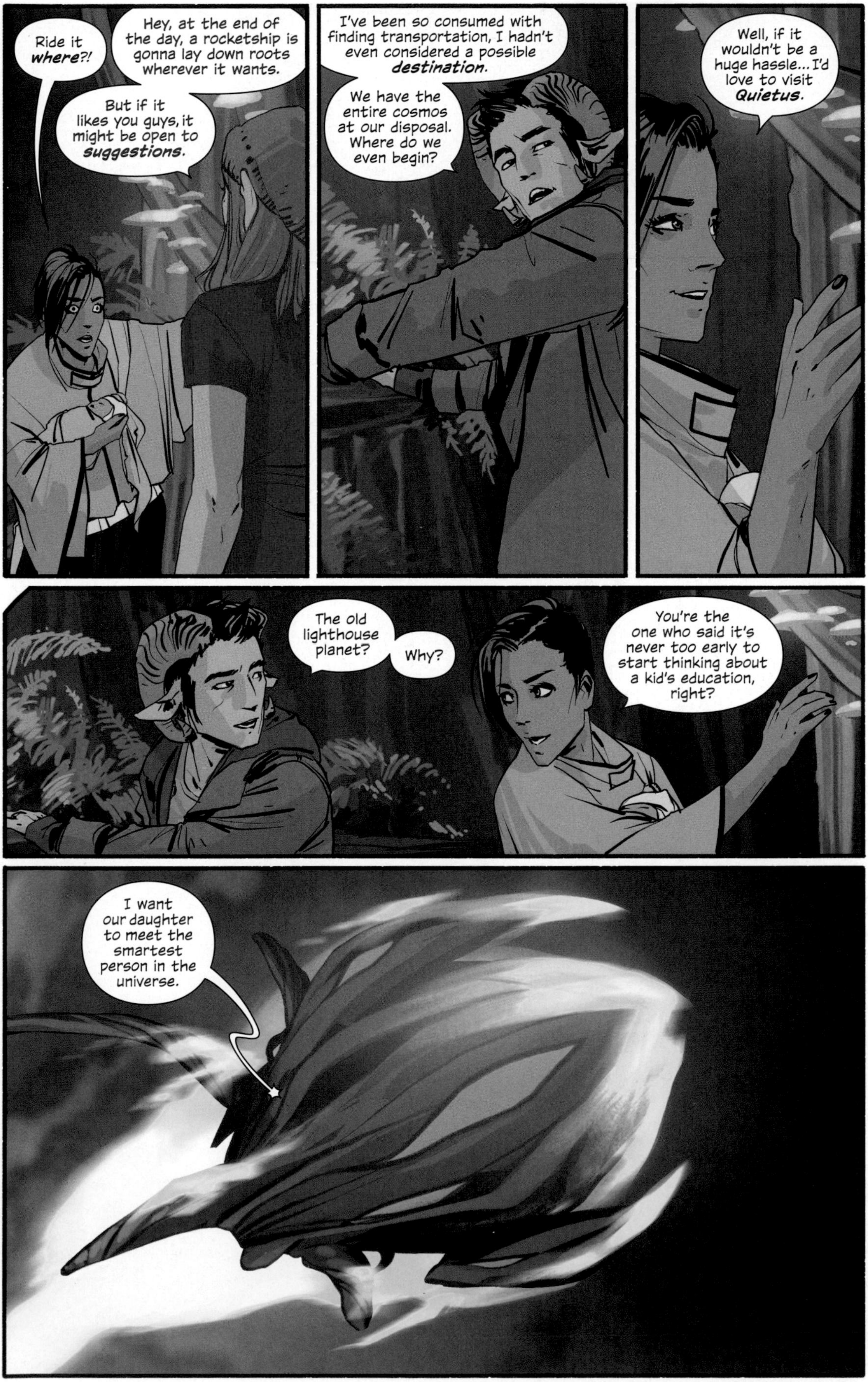
Ride it *where*?!
Hey, at the end of the day, a rocketship is gonna lay down roots wherever it wants.
But if it likes you guys, it might be open to *suggestions*.
I've been so consumed with finding transportation, I hadn't even considered a possible *destination*.
We have the entire cosmos at our disposal. Where do we even begin?
Well, if it wouldn't be a huge hassle... I'd love to visit *Quietus*.
The old lighthouse planet?
Why?
You're the one who said it's never too early to start thinking about a kid's education, right?
I want our daughter to meet the smartest person in the universe.

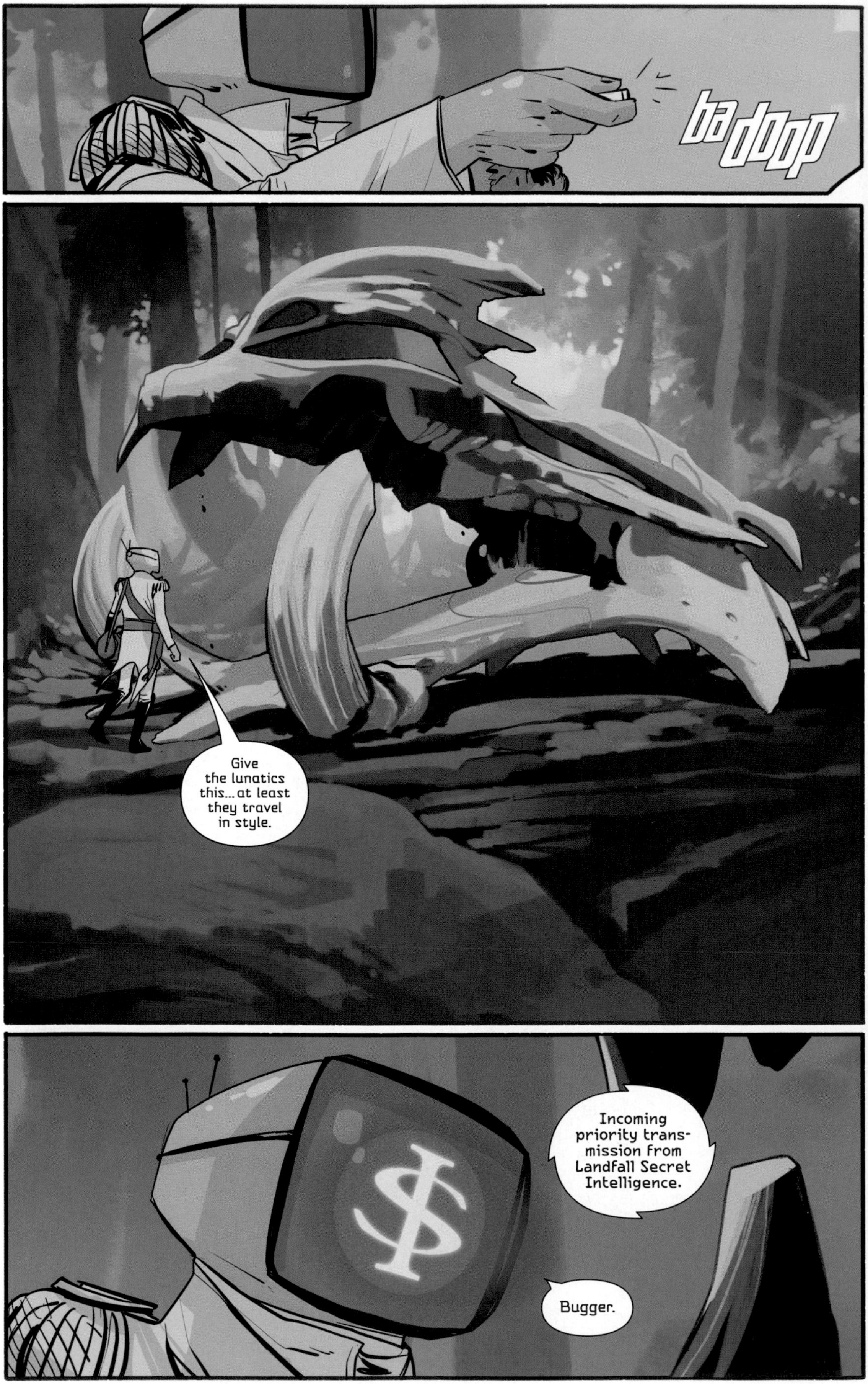
ba doop
Give the lunatics this... at least they travel in style.
Incoming priority transmission from Landfall Secret Intelligence.
Bugger.

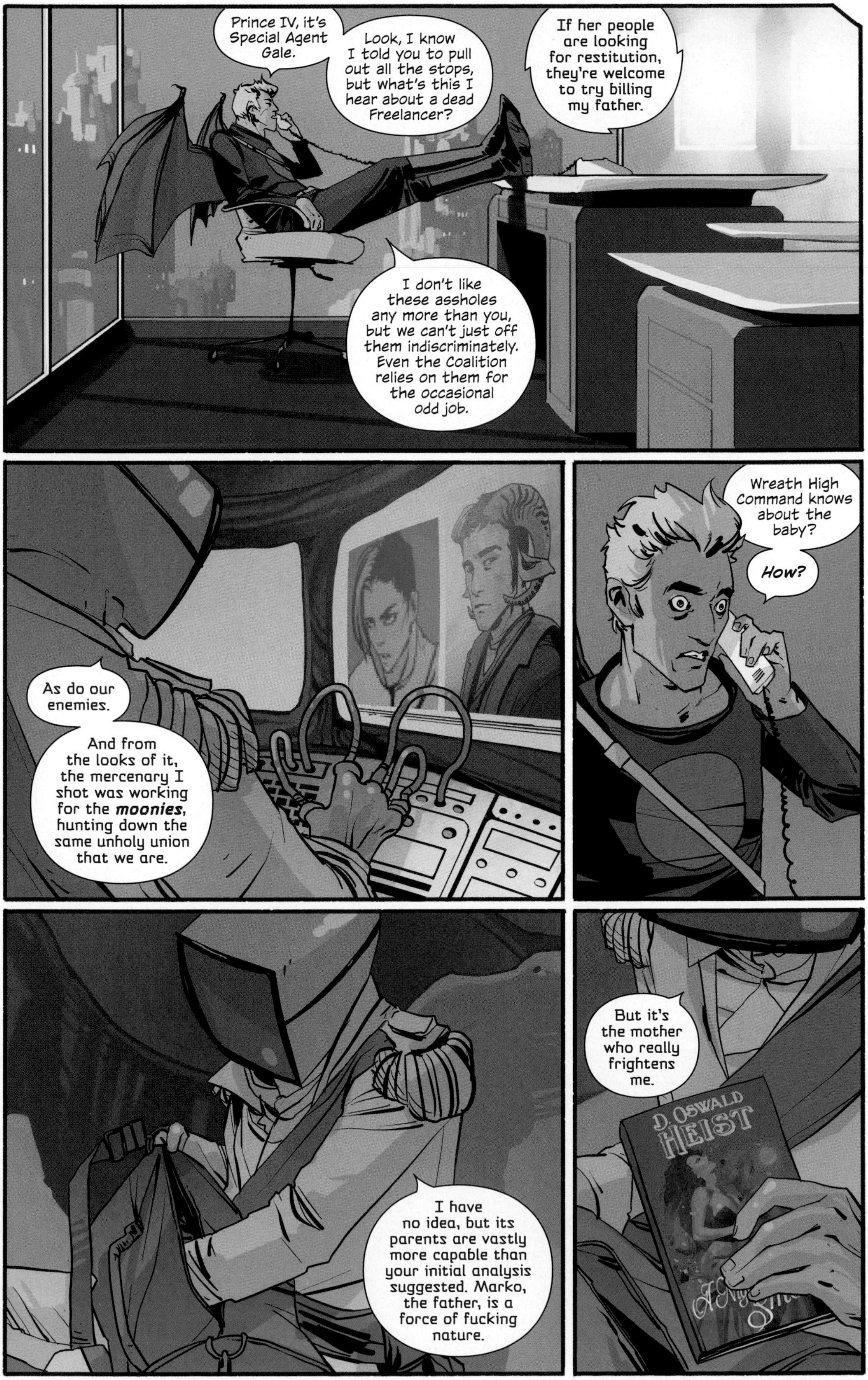
Prince IV, it's Special Agent Gale.
Look, I know I told you to pull out all the stops, but what's this I hear about a dead Freelancer?
If her people are looking for restitution, they're welcome to try billing my father.
I don't like these assholes any more than you, but we can't just off them indiscriminately. Even the Coalition relies on them for the occasional odd job.
As do our enemies.
And from the looks of it, the mercenary I shot was working for the *moonies*, hunting down the same unholy union that we are.
Wreath High Command knows about the baby?
How?
I have no idea, but its parents are vastly more capable than your initial analysis suggested. Marko, the father, is a force of fucking nature.
But it's the mother who really frightens me.
D. OSWALD
HEIST

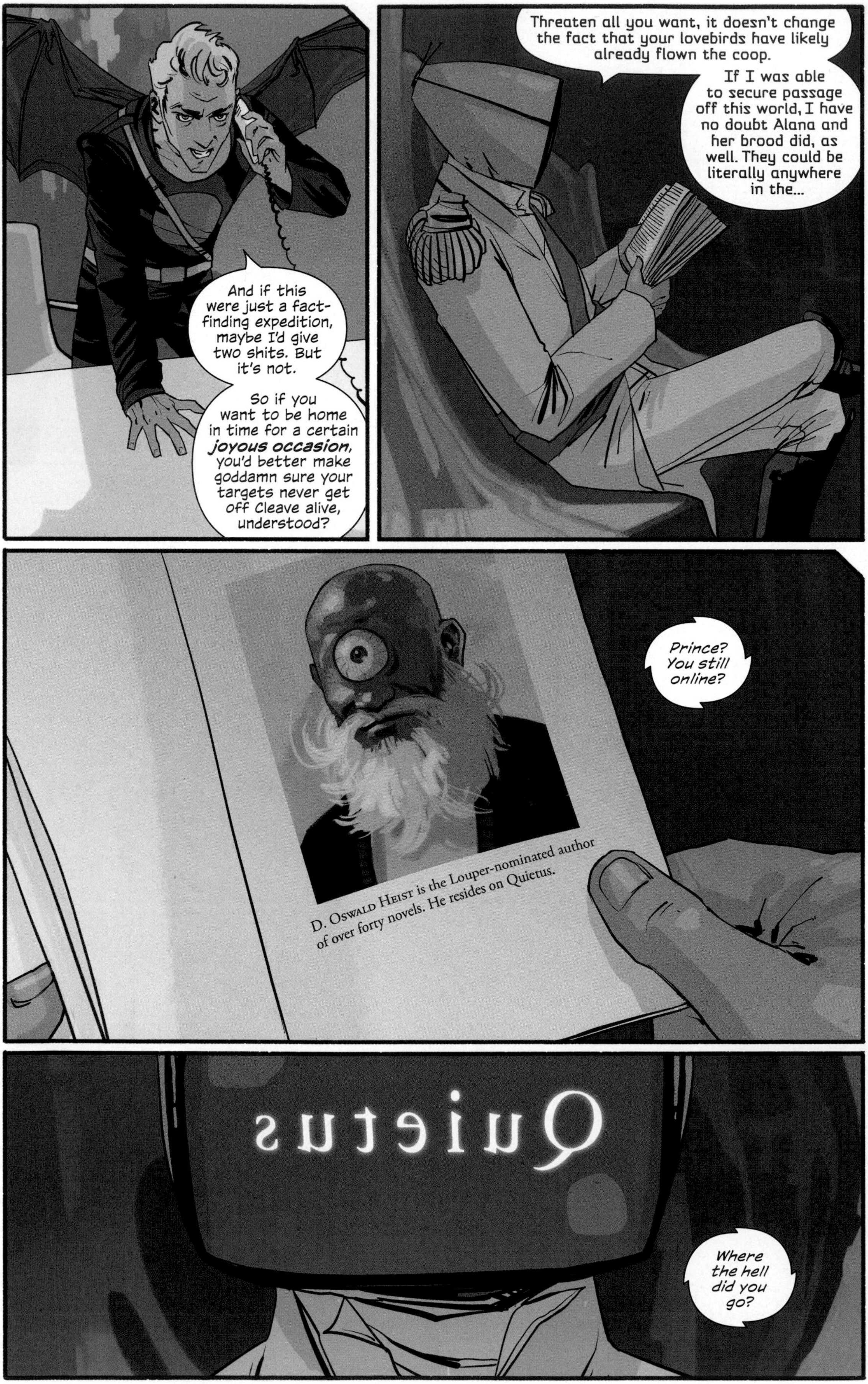
And if this were just a fact-finding expedition, maybe I'd give two shits. But it's not.
So if you want to be home in time for a certain *joyous occasion*, you'd better make goddamn sure your targets never get off Cleave alive, understood?
Threaten all you want, it doesn't change the fact that your lovebirds have likely already flown the coop.
If I was able to secure passage off this world, I have no doubt Alana and her brood did, as well. They could be literally anywhere in the...
D. Oswald Heist is the Louper-nominated author of over forty novels. He resides on Quietus.
Prince? You still online?
Where the hell did you go?

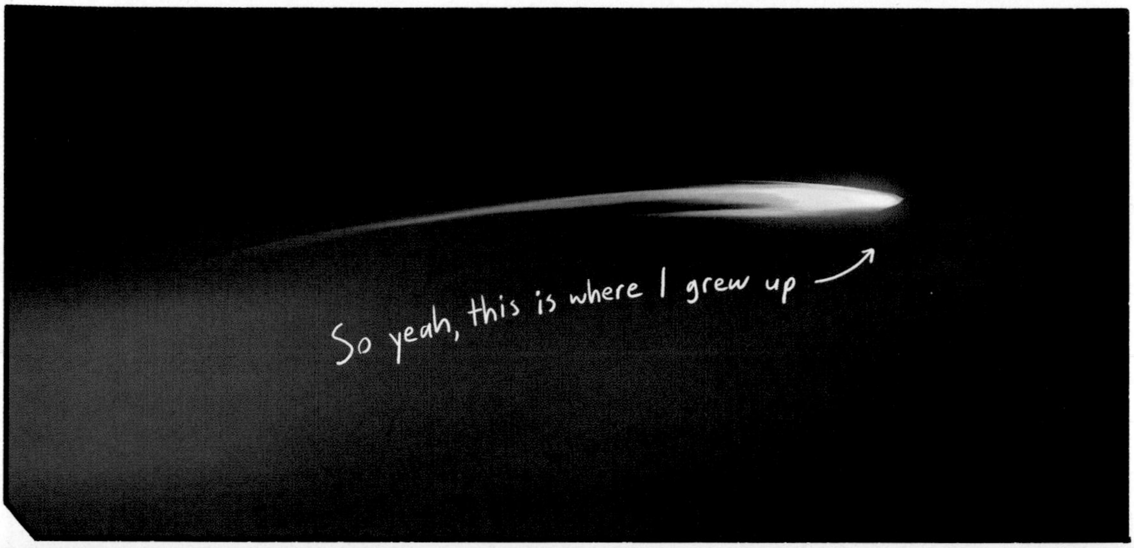
So yeah, this is where I grew up

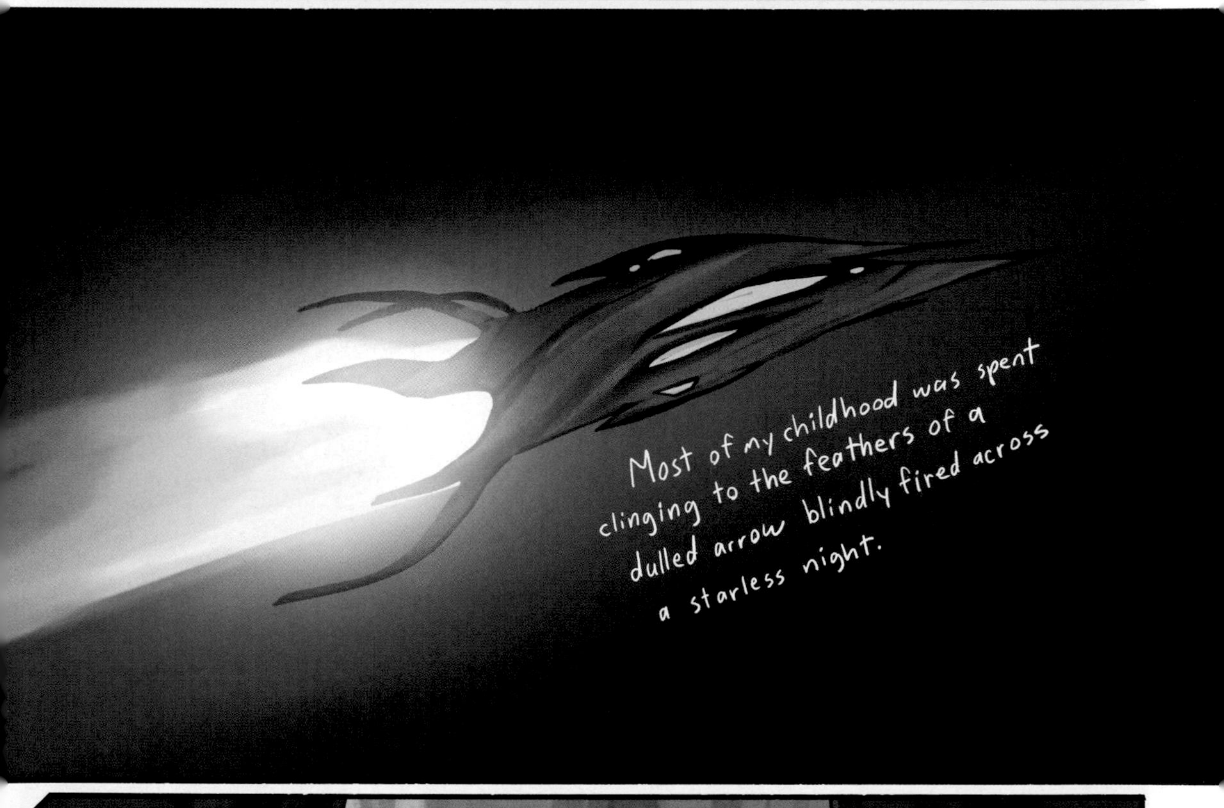
Most of my childhood was spent clinging to the feathers of a dulled arrow blindly fired across a starless night.

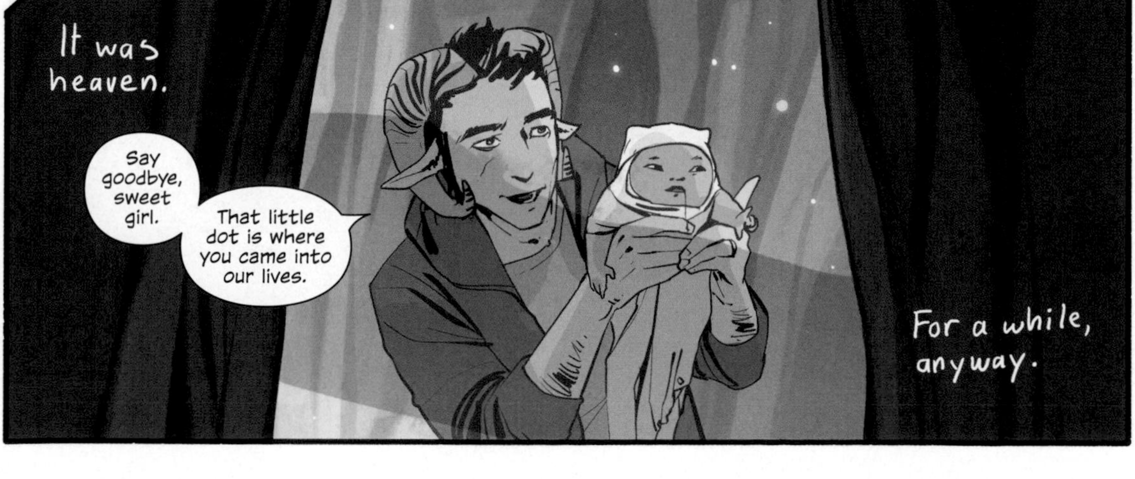
It was heaven.
Say goodbye, sweet girl.
That little dot is where you came into our lives.
For a while, anyway.

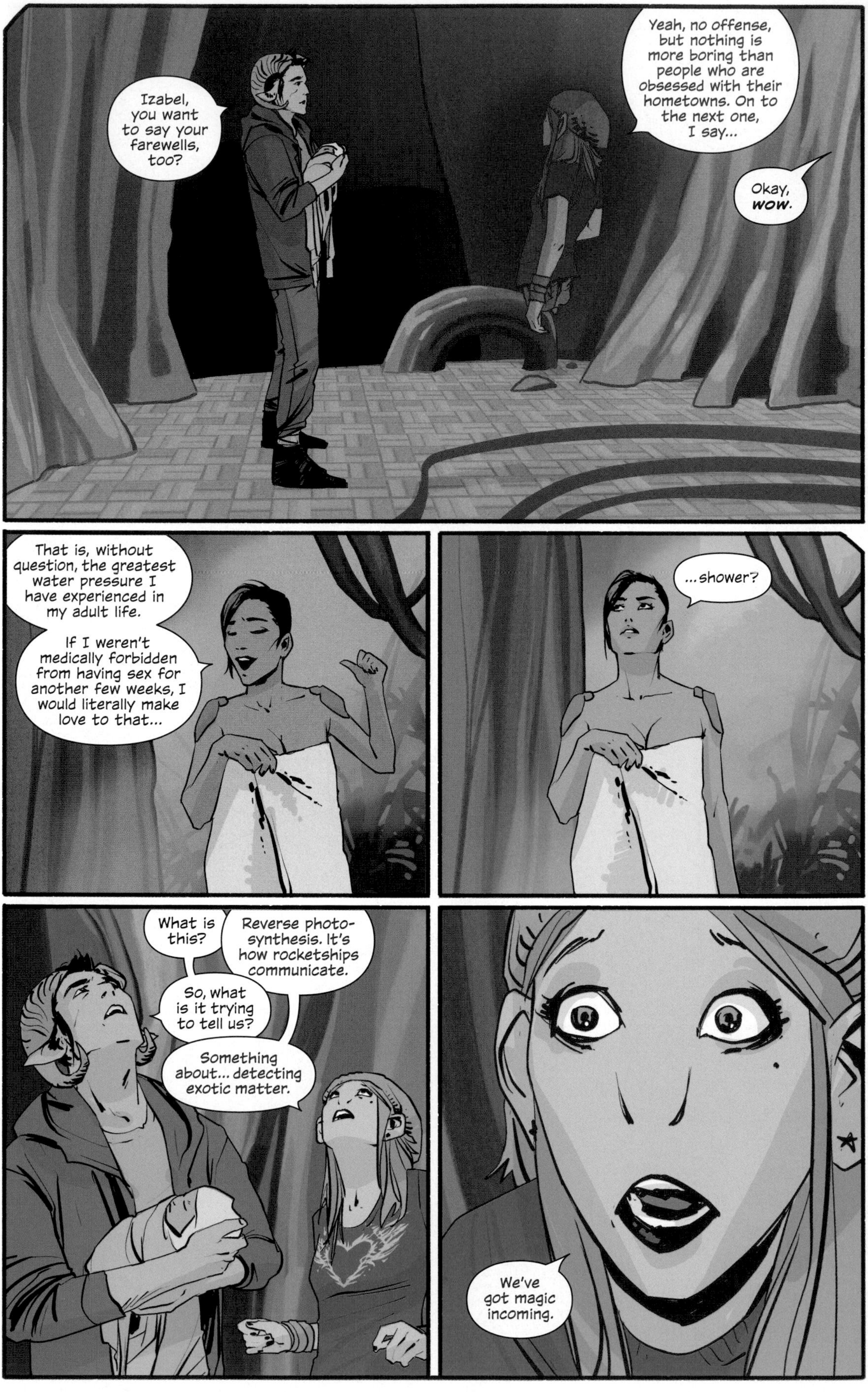
Izabel, you want to say your farewells, too?
Yeah, no offense, but nothing is more boring than people who are obsessed with their hometowns. On to the next one, I say...
Okay, *wow*.
That is, without question, the greatest water pressure I have experienced in my adult life.
If I weren't medically forbidden from having sex for another few weeks, I would literally make love to that...
...shower?
What is this?
Reverse photo-synthesis. It's how rocketships communicate.
So, what is it trying to tell us?
Something about... detecting exotic matter.
We've got magic incoming.

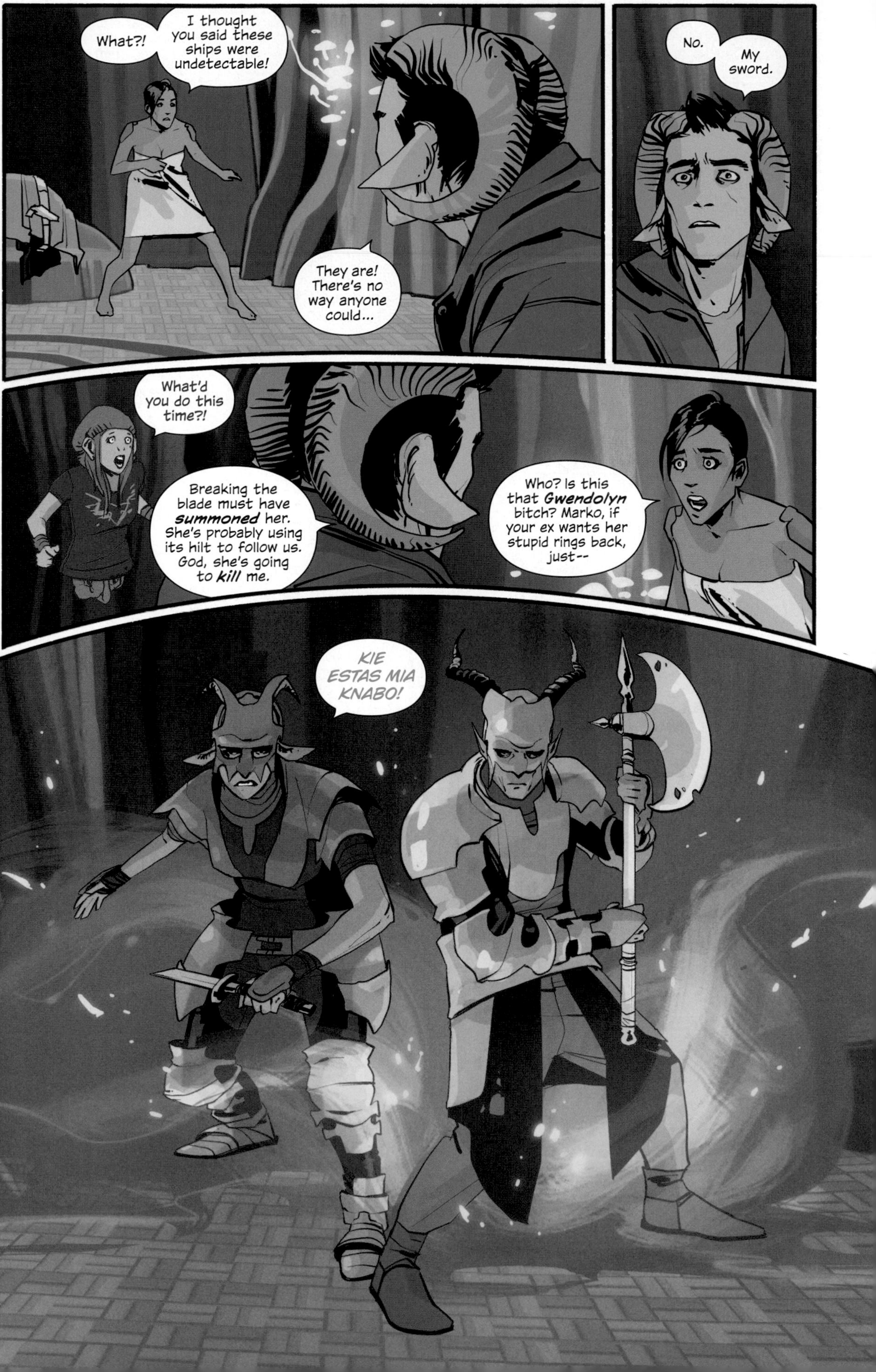
What?!
I thought you said these ships were undetectable!
They are! There's no way anyone could...
No.
My sword.
What'd you do this time?!
Breaking the blade must have **summoned** her. She's probably using its hilt to follow us. God, she's going to **kill** me.
Who? Is this that **Gwendolyn** bitch? Marko, if your ex wants her stupid rings back, just--
KIE ESTAS MIA KNABO!

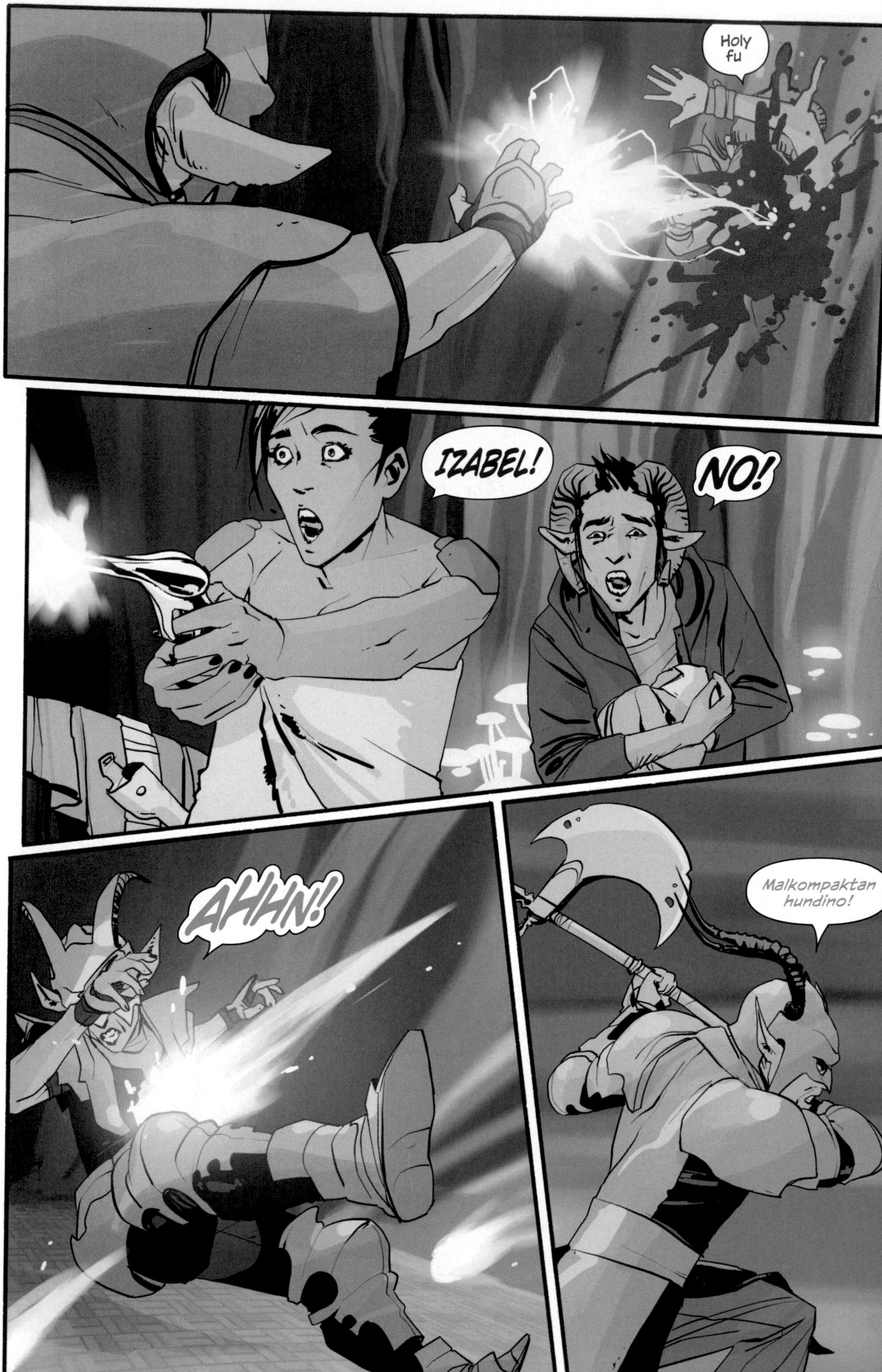
Holy fu
IZABEL!
NO!
AHHN!
Malkompaktan hundino!

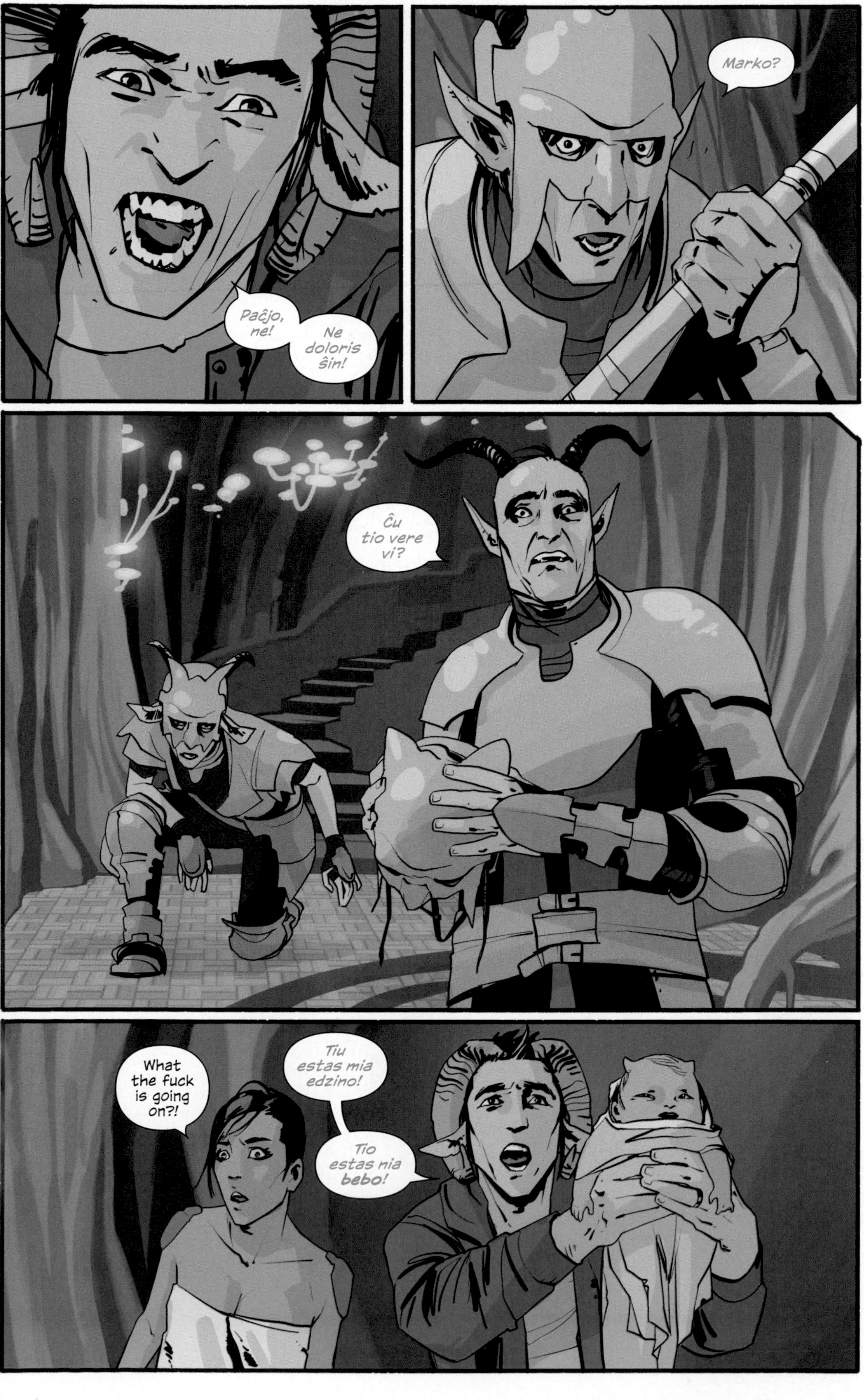

Paĉjo, ne!
Ne doloris ŝin!
Marko?
Ĉu tio vere vi?
What the fuck is going on?!
Tiu estas mia edzino!
Tio estas nia bebo!

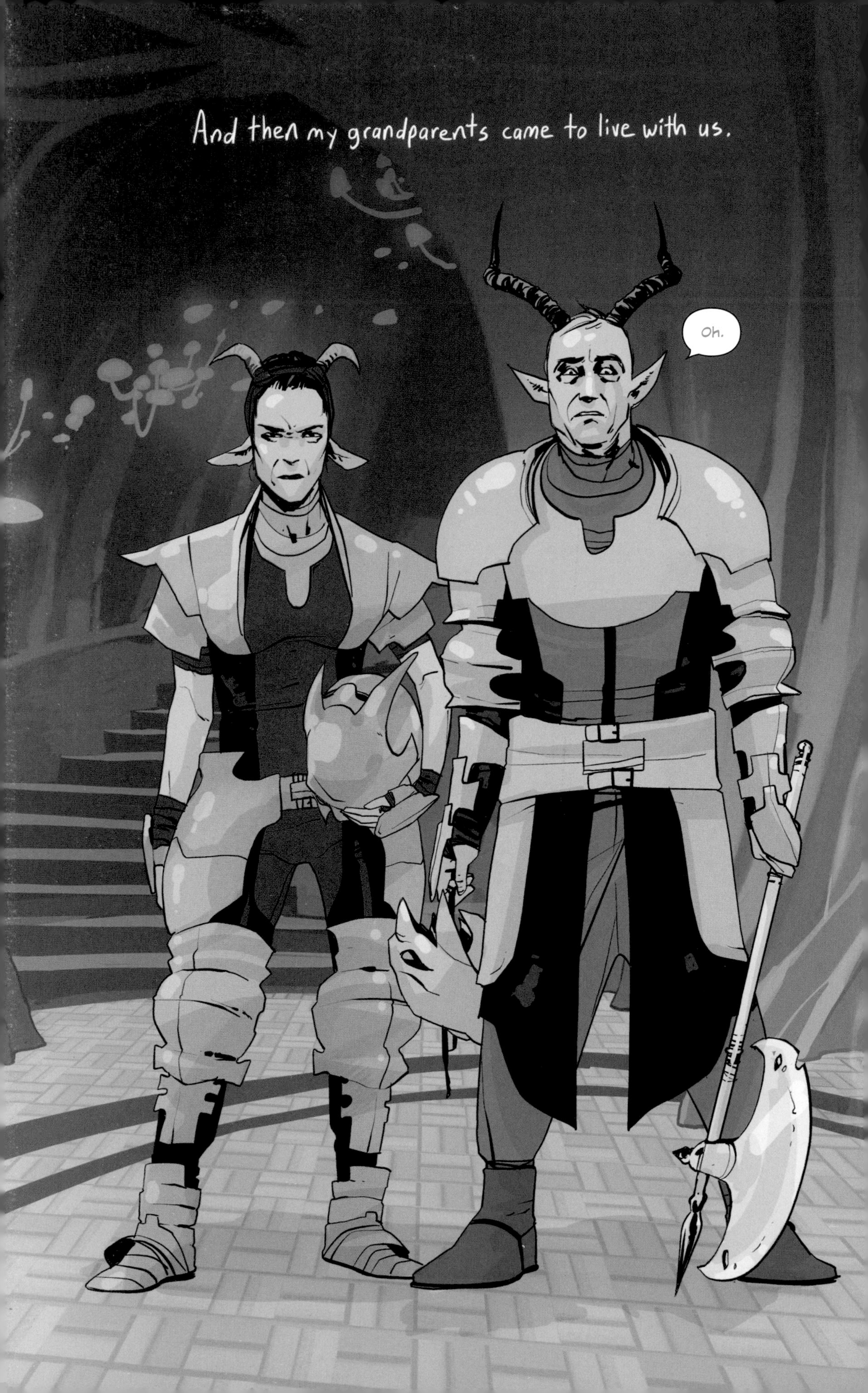
And then my grandparents came to live with us.
Oh.